The Secrets of Âlaburg

Greg Walters

English   Translation   by   Patrick   Moffatt   -   deutsch-englisch-uebersetzungen.com
Cover design: Alerim
Copyright © 2015 Greg Walters
1st edition 2020
www.greg-walters.com
contact: info@greg-walters.com
Instagram: gregwalters_author

Author

Greg Walters lives with his wife, two small daughters, and an exceptionally cheeky Labrador retriever. He is a teacher and confessed bookworm, and prefers to write at an old table in his garden--weather permitting. Greg also won the prestigious Kindle Storyteller Award 2020 in the fall of this year for his outstanding fantasy writing.

More about the author:

www.greg-walters.com
instagram.com/gregwalters_author

Âlaburg University

The Secrets of Âlaburg
The Legend of Âlaburg (Summer 2021)
The Chronicles of Âlaburg (Autumn 2021)
The Saga of Âlaburg (Spring 2022)

MARKET DAY

Sleepy, his face frozen red from the cold, Bryn was struggling to get the large bundles off Reven, his horse. Once he was done, out of breath, he unknotted the piles of animal skins, throwing them on the wooden counter of his market stand. Bryn was a slim, slightly built boy, a bit small for his sixteen years, with a thin, kind face and large, blue-green eyes. He was apprenticed to Gerald, the gamekeeper, with whom he lived. Over the winter, they would have to buy enough grain, beer, clothes, and other provisions to last the next few months with whatever Bryn was going to earn today from the skins. Soon, it would grow too cold to go hunting in the forests.

Bryn set up his stand as usual. He was hot from all the work, and sweat trickled down his face. His warm clothes, necessary in the forest, had become too bulky and were slowing him down. He hurriedly pulled off his thick-padded gloves and his fur cap. Dark blond hair fell over his face, which he kept brushing back with a flick of his hand.

Bryn arranged the skins on his counter—the snow fox skins on the far left, the rare red deer skins next to them, then the wild boar, roebuck, and rabbit skins, and, finally, the bearskin. He had been carrying that heavy skin to and from the village for months now, but no one had shown any interest.

Trade on the weekly market was getting worse and worse, especially in freezing temperatures like today. Only a few merchants from Toronham or Gerundfeld now made the long journey to Sefal to buy skins, precious stones, or forest herbs.

After several groups of merchants had been attacked in recent months in the thick, isolated forest below the Arell Mountains, many were now afraid to travel so far north.

Bryn finished setting up and stood behind the counter. With few customers about, he decided to take a look around the marketplace. Nearby, Marel had just finished setting up his stand and was busy tying bunches of herbs to the canopy. In his shack, Hondry, the village butcher, after laying out a long string of sausages and several large hams, rubbed his fat belly and stared about, looking grumpier than usual. Across the way, several village women piled rolls of dyed, handwoven fabrics on wooden tables, the colors an odd contrast to the rest of the snow-covered scene. To his side, Krell, the old hermit, tried to sell the shimmering, bright stones he had collected from the Heling River. Bryn, however, was more interested in the wooden building diagonally behind him. Zeffi's Roasted Nuts, said the bright-colored painted letters. From its chimney, smoke wafted toward Bryn, thick with the delicious smell of roasting candied hazelnuts.

I wonder if she will be there today.

Bryn had not been able to stop thinking of the dark-haired girl he'd first set eyes on four weeks ago.

His feelings left him confused. He rarely thought of girls. He never understood why Gerald talked so much to Marielle, who owned the Laughing Boar Inn, why she blushed so often in his company, why his frugal master left her such generous tips. Some of the older boys from the village were always talking about girls, especially how they looked, or making crude jokes about them that Bryn didn't understand. That kind of talk had always bored him. Wasn't it more interesting to talk about a new bow or hunting? Nonetheless, after encountering the young shop assistant in Zeffi's roastery, Bryn slowly realized that girls were more interesting than he'd thought.

Though she hadn't been there the last few weeks, every market day, Bryn would sneak around Zeffi's lopsided old hut, hoping to catch a glimpse of her. She only turned up on market days from time to time, he learned. But that didn't dampen his excitement, and now he made his way to the roastery, furtively glancing inside.

"We're still closed," a beautiful female voice said from the rear of the hut. "The sugar's not hot enough yet. Come back in half an hour."

As she came closer, Bryn saw the dark-haired girl was maybe two or three years older than him.

It was her. She was in Sefal again, finally.

"Should I tell you when it's time?" she asked Bryn, smiling.

He couldn't speak, startled by her sudden appearance. He noticed how hot his head was getting. *Oh no, I'm blushing*, he thought, embarrassed.

"Can't you talk?" she asked him kindly.

"Ah ... er ... yes."

"Well, you don't talk much, but you're not dumb," she said, smiling. "My name is Drena. I'm Zeffi's niece from Toronham. Sometimes I help out here and my uncle pays me a few guilders—but my mother doesn't like it when I travel with the other merchants because of all the robberies in the last months. Mothers, you know ..." She rolled her beautiful brown eyes. "It's nice to meet someone who isn't a bad-tempered merchant or one of those common mercenaries or soldiers. What's your name?"

Her smile was the most enchanting one Bryn had ever seen.

"Bryn," he said, still confused that such a beautiful creature would even speak to someone like him.

"Hello, Bryn," she said, offering him her hand. As if in a trance, he reached out and held it. Her skin was incredibly soft and warm. "Nice to meet you. You're the one who sells the skins over there, aren't you?"

She knows who I am.

Bryn's thoughts began to swirl, and he almost forgot to answer. "Um ... yes ... yes."

She chuckled softly to herself. "Well, Bryn, it was nice chatting with you. I have to go now or the sugar will burn. Come back around noon, and I'll give you some candied hazelnuts when Zeffi's not looking." She winked at him and turned away, dark hair swirling behind her, and disappeared into the back.

He stood there for a while, almost unaware she had gone. He slowly walked back to his stand, where he was forced to shake off his shock so he could haggle with customers over the price of his skins.

Bryn was having a good day at the market. He'd already sold several rabbit and fox skins, but the massive bearskin still sat there. The hazy winter sun was already high overhead, and Bryn wondered if he should accept Drena's invitation. Her beautiful name constantly echoed in his head. He was daydreaming about casually walking over to Zeffi's place and what he might say to her when suddenly, someone spoke and wrenched him out of his thoughts.

"Are you ssselling these ssskins here?" asked a hoarse voice.

Bryn had a hard time understanding the man's lisps and rattles. He was tall and wrapped in a black cape, with a hood cast so low over his face that he resembled a shadow. At his side dangled a large sword. And when he moved, Bryn could hear the clinking of what sounded like chainmail under his heavy coat.

"Yes, I am. How can I help you, sir?" Bryn asked, more confidently than he felt.

The stranger ran his black-gloved fingers over the display, prodding at the different skins.

"What do you want for the bearskin?" he asked abruptly.

Bryn sensed a good deal and set the price extra high for a reasonable return after the inevitable haggling. "Twenty-five guilders!"

That was a fortune, but bearskins were rare. Hardly anyone climbed that high up the mountains to even get near the fearsome creatures, let alone hunt them. Gerald was the only one in the valley who dared. Bryn hoped the stranger would not walk away.

"That'sss a lot for a sssingle bearsssskin! I'll give you twenty guildersss, lad—and not a penny more!"

That was almost double what Bryn was expecting. "Deal!"

"Wrap it up for me! I have other thingsss to do. I'll pick it up shortly before the market clossses."

Bryn took a deep breath, and just as he was about to argue he couldn't reserve the bearskin all day, the stranger said, "Here'sss ten guildersss as a deposssit. I'll give you the ressst later. Have we an agreement, lad?"

Bryn nodded, took the money, and carefully counted the silver coins.

"So we'll sssee each other in a few hoursss, lad. I hope I can trussst you," the stranger said and disappeared into the crowd.

Twenty guilders!

Bryn couldn't believe it. Gerald would be proud of him. Now they had more than enough money to see them through the rest of winter. With a huge grin plastered across his face, Bryn decided it was an excellent time to visit Drena.

As he approached the roastery, Zeffi's old, weather-beaten face suddenly appeared in front of him.

"What are you doing here, Bryn? You never have any money, and you certainly won't get anything here for free. So, what do you want?"

Somewhat taken aback, Bryn stopped, but to his amazement, he said boldly, "I've come to see Drena, if you must know."

The old nut seller raised an eyebrow. "She's not here. She left late this morning. The first blizzard of winter's about to hit, and I sent the girl off with the first caravan so she'll be back in Toronham tonight. What did you want with her?" he asked bitterly.

Bryn's heart sunk. *She's gone?* His mind began to race. He'd only just seen Drena again after so long—she'd even talked to him—and now she was gone again.

"I just wanted to talk to her, that's all," he said sadly.

"Oh, you want to talk, eh?" Zeffi said, lowering his voice menacingly. "I know what lads like you, who spend most of the year alone in the woods, want. Well, you can't have it! Get that right out of your head, Bryn! She's too old for you anyway. What would Drena want with the likes of you?" He snickered viciously.

"Besides, she'll be coming here even less now the winter storms have arrived. She'll stay in Toronham with her mother. The journey's too dangerous in all that ice and snow, even without these attacks."

He turned to the next customer as if Bryn had ceased to exist.

Hopeless, Bryn returned to his stand. *When will I see Drena again?* A peculiar, sad feeling crept upon him. Strangely enough, he'd never considered the age difference between them. Why would he? That didn't matter to him.

Over the next few hours, with his thoughts elsewhere, Bryn let himself be taken advantage of by several customers while haggling over money. All he could think about was the beautiful Drena. Thankfully, business had been sluggish since noon, and the twenty guilders for the bearskin were more than enough to make up for those poorly negotiated sales.

FOOLHARDY

The day was drawing to a close, and it had become much colder. The sunset lit up the storm clouds filling the sky. It would start to snow soon; Bryn caught that telltale metallic scent in the air. Most of the local traders had already packed up and left, leaving only a few people wandering around. Bryn started to pack his things on the back of his loyal friend, Reven. He should have gone home long ago. The journey back to the log cabin was long and dangerous in the dark—even without a blizzard. But he was waiting for the stranger who'd given him the deposit for the bearskin.

Time passed, and Bryn became more and more impatient. He was also thinking of Drena, cursing himself for not getting to know her sooner. He scanned the growing darkness around him for the stranger. He didn't want to take the ten guilders and not give the man a chance to return and pay the rest of it.

Then, it began to snow. Bryn took a moment, then decided to leave the bearskin at the Laughing Boar Inn. Everyone, sooner or later, ended up there anyway.

"Come on, Reven, old fella," he said. His breath hung in the air. "Let's get moving."

He led Reven across the empty market to the Laughing Boar, through the thin layer of snow that had already blanketed the village. He tugged Reven's reins to quicken his pace. He then tethered the grey gelding to the railing and took the bundled-up bearskin.

As he stepped inside, the heat and noise hit him immediately. He pushed his way through the crowd; the air was stuffy with smoke and spilled beer—he couldn't wait to get out. Dodging several waitresses carrying large mugs of sloshing beer, he eventually made it to the long bar.

Marielle, the broad-shouldered blond woman standing behind it, kept an eye on the lively crowd as she washed glasses.

"Hello, Bryn! What are you still doing here?" she asked, flopping her cloth down on the bar. "It's so late. And this weather's not going to get any better!"

"Hi, Marielle," Bryn replied. "Well, I was waiting for a customer who paid a deposit on this bearskin, but he didn't come back."

"Trustworthy as ever," she told him, smiling.

"Can I leave the bearskin with you? It could be one of your guests, and he might ask after me. If he does, could you give this to him if he gives you ten guilders for it? And you can keep one guilder as commission."

Marielle laughed. "You think I'd accept money from you? Who's the one who takes care of my ponies if they've been out in the snow too long? Or when Ramny's been lazy, who's always emptying the stale water in the trough? Forget it! One hand washes the other, as they say. I'm glad to return a favor for once. Besides, how could I refuse Gerald's apprentice," she said with a wink Bryn did not quite understand.

"Thank you …" he said, embarrassed by her praise. He lifted the large skin bundled up with twine up onto the bar.

"What did he look like?" Marielle asked, stowing it behind the counter.

"I can't say for sure, but he was tall, and he was armed. Maybe he's one of the guards? Guarding the traveling merchants? I remember he wore a dark cloak—but I suppose many of them wear one of those."

"I'll do my best to finish this business for you, Bryn. Not to worry." As Bryn moved toward the exit, she asked, "Are you sure you want to go out there again?" They say it's getting worse by the minute. All my rooms are now occupied, but I don't mind if you sleep in the taproom tonight. At least it's warm there. You may have to wait some time before you can lie down though. Or at least until most of the guests are in bed."

Bryn thought about it, eyeing the raucous crowd. The prospect of waiting for hours for the last drunkards to leave only to sleep on the floor made his decision pretty easy. He'd sooner sleep in his bed tonight. Besides, he knew Gerald would worry if he didn't come home.

"Thanks for the offer, Marielle, but you know, there's nothing like sleeping in your own bed. And this little bit of snow is nothing to an apprentice hunter!" He smiled.

"All right then," she replied, unknotting her brows. "Have a safe journey, take care out there, and give Gerald my regards. Tell him to come and see me again sometime! Ok?"

Bryn nodded his agreement and stepped outside. The village was covered in thick layers of snow, and the cold winds were forcing it into drifts. Bryn ran over to Reven and untied him. The daylight was all but gone, but the blizzard was getting worse. He pulled his woolen cloak tight around him and cursed himself for being so careless. He leaped into the saddle, shouting to Reven, "We have to go now—and go fast!"

Reven took off and, soon, the village was far behind them and Bryn could see the darkening forest ahead. He yelled to Reven to keep going as fast as he could, though Bryn was sure he already understood.

A DANGEROUS WAY HOME

Bryn and Reven labored through the ever-increasing snowdrifts. The tops of the Arell Mountains were no longer visible, and the path was almost impossible to follow. Even so, the old gelding trotted toward the cabin, looking forward to his warm stable and a feed of oats. Having lost his bearings in the blinding snow, Bryn could only rely on Reven to get him home safely. In his mind, he could see the outline of the log cabin in the distance. He imagined the glow of the candlelight coming through the front window and the faint, flickering golden shadows from the fire.

Damned blizzard! He thought again about how stupid he'd been to leave the market so late. But the prospect of earning twenty guilders this close to winter was too tempting, and besides, he didn't want anyone to accuse him of stealing.

Despite his predicament, his thoughts kept drifting back to Drena—how lovely she was and why he hadn't spoken to her before. Now, he had to wait until next spring. And Zeffi wasn't at all enthusiastic about his interest in Drena. Bryn sighed. *Who knows if she will even come back?*

His thoughts then turned to Gerald. How was he going to explain why he sold some of their best fur skins at such low prices? He couldn't tell him that the fur wholesalers from Gerundfeld and Toronham had preyed on his state of mind after discovering Drena had left. Even the ten guilders for the bearskin was a low price. They'd still have those ten if the stranger failed to pay the rest, but Bryn also knew Gerald would not touch it until it was clear who owned it. In any case, Gerald would want to know why he didn't bring more guilders back today. Had he forgotten how rare good furs had become?

Bryn knew this only too well. In the last months, they'd seen less and less game in the forest; even in the foothills of the Arell Mountains, there were fewer animals. Neither Gerald nor anyone else could explain it. Somehow, the animals were disappearing.

The gelding stumbled and jolted Bryn out of his anxious thoughts. Only now did he notice how cold he was. His hands felt numb. He was almost unable to hold the harness and couldn't feel his feet at all. It was so dark he could hardly see Reven's head. The snow that whipped his face also drenched his cloak and the clothes underneath, and the icy gusts of wind were making it hard to stay on his horse.

Bryn started to come to his senses and looked around. Impenetrable darkness surrounded him and made him tremble more than the cold. He tried to suppress the panic rising inside him, but the forest around him made it seem like it was getting darker and darker.

Where am I? He hadn't asked himself that question for years. He and Gerald knew the valley well. They'd traveled through it hundreds of times and were experienced trackers known for their sense of direction. But this night was different. Bryn felt as if *something* was stopping him from returning home. Not only did the wind and cold conspire against him, but his courage also seemed to have deserted him.

Bryn tried to shake off his nervousness and fear. How could he be lost? After all, he was the apprentice of the greatest hunter in the Arell Mountains. A bit of darkness and cold couldn't harm him. He pulled Reven to a stop, got off, and started jumping up and down and clapping his wet hands to regain some feeling. Then he whooped and hollered as loud as he could, hoping the noise would scare off any danger that might be lurking in the darkness.

Bryn tried to orient himself. *Where the hell am I?* He went over everything he'd learned from years of hunting with Gerald. He knew how to pinpoint his location by the stars, but they were hiding behind the clouds. He knew how to study the mountain tops and the moss on trees to work out the direction of the wind, but the peaks were no longer recognizable, and the moss was now buried under a thick layer of ice. Nothing gave him any information about where he was.

Impenetrable darkness surrounded him. *I'm alone out here.* Bryn felt sick at the thought. He wheeled around in all directions, his muscles straining, trying to recognize something. Then he stopped and tried to listen for any sound, look for any movement. But all he heard was the wind slipping through the leaves of the tall, shadowed forest.

The ancient forest of the Arell Valley was the largest closed-canopy forest in the known world. He and Gerald would often spend days, sometimes weeks, out there, hunting. To Bryn, it had always seemed endless. The upper limit of the forest was near the top of the mountains. From there, the steep, barren peaks were even more impossible to get to than a trek through the wood itself. Bryn's only hope was Reven. The old gelding knew the way home. For many years, he had been making the journey from the market back to his stable behind the cabin. The faithful animal could do it; he was sure of that. Bryn heaved his foot into the stirrup and reached for the reins to swing himself into the saddle, throwing a final, darting glance around him. As he turned to mount Reven, he thought he saw something red out of the corner of his eye.

What was that? Something glowing? Like two embers—red, like the fresh blood from a slain boar. Helplessness and panic welled up in him as he strained his eyes against the darkness. *Something is not right.* Never had he seen anything like this in the valley. *Or did I only imagine it?*

Despite the cold, he began to sweat. He pulled his hunting knife from the leather sheath at his side. He felt the weight of it in his hand and turned for a closer look at the spot where he thought he'd seen the apparition. Nothing there.

"Did you see anything, old fella?" he asked, patting the horse's neck. "Come on then, take me home!"

Reven scraped his hoof across the frozen ground as if he couldn't wait to return to his stable. As Bryn tried to mount, he heard a blood-curdling whinny. The horse reared up and leaped forward, throwing Bryn to the ground. Reven was a calm, placid creature, but something had made him crazy with fear, and he broke into gallop.

Bryn, his foot still caught in the stirrup, was dragged along, over every bump, at break-neck speed. With the reins still in his hand, he pulled himself up, out of the way of the frozen, rock-hard ground. But his back had been severely beaten, and he wasn't sure how long he could hang onto the side of the animal like this. The ground had shredded some of his clothing, which flapped in the wind. He felt the cold, wet snow penetrate every part of his body. Reven raced through the darkness. Bryn never knew the old horse could gallop at such a speed.

Bryn clawed at the leather reins with numb fingers—he was slipping. Again, his back slammed into the ground. He couldn't hold on any longer, and he could see Reven was still panic-stricken and not likely to settle. Bryn heaved himself up once more and twisted his foot out of the stirrup, his frozen hands letting go of the reins. He tumbled forward over the ground and came to rest with his face buried deep in the snow. He looked up, wiping the snow from his eyes in time to see his only hope of getting home vanish.

Reven disappeared into the night.

GERALD

"Damn rascal!" Gerald swore, peering out the window of the cabin again. It was getting darker, and the snow was becoming more dangerous. Gerald bit his lip and cursed at Bryn under his breath. *How am I ever going to make a responsible man out of this absent-minded boy?* He ran his hand over his thick, black beard and glanced out the window once more. *All these fantasies about magicians and long-forgotten kingdoms—and now girls!* Gerald knew Bryn's daydreaming was making him more and more unreliable.

The floorboards creaked under Gerald's weight as he stomped back and forth in front of the crackling fire and pushed another log into it. The smoke stung his eyes, the veins in his neck bulged. He stepped back and hurled another stream of invective toward Bryn.

Even in the coldest weather, like tonight, Gerald would only wear his regular clothes. His plain brown trousers and leather armor, which left his arms uncovered, were enough for him. Like this, it was easy for him to swing an ax to protect himself, and if he had to choose, he'd prefer that to being warm. And, besides, he didn't mind the cold as much as others did.

Though short, Gerald was a powerful man who prided himself on his strength. His small stature had prompted many to tease him or make mean-spirited jokes at his expense—

something Gerald could not abide or understand. Nobody in the Laughing Boar made jokes about him or his height twice. Once he realized he was the butt of someone's joke, their mouths were left too bloody and swollen for them to repeat it.

In Sefal, Gerald was a well-respected hunter, but he was also known as someone to avoid because of his fiery temper. Gerald had been glad when Bryn became old enough to make the journey on his own because he didn't like going there. Too many people in one place made him uncomfortable. *Although I would like to see Marielle again*, he thought, half smiling. Thinking of Marielle reminded him that Bryn was still out there.

"Cursed brat. I'll skin him alive if he doesn't show up here soon," he muttered, making his way to the wooden ladder to the loft and climbing up one more time. The loft was Bryn's domain. Once again, Gerald cast his eyes over the mess. Several fur blankets lay strewn over Bryn's straw bed. On the floor next to it were small piles of uneaten food and puddles of candle wax. Colored marbles, dried beetles, mouse heads, and various herbs were also scattered around. Gerald made his way to the small window, careful to avoid stepping on any of the clothes on the floor. Up here, Gerald had a better view of the surroundings.

He turned away from the window; there was still no sign of the boy. He saw the broken wooden flute Bryn had bought from a trader at the last summer festival propped up in one corner. But this, and the sight of this whole lovingly tended mess, only made Gerald angrier. Then his eyes fell to the other corner, where Bryn kept his hunting weapons. There wasn't a trace of disorder there. Bryn's longbow and shortbow, and a quiver of matching arrows for each, hung from two wooden pegs on the wall. On the floor was a pile of long, straight wooden sticks. Next to them were several dozen arrowheads of stone and iron, plus an assortment of feathers. Everything was at hand to make extra arrows to add to the already large stockpile. Several knives for gutting and skinning game, with sharp, well-kept blades, hung next to the bows. An unusually small one seemed to occupy a special place right in the middle.

Gerald walked over and took it off the wall. The little dagger seemed tiny in his large hand, and touching it brought forth a flood of memories. A small smile broke over his face. He turned it over in his hand. The blade was sharp and well oiled. Gerald had given it to him on the occasion of their first hunt together. The boy must have been six or seven winters old then.

Over the years, their relationship had developed in a way typical of an all-male household. They were not demonstrative of their feelings; they did not have the words to express them. Yet, they knew how they felt about each other. But it was when they were hunting that they felt the most connected to one another. Gerald had taken Bryn into his care as a toddler, and he felt more than mere responsibility for his well-being. Since their first hunt in the valley, he had taught him to look after his weapons like he would watch his own back. He put the knife back on its peg. *At least he'd learned something!* he thought—then realized the boy would become a man this summer at the Yuletide festival.

"How time flies," he muttered, shaking his head. Ten years had passed since that first hunt.

Once again, Gerald looked out the upper floor window. The blizzard had grown more severe, which worried him. And he'd never seen it get so cold this time of the year. They should have late autumn temperatures, but winter was early this year—it had arrived with a vengeance.

Where are you, Bryn? As the night wore on, Gerald's anger softened into genuine concern for the boy's safety. He knew, if it were at all possible, that Bryn would avoid riding from the village to the cabin in the dark. Because that was what Gerald had taught him. Even a good hunter and tracker should not take unnecessary risks. Something must have happened. Left to his own free will, he knew Bryn would not travel at night, especially in this weather.

DARKNESS

Bryn steadied himself on his feet, shivering with cold, soaked to the skin, trying to process what had happened. Had he really seen something? If so, what was it? Could they have been red eyes? Once again, panic flooded him, but he scolded himself and tried to repress his fear.

Though it was dark, Bryn started walking so he could at least get warm. He headed in the direction in which Reven had taken off, but he had no hope of finding the horse. The narrow forest path was unrecognizable in the snow, and the darkness made it impossible for Bryn to get a real sense of direction.

The walking calmed him down and sharpened his senses. The rhythmic movements were comforting and kept him focused. But his progress was slow as the snowdrifts were so high now that he had to wade through them in some places. Often, he sank or slipped, catching himself at the last moment, which wasted precious energy. While Bryn could still see his breath hang in the air, he used it to keep his breathing steady. It helped him stay warm, but at the same time, he felt that his strength was fading, and he knew he wouldn't last out here for long. Even so, he launched himself into the next snowdrift.

He paused at a spot that appeared more sheltered and bent forward, his hands on his thighs, taking several deep breaths. The hard slog was taking its toll. Bryn's mouth tasted of copper, and he could hear blood pulsing in his ears and rushing through his body. He was exhausted, and the thought of sleep began to lull him into unconsciousness. But Bryn knew if he rested here for even a minute more, he would never see home again.

As he struggled to straighten up, he again thought that he noticed something out of the corner of his eye—something red and glowing. Now he was sure! Bryn squinted through the dark but saw nothing. Then he noticed something else he'd caught at that first encounter with the red eyes but had forgotten entirely because his horse had spooked—the stench.

With this wind and the cold, Bryn thought he would not be able to smell anything—unless snow had a smell. Still, something was making him nauseous. The stench reminded him of moldy wood and mud drying in the sun after a flood, mixed with the bloated, decaying, maggot-infested carcass of a cow or sheep.

Bryn didn't know what frightened him more—the red eyes and the smell or the idea that he had imagined them both out of sheer panic! Still, he tried to run away as fast as possible from where the stench was emanating. But he was running deeper into the forest, in the opposite direction of home.

Silent and unseen, a tall figure followed close behind Bryn. The wind caught the hood of his heavy, black cloak, and his red eyes flashed in the darkness. He adjusted the hood to hide his eyes and ran toward Bryn.

An icy cold penetrated Bryn; he felt weak and disorientated. But he kept running as fast as he could. Even though he doubted what he'd seen and smelled, his instincts screamed that he was in danger.

Bryn plodded onward. He felt the blizzard had turned against him, forcing him backward toward the ominous presence. Dread overwhelmed him, and his stomach flipped so violently it started to ache. Glancing around for probably the hundredth time, he could see nothing, only darkness. Meanwhile, the snow was almost up to his hips, forcing him to crawl. The forest was dense and completely black with no sound from any living thing—only the wind howled in his ears. Bryn didn't know if it was exhaustion or if the forest was completely silent. His lungs were burning. He had to stop and take a deep breath. Again, his mouth tasted of copper.

The sound of a twig snapping! Bryn knew that could only be a living thing. It sounded deafening—like if he'd pressed his ear to the village church bell as it rang. The tense concentration of the last minutes had made his ears extra sensitive. Now he knew something was following him. He had to keep going, but his body refused to move.

He heard several branches breaking in quick succession, the sounds much closer this time. The disgusting musty stench filled the air. Something was coming straight at him. He took cover behind a big oak tree, unsure which direction the sounds had come from, and pulled out his hunting knife. It appeared tiny to him now, more like a toy than a weapon. Still, he pointed the blade to where he expected his pursuer to come from and held the handle with all his might.

Without a sound, a large shape emerged from a thicket a few yards in front of Bryn. It wore a black cloak with the hood up and was turning the head in all directions. Bryn watched for a moment, but he wasn't sure if the shape was looking about or sniffing the air. Suddenly, a gust of wind whipped off the hood covering the face, and the stranger froze. To Bryn's horror, he saw a pair of red eyes glaring at him.

THE CLEARING

Gerald's heart leaped. "Finally!" he called out, catching sight of the old grey gelding trotting toward the cabin through the swirling snow. He rushed down the ladder to the front door. Reven might be slow and headstrong, but he always found his way back home. But when Gerald opened the door and only saw Reven, a great fear came over him. He grabbed the reins and immediately led Reven out the back, putting him in the stable next to Olander, his own horse.

I have to find him, Gerald decided and saddled his black stallion. The chance of finding Bryn in the vast, wintery forest was slim, but he would spare no effort. On his own, Bryn wouldn't survive for long in these temperatures. *Maybe he fell off his horse?* But Gerald couldn't find a sensible reason for that. Bryn was an excellent rider, and Reven was always even-tempered and dependable. Gerald's concern grew.

He rode out into the blizzard as quickly as he could, leaving behind the cabin's warmth and protection. After a few yards, the icy wind started to die down and visibility improved. He tried to follow Reven's tracks, but it was impossible even for an expert tracker like himself. He began his search on the main path through the forest to Sefal. He rode along it for a while but stopped as he found nothing. The snow had covered any signs that could have been helpful. So he turned Olander around to find the trail they usually took to the village. But Olander was a big horse, and he made slow progress on the path once they found it because of the deep snow.

Gerald tried to cast his mind out to search for the boy—a skill he had learned many decades ago. But he was never good at it because it was too esoteric. It was clear even to the others back then that his talents lay in a completely different field. Besides not having used the skill since then, he had also taken an Oath. But the youngster's life depended on how quickly Gerald could find him. The Oath didn't matter to him now; he would deal with the Order and any consequences later.

The mental effort it took to reach out and connect to Bryn using this Mind Casting Spell was apparent on Gerald's face. Sometimes, the strain was such that he blurted out Bryn's name instead of keeping it inside like he needed to. He reined the horse to a stop and shouted to himself. "Concentrate, you old fool! Concentrate!" He stared out into the night, shut his eyes, and tried to focus. But it was hopeless. The lines deepened on Gerald's face, and his throat tightened, holding back something between a sob and a shout. At that moment, an image of Bryn flashed into his head. And then another. A clearing. The boy's face distorted with fear, his eyes wide and fixed. A huge tree. But Gerald sensed something else all too familiar, and his heart began to race. The boy was not alone. *It can't be true! Why are they looking for the boy? Why are they here in these parts? What madman would dare bring them back after so many years?*

For the first time in a long time, Gerald felt cold. He knew he could no longer risk using the spell to locate the boy; if he did, he wouldn't have the strength to make it back to the cabin either with Bryn or alone. He also knew they could sense him using it. *Bryn.* The veins on Gerald's temples bulged, and everything went dark behind his eyes. *I must stop. That's all I can do.* But it had been worth it. Gerald now had a clearer picture of the scene in his mind. And he recognized the dark, towering figure moving toward the boy with a longsword hanging at his belt. His chest pounded. He had to help the boy, but first, Gerald had to reach him. His ax might not defeat the attacker, but it would at least drive him away. At least he hoped so.

Gerald touched his spurs to Olander's flanks and drove him deeper into the forest, feverishly running the images one more time through his mind. Was that the big oak in the clearing where he and Bryn had shot their first roebuck? Gerald had no strength to mentally call out to the boy. This one clue was all he had to go on. Urging Olander to hurry, he rode toward the clearing as fast as the stallion could carry him.

Time flew. Gerald felt as if he was barely moving even though he was pushing Olander to the limit.

"Hold on, Bryn! I'm coming," he cried out, riding on through the darkness.

Bryn watched, paralyzed, as the red-eyed stranger sniffed the air and slowly crept over to the edge of the small clearing.

"I know you're ssstill here, lad," a voice hissed. "There'sss no point hiding anymore. I only want to talk to you."

But the slow, metallic scratching of a sword being drawn undercut his words. Still peering about, and with his weapon in hand, the dark figure traversed the open space, straight toward Bryn.

That voice. He'd heard the unmistakable hissing earlier today. It belonged to the stranger who'd wanted to buy the bearskin and then hadn't picked it up! *Why is he chasing me? Was the bearskin a trick to keep me in Sefal as long as possible?* The stranger agreeing to such a high price started to make sense now. He had wanted Bryn to ride through the storm in the dark. *But why?* The leather-bound handle on Bryn's hunting knife was wet with sweat. His fingers were stiff, and he had no gloves. They'd come off when he was unexpectedly dragged through the snow. The putrid smell was unbearable and got more intense as the figure crept closer. Meanwhile, having sweated through, he no longer felt the cold around him.

Slow and steady, the tall, dark man came closer. In a few steps, he would discover Bryn's hiding place. Bryn pressed himself against the big oak, his thoughts racing. Escape seemed hopeless, and he felt he was no match against this well-armed man in a fight. Bryn thought about Gerald and his lessons on sword fighting. Suddenly, Gerald's face flashed inside Bryn's head. For a moment, he had the feeling Gerald was calling out to him. Thoughts of his foster father warmed Bryn's heart despite the terror in front of him. He remembered the hunting trips, the warm nights on the porch at sunset, and the fireside chats when it rained. Bryn knew if Gerald were in his situation, he would take action and not hide like this, cowering. Bryn bit down hard on his bottom lip. After all, he was the apprentice to the great hunter Gerald McDermit, and Bryn wanted him to be proud of him.

Bryn closed his eyes for a moment. He took three deep breaths, dragging in the cold air, and stepped out from behind the tree and into the clearing. Stripped of cover, he pointed his knife at the stranger, looking more challenging than he felt.

"Here I am. What do you want from me? Your bearskin is at the Laughing Boar," he shouted, his voice trembling and high. "Give Marielle the remaining ten guilders, and you can take it with you."

In a flash, the man's head turned, and Bryn felt those red eyes burning into him. For a moment, the man appeared to hesitate, glancing about him. But when he saw the boy was alone, he lifted the massive sword in both hands and rushed forward. Bryn knew it would all be over within seconds.

Gerald did something he'd never done before. He spurred Olander to the point of driving the horse to death. Never had he done such a thing to an animal in his care, but his fear for the boy pushed him to extremes. Racing through the dark forest, Gerald relied on the horse's instincts as he could barely see the path himself. *I have to make it,* he told himself. *The clearing is not far away. Bryn, hold on!* At that moment, Olander rounded a tight bend, and his rear hooves stumbled on the slippery path. Gerald almost fell, but he grabbed the pommel of the saddle with all his strength. Once the horse had recovered, Gerald dug his heels into him hard, and the two raced on, undaunted, through the dark, freezing night.

The creature, sword drawn and running at Bryn with superhuman speed, was only a few yards from him, but the smell of decay and mold preceded him and made Bryn gag. Curiously, though, Bryn felt utterly calm and focused on what was unfolding in front of him. All at once, his senses seemed to sharpen. He became aware of every minute detail of the forest— he could see the intricate details of the delicate, greyish-green moss frozen on the trees, the unique shapes of the countless snow crystals, and even the deep nicks on the edges of his assailant's sword. The dark stranger kept coming, yet Bryn felt in these final few seconds that time was slowing down. He studied the man's powerful movements, watched each protruding muscle move, and saw the pure hatred glowing in his eyes as he got closer and closer. Bryn lifted his small hunting knife and felt an intense tingling sensation in his right hand.

Pulling hard on the reins, Gerald brought the horse to a halt. To an uninformed observer, this spot might have looked like any other path, but Gerald knew the forest better than anyone, and he leaped from the saddle. He fought his way through the snow drifts into the undergrowth next to the path, working his way over fallen trees and mountains of snow, his powerful arms frantically shoveling a shortcut to the clearing.

"Bryn, Bryn? Are you here? Bryn? BRYN!"

The gigantic dark figure lifted the longsword above his head to strike Bryn a mortal blow.

Bryn calmly watched the sleeves under the man's cloak slowly slide down his arms. What emerged from the cloak were two claw-shaped hands and arms covered in greenish-grey scales. The man's hood also fell back, and Bryn could see his face was severely disfigured and hideous. The head, covered in putrid, decomposing skin, was like the skull of a corpse and had a large hole in the middle where the nose had rotted away. But his eyes were the most frightening. Filled with hate, they stared out of the decaying skull, reddish fire boring into Bryn. *This creature has come straight from Hell*, he thought and pushed his right arm forward in a desperate, hopeless gesture to defend himself. Out of nowhere, he heard someone call his name. But it was so faint, he did not know where it had come from and had no time to look around.

Then Bryn felt as if the back of his right hand was burning. Before he could do anything, sudden, blinding light surrounded him—every color of the spectrum, like a rainbow. But he could still see that the gruesome stranger was about to strike. Then a giant sword plunged, unstoppable, toward his head.

Gerald first noticed the terrible stench as he hurried toward the clearing. *Damn it!* He knew this smell only too well. *Is it really you?! Why, after all these years?* he cursed, running the last few yards to the old oak at the center of the clearing. The tree's massive trunk prevented him from seeing Bryn standing on the other side of it, facing his attacker.

Gerald saw the clearing and put his hand over his eyes; it looked as bright as day, lit by thousands of colors. For a brief moment, he couldn't see anything. Then an unexpected gust of wind knocked him over. Without considering any possible danger, he got up and ran to the tree. He called out to Bryn, his voice almost breaking. When Gerald walked around to the other side of the tree, he could not believe his eyes.

Bryn lay on his back, motionless in the snow, his eyes closed, his hunting knife lying in his open hand, its tip glowing. *Oh no! Please, Kajal, don't let it be true!* Next to the boy was a near-circular patch of scorched earth, several yards in diameter, burnt pitch black and in stark contrast to the snow around it. Gerald narrowed his eyes. In the center was a clump of partially melted metal. Only when he looked closer and saw the charred, smoking handle did he realize it was the remains of a sword.

Gerald bent over the boy and spoke to him softly. "Bryn? Bryn, are you alright?" There was no response. The boy was breathing normally, and Gerald felt his heartbeat on the side of his neck. He did not seem to have any external injuries.

Nevertheless, he had to get him away from here and to somewhere warm. At the cabin, Gerald could examine him more closely. He removed the knife from Bryn's barely warm hand and slipped it into his belt. He picked the boy up carefully and carried him in his arms, as if he were a small animal, back to Olander. He lay the boy on the horse and, without letting him go, jumped up behind and held him.

"Go, Olander," he whispered, his voice hoarse and exhausted, and without delay, the horse bolted as fast as it could for home.

RECOLLECTIONS

Gerald crept into the quiet, warm cabin and carried Bryn to his room. He undressed the boy and put him to bed under several fur blankets. He watched Bryn for a moment, then put a hand on his shoulder, and shook him gently.

Bryn opened his eyes.

"Gerald? Gerald," he whispered, his voice croaky. "I've been dreaming about you." Then he fell back into a deep sleep.

Gerald stroked Bryn's sweaty hair with his big, rough hand. "I know, Bryn. Sleep now. Sleep will give you your strength back."

He sat down beside the bed, laying his double-bladed ax on his knees and peering out the small loft window into the darkness.

Upon waking, Bryn's first thought was that he needed water. *Why am I so thirsty?* His throat burned, and his mouth was dry. It took all his strength to sit up and look around. Disoriented, he was slow to realize where he was. Gerald was asleep in a chair next to the bed, fully dressed, an ax on his knees. He seemed to have spent the whole night like that, which seemed strange. Bryn had never seen the huge ax either, and he'd thought he knew all of Gerald's weapons. But right now, that riddle could wait; there were plenty of other things on his mind. Bryn pulled off the blankets—he was getting too warm—and stretched his stiff limbs. Every bone ached.

What happened last night? But what little recollection he had triggered a rush of adrenaline through his body, and he panicked. He flushed even hotter, his stomach tight and painful.

But something else was more important. Bryn felt he needed to drink gallons of water straight away; otherwise, he'd die of thirst. Next to his bed was a jug of cold water and a wooden board with coarse bread and dried meat. He reached for the jar's handle, but he was still so weak that it slipped from his fingers. The jug crashed to the floor.

Gerald jumped and raised his weapon with a ferocious expression. He looked around, smiled, and said in a calm, deep voice, "You seem to be doing better, if you're breaking our dishes again!" He felt Bryn's forehead. "You're burning up! I guess you'll have to stay in bed for a day or two. But it could have been worse, much worse."

Gerald caught himself frowning at the boy and tried to muster a smile. "So, how do you feel?" he asked, a little too cheerfully.

"Water," was all Bryn could say.

"Yes, of course," mumbled Gerald, looking at the remains of the jug. "I'll get some more water. But this time," he added, smiling, "in something that's not too heavy."

After a while, he returned with the small, colorful wooden mug Bryn had used as a child, filled with steaming herbal tea. He handed it to the boy, grinning. "Can you handle this one?"

Grimacing, Bryn sat up, and took the mug with both hands. The heat of the tea penetrated his palms, and, sipping from the mug, he noticed a calm spread through his body. Last night's fears seemed to fade away. Gerald made sure he drank it all, and Bryn eagerly complied: it not only quenched his thirst but also soothed his aching throat.

Gerald eased himself onto the end of the bed and studied Bryn's face. "Can you tell me what happened?"

Where should he start? *Not with Drena, that's for sure.* At the mere thought of her, he felt a pleasant uneasiness in his stomach and his heart began to beat faster. Then, he remembered. The furs! Drena's departure had blindsided him, and he'd failed to haggle hard enough and sold some of their best pelts for less than their worth.

"Gerald, I sold some of the furs for—"

Gerald waved it off. "We can talk about that later. I want to know what happened after you left the market."

Bryn let himself fall back against his blankets. He thought about what he should and should not say. His memories of last night were still fragmented, but even what he could remember hardly seemed real in the cold, hard light of the day.

"Well?" Gerald pressed him.

Bryn swallowed loudly and pulled a face to play up his sore throat. But Gerald's face showed no sympathy. A fever didn't mean he couldn't get explanations from the boy.

"I …" Bryn began, making up his mind on what he should say. "I don't remember all of what happened yesterday."

Gerald nodded, running his hand through his beard. "Please tell me everything—anything at all, no matter how insignificant."

So Bryn began talking. He spoke about the market, the furs he had sold too cheap, and, after some hesitation, even Drena, and was surprised when Gerald responded with a conspiratorial wink. He spoke about the stranger's interest in the bearskin, how he'd waited too long to return home because he didn't want to cheat the man out of his money, how he'd accidentally fallen off his horse—but he deliberately neglected to mention the red eyes.

"… and the next thing I remember is waking up here this morning. I must have hit my head when I fell from old Reven. That's why I remember so little," Bryn said, carefully.

Gerald's eyes narrowed. "And that's all?"

"That's all I can remember." Bryn turned his eyes away. *Why should I tell Gerald about it? He wouldn't believe me anyway.* Bryn was sure Gerald would only ask him to stop dreaming about magicians and conquering heroes and live in the real world. *I'm not even sure now if I saw the gruesome creature with the red eyes.* But the goosebumps on his arms proved that the dark creature's memory was painfully real, unlike anything he could have imagined.

"Where's the money you made yesterday?" Gerald asked flatly. Bryn pointed to his trousers. Gerald grabbed them, rummaged around the pockets for the small purse, poured the coins into his large hand, and started counting. "Are the stranger's ten guilders here as well?"

"Yes, that's all the money from yesterday's sales. I'm sorry I didn't do better," Bryn replied, perplexed by the sudden change of subject.

To his astonishment, Gerald gestured at him to stop apologizing and stuffed the money in his pocket.

"Don't you worry about that, my boy. The important thing is that you're back here, and you'll soon be well again." He got up. "Sleep a few more hours. I'll make us something to eat in the meantime so you can regain your strength," he added before he went down the creaky steps.

Bryn sighed. He struggled to rid his mind of last night's frightening memories. But eventually, his thoughts turned to Drena, and he fell fast asleep, dreaming of her.

ONLY HALF THE TRUTH

The sun was already low, and Bryn headed for the ladder and clambered down from the loft. At the bottom, he felt dizzy and held the side rail.

Gerald was nowhere to be seen. Sunlight streamed through the living room's large front window. Dust particles danced in the yellow light. He warmed himself momentarily by the few embers still glowing in the hearth and made his way to the kitchen, using the backs of the old, green armchairs as support. The small table in front of them was always a mess of leftovers, dirty glasses, weapon parts, and broken arrows—the usual chaos from two single men. Once again, Bryn had to stop because his legs refused to work. Then he headed for the kitchen.

The small kitchen was warm and smelled delicious, and his stomach started growling. But then, he had slept all day with nothing to eat. A fire was burning in the stove, with several pots and pans on the thick iron plate. His mouth watered. He lifted the lids to see what was for dinner. Fried green beans with bacon. Mashed potatoes mixed with carrots, which had a light orange color. Under the lid of the large cast-iron pan, a juicy venison steak bubbled in a thick brown sauce.

Bryn swallowed several times; everything looked so good. He held the heavy lid in one hand and fished around in the basket on the shelf above for a wooden spoon with the other. As he was about to dip it into the delicious sauce, a deep voice behind him made him drop the lid.

"Well, if you have the strength to be snacking," said Gerald, smiling, "you might as well set the table. I'm going to get washed."

Bryn hurried, as best he could, to set the table.

Soon, they were having dinner at the small kitchen table. Bryn ate quickly even though the food was still too hot to swallow. Before long, the meal was finished, and they started to nod off in front of the empty dishes.

Bryn gave a long yawn and stretched. As he got up from the table to clear the plates, Gerald stopped him. "When will you tell me who attacked you yesterday and how you made him run away?"

Stunned, Bryn dropped back down on the wooden chair. "Y … y … yesterday? An attack? How do you come up with that?" But Gerald's stern look, he knew, meant all further attempts at a cover-up were futile.

"Tell me the truth, Bryn."

Bryn pondered over the incident. Much of what was blurry this morning seemed clearer now. Still, rocking silently back and forth on his chair, he couldn't put it into words.

"Gerald, I …"

"Describe the smell, Bryn, if you can."

How does Gerald know about the smell? I've only been able to remember it the last few minutes myself. But the expression of mild disappointment on his foster father's face was too much for him.

"It smelled like rotten wood and old mud—like the smell of death."

Gerald nodded, and, strengthened by this, Bryn continued, "I only saw his face for a moment. It was horrible. Worst of all were the eyes; they seemed to glow red, staring at me, filled with hatred. I think he wanted to kill me."

Bryn faltered for a moment and took a breath.

"The creature held a longsword in his claws and lifted it above him as if he wanted to cut off my head." He shuddered.

Only after he said it did he fully comprehend what had happened last night—someone had tried to kill him. Bryn had tears in his eyes, and his heart was pounding. Gerald put his arm over his shoulder, and slowly, Bryn calmed down.

Now that the truth was out, Bryn's thoughts settled. *But what has the smell got to do with the attack?* Bryn took a long, slow breath.

"Gerald, how did you know there was an attack? I didn't mention it this morning. I didn't think you'd believe me. And I couldn't remember everything then anyway," he added remorsefully.

Gerald was silent for a while, but he was fidgeting with his hands.

"I recognized the stench. How could one forget it?" he said under his breath. "Many years ago, even before you came to me, I had already noticed these disgusting smells"—Gerald pointed out the window—"up there, below the peaks of the Arell Mountains. I had been chasing a wounded grizzly bear for days when I suddenly noticed this deathly smell. Instinctively, I hid behind a rock. Until now, I've never told anyone what I saw there."

The old hunter leaned back and took a long sip of his brandy.

"From my hiding place, I could see the stinking creature. Its red eyes shone in the early twilight. Suddenly, I saw the bear coming out of a thicket—a massive animal that was already weakened, but still a serious opponent. The creature had also noticed him. In a movement almost too fast for my eyes, the creature ran toward the bear. I saw it cut off the bear's head with a single blow from its huge, clawed hand. The creature sank its teeth, and then its head, into the animal's bloody carcass, devouring it. I used this moment to creep away and head into the valley. Never again have I run so far in so short a time. Since then, I never hike so far up and avoid hunting there too. But now these creatures seem to have come down into the valley."

A lump gathered in Gerald's throat. He could not, and would not, explain the whole truth about these vile creatures to Bryn. *It is better for him.* Gerald tried to chase away his pangs of conscience with that thought.

"Good thing you came in time to drive the creature away; otherwise, it would have eaten me."

But Gerald did not return the smile or look pleased like Bryn had expected. Instead, he only nodded, his mind elsewhere.

"Yes, we must be grateful for that." Gerald kept quiet about the tremendous scorch mark on the ground and the charred sword. More warmly, he said, "Oh, by the way …"

He handed Bryn his hunting knife, much to Bryn's surprise and delight. He took it and put it in his belt. Had he looked more closely though, he would have seen that the blade was slightly blackened.

A LATE-NIGHT INTRUDER

Bryn and Gerald cleaned the dishes and the kitchen together. Afterward, Bryn noticed he was more exhausted than he wanted to admit. Gerald sent him to bed. Bryn gladly obeyed, and, after a few moments, fell asleep.

The door to the henhouse creaked, but not in a familiar way, waking Bryn from a restless sleep.

Something was not right. Several times before, the larger foxes had tried to get inside the stable. But they hadn't been able to open the massive wooden door, and it had annoyingly squeaky hinges. Maybe they were trying to get at the chickens now. Reluctantly, Bryn got out of bed. The room was so cold he could see his breath in the air. He went to the window and looked down at the front yard and the chicken coop on the far-right corner of the property. The night was clear, and the stars and moon shone brightly. The snow-covered forest, from up here, looked almost infinite. In the wind, the white-powdered fir trees swayed back and forth. Bryn pressed his face against the window, his breath fogging up the glass. With his shirt sleeve, he removed the ice flowers that had formed in the corners of the window. But he had no time to admire their beautiful shapes tonight; his attention was on the henhouse.

A low picket fence marked out the coop, and Bryn could see no sign of an intruder. He shrugged and was about to return to his warm bed when something caught his attention. There were tracks in the snow. Even though Bryn was an experienced tracker, he'd never seen tracks like these before. They were quite big, with six or seven toes, and he couldn't be entirely sure at this distance, but they looked like they had claws. *Damn, I have to save the chickens!* He slipped on his thick-padded fur jacket and his winter boots and scrambled down the ladder.

Had Bryn stayed a few seconds longer at the window, he would have seen a towering, dark figure emerge from the henhouse and wipe the blood from its ghastly snout. He also would have seen it look up at the window with its red eyes, familiar and glowing.

Bryn tip-toed across the living room as fast he could so as not wake Gerald. The fire was only smoldering now, but it was still warmer here than up in his bedroom. Through the window the moonlight seeped in, casting long, eerie shadows of the armchairs. This sort of thing usually played tricks on Bryn's imagination but not tonight. He had to save the chickens—the eggs were an essential source of food for them in winter. Now, he felt safe, stronger; he was not in the forest, he was home.

He carefully opened the front door. The cold wind immediately hit him and pulled at his clothing. He stepped out, and his shoes sunk with a crunch into the fresh snow. He closed the door gently and headed over to the strange tracks. Kneeling, he ran his hands over them. It was clear they belonged to a massive creature with seven toes, each with long, sharp, hooked claws. He ran his fingers over the imprints in the snow once more and rose to his feet. The wind had picked up, and Bryn grabbed his jacket collar to close it. Heart pounding, he followed the tracks toward the chicken coop.

The icy air from the opened door had swept into Gerald's room and woken him. The chill soon passed, but he could not fall asleep again. *Did I not lock the doors properly, or is there another window open?* he wondered, getting up to look for the draught. After checking all the windows on the ground floor, he pulled the front door hard to make sure it was closed correctly. *Perhaps I only had a bad dream; hardly surprising given the events of yesterday.*

With all the walking about, he also had to answer the call of nature. It was only a few yards to the dung heap behind the house, but in freezing weather like this, the trip always made Gerald grumpy. He shuffled back to his bedroom, put on his coat, and returned to the kitchen to put on his heavy, fur-lined boots next to the door. Any sleepiness he might have felt evaporated with the gusts of wind that greeted him when he opened the door. Grumbling to himself, he stomped through the small garden toward the dung heap. *At least there's a full moon, so I won't pee on my boots like last time.*

As Bryn reached the chicken coop, he saw the henhouse door was slightly open. He cursed himself for not bringing his knife, which was under a pile of clothes on the chair next to his bed. When he opened the door further, Bryn saw drops of blood splattered on the ground. His body filled with adrenaline. He steadily backed away from the henhouse, heading for the cabin as quickly and quietly as possible. Without a weapon, he had few options. *I have to wake Gerald. Together, we can drive off the intruder.*

As he turned to make a run for the cabin, he spotted a dark figure with red-hot eyes crouching on the snow-covered roof of the henhouse, watching him. Bryn went rigid, and his nostrils were filled with the same stench as the night before.

Around the back, Gerald was emptying his bladder and groaning. The warm fluid steamed and left yellow marks on the snow-covered dung heap. When he finished, he headed to the kitchen door. But he thought he saw something out of the corner of his right eye—movement on the henhouse roof. There seemed to be something like a giant bat about to launch itself off the roof into the front garden. But when he looked again, he saw nothing. Suddenly, the wind changed direction, and he smelled something musty.

Then he heard a scream.

The creature leaped down with such force that it left the old wooden henhouse creaking and swaying. Bryn screamed in fright at the sight of his attacker, or a similar creature, standing in front of him. Frozen with fear, he could only wait for the inevitable blow.

Gerald ran as fast as his stocky legs could carry him into the storeroom where he kept his weapons. The double-ax, which he had removed from its hiding place under the floorboards only yesterday, was luckily lying at hand. *I should not have been so careless,* he scolded himself. Gerald had assumed that Bryn's attacker was dead. While the boy had slept, he had taken a closer look at the clearing. Although the charred handle was buried under a layer of fresh snow, he found it easily enough; bits of flesh from the attacker's hand were stuck to it. He also found a few claws and bloodied shreds of skin scattered around the area. Having gathered the mortal remains of the creature, Gerald set a fire and burned them in the belief that this was the end of their enemy. Then he had mounted Olander and ridden home.

Why was I so stupid! I should have known there would never be just one. He cursed himself again for not watching over the boy like last night. Finally, with his double-ax in hand, he headed for the front door, leaving behind a trail of wet footprints on the polished floorboards—a punishable offence under different circumstances.

The first thing Bryn heard was scornful laughter.

"Are you ssscared?" hissed a hoarse voice, which erupted again into terrifying laughter. "It'sss only right you're ssscared, but it won't be for long becausssse now you're going to die!"

Gradually, the creature came closer. Escape seemed impossible, and the stench became more and more unbearable. *I have to stall for time!*

"What … what do you want from me?" Bryn demanded, though his voice trembled.

"How tragic. You don't know why you're about to die," the beast mocked. "But I'll make a deal with you. If you tell me how you killed Kaull yesssterday, I'll explain why your life is over."

So I killed the creature last night! Bryn had no idea how. "I can't tell you. I don't know myself."

"Oh, what a pity. Then I guesss it'sss time to die, Bryn."

But just as the creature lunged at Bryn, Gerald's heavy ax split open the back of its skull. The demon's shrill cry almost burst Bryn's eardrums as dark greenish-yellow blood spurted from the gaping wound.

Gerald yanked the ax out with a terrible squelching sound and struck another blow from behind. But the beast turned around and lashed out with its long, sharp claws at Gerald's head. Gerald dodged the blow, graceful like a cat, showing all his hunter's prowess, and tumbled to the side. The claws tore through the air.

Gerald rolled onto his back and leaped to his feet in one smooth movement. As soon as he regained his footing, he struck again. This time, the blade plunged deep into the side of the attacker's body. Weakened and blinded by the blood now flowing over its contorted face, the creature hissed, stumbling toward Gerald, who was lifting the ax for the final blow. With a little hiss, the powerful weapon cut through the icy air, hitting the beast on the side of the neck. The head thudded to the ground. Its body toppled over. Gerald and Bryn looked on as a torrent of unnatural, green-colored blood gushed from the steaming slit in the middle of its chest.

Gerald turned to Bryn, his face splattered with blood. "Are you all right?"

Bryn stared at him, speechless, but managed a nod. Gerald came closer and put his hand lightly on Bryn's shoulder, gently leading him back inside.

ON THE RUN

Still trembling, Bryn sat down with Gerald's help on one of the armchairs. As soon as Gerald felt he was safe there, he threw some fresh logs into the embers and stoked the fire. Then he closed all the shutters and locked the back door. Gerald carried his huge ax with him the whole time, its blade shimmering a strange blue. After securing the cabin, Gerald came over to Bryn.

"I'll have a look around outside. You stay here! Understood?"

Bryn, still numb with fear, nodded and curled up in the large armchair. Gerald wrapped him in a warm blanket and left.

The click of the door made Bryn bolt upright in fright.

"Everything's alright; it's only me," Gerald reassured him. "Go back to sleep. The next few days are going to be exhausting."

Bryn realized he'd been asleep for a while and eased back into the chair. He watched Gerald as he fell into the chair opposite, the ax at his side, his eyes fixed on the front door. Bryn was soon asleep—but it was restless. He dreamt the bloody face of his attacker was standing in front of him. The recurring nightmare kept waking him, but when it did, Gerald comforted the boy and helped him go back to sleep.

The sun was up. Gerald flung open all the shutters, and cold, fresh air rushed in. He looked out at the forest, big, dark rings under his eyes.

"Bryn, it's not safe here anymore," he said, his voice somber. "These creatures are now in the valley, and more of them will come for us. We're too isolated here, so I have saddled Olander and Reven and packed the essentials. We leave in half an hour. Get cleaned up. You can take one special thing from your room with you—and that's all. We leave the Arell Valley and Sefal today."

Hearing these words sent a thousand thoughts through Bryn's mind. He was afraid here, but at the same time, he didn't want to leave. The day before yesterday, he'd imagined what to say to Drena when she returned to the market in spring. But now, he feared for the safety of the villagers. Besides, this was his home, and he did not want to leave so quickly.

"Gerald, are you serious? We can't just run away from here without warning the others."

"I already did that when you were sleeping," he said, not looking Bryn in the eye.

Bryn searched for something to convince Gerald not to leave. One thing was clear; he should not mention Drena. "The skins, Gerald! What about the skins in the shed and the cellar—do you want to leave them behind? What are we then going to live on, and where are we supposed to go?"

"We'll be fine. I've put some money aside, and where we're going, you and I may be able to hire ourselves out. In any case, we'll be safe there. You will be safe," said Gerald with an insistence that invited no objection. "Now, pack your things. You have twenty-five minutes."

Cursing to himself, Bryn climbed up to his room. His thoughts only revolved around Drena, and he racked his brains on how to persuade Gerald to stay so he could see her again. Looking around at his little world filled him with sadness. He didn't want to leave; this was his home. Bryn collapsed on his straw bed. *What should I leave behind?* It was a difficult choice. How do you decide what to take from your previous life and what to leave behind?

Finally, he stood up and took his bow and a quiver full of arrows from the wall. He also took the hunting knife from under the clothes on the chair and put it in his belt. He put on a thick linen shirt and his woolen cloak. He looked down at his colorful marbles, the dried mouse head, and his flute, none of which could make the journey with him. Finally, he dug out a crumpled papyrus bag from under the bed and opened it. He could still smell the sweet aroma of candied nuts. On the day he'd first seen Drena, he'd used all his pocket money to buy them. And though she hadn't noticed him, he hadn't been able to get her out of his head since then. He carefully stuffed the bag into his shirt pocket, closed the clasp of his cloak, and took one final look around.

Closing the kitchen door behind him, Bryn saw that Reven and Olander were already saddled and carrying several large saddlebags. They scratched their hooves in the snow, steaming white breath puffing out of their nostrils. He patted them and tied his own few belongings to Reven's back. Gerald had packed plenty of provisions. But he had also stowed away some weapons and warm furs that would be useful in this weather. Bryn knew that a journey through the Arell Forest in the middle of winter was not without risk. As if the cold and wild animals weren't enough, Bryn also knew that creatures who wanted him dead were lurking out there. Goosebumps ran up his spine, and he fastened his cloak even tighter.

"Are you ready?" Gerald shouted from the stable.

Bryn had to think about it. "Yes …" he said quietly.

Soon, the two hunters were far from home, riding at a trot side by side through the snow-covered forest.

THE FOREST INN

Bryn and Gerald were following the ancient path the villagers called the Royal Trail. In the old stories, the trail was one of the first to cross from one side of the kingdom to the other. Bryn loved hearing stories of the former times, but Gerald didn't want to know anything about them, so Bryn couldn't talk about them to distract himself from his darker thoughts. When they set out, Bryn had tried to get Gerald to tell him where they were going, but he only gave cryptic answers or repeated something reassuring.

"We'll be safe there, Bryn, that's all you need to know. Safe."

So the hours passed uneventfully, apart from riding around the usual fallen trees, or the occasional clump of icy snow that fell down the back of their collars from the overhanging branches.

Over the day, it got colder and colder, and the path continued to narrow, so Gerald instructed Bryn to ride ahead of him. This, Bryn understood, was a precaution, even if Gerald hadn't called it that. And he also did not fail to notice the big ax hanging directly from Gerald's saddle and the way he studied the forest as he rode.

Meanwhile, Bryn pondered what the creature might have meant by asking him, *"Tell me how you killed Kaull."* It seemed pointless to approach Gerald again. He was still pretending they were on a long trip and not on the run, even though Bryn had seen the tension on his face. If his questions were to remain unanswered, Bryn thought he might as well daydream about something pleasant—Drena.

And so passed the first day of their escape.

So far, the forest canopy had shielded them from most of the sun's light and warmth. Now, the sun was setting. Gerald looked at the faint, golden light falling on the boy ahead of him and became more agitated.

"We must find a place to stay for the night." Gerald's deep voice broke through the hours of silence. "It shouldn't be much further, but I haven't been this deep in the woods in years. Give Reven a little push. I don't want to have to spend the night on this damn trail."

We've been riding for hours already. Where are we going to find a place to sleep in this wilderness? thought Bryn. Their cabin was so deep in the forest that many villagers thought they lived in the wilderness, but now they were somewhere much deeper.

"I smell smoke!" exclaimed Gerald, suddenly flying past him on Olander at a speed Bryn had never seen from them before. Bryn kicked his heels into Reven's side and took off after them. But the next moment, Gerald rounded a bend and was gone. Bryn shouted at Reven to go faster. After a few hundred yards,

he found himself at the edge of a clearing and pulled the horse
up. In the middle of the clearing stood a traditional-looking
building made of exposed timber framing and plaster. In the
approaching darkness, the lights inside gave a welcoming glow.
He slapped the reins and trotted over to Gerald, who was waiting
by the front door. From the smoke spiraling out of the chimney,
Bryn knew it was going to be warm in there. As he came closer,
he saw a sign, with old-fashioned lettering carved into it, hanging
above the door—*The Forest Inn.*

"Wait here a minute," said Gerald. "I'll see if we can get a
room for the night." He pushed open the heavy wooden door
and disappeared.

Bryn climbed down from Reven and rubbed his thighs. He
hadn't ridden so much for a long time and just realized his hands
and feet were numb. He thought a look around would warm him
up, but he noticed another sign next to the door.

This House is under the protection of the Peace Keepers.
Breakers of Oaths are not welcome.
Beds available for our smaller guests.
The use of any 'natural talent' or 'gift' is strictly forbidden in the public
bar.
Fraternity symbols must be concealed at all times.
Fresh tripe every Wednesday.

Apart from the tripe, which he disliked anyway, Bryn had no idea what the rest of the sign meant. As he went to reread it, the door opened, and Gerald stepped out.

"Why are you hanging around here? Take the horses around the back to the stable. Feed them, groom them, make sure their coats are dry, and then come in. Tonight, we'll sleep here."

A while later, Bryn entered the dining room, gleaming with sweat and tired from his chores. The murmur from the few guests inside stopped for a moment, then began again. The place was warm, and everything about it felt comforting. Down one wall was a row of tables in booths with carved partitions, where people were eating and drinking. The massive stone and timber walls, rendered with clay, also added to the homey atmosphere. But the focal point was the mighty open fireplace at the rear of the building where a big fire was blazing.

Gerald was at the bar, having a lively conversation with the broad-shouldered older man polishing glasses behind it. But when Bryn appeared, they both fell silent, and Gerald sat back on his stool to look over to the menu board on the wall.

"Yes, so, ah … we'll have the vegetable soup and bread," he muttered to the man, "a glass of your finest red wine for me, and a mug of table beer for the boy."

The innkeeper nodded, glanced at Bryn, and headed to the kitchen. Gerald pushed the stool back and showed Bryn to their table.

No sooner had they taken their seats than the food arrived. Bryn looked at Gerald, but he had his head down and was fiddling with his sleeves. Two large bowls of hot soup landed in front of them, plus a board with a warm, crusty loaf on it. Bryn was starving, and he plunged his wooden spoon into the thick soup. He'd only eaten dry bread and stale cheese on the ride and never imagined there'd be a proper, warm meal for supper. And the soup tasted good too, especially with the dollops of sour cream on top.

"The innkeeper has given us a room up in the roof," Gerald whispered, looking around the room. "A quiet night in the warmth will do us good. I don't think we're in any danger here from our … visitors."

Bryn responded with what had been on his mind most of the day. "Can I ask something?"

Gerald could only mumble and nod a yes, his mouth crammed with bread and soup.

"The last of our 'visitors' asked me how I killed Kaull," said Bryn, drawing quotes in the air. "What did he mean by that?"

"Shhh!" Gerald hissed, crumbs shooting out his mouth. "You're not going to discuss that sort of thing in public!" He looked around at the almost empty dining room and pointed at Bryn's bowl. "Eat your soup and stop worrying so foolishly. Your mind must have played a trick on you. I do not believe these animals can speak," he spat out.

And that was the end of the conversation. Gerald wiped his bowl clean with what was left of the bread and tugged at a loose thread he found on his sleeve.

In the harsh silence, Bryn sipped his beer, thinking hard about everything that had happened. *No, you're mistaken, Gerald. I heard it, and it spoke.*

After the meal, they went straight to their room. Both were tired after two nights without decent sleep, and tomorrow, they had to be up bright and early again. In the end, they were glad to sleep and escape the uncomfortable silence between them. Bryn snuggled into the warm, white sheets and turned to Gerald, who was in the bed on the other side of the room.

"Are we safe here, Gerald?" he asked quietly.

"You can sleep in peace," came Gerald's deep, soothing voice. "The Forest Inn is a safe place, almost as safe as where we're headed." With a hearty yawn, he turned over.

"Where are we going?"

But all he heard was Gerald's deep breaths, followed by snoring.

THE PANRA PASS

The two exiles set off before dawn. In their hands were two small bags the landlord had given them for their breakfast. Bryn pulled on the reins and looked inside his bag, taking out a warm cinnamon pastry and smiling. The sun was coming up, and, for the first time in days, he felt good. *It's true what they say about a good night's sleep.* Then he squeezed Reven with his heels, and they trotted along the snowy path further south.

They had been riding in silence for some time when the trail widened. Soon, Bryn heard Gerald's horse coming up next to him.

"To reach our destination, we have to go over the Panra," said Gerald, looking straight ahead. "It's the highest mountain in the Arell Mountains. To get over it, we need to take the mountain pass. It's a dangerous place in this weather. Even in summer, it's not without its dangers." Gerald glanced over to Bryn. "There's one more thing. We cannot take Olander and Reven over the pass. We'll have to leave them behind. I'm sorry, Bryn."

Bryn's face went blank. The horses had been part of his life for as long as he could remember. To abandon them meant his past life would be gone forever.

"Gerald, you can' t be serious? You love them! They're the best animals you could wish for."

"You're right, son. But I have no other option," he said, his voice tight. "The important thing is getting you somewhere safe and away from those creatures. I will make any sacrifice for that." At that, he dropped his horse to a slower trot and fell in behind Bryn.

The silence between them grew. *What else will I lose?* Bryn wondered. *Reven, my friends, my home, Drena—what comes next? All I have left is Gerald.* He peeked over his shoulder at his foster father, who was scouring the surroundings. Ice crystals had formed in his dark beard. Yet, under his cloak, his arms were bare. *Hard shell, soft heart*, thought Bryn. *But I have to trust him.* He spurred Reven to a faster trot, determined to get out of the cold, the uncertainty, and the fear to this place where he would be safe.

By late afternoon, the path had become narrower and steeper. Large rocks and loose gravel made it difficult for the two horses to find a firm footing. And it was getting colder and windier the higher they got.

"Stop!" cried Gerald. "Stop, Bryn. It's no use anymore. From here, we go on foot."

This moment was what Bryn had been dreading. The stiffness in his legs made it hard to get out of the saddle. But it was time to say goodbye to Reven.

Gerald went to Olander, spoke to him, and then came over to Bryn. The wind was strong, and Gerald had to shout in Bryn's ear. "Unsaddle Reven and take only the necessary things with you. We shouldn't be on the pass longer than a day or two."

Bryn hefted the saddle off Reven's back, filled his knapsack with food and warm clothes, and put it over his shoulders. Finally, he slung his bow and quiver over his neck and swung them over his shoulder. Wiping tears from his eyes, he walked around to Reven and put his arms around the animal's neck.

"Take good care of yourself! Alright?" The horse's ears flicked, and he scraped a hoof in the snow. Bryn hoped it meant the gelding understood him and walked back to Gerald.

"Ready?"

Bryn nodded, wiped away his tears, and started climbing up the pass. If he had turned around, he would've spotted Gerald say something to Reven and seen the animals walk calmly back to the valley.

Bryn and Gerald were making plodding progress. The wind was so strong that they had to brace themselves against it. It had also begun to snow. They had covered quite a distance after two hours, but the pass was still a long way off. The sun had already set, and darkness began to creep over the lonely mountain path. As night fell, the temperatures also began to plummet. They would not survive the night without shelter.

"We need to rest," yelled Gerald. "Look for a sheltered spot nearby."

Considering the cold and the biting wind, Bryn thought this would be impossible. But he didn't say anything.

Tired, they trudged on, without any sign of warm or safe shelter. Meanwhile, it had become dark.

Bryn strayed a little off the path and stumbled over a branch. Cursing, he looked at what tripped him. There were hardly any trees growing at this height, but this one seemed to be the exception. Because of the masses of snow, the wooden giant had partly fallen over. Now, its large, needled branches hung low above the ground, forming a small, natural cave. Here, they would be at least a little protected.

Bryn called out to Gerald, who was already quite a few yards ahead and hard to see in the darkness and falling snow. Louder, he called again, "Gerald, I found something!"

Gerald turned to see Bryn waving frantically at him. Bryn pointed down to the side of the path. Gerald whistled his approval and came down.

"Great idea, son. You might make a decent huntsman after all."

They crawled under the low-hanging branches, trying not to shake off the snow, which should add extra protection from the cold. Bryn soon realized the tree only offered limited protection from the wind and frozen ground. Furthermore, the snow melted due to his body heat, and the bottom of his trousers grew wet. They would never be able to start a fire in this weather, especially since they didn't have any dry wood. But there was no better shelter for tonight. Bryn thought longingly about last night's inn. He also realized how unprotected they were on this lonely mountain path. Gerald seemed to think so too. He had the ax on his knees again, with both hands resting on it.

"Try to sleep, Bryn. I'll keep watch. I can cut off the heads of a horde of these creatures if I need to."

They sat close together. Bryn had never been so cold in his life. *I won't be able to sleep a wink here.* Yet, sometime later, Gerald was shaking him roughly.

"Wake up!"

Bryn needed a moment to realize where he was. He was cold as ice, and his neck hurt—the first sign of an imminent cold or worse.

"What is it?" he asked in a husky voice.

Gerald lifted a finger to his lips. "I heard something," he said, a hushed whisper that Bryn struggled to understand. "Let's hope it's only an animal lost up here because of the storm."

Bryn didn't think he could get any colder, but now, an icy shiver ran down his spine, and the hair on the back of his neck stood up. *They've found us! No animal is running around up here in this weather. Of all the places to be, and no help about.* His stomach tightened painfully at the thought.

Gerald saw the look on Bryn's face. "I'm going outside for a look," he reassured him. "Grab your bow and arrow and have it at the ready until I come back."

"Don't leave me on my own, Gerald," Bryn cried loudly.

"Shhh." Gerald covered Bryn's mouth and thought for a moment. "All right, then come with me. I suppose you're no safer here than out there. Cover me with your bow."

Bryn took his weapon and crawled out of their shelter behind Gerald. Outside, the wind tore at him, and the cold was indescribable. Snow whipped into their eyes. Bryn pulled his scarf in front of his face to protect himself a little and looked around. Pitch-black night surrounded them. Gerald had lifted his ax, ready to fight. He walked ahead into the darkness, and Bryn followed him. There were no traces of their late-night visitors. Suddenly, Bryn heard a kind of howling behind him, but the howling wind made it impossible to identify its source. Panic-stricken, he turned around. There was nothing there. Immediately, Gerald was by his side. The tension in his face made him look even more threatening, but it gave Bryn great comfort. They stared into the darkness, defying the driving snow. But neither of them could see anything.

"We can only stay out here a few more minutes," Gerald shouted over the wind, "or we'll freeze to death."

Bryn nodded. His strength was fading, and he knew it would lull him into a deceptive tiredness that would spell his death if he gave in.

They circled the tree. Again, Bryn thought he heard howling, but he wasn't sure. Then, out of the corner of his eye, he spotted movement. Something was sprinting toward him.

"Gerald!" Bryn yelled.

Though Gerald was only a few yards to his left, he was facing the other way and didn't hear Bryn over the howling storm. Bryn's heart thumped in his chest. *They've found me!* He was no longer conscious of the biting cold—only of the figure racing toward him. But his hands were numb. Three times, he fumbled to nock an arrow on the bow—and then dropped them both. In his panic, he had forgotten everything he had learned, and he ran toward Gerald. After two unsteady steps, he tripped and fell into the snow, turning to see the creature almost on top of him.

The impact had driven the air out of Bryn's lungs, and he'd scraped his knees on the frozen earth. He tried to get back on his feet but stumbled, and the creature ran into him and knocked him down. He couldn't react anymore. *Now they have me!* he thought as some kind of animal tried to push him over. Bryn closed his eyes and held his hands in front of his face, braced for the inevitable.

Something rough and wet touched his nose and licked it. Bryn opened one eye and found himself staring at white-yellow fangs. It was only a snow fox, standing trembling above him, licking his face. Even more, the animal seemed to want to cuddle up to him. Laughing, Bryn tickled the animal's ears and called out, thrilled that he was still alive.

"You scared me! What are you doing here in this weather, little fella?"

The animal stared at him with dark eyes, licked his face, and scratched at Bryn's upper body with its little paws.

Suddenly, Gerald was beside him, the ax lifted above his head.

"Gerald! Stop, it's fine. It's all right!" Bryn yelled.

Gerald burst into laughter. He dropped to the ground with a laugh so contagious that, soon, both were in fits. Gerald could hardly speak.

"Such great hunters," he spluttered, "that a little snow fox can fool us like that!"

They crawled back under the fallen tree, and the snow-white fox followed after them. As Bryn sat, it put its snout through the entrance, a bit of snow trickling down its black nose.

"Come in, that's a good little fella. It's warmer in here." The fox padded in, its eyes fixed on Gerald, who was smiling at it, and crept over to Bryn. Bryn picked it up and noticed how much warmer he felt with the furry little creature in his arms. And even though the damp fur smelled a bit, it didn't bother him. The smell was strangely familiar, although he didn't know why.

Cuddled up with the small animal, Bryn fell asleep almost immediately.

Bryn felt like he'd just closed his eyes when Gerald woke him gently. "We have to be going."

Bryn looked around for the fox, but it was gone.

"He disappeared earlier when you were fast asleep. But who knows, maybe you'll see him again. In these parts, they have a saying, 'The Panra Never Forgets,'" said Gerald, winking.

Still, Bryn didn't get to say goodbye to his little friend. He gave a deep sigh and picked up his few belongings. When he stuck his head out from between the branches, a dark night greeted him. Gerald let him sleep for only a few hours; he knew they had to keep moving. They both noticed it was much colder outside the shelter. Bryn began jumping up and down to get his blood circulating. Gerald pushed him on up the mountain pass, and Bryn was soon much warmer than he ever wanted to be.

They made it to the summit of the pass as the sun was rising. The weather had improved too, and the view over the Panra Valley was spectacular. Thousands of snow-covered trees lay majestically below them, some of their tops glowing pink in the winter dawn. But Bryn could not see this safe place of Gerald's anywhere. He asked Gerald where they were going.

"We have to go down even deeper first. Then you will see it. You can't miss it," Gerald answered and didn't explain any further, beginning their descent.

A few hours later, Bryn saw a large, dark object far away, on the side of a small mountain on the opposite side of the valley. But it was another hour before he realized it was the outline of a castle. Meanwhile, the weather had worsened. The sun had been driven off by dark, grey clouds, and the smell of snow was once more in the air.

THE LEKAN GATE

Slowly, Bryn and Gerald made their way toward the massive fortress. Bryn could now see a formidable, dark stone wall surrounding it and a steep, stony path leading to the main gate. As they climbed, the path became narrower, the ground falling away to a sheer drop on either side. The bitter alpine winds chilled Bryn to the bone, and he pulled his cloak tighter around him. *First up and then down, and now up again!* he complained to himself. But Gerald didn't seem bothered by the weather or the steep path. He was climbing without a hint of tiredness or effort. Bryn envied him.

"We're almost there!" Gerald said, making Bryn jump. They had not spoken to each other for hours to conserve their strength. Apart from the howling wind and the occasional cawing of some large crows, they'd heard nothing. Bryn lifted his head toward Gerald, who was in front of him, and immediately, the wind stung his eyes, making them water.

"It's not far now, Bryn. You should see the gate around the next bend."

Bryn muttered something under his breath.

But that was all Gerald needed. He gave a quick nod and trudged on, expressionless, defiant in the face of both wind and mountain.

Almost there? And then what? He hasn't told me how this castle and its people are going to help us! Even now, as it towered over them, Gerald refused to say anything. *All he ever says is, we will find protection there, you'll be safe there.*

Exhausted, Bryn slogged on, his strength all but gone. He had never covered such a great distance in such a short time and was about to suggest they rest when he saw the large gate. It was so big that he wondered who could even open it. He stopped, bent over with his hands on his thighs, and took a deep breath. He eyed up the wood and wrought-iron gate, and a faint smile crossed his face. *We're here!* He couldn't believe it.

Gerald was already at the mighty gate and beckoned Bryn with an aggressive wave of his hand.

"Come on!" he yelled in frustration.

With the end of the journey now in sight, Bryn rallied his remaining strength and staggered forth. Breathless, he made it to Gerald and dropped his pack on the ground.

Up close, the castle entrance was bigger and more intimidating than Bryn first thought. Somehow, it filled him with dread. Like an oversized eye, the gate seemed to be watching the two strangers. Bryn shuddered at the thought but wanted a closer look. Carved into the wood were scenes from a battle, depicting cruel and atrocious acts—a fight between thousands of fierce-looking soldiers and dragons and other mythological beasts.

Some even had eyes made of colorful gemstones the size of Bryn's fist.

Especially striking was an arrangement of numerous gemstones that changed color with the angle of view. They appeared to stream out of the hands of a small, old man with an oversized hat, a beautiful woman with long hair, and a muscular man with an angular face. The three characters formed the center of the scene. The gemstones flowing from their hands got smaller and smaller at the edge of the scene. They framed and flooded the entire battle as if they wanted to influence it. But Bryn wondered why they didn't shoot their magical stones at the hideous monster standing behind them. He studied the picture, which looked more like a monumental work of art than a mere castle gate. He had never seen such fine metal and woodwork, and the many precious stones must be of immeasurable value.

But there was something strange about this gate. Bryn needed some time before he noticed it. It didn't have a lock or a handle. The whole gate seemed embedded in the wall without any indication where and how to open it.

"How do we get in? Is this a gate or just a work of art to blind poor travelers like us?"

Gerald chuckled. "No, my impatient young friend, this is the Lekan Gate, and it opens only to those worthy enough to enter the Castle of Âlaburg. Place your hand on one of the gemstones."

Bryn frowned, but knowing Gerald rarely tolerated being contradicted, he put his right hand on a small stone. The multicolored gemstone felt smooth and cool at first, but suddenly, it became noticeably warmer and seemed to pulsate. Frightened, Bryn wanted to pull his hand back, but some invisible force stopped him. His hand refused to obey him.

WHAT IS YOUR DESIRE? a voice boomed in his head.

Bryn cried out in shock. He struggled to free his hand from the stone, but the more he tried, the tighter it held the pulsating, glowing gem.

WHAT IS YOUR DESIRE, BRYN?

For a moment, Bryn stopped struggling. *How does the gate know my name? And why can it speak?*

"How do you know my name?"

YOU ARE NOT THE ONE ASKING THE QUESTIONS, BRYN. TELL ME, WHAT IS YOUR DESIRE?

Bryn tried to think of an answer. *Why does the gate want to know something about me? It already knows who I am!* So Bryn just said the first thing that crossed his mind.

"We want to come in!"

Bryn thought he heard a short laugh in his mind.

THAT IS A WISE ANSWER TO A QUESTION FROM A GATE, MY BOY. BUT TELL ME, WHO IS YOUR COMPANION?

In his mind, Bryn answered, *"Gerald, the gamekeeper."*

Again, a short laugh, or something similar, flared in Bryn's head.

SO HE IS A GAMEKEEPER AT THE MOMENT. VERY WELL. IS HE YOUR FRIEND, YOUNG BRYN?

"Yes, you could say that."

There was a moment of silence.

ARE YOU SURE YOU WANT TO ENTER ÁLABURG? MANY DANGERS LURK WTIHIN THESE WALLS, AND YOUR PATH WILL BE ONE OF THE MOST CHALLENGING EVER TAKEN HERE. BUT AT ITS END, GREAT KNOWLEDGE AND EVEN WISDOM AWAIT YOU.

"Yes!"

The answer came from Bryn's mind before he could think about it. He had heard the warnings of the gate, and they frightened him. But deep in his heart, he knew that he had to and wanted to say yes.

A QUICK DECISION, BRYN. AND MUCH APPRECIATED. THEN I WELCOME YOU TO ÁLABURG, A PLACE OF FRIENDSHIP AND PEACE. MAY YOU INCREASE THE GLORY OF YOUR NATION AND BRING PEACE TO RAZUCLAN. FROM THIS DAY ON, THE LEKAN GATE IS ALWAYS OPEN TO YOU.

The large door opened without a sound, presenting a view of the courtyard of the castle.

Excited, Bryn turned to Gerald. "The gate spoke to me, and it knew my name. Do you hear? A gate spoke to me! And it said something about friendship and peace—"

"Yes, yes, that's great, but now let's go in. I want to get out of this cold."

Stunned by Gerald's reaction, Bryn stopped. "You knew it would talk to me?"

Gerald glanced down at the boy and smiled. "I had hoped so. Now, get in here before it changes its mind. And please stop with the questions!"

They entered the courtyard in silence, but Bryn's eyes were wide with excitement.

Several people with thick hoods covering their faces scurried about the vast space, but nobody seemed to take notice of the two newcomers. A group of tall, slender people ran past the two in a hurry, but Bryn couldn't make out their faces. They also had their hoods pulled down hard against the cold. Only their blond hair stuck out from under their robes. A little way off, Bryn could see two tiny figures asleep on a bench under a mighty tower at the center of the castle. A thin layer of snow had already covered them and the empty bottles scattered around them. The reddish stain in the snow nearby told Bryn they had been celebrating a little too hard the night before.

Bryn noticed a young man staggering toward them with a half-full bottle of wine in his hand. But before the drunken stranger could reach Bryn, Gerald stepped in and grabbed him by the collar. The young man launched into a slurred, incomprehensible tirade and tried to strike him. But Gerald held him in a vice-like grip. Bryn saw Gerald whisper something to the young man, who froze. Although Bryn would never have thought it possible, he became even paler. Then he bowed oddly and left, almost slipping twice in the snow as he made his escape.

Gerald came back with a face that could have soured milk.

"Who was that?" Bryn asked.

"Nobody," Gerald snapped. Bryn didn't dare probe further.

Gerald dragged him deeper into the courtyard. The defense tower, under which the two little figures were sleeping, was so high that the top remained hidden in the low-hanging clouds. As if wanting to protect it, several other buildings surrounded it, all in different styles. Everywhere Bryn looked, he could see various little towers on all the castle buildings.

Some of the buildings seemed to be made entirely of wood, although Bryn couldn't see a single nail anywhere. They looked like they'd grown there instead of been built. One of the most prominent towers looked like it was made from one massive tree; its dark, shiny wood was so smooth. The strange building had no doors, but hundreds of windows, flowers, and other plants were growing over it. The sea of flowers was quite a sight, and their sweet smell blew over to Bryn. He was so excited he failed to realize none of these plants should be in bloom now.

Right next to the wooden houses were several exposed timber-frame buildings with plastered walls and shingles on the roof. Bryn had seen these in Sefal and many other villages. They had standard wooden doors and leadlight windows, and their towers were of medium size and quite dull. In front of some of the windows stood a few stunted plants, no way comparable to the floral splendor next door. Several floors up, hard, frozen laundry was hanging out to dry, and behind some windows, a cozy, suffused yellow light was burning. *A bit like in Sefal,* Bryn thought to himself, feeling homesick.

Several small buildings followed, which appeared to be made wholly of granite. Compared to the tree houses, they looked clumsy, but they were artfully decorated with hundreds of stone carvings. Some of them seemed so realistic that Bryn had to blink to see if they were real or not. It was noticeable that the granite houses had the fewest and lowest towers. Also, their windows and doors were all tiny, as if for small children.

To the right were some pitch-black housing blocks with tall, jagged, angular towers. These houses lacked any decoration. The iron-reinforced doors looked forbidding. The windows had thick steel grilles, and you could not see into the rooms behind them because they were so dark. The tops of the towers were also adorned with grotesque-looking skulls. *And who might live in there? Or is it a prison?* Bryn pondered and turned away. The sight of those buildings gave him goosebumps.

They then came across a garden planted with herbs; Bryn spotted rosemary, thyme, and mint. He could also see wild strawberries that, despite the cold, were full of ripe fruit. A narrow path wound through the plants toward a small stone cube at the base of a high wall. The cube's walls were whiter than white, nearly too bright to look at. It had no windows or doors, but Bryn detected wisps of grey smoke rising from a chimney on the flat roof. And it seemed to have been hewn from a single piece of rock.

"This way, Bryn," said Gerald, pointing to the cube.

TEJAL

As they followed the path along the wild strawberries, Bryn heard a faint voice giggling. It was so infectious and full of joy, Bryn started grinning himself.

"Oh, Gerald, it's so good to see you back!" several voices tittered.

"Yes, it's been so long. We missed you. Where have you been?" asked another.

Then a choir of a hundred voices began asking the same questions. "Where were you, Gerald? Where have you been?" The voices giggled so much, it sounded as if they were teasing him.

"Gerald, who is saying this?" asked Bryn.

"Nobody! Don't listen. It's best for both of us."

"Don't listen? Gerald, where are your manners? Don't you like us anymore?" the cheerful, high-pitched voices asked in unison.

Gerald mumbled something incomprehensible and pushed Bryn's shoulder to keep him moving forward.

Suddenly, Bryn noticed movement. It seemed as if the wild strawberries were alive. Then he saw tiny creatures crawling all over them. Their small heads looked like a strawberry—only with a woman's face, and they laughed non-stop. Their bodies were slim and green, but Bryn couldn't tell if it was their clothes or their skin that resembled the color of the plant's leaves. The tiny, transparent wings on their backs began to flutter and carried the little creatures over to the two of them.

"Have you forgotten us, Master Gerald? How naughty of you!" Again, hundreds of tiny giggles filled the air. The little creatures flew up to Gerald and tugged on his beard and ears with their small hands. "Gerald, when are you going to tell us another story? When?"

Gerald swatted at the creatures fluttering around his head. But Bryn noticed that Gerald, who was usually quite rough, was careful not to hit any of the delicate little beings.

"Who is your new companion, Gerald? Tell us about him! Tell us about your adventures!" The little strawberry women laughed to themselves.

"My dear Samuusen, please forgive me, but I don't have time now. Tejal is waiting for us. But I will make up for the lost time and tell you stories of the world outside," Gerald said, bowing low. "Please let me and young Bryn pass."

"Very well, Master, but remember your promise. We'll be waiting for you, and, next time, we won't make it so easy for you to pass." With a last tug on Gerald's reddening ears, the strawberry creatures flew off, giggling.

The garden fell silent, but a sense of sadness fell over Bryn as he watched the little creatures flutter away. Bryn sighed and went on with Gerald. Asking any questions about the strawberry women, he knew, were pointless.

They made their way to the cube. The shimmering white surface was so disconcerting that Bryn needed to slightly turn his head away. But now, in his peripheral vision, Bryn could see the building had a door. Dumbfounded, Bryn forced himself to look directly at the cube again, but the door disappeared. *Strange*, he thought. *So, when I turn my*—but before Bryn could finish moving his head, it appeared again out of the corner of his eye. And when he looked back, it was gone—and so was Gerald.

He shouted Gerald's name, but there was no answer. *He must have gone in already.* Bryn tilted his head, shifted his eyes sideways until they hurt, and stumbled toward the cube. But in the end, it wasn't that difficult. When he was directly in front of the cube, the spell seemed to break, and the door appeared. It had a golden handle in the shape of a dove carrying a snake. It was heavy in Bryn's hand, and he turned it.

"That took forever," said Gerald gruffly. "You just look through your fingers."

Bryn's eyebrows arched. *He's been in here before.*

"Wait here until I come back," Gerald added, pointing to an uncomfortable-looking bench. "If you need anything, contact Gwendolin." Gerald nodded toward a blond girl sitting at a large desk. Then he went through a massive door that slammed shut behind him.

Bryn took a seat on the bench. He was right; it was uncomfortable. Somehow, it forced him to sit completely straight. If he tried to wriggle about and make himself comfortable, it gave him a sharp bolt of pain or he slipped off the wooden seat. So Bryn sat there stiffly, but his eyes were free to wander. The room itself was modest, and several, brilliant white lamps hung from the ceiling. The walls were not as dazzling as they were outside but more cream-colored. And everywhere, there were cabinets filled with trophies. Above these hung large oil paintings of stern-looking characters in colorful costumes. But before Bryn could make any sense of it, he heard a high voice behind him.

"Who are you?"

Bryn jolted, turning around to see the pretty blond girl staring at him.

"Are you talking to me?" he asked, wide-eyed.

"Well, who else? There's nobody else here," she sniggered. "I am Gwendolin, and I'm one of the sisters and brothers of the Elbendingen fraternity. And you?"

Bryn noticed his head getting hot. Girls intimidated him, especially pretty ones, but he tried not to look too flustered.

"My name is Bryn—I have no brothers or sisters."

The girl chuckled to herself. "No, you fool. It's not about real siblings. It's about—"

Right at that moment, a woman's voice sounded throughout the room.

"Please leave our guest alone and finish the account for the papyrus order, Gwendolin. We're not paying you to be Âlaburg's biggest gossip."

The girl turned pale and immediately began to rummage through a stack of documents, ignoring Bryn.

"It's almost finished, Grand Master Tejal. Please forgive me." She began scribbling something down. But she knocked over the pile of papers, and, trying to gather them up, pushed another stack onto the floor. Bryn watched, bemused, at the chaos unfolding in front of him.

The slim, fair-haired woman, almost hidden behind her large desk, looked up.

"Why have you come here, Master Gerald?" she asked coldly. From her intonation and expression, it was clear she was comfortable giving orders and having them obeyed. The precious-looking rings on her fingers clacked on the dark, polished wood as she spoke. "Is it because of the boy out there? Do you remember the last time you found a student and brought her here? It all but destroyed this institution."

Gerald squirmed. When he stood before Grand Master Tejal, he always had a lump in his throat. Her stern gaze and imperious-looking bun intimidated him in a way only a few beings in Razuclan could do. The formality she now used to address him also made Gerald feel uncomfortable—so did Tejal's black, tight-fitting robe.

Even so, Gerald knew the Chancellor's anger at him was justified given the circumstances. He had made many mistakes. But that was a long time ago, when he and Tejal were much closer—a former life. But now, how was he going to—

"So?" prodded Tejal.

"Yes?" he blurted out, forgetting where he was.

"Yes, what? Be more specific! Why have you returned after so many years? Why now and not when we needed you—when I—when we sent for you?" She glowered at him.

Gerald swallowed hard and wished he had something to drink. His throat was so dry.

"I'm here for Bryn. That's the boy out there. I would like him admitted."

Tejal's gaze darkened as she fixed Gerald with a piercing look. "I've heard that from you before, and we both know how that turned out."

"No, no, this is different. The boy is special. They're looking for him. I had to bring him here. This university is the only place he'll be safe."

"They're looking for him, you say. Is this supposed to be an admission criterion for us now? That somebody is looking for somebody?" she said, staring Gerald straight in the eye.

"Of course, I don't mean it that way, Grand Master," he said, lowering his gaze. "The boy is special. He might be our best hope."

Tejal rolled her eyes. "I never thought you'd be one to believe in hocus-pocus, Gerald." When the Chancellor realized she'd used only his name, she cleared her throat. "Our only hope is this university and not some chosen one for the mob to worship. I leave such daydreams to our venerated religious Masters. What is his fraternity?"

"I couldn't determine it."

Astonishment spread over Tejal's face. "Students here learn to do this test in their first semester. I have every right to expect a Master, even a former one, to perform it."

Gerald struggled to remain polite. "I know how to do the test, but Bryn's result was … strange."

"Strange? What do you mean? Be more specific!"

"I can't describe it. The best thing is for you to test the boy yourself," said Gerald, more confident now.

"Ha, you think I don't see what you're trying to do? You want to make me curious, so I test him here. But if I do that, I have to take him in because the fraternities' spells then bind me to assign him. No, I won't make it that easy for you. I will test the boy, but under one condition, Gerald," she said, smiling wryly.

Gerald grew restless. He'd suspected this conversation might take such a turn but had hoped Tejal's curiosity would spare him any conditions. "And what is that?"

"You know what it is. I want you to stay here and take up your old position. As you know, it's been vacant for some time."

Gerald drew a deep breath and tried to respond.

"Spare me your arguments. This is my condition. Accept it or leave the university with the boy immediately."

Gerald's shoulders slumped. "I thought you might ask me to do that, Tejal. "But you know I can't …"

Tejal raised an eyebrow, and Gerald fell silent. For a moment, the two just stared at each other.

"All right. All right," said Gerald. "Test the boy."

Tejal laughed to herself and touched her hand to her larynx. "Gwendolin, would you please send young Bryn in."

THE TEST

Bryn opened the door to the office and went in, his heart pounding harder and harder with each step. Tejal looked him up and down, and Bryn saw the immediate displeasure on her face.

"He's not that big. I imagine he doesn't pose any particular threat," Tejal said to Gerald as if Bryn wasn't there. "Greetings, my name is Tejal. I am the Chancellor of this university. From now on, you will address me as Grand Master or Chancellor. You will also bow formally before the other Masters of this great institution and me. Well, don't stand there, boy, bow. Has Gerald taught you no manners at all? It appears not—but that's not surprising when you consider his own. What's your full name?"

The constant stream of information and questions left Bryn speechless. He gave a slow, awkward bow. Overwhelmed by what was happening, his face turned bright red, and he looked to Gerald for help.

"He can be a bit shy sometimes," Gerald whispered.

"Or is it possible he's not too bright?" she asked, raising her voice. Again, Tejal asked Bryn for his name, only this time, she spoke slowly and over articulated each word.

Bryn was annoyed by her arrogance and spitefulness. He wasn't stupid. After all, he hadn't been Gerald's apprentice all these years for nothing. He could read and write, unlike most of his peers, and his math was so good nobody could cheat him at the market. He had also been one of the best trackers and trappers in the valley and had already shot his first roebuck years ago. He became angry and looked Tejal square in the eye.

"I'm not stupid. My name is Bryn McDermit."

At that, a slight, almost imperceptible smile flitted over Tejal's otherwise stern face.

"Well, he might not be deaf, but he's certainly impudent. As his guardian and educator, Gerald, I suggest you try another approach with the boy. Should—I repeat—*should* the boy be accepted, his impertinence has already earned him his first punishment."

She became thoughtful for a moment and turned to Bryn. "So, tell me how old you are."

"Sixteen, Grand Master," he replied softly.

"Well, there you go. Seems you do know about numbers. Sixteen. That's young for a human student. But then again, no one knows how old the dwarf students are either." She said the last part more to herself than anyone else.

Before Bryn could think about what Tejal meant by dwarves, she moved on to the next question.

"Who are your parents, Bryn? It's nice you have Gerald's name, but he's not your father, is he?" She glanced at Gerald and raised an eyebrow; Gerald shook his head briskly.

Again, Bryn's face reddened. He hated strangers asking him about his parents. All his life, he'd asked himself the same question but never found an answer. It was even worse to admit he had no parents. He stammered out his usual response.

"How can you not know who your parents are? Gerald, what does this mean?"

Gerald cleared his throat. "Well, I found Bryn in the woods one day. I was fox hunting. I followed the animal to its den. When I realized it had cubs, I gave up the hunt and was about to return when I saw him." Gerald pointed his thick index finger at Bryn. "He was lying in the warm burrow, playing with two small fox cubs. They seemed to get along. Bryn was fearless in dealing with the little predators, and they treated him gently. Also, the mother animal seemed to have already accepted him as one of her own. But he couldn't have been there long. His clothing was still clean."

Hearing this, Bryn understood why the little snow fox's smell had seemed familiar to him last night.

"Still, it was clear I couldn't leave him there. After several attempts, with the vixen defending the boy like her own offspring, I grabbed the boy and pulled him out. The next day, I went to the village council. I believed the mother would soon be found. There are very few people down in the Arell Mountains, and they all know one another. But none of the women were missing a child, and there were no rumors about abandoned children. So, the council decided the child should stay with me. It had been a harsh winter too, and none of the others were confident they could manage another mouth to feed. So, after some back and forth with the council, I agreed to raise the child as my own."

Tejal listened and nodded along to Gerald's story. "Do you have any guesses about the parents?"

Bryn's eyes widened; he was eager to hear more.

"No, I don't," Gerald murmured, shooting Bryn a furtive look. "I have no idea who Bryn's natural parents might be. And finding him deep in the forest was pure chance."

"Very well. The matter of his parentage is not important either. The test will determine which of the nations he belongs to and which fraternity we can assign him. These attacks by the enemies of peace are a recognition he has the gift. I'm convinced they wanted to prevent him from coming here. Gerald, it was wise of you to bring him," Tejal admitted in a conciliatory tone. "Especially in these times, we cannot afford to pass on any gifted person. Razuclan needs trained protectors of the peace."

The Grand Master turned to Bryn. "Come to me."

Gerald nodded to Bryn, who stepped forward and bowed again. Tejal acknowledged this gesture with a smile.

"Bryn, this is Âlaburg University. Here, we teach whatever is necessary so peace and friendship can reign among the four enlightened nations," she said solemnly. "Only a few are allowed to enter through the Lekan Gate. That it has chosen you is a good sign. It means you belong here—that you have the gift.

"But your fraternity will be more decisive for you and your future here. It will be your family for the next several years and help guide you through your education. Even after you graduate, you remain connected to your fraternity for life. Âlaburg has four large student fraternities or brotherhoods. Of course, the latter term is not correct because, naturally, we also have female students here." She almost seemed to wink. "The honorable fraternity of Elbendingen is for members of the ancient nation of high elves. Not only are they skilled summoners and magicians, but they also equal the other fraternities in almost all other respects.

"The Ølsgendur fraternity is home to the dwarves, recognized for their artistry and craftsmanship. It is they who built the Lekan Gate as well as many of the other incredible buildings and works of art here. But they are also brave warriors and the best mathematicians in Razuclan.

"Only the Řischnărr fraternity can claim to be a true brotherhood. It accepts only the proud sons of orcs, the greatest and most powerful warriors of the known world. All enemies should fear their physical strength and their fury. Few can match an orc in battle, and you should never make an enemy of any of them.

"The fourth is the Bond-of-Faith fraternity, and the one open to humans. The test will likely bind you to this one. The majority of these people are powerful religious scholars who can interpret the stars and summon the gods' power. Many great wizards and warriors have come from this fraternity over the centuries. Humans are the most adaptable nation in Razuclan, and this affiliation would allow you to pursue any path in life you choose. Now, let us begin. The test for placement is straightforward and painless."

Bryn stood in front of the Grand Master, fidgeting with his hands. *What was she talking about? A gift? What was it? Wizards, elves, dwarves, and what the hell is an orc?*

Tejal took Bryn's hands in hers. "Open your mind to me! The incantation I am about to speak will reveal where you belong. The powers within Âlaburg will assist me. The spell cast on you will also allow you to move about the grounds undisturbed and enter your fraternity house. Furthermore, it forces everyone to use the common language, the one most spoken in Razuclan, the human language. So, this will not present any problems for you. We use this spell so everyone can communicate with one another and follow the lectures."

Bryn pulled his hands out of hers. "But what do you mean by the gift? And who are these enlightened nations?"

Tejal glared at Gerald. "Why does the boy ask me such questions, Master? Surely, he does not cling to the belief common in humans, who, in their delusional self-absorption, think magic exists only in fairy tales?" Turning to Bryn, she asked, "Haven't you heard of the four enlightened nations?"

Bryn bit his bottom lip and shook his head.

"Gerald, have you taught him nothing? The boy doesn't even know the basics about Razuclan or Âlaburg! You were a Master, and you tested him. Even if you were unable to interpret it, surely you understood he must have this basic knowledge if he is to stay alive," Tejal said sharply. "You humans! Even now, after everything that has happened, you still deny the true nature of our world …"

"That's not the way it was," Gerald defended. "You know I don't think that way. After I tested him, I thought I was wrong, and the boy was not gifted. The magic mark did not appear. Not even for a moment. Because of the great distance from Âlaburg, I had not expected it to appear permanently. Yet, even with my limited ability, I did expect to have seen a flash of it. But there was nothing. Why would I talk to him about such things and make his life unnecessarily complicated if he is not gifted? I wanted to protect him from this world and all its problems. I wanted Bryn to have a quiet and normal life—but that's all over now!"

Tejal turned to Bryn. "The world is more complicated than you humans make it out to be. Humans are not the only enlightened nation in Razuclan. You have a lot of catching up to.

Your fellow students were all trained from birth after the test showed they were gifted. For all nations on the continent, it is an honor to be thus and to be accepted into this university."

Bryn's mind was churning. *Elves, dwarves, wizards* ... Gerald had always scolded him for being a dreamer when he asked about the old legends of wizards and wars between mythical creatures.

Now Bryn had just learned these were not fairy tales.

Tejal tapped Bryn on the shoulder and turned him to face her. The Grand Master smelled of flowers, and Bryn saw her skin was flawless except for the faint wrinkles around her mouth. Her teeth were as white as snow. He hadn't realized how attractive she was. But now, standing close to her, his stomach was in a knot, and he had to swallow several times, his throat dry.

"I know this is all new and confusing for you. Put your hands in mine. Trust me. When the test is over, all your questions will be answered."

As soon as his fingers touched her soft skin, her hands closed around his with a power he had not expected. Tejal looked into his eyes.

"Try to relax, Bryn."

But for Bryn, between the collapse of his world view and the unfamiliar closeness to a woman, relaxing was impossible. In the end, he forced himself to take several deep breaths.

"Well done," Tejal encouraged him. "I will now connect the two spirits. I act only as a spectator and medium; the university will choose the correct fraternity for you. Are you ready?"

Bryn's nod was almost imperceptible, but Tejal seemed satisfied and began to murmur.

"Come, Âlaburg, hearken unto my call,

A decision is needed; a selection must befall.

A student comes here and choose you must,

If he is to learn and serve like us.

To a fraternity now he must be bound,

And bring it honor once it is found.

No matter which you shall announce,

He shall fight for peace, and our adversaries denounce."

When the Chancellor finished chanting, the light in her office began to flicker. The books on the shelves started to move, and it seemed as if the whole room was shaking. The door flew open, and a mighty, icy wind whirled about, picking up all the documents and flinging them around. As Gerald lifted his arms to protect his face, a violent flash of energy tore through the room, creating tremendous heat.

Bryn and Tejal were both in a trance and didn't notice anything. But Gerald had to hold on to a bookcase several times to avoid falling over and being hit by flying objects.

The office was utterly engulfed in chaos, but around Bryn and Tejal, all was calm.

Then, as suddenly as the commotion had started, it ebbed away. At first, the stillness seemed unreal to Gerald, and it took a moment before he released his grip on the bookcase.

Gwendolin appeared at the open door, her hair disheveled, and her eyes flitting about the room.

"What happened?" she asked, her voice trembling.

Gerald couldn't answer her. He could not think clearly and stared about the destroyed office. Loose sheets of papyrus and torn books were strewn everywhere. Paintings lay scattered on the floor, partly torn or burnt. Several trophies had tumbled through the door and formed an indescribable mess with some of Tejal's potted plants. Only Tejal's desk appeared undamaged, though there was nothing left standing on it.

Gwendolin crept through the door but slipped on some spilled ink and fell into Gerald's arms. Hanging askew in his firm grip, she repeated her question. But Gerald was still speechless. Nothing had prepared him for this.

THE RIGHT FRATERNITY

Bryn concentrated on his breathing, trying to focus on the pleasant, cool air flowing in and out of his lungs. With each breath, he became calmer and more determined. Bryn thought only of this eternal ritual of life. Breathe in, breathe out, breathe in, breathe out. Bryn sensed he was disconnecting from the world around him, sinking into a pleasant trance. Then he heard a loud humming, and his head began to ache. Suddenly, as if he'd been hit by a wave of icy water, he was wide awake again. But now his senses were so sharp, they almost overwhelmed him. He marveled at the richness of the colors he could see—and his hearing was so acute, he could pick up even the slightest sound.

The hum in Bryn's head was his blood rushing through his veins. But he was also able to distinguish other things, like the scents Tejal was wearing. Bryn realized it was a mix of lavender and rose, with a little bit of rosemary. She had been to the garden, maybe to see the Samuusen. The fragrance was intoxicating and gave Bryn goosebumps. But now, the amount of detail he could see in Tejal's office began to make his head spin. It hurt. When he looked at the desk, he saw every grain of the wood in it. He could count the eyes of the tiny spider in the corner of the ceiling and see the delicate web of silver threads shake gently every time it moved. It was too much for him to process.

But there was another sense, something Bryn had never known before. Gradually, the Chancellor's office began to blur out of focus. All at once, thousands of beams of colored light flooded the room. It was as if the windows were diamonds, splitting the light from several suns into millions of rays. Amazed, Bryn reached out for one of the flowing ribbons of color, but it eluded him. Like streams of water, they kept changing direction. But, finally, by using all his mental strength to imagine himself holding the energy in his hands, he was able to grab one of the translucent ribbons. It made his hand tingle.

Bryn grabbed a red ribbon first, then a yellow one, and, finally, a blue one. The three then fused into a dazzling mix of continually changing colors—like a rope braided from a rainbow. But, after a few seconds, it slipped through his fingers, unraveled, and the colors swirled through the room once again. Seduced by the sight, Bryn wanted to hold them one more time and focused all his attention on the colors.

Stop, Bryn! Leave the colors and come back, implored a voice in his head. But Bryn was not interested in listening. The colored ribbons were too fascinating. He tried to reach for them again.

Bryn, you must come back, the voice called with more urgency. *Fight it!* The fear in the voice forced Bryn's thoughts to clear, and the colors in the office faded a little. It felt like someone was pulling him out of the water by the collar. The brilliant colors faded, then disappeared, and he found himself gasping for air as if he'd just run a thousand yards. Bryn became conscious of his surroundings again but was overwhelmed by a deep sense of loss now that the colors were gone.

Tejal stood pale and trembling in front of him, trying to catch her breath. Her immaculate hair hung in sweaty strands across her face, and she fixed Bryn with a penetrating stare. Looking away, he saw Gerald propped up against a wall with Gwendolin still in his arms and assessed the indescribable chaos in the room. *What happened to her office?*

"I almost lost him," Tejal whispered to Gerald, her voice trembling. Then she swept back her hair with a dismissive wave of her hand. "Show me your left hand."

Bryn did not respond but watched unblinking as the Chancellor sat down in a chair next to him. He would have liked to sit down too, but the only other thing still standing in the office was the desk. Bryn, drained and unsteady, lowered himself to the floor.

"Your hand, Bryn. Please show me your left hand. We don't have much time. The Binding Spell is weak at first."

Bryn's eyes rolled back in his head, but he heard the urgency in her voice. He lifted his hand slowly up to his face. It looked like it always did.

Meanwhile, Tejal seemed to have regained her strength. She stood from the chair and knelt next to him. She took his left hand and gently turned it over, but there was nothing there. The back of his hand was completely unchanged. Tejal looked confused, and a hint of disappointment lingered on her face.

"I don't understand," she murmured. "It took so much of my strength to get him out of the realm—you were right, Gerald, this is impossible to understand. Never before have I had such difficulty bringing a student back from the test. Nor do I remember ever having this kind of reaction outside the test sphere. At most, a book fell off the shelf! But this one …" she trailed off, her attention shifting from Bryn to the ruined remains of her office.

Finally, Bryn began to realize where he was and sat up. He crawled the few feet to Tejal's great desk, grabbed the edge of it, and tried to pull himself up. Gwendolin went to help him but gave a sharp scream when she saw his hand.

"Look, Chancellor," she said in an unnaturally loud voice. "He has the mark on his right hand!"

Bryn stood up and leaned against the desk so he wouldn't fall. Tejal approached him and, without a word, took his right hand and examined the back of it.

"What is this?" she asked herself. She lifted Bryn's limp arm and showed Gerald the slowly fading black mark. "A circle, Gerald. A perfect black circle."

Only then did Bryn notice the itching and burning sensation on the back of his hand. Though the examination was not over, he pulled his hand out of Tejal's and looked at it himself. It was hardly visible and seemed to be fading away, but it was most definitely a black circle on the back of his hand. And the more it disappeared, the less his hand hurt.

Without warning, Tejal shouted at Bryn and Gwendolin. "Both of you leave the room immediately and wait for me in the secretary's office! Not a word to anyone, especially you, Gwendolin, unless you'd like a new job cleaning the orc toilets until you graduate."

"What are we going to do with him?" Gerald asked after the two had left. "The test may not have yielded the desired result, but he has magical talent. That much is clear. The reactions in the last few minutes prove this."

Tejal nodded wearily and began to pick up scrolls of papyrus and trophies and put them on her desk. Then she raised her arm and a narrow beam of golden yellow light shot from her hand. The light wound around her chair lying on the ground, lifted it up, and it flew back behind the desk. turned it to make it stand behind her desk. Tejal sat down with a heavy sigh.

"I have no idea what to do, Gerald. If he were a normal student, one of the House Masters would be here now to collect him, as the bond would have been made. But as you can see …" She gestured at the empty office. "Nobody has come."

"You can't make him leave! They'd come for him," Gerald yelled, thumping his fist on the desk. "He would not survive outside these walls, or, worse, they might try to use him."

"Calm down," said Tejal. "I'm well aware of all this. I will not let him go, but none of the four fraternities will accept him as a student. I'm not even sure if he would get past the fraternity houses' protective spells or be forced to spend the night outside the entrance. No, we have to find another way. Given his obvious gift, he must receive training, if only for his protection and that of Razuclan. After all, you, more than anyone, know what a gifted person can do without adequate training." Gerald lowered his eyes. "In effect, there is only one solution that everyone will accept. It won't make life easy for him here, but …" Tejal folded her arms, leaned back, and pondered for a moment. "The White House is open to any student."

"No!" Gerald exploded. "You can't be serious. The fraternity of the bastards?"

"Mind your tongue!" snapped Tejal. "Every student at this institution is equal when they have the gift. Your fraternity is only part of who you are. Our principal mission here, which you, above all others, should realize, is to ensure the peace between the four great nations of this continent. So, until I understand what the black circle means—and on the wrong hand—White House is our interim solution. I will search the archives and consult with several fraternity Masters and others."

"I know you're right," Gerald grumbled and looking dazed. "It's just … White House …"

"It is decided then!" Tejal said sharply. "You will have your way, Gerald. The boy will be admitted. But, for the time being, I'm binding him to White House."

She moved her left hand as if to catch something, and a crackling sound echoed through the room, leaving it smelling burnt, like molten metal.

"It is now done. Bryn is a student at Âlaburg," Tejal said with a smile. "Will you tell him the good news, or should I?"

DECISIONS

In his confusion, Bryn almost slipped when he sat on the bench in Gwendolin's office. The seat was uncomfortable, but he tried to organize his thoughts nonetheless. *So all those characters in the fairy tales old Maana told the village children were real!* But what overwhelmed him the most was his experience with the shimmering colors.

"Is it always like this when you get a new arrival?" Bryn asked as Gwendolin sat down behind her desk.

"No, usually not so much gets broken," she said with a cheery smile, covering her unease.

"Are there real elves and dwarves at this school?" Bryn asked when he realized Gwendolin was not going to instigate any more conversation.

"Yes, of course!" she answered, laughing, more relaxed now. "May I introduce myself? Gwendolin, Elbendingen fraternity, second semester, and student head of the house. Oh, and yes, I'm an elf. Always at your service." She came out from behind her desk, grinning mischievously at Bryn, and gave a little curtsy.

"So, you do exist," Bryn stammered. Taking a closer look at her, he noticed her pointed ears, the slightly slanted eyes, and how unusually pretty she was.

"Oh yes … and you'd better not say school," Gwendolin added. "Âlaburg is a university. Everyone here has already finished school. Only the best of the best study here to improve their skills. Each generation's most gifted have the chance here to unleash their magical potential, to help shape and protect Razuclan."

"Magical potential? Who else is here besides dwarves and elves? Wizards with long beards who turn humans into frogs? Man-eating monsters?" Bryn said to himself a little too loudly, much to Gwendolin's disbelief.

"Yes, all this and much more," she replied, giggling. "Âlaburg has many fantastic, mysterious things in store for inquisitive and talented students. After your performance in there," she said, pointing to the Chancellor's door, "you clearly have certain talents. But whether these will prevent you from being turned into a frog or eaten, only time will tell." She smiled at him.

"Gwendolin!" thundered Tejal's disembodied voice. "I told you to refrain from talking to our new guests. Now, please finish the new papyrus filing system and settle Řischnǎrr House's soap account! And Bryn, come into my office!"

Taking a deep breath, he left the hard bench and went back to the Chancellor's office. Gwendolin looked up and gave him an encouraging nod, though he thought she also made a small movement with her hands to mimic a frog hopping.

"Bryn, you are to bow when you stand in front of the Chancellor," Gerald told him, closing the door behind them. Bryn's bow was reluctant and clumsy, and he felt ridiculous doing it, considering the state of her room.

"We have made a decision," said Tejal. "You will be admitted to Âlaburg and educated in the Seven Wisdoms of Razuclan. Starting tomorrow, you will begin lessons in Magic, Combat, Healing, Summoning, History, Religion, and Math. And should you graduate after many years spent studying these disciplines, the path is open for you to join the Driany Order and work for peace and security on the continent. There is no greater honor than to become a member of the Order." She shot a sad, sideways glance at Gerald, who appeared not to notice.

"Fame, wealth, power, and honor await you, Bryn, should you be gifted enough to follow this path. But do not become blinded by such rewards. A rocky and perilous path lies before you," she warned him, "for the most part because you are one of the youngest ever to gain admission here. But one thing I can promise you. I will personally help you overcome your challenges—as will all the Masters of this university." She cleared her throat and moved closer to him. "Tell me, when I held your hands and everything became blurry, what color did you see?"

Stunned, Bryn stared at the Chancellor. "You knew this would happen?"

"Of course! As the chancellor of this high institution, I have tested and accepted many new students. And I was also subjected to this same selection process," she said with a slight smile. "So, Bryn, describe to me the color that you saw."

Bryn wondered how to put his experience into words. "At first, I didn't notice much. Then everything appeared as if I was looking through a fog or a thick glass bottle. For some reason, my head began to hurt, and suddenly, I could see and hear everything in great detail. By the way, you have a spider sitting up there," he said, pointing his chin toward the corner of the ceiling. "And then came the colors."

"There was more than one?" asked Tejal.

"Yes," Bryn answered. "First, a red ribbon, then a yellow one, and in the end, I saw a blue one."

"My goodness, all three colors," whispered Gerald, loud enough for Bryn to hear.

Bryn continued, unaffected by Gerald's comment. "I tried to grab them, but they kept evading me. It was like trying to grab a stream of water. After a few attempts, I managed to hold them, and they melted into a single strand that shimmered in all the colors of the rainbow. It was beautiful," he added as if in a daydream. "Beautiful!"

Tejal, who up until now had listened to Bryn without emotion, looked excited. "You saw three colors? Were you able to bring them together? Think carefully. These answers are critical."

Bryn nodded, not saying a word.

"By Tamir—all three colors," cried Gerald. "All three!"

"Enough of this superstitious nonsense, Gerald," railed the Chancellor. "I will have to think about your observations, Bryn. The test did not match you with one of the four fraternities."

Bryn's shoulders slumped, and he looked at Tejal pleading. Where would he and Gerald go then?

"But that does not mean you will not be admitted to Âlaburg. You certainly have the gift! Not to train you would be a waste of your talents. So, until we can check your test results, I am assigning you to White House. Fortunately for you, the new semester starts in two days, and many of the students will return tomorrow after their holidays. Also, tomorrow, there will be an official ceremony for all the new students in the assembly hall. You are now a student here, Bryn, and a member of White House." Then she put her hand on her larynx. "Gwendolin, please contact Morlâ. Tell him to come to my office at once."

"Congratulations, my boy," said Gerald as they waited for Morlâ to arrive. "A student of Âlaburg! I'm sure you will do great things," he said, giving him an awkward hug. Bryn thought he saw a tear in Gerald's usually stern eyes, but there was nothing there when he looked again.

After a while came a knock at the door.

"Come in!" Tejal called.

A brown-haired boy entered, perhaps a head shorter than Bryn. Looking closer at the newcomer, Bryn noticed that although he was quite small, his face looked older than his size would suggest. He also had a little goatee under his chin. He bowed to Tejal and Gerald.

"Morlâ, good, you're here," Tejal said.

"Chancellor Tejal," he replied, his unusually deep voice more like a grown man's. "How can White House be of service to you?"

"I have a new student for you," said Tejal, pointing to Bryn, who was shifting sheepishly from one foot to the other. "This is Bryn. Until there is a final decision, he will be a student of White House. I would like you to mentor him in all matters relating to Âlaburg and show him some of the university's more unique features."

Morlâ then bowed again. "It would be an honor. White House will not disappoint you, Grand Master Tejal."

She then turned to Bryn. "Go with Morlâ. He will take you to your quarters and show you the university's most important buildings. I wish you a good start in your first semester, Bryn. Oh, one more thing. You will report to Âlaburg Gardens at the end of the week. I have a lot of work for you there. I think thirty hours of punishment should be enough to remind you to show me and the Masters here proper respect in the future." And with a casual gesture toward the door, Tejal let Bryn and Morlâ know they could leave.

Morlâ bowed again and discreetly pressed his hand to Bryn's back to remind him to do the same.

As they left the office, Bryn glanced back and overheard Gerald and Tejal talking. "I welcome you back too, Gerald. Before I forget, you'll need this—since I assume your Oath still stands."

She handed him a pair of rusty garden shears from the drawer. Gerald blushed and started to answer, but the office door closed, and Bryn could no longer hear their conversation.

MORLÂ

"Pleased to meet you, Bryn. I'm Morlâ," He pushed out his hand with a friendly smile, and Bryn shook it. "I'm in my third semester here and was just elected as the student head of White House. But it was no big deal; I was the only candidate." He laughed, slapping Bryn on the shoulder so hard that it made him stagger forward. "The best thing would be to first show you around the university grounds and then where you will be sleeping. After that, we'll go stuff our faces. I'm starving."

He led Bryn out of the Chancellor's building and through the Garden of the Samuusen. The vast, snow-covered university courtyard was entirely in the shade of an enormous defense tower.

Bryn's stomach growled. *It must be late afternoon already.*

As they strolled, Morlâ decided to play tour guide. "See the buildings far left, with flowers on the front, that look like they were hewn out of a tree?"

Bryn nodded.

"This is Elbendingen's fraternity house. The elves live there," he whispered disdainfully. "They think they're all perfect and don't want anything to do with anyone else. Although I have to admit, the girls are stunning! And they have absolutely no interest in anyone from White House, so don't waste your time.

Take my word for it." He shivered as if to shake off some nightmare. "Well, never mind … and then we have the old sheds next door, the ones with the half-timbered facades …"

Bryn felt homesick looking at them and hoped he would be sleeping there tonight. Morlâ noticed the change on Bryn's face. "Unfortunately, they're not where you're going. Not yet, anyway. They belong to the Bond-of-Faith fraternity. Your kind lives there. You know, overgrown good-for-nothings who pray all the time—humans," he quipped and slapped Bryn on the shoulder. Once again, Bryn staggered forward. He had tried hard not to lose his balance this time, but he realized the dwarf was pretty powerful. And Morlâ had been standing on tiptoes!

He continued walking around with Morlâ, who was still enjoying himself. "Do you see the magnificently designed houses next to the primitive huts and feeble towers? That is Ølsgendur House, the fraternity of well-bred, highly-gifted dwarves," he said in a resonant voice. "This is the building where I should be staying tonight—and every night. But that's another story."

"Are you a dwarf?" Bryn burst out. "A real dwarf?"

Morlâ laughed. "No, sonny, I'm just small for my age." But then he came close to Bryn. "Never ask this question to another dwarf here in Âlaburg. They will be deeply offended, and the whole of Ølsgendur will be displeased, and you will have a pile of problems. Got that, Bryn? What I'm telling you is important."

Bryn nodded uneasily.

"Good!" Morlâ walked away, muttering to himself, "Am I a real dwarf? Really! I'm in White House because I can't—" He realized he was on his own and called back to Bryn. "Come on! It's become too cold out here—and I don't like talking to myself."

They walked on, and then Morlâ stopped and pointed. "And while we're talking about not offending anyone and honor and so on, be careful with this lot." Bryn looked at the dark, prison-like houses and towers on the far right behind the defense tower. "You'd better not speak to them at all. Orcs from the Řischnărr fraternity have no sense of humor. None. They will crush you if you look at them sideways. So avoid them. Unless, of course, you're able to summon like the great Tamir the Wise," he added with a grin.

The two students hurried across the university grounds. They passed the bench where the two dwarves had slept off their big night. Though the two drinkers had gone, Bryn could see the reddish mound where their stomachs' contents had hit the cobbles a few hours earlier. He felt queasy.

"Start of semester party" said Morlâ. "It was quite orderly this time. But there are always a few idiots who don't know how much beer and wine they can drink."

Soon, they were standing in front of an insignificant door at the bottom of the defense tower. Sitting next to it was a demonic-looking statue with a big mouth.

"Put your left hand in," Morlâ insisted, pointing to the gaping mouth and sharp fangs.

Bryn inched his hand inside; it snapped shut and bit him.

"Ouch, what the hell?" Bryn yelled, trying to free himself. "Is this a joke, Morlâ? Can you help me? This thing is going to take my hand off."

Morlâ turned pale. "What the Ûduliý?! I thought you took the test, and Tejal assigned you to this house?" He ran toward the gargoyle and tickled it between the ears, and the pressure on Bryn's hand eased a little.

"Pull it out if you can," cried Morlâ. "I've never seen anything like this." Again, he ran his hand over the granite beast's ears, and its jaws opened a little wider.

Bryn seized his chance and pulled out his hand.

"Phew, thanks, Morlâ. What was that? Is that how you greet new students here?" he asked the dwarf with a reproachful look.

"No, no, not at all. I'm sorry. It wasn't a joke. This old head is our house totem. Only White House members can open the door by putting their hand with the magic mark on it. All other students are forbidden to enter. Their mark will not work here. Fortunately, it's ticklish behind the ears." He ran his hand lovingly over the back of the gargoyle's head, and the mouth opened wide again. "We have to see the Chancellor straight away! You can't get in here if the gargoyle doesn't permit it. Even if I open the door for both of us, the protective spell will stop you coming in. Old Tejal will be furious that we have to go back to her, but …"

But Bryn had an idea. He pushed up his sleeve and put his right hand down the monster's throat. They both heard the door click, and it swung open without a sound.

White House

"Oh, man! The right hand," said Morlâ, shaking his head. "I've never seen that before. Now, that is strange—but Âlaburg never ceases to amaze me. Well, come on in!" Morlâ stood in the doorway and pointed to a flight of descending stone steps. "Welcome to White House."

Bryn's eyes sparkled with excitement. "It must be a special honor to live in the castle tower?"

Morlâ laughed but stopped when he noticed Bryn's baffled expression. "Ah … I thought you were joking. We're not *in* the tower, we're *underneath* it. White House's rooms are in the basement—along with several broken school desks, some moldy stuffed animals, and a stack of worn-out sports mats. But, so what? We're all only passing through—even if some of us are taking a little longer than others."

"Passing through? I know Tejal hasn't decided which fraternity I should be in, but I thought, while I'm here, White House would be my home."

"Oh, my dear boy … you have no idea about Âlaburg, do you?"

Bryn bit his lip and shrugged. "Up until an hour ago, I thought you—I mean, dwarves, only existed in fairy tales."

Morlâ smiled. "Well, I guess we'll have to start at the beginning, but come in first. This dwarf's bottom is starting to freeze."

The well-trodden steps were lit with torches. As they headed down, Bryn noticed a pungent smell, which became stronger the deeper they went. It was a mixture of dust, boiled cabbage, spilled beer, and body odor. At first, Bryn had to breathe through his mouth, but he couldn't keep that up for long. At the bottom of the stairs was a comfortable but neglected and slightly dirty common room. Several small, red armchairs were scattered around a big, crackling fireplace. Many of them had straw filling coming out of holes in the worn upholstery. And there seemed to be a problem with the fireplace. Now and then, dark smoke spewed back down the chimney into the room.

Morlâ flopped into one of the chairs and invited Bryn, who now looked exhausted, to sit next to him.

Morlâ folded his arms and looked up at the ceiling. "Seems you have no idea about Âlaburg University, so I will try to enlighten you. The university brings together children from the four enlightened nations of Razuclan to protect the peace on the continent. Each nation tests its newborns for the gift. If this test is positive, which is rare, then the child comes here after they come of age. The Lekan Gate tests them again, and only those who truly have the gift can pass—this is the actual admission test. After this, the Chancellor checks your strength, and you get assigned to a fraternity. The four fraternities, or houses, are Ølsgendur, Bond-of-Faith, Elbendingen, and Řischnărr." Morlâ stretched his arms and yawned. "It seems the gift gets passed on less and less in Razuclan. So, lucky you, the House Masters are utterly obsessed with accepting new students."

Morlâ threw his feet on the low table in front of him, unconcerned with the empty bottles and beer mugs he knocked over, and continued, "Those whose result is not clear come here to White House until the Masters, in their wisdom, agree which fraternity they belong to. That's why you're here."

"But didn't you say earlier you could end up staying longer?" said Bryn.

"You're a bright little fellow," Morlâ replied, "but you're right. Some students stay here at White House for their entire time at the university. In fact, that's the case for most students without a fraternity who come here."

"Why?"

"Why? Because this is the unofficial bastard's fraternity," Morlâ spat out. "You come here when the spell determines you're not pure." He made quotation marks in the air. "The fraternities do not like to accept students from mixed backgrounds. So those that do have their education under the tutelage of White House. That's why it's called White House. We're like a blank sheet of papyrus. It means, on the one hand, we do not know where we belong. But on the other, it means the possibility of determining one's own destiny. Because rarely does one of us bastards prove so talented that one of the fraternities takes us in."

"So you're a ... I'm a ... we're both—"

"It's best you don't ask anyone this. Have you got that? Man, you've got a lot to learn," he said with a sigh. "If you must know, I am a real dwarf. I know who my parents are, I look just like them, and I share a resemblance with my eleven siblings. My problem was my test last year. I stood in front of Tejal—and I remember being surprised by her beauty and how good she smelled—and nothing happened! There was no magic—well, not that kind, anyway. I didn't see any colors, and no mark appeared on my skin. Ølsgendur refused to take me in. But since the gate had let me in, the university couldn't send me away either. So, until some magical powers show up in me, I'm here in White House. Nothing arrived last semester! Anyway, that's all I'm going to say about it."

"Sure thing, Morlâ," said Bryn, nodding. But their conversation paused uncomfortably. "My situation's the other way around. I've seen the colors, but I don't know who my parents are. Tejal may find them, and then I can join my fraternity. And I'm sure your abilities will start developing soon too!"

"Maybe …" said Morlâ, trying to smile. "It's possible we'll only be in White House for a while. But until then, we'll make the best of it, won't we?"

"Absolutely!"

Morlâ jumped out of his chair. "Come on, let's get something to eat. I'll show you where to get a proper meal," he said in a conspiratorial tone. "This time of the day, the university grounds should still be pretty empty. Many people are sleeping it off or won't return home from semester break until evening. So it's an ideal time to show you some secrets. Your belongings will be sent down here later anyway, and then I'll show you to your room."

They scampered up the stairs. Morlâ led his new housemate down a path past the fraternity houses to where it split on either side of an overgrown garden. They took the right fork, but when they came out of the bend—even though Bryn was getting hungry—he halted.

In the distance, across a wide courtyard and in front of the high castle wall, stood the most incredible building Bryn had ever seen. It was four stories high and made of massive red bricks, with hundreds of different stained-glass windows all over it. The building had four corner towers and a small dome in the center of the roof.

"What are those things sticking out of it?" Bryn asked.

"Out of the dome? They're for looking at the stars."

Bryn was impressed, but then he saw the four large signs on either side of the entrance, embedded in the stone, and his eyes widened even further.

On the far left of the entrance was a giant flower. Even in this dim light, it glistened in different colors. Bryn wondered how it'd look in bright sunshine, and then his eye caught something else. Next to the flower was a large iron hammer with a wooden handle. Bryn thought it looked perfect for beating metal—or skulls. To the right of that was a huge, simple wooden ankh. Bryn was familiar with this type of cross, which had an oval loop in place of an upper bar, from the Kajal churches back home. But this one was black and so smooth and polished that it gleamed. On the far right, in stark contrast, was a grotesque skull. Its pointed horns and massive fangs made Bryn's skin crawl.

"What is this building? And these symbols, or signs, whatever they are, around the doorway—what do they mean?"

"Well, this is the main building of the university of peace and friendship. Every day from the day after tomorrow, this is where you will come to study. As for the symbols, they should be self-explanatory for a smart lad like yourself!" said Morlâ, grinning.

Bryn thought for a moment. "Well, I know the ankh. I've seen many of them, so this must be the symbol for the humans."

"Very good! The contestant scores a point! And the other three?"

Bryn looked at the signs, and his mind flooded with memories of old Maana telling fairy tales on the market and the old counting rhyme they would sing when she needed to take a break.

In the land of dwarves,

In the mines so deep,

The wee folk who toil down there,

Wield hammers as we sleep.

Most beautiful are the elves, of course,

This much we know is true,

You see their gift in all the flowers,

And every drop of dew.

Still, beware of all the shadows,

If you go out at night,

The laughing skulls who hide in there,

Are not a pretty sight!

So should you be out after dark,

And hear that creature's laugh,

Your fate will tears and sorrow be,

If you wander down that path!

Finally, Bryn stopped whispering it to himself. "The flower stands for beauty, so it represents the elves. The hammer means work and skill, so that must be the dwarves. The ankh represents faith, and we know that's for the humans, but the skull ..." said

Bryn screwing up his face. *What did Tejal and Morlâ call the ones who lived in the dark houses? Urgs?* "The skull must represent the urgs!"

Morlâ applauded. "Congratulations. Three out of four! However, the skull represents the orcs. Remember the name, so you know who's beating you up over the next few weeks," he added with a wink. "Now, let's go inside and get something to eat. I'm almost starving."

Bryn was about to say yes when Morlâ took off toward the building, his short legs carrying him across university grounds faster than Bryn would have imagined.

FILIXX

Almost out of breath, Bryn came to a skidding halt next to Morlâ, standing in front of two massive, reinforced doors. They were shut and had no door handles or even a keyhole. Bryn scratched his head and leaned back, his hands on the small of his back as he examined the giant entrance.

"How do we get in there? Isn't the university closed during the holidays?"

"Of course not!" said Morlâ, who, to Bryn's surprise, didn't seem the least bit out of breath. "We're supposed to study all year round. But without formal approval, you can't get in during the holidays. But come this way."

He led Bryn around the side of the enormous building to a small door hidden under a mass of ivy. Bryn would never have discovered this by himself.

"Give me a hand," said Morlâ, trying to hold back the curtain of vines.

Bryn held the ivy open, and Morlâ knocked on the door several times in a loud, complicated rhythm.

"What's he doing in there?" Morlâ muttered into himself. He was about to knock a fourth time when a crack appeared in the door.

"Who's there?" asked a high-pitched male voice.

"It's me, Morlâ! Who else would it be?" Morlâ pushed at the door.

"Morlâ?!" the voice sounded. "We agreed you wouldn't bring anyone here when the kitchen is supposed to be closed. I could lose my kitchen access—end of story, and then where would …"

"Yeah, yeah, yeah, and then you'd only be able to feed yourself ten times a day! Bryn is all right. He's the new guy in White House. Now get out of the way, I can't move you and the door," he said, winking at Bryn. Morlâ strode inside, followed by Bryn, who had to duck his head in the small doorway.

Behind the door was a spotlessly clean room with a light-colored earth floor. Hanging on an iron rack were several great pots and pans that Bryn thought looked big enough to feed an army. On the bench opposite sat a big jar of ridiculously long wooden spoons and ladles and a pile of carving knives and forks. Several well-scrubbed, slate-topped tables stood in the middle of the room. In the far corner, Bryn counted eight large, wood-fired stoves. The one that was lit held a medium-sized pan big enough to cook dinner for eight to ten people. Bryn could hear it sizzling away, and the smell was mouth-watering.

"My lamb fillets better not be burnt," said the cook, who was in a white apron, hurrying to turn the meat.

"I hope so too, Filixx, because we're famished," said Morlâ. "It smells delicious, by the way."

"I only made enough for myself."

"Well, there's more than enough for all us then!" said Morlâ, walking over to him. "With the portions you usually eat, you won't starve sharing your afternoon snack with us." He clapped Filixx on the shoulder. "Oh, by the way, may I introduce you two? Bryn, this is Filixx. Filixx, this is Bryn." He pointed each one out to the other.

"Pleased to meet you," said Bryn. Filixx nodded and went back to his pan. Bryn figured Filixx was a bit older than himself, around seventeen or eighteen. He had straw-blond hair and a handsome face, which was somewhat distorted because he was also exceptionally fat. He had a round head and an excessive, bulging chin. His dark eyes were friendly and intelligent, set above bright red cheeks that wobbled when he moved. The rest of his body was also marked by fat. His arms were thick like little tree stumps, and Bryn couldn't distinguish between what was muscle and what wasn't. Over his white trousers hung a considerable belly, and his short legs seemed to bend under so much weight. Even so, he scurried nimbly back and forth between the sizzling pan and the spice rack and pantry at the other end of the room.

"Filixx is also a 'provisional' member of White House," said Morlâ, using air quotes. "He's an excellent cook and makes sure we eat the best food in Âlaburg. And as you can see"—he gestured broadly at the kitchen—"he has this fantastic place to prepare it! You will be grateful for that, Bryn, believe me.

Speaking of food, how's our lamb doing? Filixx, my dear boy, is there anything I can do?"

Filixx kept moving things around the pan. "The meat is done, but the mushrooms need more time to braise." Without taking his eyes off the food, he pointed to a tall, open cupboard stacked with dishes. "Well, set the table then!"

Bryn fetched plates from an upper shelf while Morlâ grabbed cutlery from a lower drawer. They set one of the tables, and Filixx dropped the pan on it and began to serve. Bryn and Morlâ grabbed some stools, and the three sat, greedily bent over the sumptuous feast.

Filixx glanced sideways at Bryn. "Hope you like it," he said, his cheeks bulging with food.

"It's fantastic as always, Filixx," Morlâ sputtered, spraying chunks of food over the table.

"It's delicious," added Bryn, cutting another slice of meat. "You put fresh thyme on this. And what kind of mushrooms are these, Filixx? They taste fantastic—especially the sauce."

Filixx stopped chewing and looked at Bryn, a little curious.

"Never ask him for the recipe though," said Morlâ with a laugh. "However, the best cook in Âlaburg will always accept praise—and plenty of it!"

Filixx hummed to himself, gathered a pile of mushrooms on his fork, and shoveled them into his mouth.

Silence fell over the three. They were enjoying their meal—especially Bryn, for whom exquisitely prepared, expensive cuts of lamb were something special. He had never tasted food like this before. When Bryn finished, he sat back from the table and rubbed his belly.

"Yep! I couldn't eat another thing either," said Morlâ, picking his teeth with a fingernail. "Well done, Filixx. Bravo, and many thanks."

Filixx, who had eaten more than both of them together, mopped up the last of the sauce with a piece of bread and held it up in a toast. "To White House!" Then he pushed it into his mouth.

"To White House!" said Morlâ.

Filixx wiped his mouth on his apron and turned to Bryn. "You're new, and they sent you to White House. Hmm. Why aren't you over there with your human brethren, saying prayers with all the other praying mantises. How come they sent you to the house of bastards?"

Bryn blushed, not knowing what to say.

"There's no need to get embarrassed. Why must everyone be so sensitive and make such a secret of it? You're almost as bad as Morlâ," Filixx said, grinning at him. "Well, with me, it's no big secret. Dwarf mother and elf father. I never met him, but I was the tallest dwarf on the mountain, so ..." he trailed off, staring into the distance. "Anyway ... it was clear to me pretty early I was different from the others. On my twenty-fifth birthday, my mother told me about my father. She thought I was always too young to know! But when I couldn't get through the door without getting down on my knees, she finally told me everything. It would have been nonsense anyway to wait until the coming-of-age ceremony. Everyone could see I wasn't a real dwarf." He sighed. "But then, the priests discovered I had the gift, and I came here."

"And now Filixx has several bastard friends. Isn't that right, Filixx?"

"Yes—especially when I'm cooking!"

Morlâ turned to Bryn. "Speaking of bastards, what's your story Bryn?"

Bryn cringed.

"Oh, come on. You're amongst *friends*," said Filixx with a laugh.

So, Bryn told them about Gerald and the attack on his way back from the market. He also confessed that, up until a few hours ago, he thought elves and dwarves were mythical creatures and that he never would have expected to be sitting at a table with any of them.

Filixx shook his hand and gave him a standing invitation to the kitchen whenever he was hungry. He drummed the secret knock on the table with his fingers.

"Now, remember this, so I know it's you."

MORLÂ'S DWARF CHALLENGE

"Morlâ, how old are you?" asked Bryn as they stepped through the ivy-covered door and headed for the tower.

Morlâ laughed to himself. "I'll give you three guesses, and if you can determine my age, you can be my roommate. If you don't come up with the right answer, you'll have to move into room number four. Stinky's room. And you won't like that." Morlâ stopped and turned to Bryn. "I'm the student head of White House, and we haven't had a House Master for ages; if you lose, you will have no one to complain to. Are you all right with that?"

"All right," said Bryn. "Give me a few minutes to think it over."

Morlâ bowed extravagantly, a gesture of consent.

As they strolled through the university grounds, Bryn thought about what Filixx had told him. *He said his mother thought he was too young at twenty-five to know about his father and wanted to protect him. And at that age, he had yet to have the ceremony of his admission into adulthood. Now the question is, at what age do dwarves have that rite of passage? And I wonder if Filixx is older or younger than Morlâ? In any case, they are both older than twenty-five!*

"Can you give me a hint?"

"No!"

Bryn thought about it further.

When they arrived at the tower, Morlâ took out a golden disc he wore around his neck on a chain. He slid it into the gargoyle's mouth, and the door opened.

Bryn meant to ask Morlâ about the disc, but he was too busy with the question of Morlâ's age to think on it further. They went downstairs to the common room, which still had a strong smell but was warm. Bryn and Morlâ dropped into a couple of armchairs and sat staring into the crackling fire.

"So, Bryn, time's up," said Morlâ. "I have to assign you a room."

"Are you older or younger than Filixx?"

But all he got was silence and a stern look.

"All right, I won't ask again." Bryn stood up and began to wander around the room. "Filixx said twenty-five is still young for a dwarf, so you are older than that." He studied Morlâ's face in the hope of seeing whether he was on the right track, but it was unreadable. Bryn sighed. "Are you thirty years old?"

"Wrong answer. Two guesses left."

"Are you thirty-five?"

"One guess left. Then we'll put your things in with Stinky— and I can keep my single room."

Bryn wouldn't share a room with someone called Stinky. The reason for this nickname was obvious. He was getting desperate. *Morlâ has been here for two semesters now. Hmm ...* But that didn't help him. Then he had a brilliant idea. *For us humans, the number seven is significant. On my seventh name day, I was allowed to go hunting with Gerald for the first time. Next summer, for Yuletide, I become a man because I'll be seventeen. In three times seven years, at twenty-one, I'll be considered an adult.* He felt he was now on to something. *The dwarves, who seem to age much slower than humans, are probably similar; only the time difference would be greater. Perhaps twice as much? Then Morlâ would have come here as a man, at about twenty-eight. That plus the time he's been at the university ...*

"What is it then?" asked Morlâ. "Tell me—"

"Wait, I have to do a quick calculation." After a moment, and risking everything, he presented Morlâ with the result. "You are twenty-nine years old."

Morlâ was astonished. "How do you know that? No one who wasn't a dwarf has ever guessed my age. Can you read my mind?" he asked, half joking and half serious. "If so, that was dishonest, and you should have told me."

"No, no," Bryn reassured him. "I did a little math."

"I don't understand," grumbled Morlâ.

"You don't need to. So, you better show me *our* room," Bryn said, beaming.

"All right, roommate," sighed Morlâ, standing up. "Follow me. I'll show you the legendary White House room number one."

They crossed the common room to a set of small, wooden stairs. It had three steps, which led to a red, oval door with a worn gold door handle resembling a lion's head. Morlâ opened it and showed Bryn a long, dim hallway lit by several spherical lamps that ran along the wall.

"Over there." Morlâ pointed to two white doors on the right side of the hallway. "These are the washrooms. We have running water, and sometimes, it's even warm!"

On the other side of the hallway were several doors of various colors with golden numbers painted on them. The first door was black with a golden eighteen, the next was purple and had the number seventeen, and so it was all down the hallway.

Bryn looked at the different doors with anticipation.

Near the end of the hallway was a dark green door with the number four on it. It was heavily damaged and hung crookedly on its hinges. It didn't close properly and looked as if huge claws had left deep scratches in the wood. And the golden four hung upside-down on a nail.

Morlâ pointed it out as he passed. "I was so sure you were going to end up in there."

Finally, they came to a blue door, and Morlâ rummaged in his trouser pocket for a small, silver key. The large lock clicked, and Morlâ pushed open the door.

"Welcome to room number one. Your new home, Bryn. May we both have successful and good times here and do honor to Âlaburg and White House."

Bryn stepped tentatively into the small, windowless room. A few small lamps were already lit and bathed the space in a pleasant light. Each half of the room had a wooden bed. The one on the right had been made up with a big, comfortable pillow, new bed covers, and a thick, warm blanket.

The left side of the room clearly belonged to Morlâ. On the walls hung some charcoal drawings of other dwarves. Bryn guessed they were probably family. On his desk lay sheets of papyrus covered with runes, which Bryn could not decipher. Neither could he identify the remains of the food scattered over the desk. Morlâ's bed was unmade, and the covers needed washing. In the corner was a big leather satchel filled with old books, writing tools, and papyrus. Morlâ seemed to have carved strange signs or symbols on the outside of it, but Bryn decided to ask about them later.

Next to the satchel was an object that caught Bryn's attention. It was a long, bent iron rod with a wooden handle. At the end of the rod was a golden star, which sparkled despite the dim light. Before he could ask about it, Morlâ started shouting.

"Damn! Damn it! How did she know?"

Bryn looked at Morlâ and followed his gaze to Bryn's bed. On the snow-white blanket lay the few belongings Bryn had taken when he fled the cabin with Gerald. There was also a leather satchel like Morlâ's. Next to that was a white sash with a strange, interwoven black emblem and an envelope with a red seal.

Morlâ was angry. "Did you discuss which room you would be in with the Chancellor? Are you her new little darling, now, are you?"

"Morlâ, think about it," Bryn said, getting annoyed. "You chose this room for me, remember?"

The dwarf murmured to himself. "You're right, but how does she know everything, and how did she get in the room?" Then he turned pale and began to rummage through the messy pile of papyrus on his desk.

Bryn fell back onto his bed. It was soft. He stretched out his arms, smiled, and broke into a huge yawn—that's when he remembered the envelope. It was made from thick, cream-colored papyrus and felt good in his hand. He took a closer look at the seal. It depicted a dove with a snake in its claws. The writing below it was indecipherable, as if it was done in a hurry. As Bryn broke the wax, a small, silvery whirl flew out from the seal. It spiraled to the ceiling with a soft ringing sound and then disappeared. He glanced at Morlâ for an explanation, but he was still sorting through his desk. *This university is a strange place*. Inside the envelope was a letter written in black ink with meticulous handwriting.

From:

Raisar Merhorna Elisa Tejal

Grand Master, Chancellor, Keeper of the Seals, Supreme Peace Keeper, Healer

To:

Bryn

White House

Room no. 1

Dear Bryn,

Welcome to Âlaburg. As Chancellor, I am delighted to welcome you as a new student and a future guardian of peace. Unlike your fellow students, you do not know anything about the true nature of Razuclan. Therefore, you will have to learn twice as much as they do. But I am sure you will succeed. Your talent is extraordinary, if what happened in my office earlier is any indication. Please do not talk about what happened with any Master or student. And above all, do not mention that in my test, you saw three colors! This is for your own good. I will find out what this means, and then you and I will talk and decide how to continue.

Enclosed is your timetable. Morlâ will help you find your way around as you both are taking almost the same subjects. He did not make significant progress in any subject except Math in the last semester. He will be repeating all the others. Morlâ will explain everything else and show you around.

PS: Don't forget your punishment on the weekend in the gardens.

PPS: I have made Gerald the acting House Master of White House; inform Morlâ about it. He can pass this on to the other residents.

PPPS: You do not need to hide this letter; no one but you can read it.

PPPPS: This does not apply to your timetable; you must show it to your Masters before starting all your lessons.

In friendship and peace!

Tejal (Grand Master, Chancellor, etc.)

Bryn read the letter three times until he was sure he had understood it. He could hardly believe it. He was a student of Âlaburg, and Gerald was his House Master! The events had come thick and fast in the last few days, and Gerald had a lot to explain.

Bryn put the letter down and noticed Morlâ looking at him with suspicion. But he didn't want to tell him what was in it right now, partly because Tejal had asked him to and partly because he was still annoyed with the challenge Morlâ had set him over the room.

"Gerald will be the new House Master of White House, and we both have the same timetable. The rest of the letter is only a bunch of welcoming words."

"Gerald as in your foster father? I've never heard of a *Master* by that name."

"I have never heard of such a *Master* either."

"This is going to be fun. We here in White House don't have an official House Master because we are not a fraternity. That's why there is only one tutor here. Usually, the untainted, virtuous lecturers are too respectable to accept a position here. For decades, White House students have managed their own affairs. Who knows what kind of improvements Gerald may try to bring about here? We'll see. But I have a few things to sort out now, Bryn. I'll see you tonight at the latest." Then he grabbed some sheets of papyrus off his desk and raced out of the room.

Morlâ's heavy footsteps echoed down the hallway, and Bryn heard the door to the common room slam. His new home fell quiet. Only then did he notice how exhausting the last days had been. He threw the things on the bed to the floor and curled up in the blanket. But his final thoughts before falling asleep were of Drena.

ANSWERS

Bryn woke with a slight headache, and, for a moment, he didn't know where he was. His mouth was dry and tasted terrible. He needed more sleep. Then the events of the last few days came flooding back to him. But Bryn didn't know whether to be happy or sad about these sudden and profound changes in his life.

On the one hand, he missed Drena, although he didn't even know her well. But on the other, the secrets of Âlaburg were out there, waiting to be discovered. There was something magical about this place; Bryn understood that much.

Even though he was still a bit disappointed with Morlâ, Bryn was looking forward to sharing a room with him, and it compensated for the loss of his bedroom back home. Bryn had often been left alone there while Gerald was away hunting for days on end. And his contact with others had been limited to the few festivals and market days in Sefal. Here, he was among his peers. Bryn had yet to see what elves and orcs were like, but he seemed to get along with dwarves pretty well.

He was looking forward to studying at a university. Gerald had taught him to read and write, and Bryn knew about hunting and weapons. But Âlaburg's curriculum differed considerably from these subjects. He looked again at Tejal's letter and studied his timetable in detail. Monday to Friday, he had lessons from eight until early afternoon, which included several breaks. There was a break at noon for one hour, which Bryn noted with delight. *Maybe life here will be even better than in the forests.*

I wonder what subjects I'll be studying? Bryn could imagine doing Math, History, and Religion, but he couldn't believe Magic was a subject. *Do they teach real magic here? Maybe it has something to do with the colors I saw in Tejal's office?* But Bryn would have to wait until Monday morning to find out.

On Monday afternoon, his schedule said Healing. He didn't want to become a nurse, but maybe the Combat classes had so many injuries, everyone had to train in Healing? *Do they use real weapons here, or is it only about physical self-defense?* Bryn couldn't fathom some of the subjects in his timetable. *Summoning is scheduled for Tuesday morning, but what is that?* He slapped the timetable down on his bed. He was thirsty again, and getting out of bed was more of a struggle than expected.

Bryn ventured into the empty hallway, and instantly, the lamps came to life, flickering with yellow light. He stepped toward one and gently ran his hand over its curved surface. It was cool to the touch, and behind the opaque glass, there was no candle or anything like that. All he could see was the dust he had disturbed, which was now tickling his nose. Bryn shrugged. Âlaburg would likely present many such mysteries to him over the next weeks, and it would be better to take them for granted. That way, they would not distract him too much from his lessons, and in any case, he would not get answers to all his questions.

Bryn headed slowly to the common room to check if any more White House residents had arrived. He opened the red oval door and peeked in, but the place was empty and quiet except for the fireplace's occasional crackle. Bryn looked around and saw something embedded in the far wall. It was a water fountain in the shape of a small monster. It was laughing, and when he got close, it stuck out its tongue, and water poured from its mouth and into the stone basin below. Bryn bent down and cupped his hands under the cool jet of water and drank until he was no longer thirsty. Just as he was wiping his mouth, Bryn heard heavy footsteps coming down the stairs and stilled. *Gerald!*

"Hello, Bryn," he said when he discovered his former apprentice. "I'm glad I found you so soon. I have a few things to explain to you." He sounded embarrassed. "Can we walk for a bit?"

They trudged up the stairs to the front door and then out into the university grounds, which now had an amber glow from the evening sun.

They wandered for a while, but Bryn could sense Gerald getting agitated as they crossed the central courtyard.

"I don't even know where to start, Bryn. What do you want to know?"

"Tell me about magic."

Gerald laughed to himself. "As you can see, magic does exist! It is to Razuclan as clouds are to rain or day is to night. But many people have forgotten about it or suppressed the truth of it. Though not everyone; otherwise, there would be no human students at this university. The wealthy, educated high nobility have been using magic in secret for centuries. But they teach the common people it only exists in fairy tales. They want their sons and daughters in the Bond-of-Faith fraternity to rule the human kingdom with the help of magic. The stories you often spoke of are, for the most part, true. There are beings in Razuclan able to cast spells."

Suddenly, Gerald fell silent and backed away from Bryn. "I cannot and will not tell you any more about this subject even though I know it's of particular interest to you." Gerald dropped his head, and Bryn could see him retreat into himself. "No, I'm not the right person to talk about this. The Mind Casting Spell in the forest was an exception. But since I took the oath …" When Gerald realized Bryn was listening to him, he fell silent.

Bryn could not believe what he'd just heard. "But why did you pretend all these years there was no such thing as magic? Why didn't you tell me about this place?"

Gerald looked up. "I wanted to protect you from this world, Bryn! That was all; you must believe me. When you were a young child, I tested you but misinterpreted the results." Gerald shook his big head. "Me and magic! I thought you didn't have the gift and that the Order's troubles wouldn't affect you. That's why I trained you for a secular profession as best I could, but then came those—"

"—monstrous creatures!" Bryn finished. "What are those beasts?"

"They're called Vonnyens." Gerald started walking again, with Bryn close by his side. "Nobody knows exactly where they come from. All we know is that they have a Master who gives them orders."

Bryn wanted to know who this master was, but Gerald interrupted him.

"Let me speak, boy! I wasn't honest with you when I said I knew little about these beings. I told you the first time I saw one was when I was chasing a bear up in the mountains decades ago. But the truth is that I have fought the Vonnyens before that. Several times, in fact, on behalf of the Driany Order. Many years ago, after this place was founded, there grew resistance from the four enlightened nations about learning together and from each other. Soon, a group of insurgents formed. They wanted to bring about a rupture between the four nations and trigger a new war. They used the Vonnyens for this. I don't know if they bred them, summoned them, or took them from the earth's depths. But in any case, because of their raids, a great war was almost started again in Razuclan.

"It was clear to everyone that this war would have meant the end of the four enlightened nations because they would slaughter each other. The peace negotiations after the last great battle between the nations had been difficult. Today, weapons and spells are much more powerful than they were then. Another war would mean the end of life in Razuclan as we know it. The battle with the rebels raged for many years. I was a member of the Driany Order by then. We were sent in small groups on several missions throughout Razuclan. On those missions, I fought against Vonnyens several times but never on my own. I always had my brothers and sisters of the Order, who were trained here at Âlaburg, watching my back.

"With united forces and great sacrifices, the Order succeeded in ending these attacks. Much suffering was brought upon Razuclan, and many innocent people suffered from the bloody clashes. The rebels were caught and punished. I had no more desire for fighting and magic; it had all been much too painful for me. That was also one of the reasons why I retreated into solitude. Since then, the Vonnyens have seldom appeared again in the human lands. Until the day one of those creatures attacked you in the forest. I knew then I could no longer hide from the world."

"Why did they attack me of all people?"

"I don't know. It may have something to do with the gift you carry inside you. Even in the attacks of that time, the victims were always those who had the gift. The ringleaders of the uprising wanted to use the Vonnyens to destroy the magical talent of Razuclan. But why you were the first to be attacked after such a long time, I don't know. Even the Chancellor hasn't been able to explain it yet, but she will. Tejal is a master in solving mysteries and always has an answer to the questions asked. But one thing is sure; you are safe within these walls."

"Can I ever leave the university again?" Bryn asked, frightened.

"This is a difficult question. For the moment, at any rate, you must not leave these walls. I wouldn't try to sneak out either. Tejal has taken some precautions that will prevent that and only get you more punishment. Besides, you can't leave Âlaburg against her will. But you will be trained here and learn how to defend yourself against attackers. As soon as your level of training is appropriate, you will even have to leave Âlaburg. At the end of the semester, a small group of the best students will be sent on a peace mission somewhere in Razuclan. I am sure you will be among the best in Âlaburg."

"That creature asked me how I killed his companion. Why did he ask me that?"

"I don't know. No one knows what goes on in the minds of those monsters. This is the first time I've heard Vonnyens can speak. Perhaps you imagined it. Or no one who heard it ever survived to tell the tale. I think you intuitively performed some primal form of magic in self-defense. When I came to the clearing, I could sense there'd been a strong discharge of energy. And the ground was scorched where your attacker had been standing. All that was left of him were a few steaming bits and pieces. Your dagger also glowed, which also indicates a discharge of energy."

Bryn couldn't believe he had cast a spell to fend off an attacker.

"That you could kill a Vonnyen all on your own shows you have powerful magic—and that you have much to learn, so as not to hurt yourself or others."

"Will you teach me? Aren't you a Master here?"

Gerald snorted and came to a halt. "I was a Master here, but then …"

Bryn came to him, waiting for more. Due to their animated conversation, he hadn't paid attention to the surroundings. Now he realized they were standing in front of the vast, overgrown patch of the forest he and Morlâ had come by before.

"Welcome to Âlaburg Gardens, Bryn," said Gerald with outstretched arms. "My task is to return this place to its former glory. That was Tejal's condition, but at least it's better than having to teach again. Over the next few weeks, you're going to help me."

"And," said Gerald, pulling out the rusty shears Bryn had seen in Tejal's office, "she has forbidden the use of magic in the garden."

THE NEWCOMER

Gerald brought Bryn back to the tower. It was now completely dark and impossible to see the top of it. Still, lights were burning in many windows of the other houses. He gazed longingly at the timber houses of the humans. But right now, the Bond-of-Faith fraternity was denied to him.

After Gerald had left, he put his right hand in the gargoyle's mouth and grimaced. The White House door opened. As he started down the stairs, he heard voices coming from the common room. He'd heard several White House students had returned from their vacations. At the bottom of the stairs, Morlâ rushed toward him.

"Bryn, where have you been? I was getting worried and thought you got lost on the grounds."

Bryn was touched. "Sorry. I was with Gerald. We had a lot to talk about. But, in the future, I will make sure to give you notice."

Morlâ frowned at him, unsure whether the apology was serious or not. "I hope so," he said, winking at Bryn. "Come on. I'll introduce you to the others." He grabbed Bryn's forearm and pulled him into the packed common room.

"Hey, everybody, listen up," he shouted into the excited chatter. "We have a newcomer. Let me introduce you to Bryn.

He has as distinguished a family history as the rest of us. I'm sure you all will support him as much as you can because he's not too bright—a typical human being, in other words!" The room broke into laughter.

Bryn was uncomfortable with both the introduction and the attention that followed, but he smiled and looked at everybody. Some seemed more friendly to him than others, and some just nodded. He noticed he was blushing. Thankfully, everyone soon returned to their conversations and tales from their holiday adventures.

"Come, I'll introduce you to a few others," said Morlâ, pushing Bryn toward a strange-looking trio.

One of them was Filixx, and his massive body stood in stark contrast to the other two. They were skinny, pale, and remarkably tall. They also looked exactly alike and had strange red eyes and snow-white hair.

"Meet Rulu and Ulur."

The two gangly boys turned in unison. "Welcome to White House, Bryn," they said together in a high-pitched voice. The boys held out their soft, oversized hands, and Bryn shook one and then the other. He noticed their ears were pointed like Gwendolin's and that they were twins.

"They're twins," whispered Morlâ as he pulled Bryn over to the next group. These were dwarves; Bryn could tell that much from their height. The unique thing about them was they were all ancient, even by dwarf standards. Their skin was wrinkled, their long beards were grey, and three of the five had only a little hair left. "May I introduce to you the most senior students of Âlaburg. This is Toulin, Houlin, Kaneg, Worin, and Lebos—also called the Five Wise Ones. Whenever you have questions about history, ask them. They have experienced most of it themselves."

His comment earned Morlâ a stern look from the five. Yet, they all shook hands and kindly offered to help Bryn with any history questions.

Finally, Morlâ led Bryn over to the far corner of the room to meet a group of girls. They were amusing themselves over something, but when they saw the boys coming toward them, they burst out laughing.

Morlâ put his mouth up to Bryn's ear. "I would like to spare you the encounter with these four, but then they might not let me copy their homework for a few weeks. Then I won't be admitted into next semester again, and I'll end up like our Five Wise Ones from before."

Bryn was blushing again. Nevertheless, Morlâ pulled him firmly toward the girls, each of whom looked very different. One was medium-sized, dark-haired, and a little plump and seemed to be the four's quietest. The ringleader was tall, slim, and blond. She spoke and laughed the loudest; her appearance reminded Bryn of Gwendolin. The other two were roughly a mix between the pretty girl and the smaller, chubby one. All three seemed to hang on the blond girl's every word.

"Hello, my dears! How lovely to see you! Did you have a nice holiday?" Morlâ asked.

At first, the young women pretended not to notice them and kept laughing. Then the leader turned around. "Hi, Morlâ. I thought you might have grown a bit taller over the holidays. Hmm. What happened?"

Morlâ blushed a little, something Bryn would never have expected, but kept beaming at them, nonetheless. "Ha-ha, now that's funny! Every semester, the same joke, Karina. Delightful!"

Bryn heard the caustic undertone, though he couldn't tell if the girls did. They gave no indication of it.

"And here's our new housemate, Bryn," said Morlâ. He pointed at Bryn standing next to him.

An uncomfortable silence followed. The girls had no intention of welcoming the new student. Bryn noticed his head getting hot. *Oh, no. Not again.* This happened every time he met girls. Finally, Karina extended her listless hand to Bryn. The other three did the same and introduced themselves as Malin, Elina, and Hela. Only Hela, the somewhat plump girl, laughed openly to his face.

After this little exercise in humiliation, Morlâ and Bryn decided to go to their room.

Morlâ opened the door and gave Bryn a small, silver key. "Take good care of this; it's enough that Tejal's snoops around here. After all, the whole university doesn't need to know what we get up to."

Bryn threw himself on his bed. Only now did he notice how cozy and warm the room was even without an open fire. Warm air came out of an iron grill in the wall. When he asked Morlâ about it, he just shrugged, and Bryn put it down as another of Âlaburg's wonders.

There was a knock on the door.

"Come in," cried Morlâ. Filixx stuck his head into the room.

"Have you two had dinner yet?" Before they could say no, Filixx dropped a basket filled with delicacies on Bryn's bed. He took out a warm loaf of bread, half a ring of salami, a large wedge of yellow cheese, some lard and butter in clay pots, four hard-boiled eggs, and some salt. He also pulled out a knife and a wooden board for each of them. "I've already eaten in the kitchen—but a second supper never hurt anyone!" And with that, he began to cut three thick slices of bread.

The three of them sat on the beds in silence and ate. After, Bryn felt he had never eaten so well in his life.

They shook the crumbs off Bryn's bedspread into the corridor, and Filixx said goodbye. It was late, and early tomorrow, they had the welcoming ceremony in the dining hall.

Bryn and Morlâ put on their pajamas and crawled under the blankets. After a short time, the light in the room went out.

Bryn became alarmed.

"Don't worry," said Morlâ, "it happens at the same time every night, so we little students get enough sleep." Then he rummaged under his bed, took out a small oil lamp, and lit it. "If I were better at magic, I could conjure a werelight, but we'll have to use this until then." He passed it to Bryn. "So, your Gerald will be our new House Master. Is he a good Master?"

"I have no idea," Bryn replied. But when he thought about Gerald, he realized how happy he was to have him so close.

After a while, Morlâ was snoring softly, and Bryn blew out the lamp and fell asleep with a smile on his face.

THE SPEECH

Bryn woke early and daydreamed about the ceremony later today in honor of the new students. Morlâ was still asleep and snoring. Bryn studied the pole with the shining golden star propped up against the wall between the two beds. Again, he wondered what it was and decided to ask Morlâ about it later that day.

When he tried to touch the shining star, Morlâ rolled over to face him, his eyes still closed.

"Better not touch the Harel Star," he warned Bryn, "unless you want to sit through the welcome ceremony with severely swollen fingers."

Bryn pulled back his hand. How did Morlâ know what he was about to do? And why was such a beautiful object so threatening?

"Morlâ, you still awake?"

"Yeah …"

"What is a Harel Star?"

Morlâ opened his eyes and slowly sat up. "That, my young friend," he said, yawning, "is the pride and joy of White House. And I, as its student leader, have the privilege of being its custodian. It is the objective of a game called Starball. It's a game of combat and magic, where you try to capture your opponent's Starball. And this one here is ours! White House has never won the championship. Maybe you would like to join the team? You might make a good Starball player. Who knows? Our next training session is Tuesday afternoon. I'm putting together a new team for the semester. I hope you'll sign up. For the last few semesters, White House hasn't had the four players needed to form a team." Morlâ saw Bryn's quizzical expression and shrugged. "I'll explain the rules on Tuesday. Come on, we better hurry."

Morlâ jumped out of bed, and Bryn, already dressed, and sat on the bed and watched as Morlâ put on his White House sash. It was crumpled and slightly dirty, hardly white at all. Unfortunately, it was far too long for him, so he had to wrap it around himself twice. Bryn stifled a laugh.

"Must we wear these silly things?" he asked.

Morlâ glanced at him sideways and squinted. "Of course … especially today! It's not necessary for normal school time, but at festive events or ceremonies, all fraternities wear their colors— even White House, though sadly, we have no fraternity color."

Bryn stood up and put on the sash Tejal had given him yesterday. Like the swirl he had seen when he broke the seal on her letter, a small black symbol was woven into the brilliant, clean, white fabric.

"Are you ready?" said Morlâ growing impatient.

Bryn smoothed down his sash once more, and they stepped out into the hallway. It was crammed with students in white sashes talking loudly and laughing. But one person stood out because he was about two heads taller than all the others with shoulders at least twice as wide. The unknown student had the hood of his dark cloak pulled down over his face but was not wearing a sash.

"Who's that?" asked Bryn.

"It's Stinky from number four," Morlâ said, pointing to the ruined green door. "You'll meet him soon enough—and better not call him that to his face either. Ok?"

Bryn nodded. He let the crowd carry him into the common room. A surprise awaited him there. Gerald was waiting for his new charges. He had combed his hair and trimmed his beard, and his sash was flawlessly white and immaculately ironed. Bryn had never seen him dressed so formally. For a brief moment, their eyes met, and Gerald winked at him.

"Students of White House," Bryn's former hunting master began solemnly, "my name is Gerald McDermit, Knight of the Order and Keeper of the Gardens of Âlaburg. I am your new House Master. Any questions or concerns you may have, please feel free to contact me. I am also here as a mediator if there is a dispute between individual students or even with Masters. I will decide on what further action to take in these cases. I expect you to honor White House, live up to the university's ideals of peace and friendship, and uphold these values in the outside world. As students of this unique part of the university, it is precisely from you that I expect excellence and outstanding grades in all Seven Wisdoms. I also want to see the Starball team finally play again and win."

The students seemed impressed by his speech and occasionally raised their voices in approval.

"This semester," said Gerald, thumping the table, "I would like to see you among the university's most outstanding students in sports and lessons."

At this, all the students began to shout.

Bryn was also carried away by the enthusiasm, as was Morlâ, who had probably forgotten for a moment he was more interested in joining the dwarves' fraternity.

The cheerful crowd of students then moved up the long set of stairs to the castle courtyard. There, Bryn saw many more excited faces. *Gerald did well*, he thought. The new House Master had made the students happy about being a White House member and used their outsider status to motivate them. Bryn was proud and glad to see this new side of him.

On the way to the university building, the students of the four other fraternities joined their procession. From the Elbendingen fraternity house came a medium-sized group wearing bright yellow and blue sashes with a small, blue flower woven on the yellow side. Bryn saw many beautiful, slim faces with flowing, long blond hair—both girls and boys. The students seemed to be in an excellent mood, always laughing and teasing each other.

Some of them had used their fraternity colors in their clothes, so you could see many yellow and blue caps, scarves, and even trousers that had one yellow leg and one blue leg. So light-footed was their walk that they seemed to be floating. But Bryn could also see the elves were only concerned with themselves, even when their group started to mix physically with White House members.

In front of the Bond-of-Faith fraternity house, Bryn saw younger and older people dressed in red and yellow. On the red side of their sashes was a yellow ankh. They seemed to have at least three times as many students as Elbendingen, not to mention White House. They behaved just like ordinary humans. The boys pushed and shoved, while the girls moved together in small groups and giggled about everything. Occasionally, a few left the fraternity house hand in hand, staring into each other's eyes. Due to their bright fraternity colors, the human students were even more noticeable than the elves. Red shirts and yellow trousers were the order of the day. They were also wearing red and yellow coats and headgear. Though they were colorful and cheerful, Bryn could not ignore some students' derogatory remarks about the fraternity members from the 'bastard house.'

About three hundred feet before the sharp right turn at the entrance of the garden, the motley group of students passed the

Ølsgendur fraternity house. There, they were joined by a group of short people wearing blue and red sashes, which had a red hammer on the blue side. Bryn noticed that there were about as many dwarves as elves. It was also noticeable that the dwarf students mostly limited themselves to wearing only their sashes to show their house colors. He could not find blue and red clothes anywhere. The dwarves also avoided mixing with the other students and walked in a blue and red block ahead of them. But the dwarves were quickly caught up to by the other students, forming a colorful and happy group.

Then Bryn heard a sound like an army marching. He stretched his neck to see where it was coming from and saw many students dressed in black marching in lockstep in rows of five. As they advanced, Bryn could make out the emblem on their otherwise black clothing—a white skull. Tall and muscular, each student also had the hood of their black cloak pulled down, making it difficult for Bryn to see their faces.

The students of Řischnärr fraternity, thought Bryn, excited. *Finally, I will get to see an orc.* As the formation of orcs drew closer to the colorfully attired crowd of students, Bryn could see their faces. They all had a heavy brow ridge, and their skin looked dark green or even black. Several of them had light-colored scars on their faces, and out of their heads grew small, sharp horns.

Bryn noticed the pace of the students slow down as if nobody wanted to walk with the orcs. Seeing this, the Řischnärr students marched through the university's main entrance by themselves. Only then did the more jovial crowd saunter in.

Álaburg University! Bryn thought in astonishment as he stepped through the door. He found a medium-sized room behind the entrance, which Morlâ called Remter Hall, with walls made of the same red brick as the outside of the building. Bryn marveled at the vaulted ceiling and the flowers carved on the marble columns' capitals that supported the stone arches. And at the apex of each arch, there were beautifully ornate keystones.

On the walls hung several display cases piled with dusty goblets and statues of some distinguished representatives from the four nations. Next to them was a giant bulletin board covered in what looked like several front pages of a student newspaper and some handwritten articles in the common language. As far as Bryn could make out, they were about religion and history. Other articles were so yellowed and torn that their authors had probably passed their exams many years ago.

As Bryn drew closer, he saw one of the front pages had been scribbled on. This was probably a piece about Tamir the Wise, whom Morlâ had already mentioned. It had perhaps said:

… *then Tamir realized the true nature of the summoned beings* …

But a prankster, using thick black ink, had changed it to:

… *then Tamir realized the true meaning of the food in the dining hall and cast his famous spell of forgetting* …

It made Bryn smile. Then Morlâ pulled him by the arm through an open double door to join the other students in a vast room filled with several long tables and chairs all arranged in neat rows. The place smelled of old fat, boiled milk, and steamed cabbage. Down the middle of each table was a table runner in one of the fraternity colors. At the far end of the room was a podium with an emblem of the dove with the snake in its claws on the front.

On the far left, Bryn saw a table with a yellow and blue runner where the elves took their seats. Next to it, three long tables in red and yellow were set for the human students. Then followed a table decorated with a blue and red runner, where some dwarves were already sitting. On the far right were three tables with black runners, where the orcs sat with grim faces, not saying a word even to each other. There were also tables in the rear left corner of the room, covered with runners of different sizes in various white shades. Morlâ pushed Bryn toward them.

Morlâ sat on a wobbly chair and instructed Bryn to take a seat. Filixx arrived, sat next to Bryn, and smiled. "Today, you get to experience Tejal's '*let's-all-love-each-other*' speech. It gets harder to sit through the more often you hear it."

Suddenly, a commanding voice roared, "Quiet! Can I have quiet, please!"

Bryn crooked his neck and recognized the Chancellor standing behind the podium. The dining room immediately fell quiet.

"Dear students, I welcome you to the new semester at Âlaburg. I'm sure your semester break was, as always, far too brief …"

Some students laughed, but Bryn thought it sounded more forced than genuine.

"… yet you all found your way back here to finish your education and diligently continue your studies."

Morlâ rolled his eyes.

"I would particularly like to welcome all the new students joining us this semester. Exciting times await you at this institution; you will learn things you might have thought only existed in fairy tales."

Despite the distance, Bryn felt her look directly at him.

"After your training in the Seven Wisdoms of Razuclan, any career will be open to you. Whether you join the Driany Order and help secure peace or take another path, you will be immensely sought after. Kings will ask for your advice, and people from all nations will ask for your help. But you must be mindful that your education and talent also comes with responsibilities. More than sixty years ago, our four nations finally attained lasting peace. The centuries before were marked by conflicts between orcs, elves, dwarves, and humans. Time and again, our ancestors found reasons to wage war and kill each other."

Tejal paused dramatically for effect.

"But the wisest representatives of the enlightened nations concluded that a treaty would ensure lasting peace. The children of the elves, humans, orcs, and dwarves were brought together to meet and work together. At the borders of the four nations, where they all meet, this university was founded. Âlaburg. The place was well chosen—it is a former site of many wars and now a reminder of peace. The flow of energy necessary to use the gift is especially strong here. Even the ancients used this place to create unimaginable wonders that still characterize Razuclan today, like the Glowing Waterfalls of Rolarm or the Singing Rocks of Đykordin. I could list the magical marvels here forever."

Again, the Chancellor paused and, searching the room, seemed to look into every student's heart. Still, Bryn had the feeling she was looking directly at him. A glance at his fellow students told him they probably felt the same. There was complete silence as everyone listened, spellbound to Tejal's words.

"At the end of this semester, we Masters will select exceptionally talented students to participate in these wonders of Razuclan or contribute to new ones. Those selected will be sent on a mission to one of the four nations to support the Driany Order's work. Adventure, glory, and the highest honors await many of you this semester."

Bryn saw that Filixx, who'd been cynical about Tejal's speech, was now listening attentively to it.

"I wish you a successful and peaceful semester, and may your achievements be outstanding. As the most gifted students in the land, I hope you will lavish further wonders upon Razuclan."

Out the corner of his eye, Bryn saw Gerald rise out of his chair. He felt this was rude, that it spoiled the solemn mood of the moment, and was starting to feel ashamed of his foster father when four other people, each seated at the head of the connecting tables, also stood up.

Tejal's somber voice rang out. "Does the House of Ølsgendur swear to uphold and defend the peace in Razuclan?"

A deep voice, unexpected from the short dwarf with a long, grey beard, answered, "We swear it."

Tejal made a sudden movement with her hand, and all the dwarves raised their left arms to show the Chancellor the back of their hands. Bryn could see they all had a glowing hammer, the symbol of their fraternity and a sign of their magical powers, on the back of their hands.

Tejal asked the same question to the houses of Elbendingen, Bond-of-Faith, and Řischnǎrr, and the ritual was repeated three more times. Flowers and ankhs appeared on the elves and humans to confirm their fraternity and oath to the university. Bryn could not make out the sign on the back of the clawed hands of the orc students. *Maybe it's because of their dark skin*, he reasoned.

Finally, the Chancellor addressed the members of White House. Bryn noticed that in her speech and the ceremony that followed, she kept changing the fraternities' order. Bryn presumed this was to ensure none of the four houses felt they were being favored. White House, though, was always mentioned last—or left out altogether!

Gerald, in his deep baritone voice, took the oath for White House.

And again, Tejal gave the strange-looking gesture.

Bryn noticed his right hand was tingling, and the dark circle had appeared on his skin as it had in Tejal's office. He felt an irrepressible urge to raise his arm and show the symbol to everyone in the hall. And that's precisely what he did! But the expressions on the faces in the room left him bewildered. Among all the arms raised, only Bryn had his right arm up, with the mysterious circular mark on the back of his hand clearly visible and glowing for everyone to see.

BREAKFAST

After the swearing of the oaths, Tejal announced it was time for breakfast, and hundreds of students formed a long line down the servery counter. But Bryn, Morlâ, and Filixx decided to wait until the initial rush had subsided.

Bryn used this time to take a closer look at the others from White House, especially those he hadn't met yet. But as he glanced around the table, he saw that most of the other students in the room were staring at him and whispering, and if he caught anyone's eye, they quickly turned away. Bryn dropped his head and kept his gazed fixed on those at the table.

"Aren't you the popular one," Morlâ whispered.

Opposite Bryn sat a group of three petite, brown-haired girls who clearly had dwarf blood. One was looking at his right hand from the corner of her eye. They got up together and headed to the counter. Next to Filixx sat two older, human-looking boys who seemed to be in their early twenties, their faces buried in their plates. Somehow, they had already managed to get some food and were cramming it into their mouths.

His gaze then fell on the student at the end of the table; he was wearing a hood. Bryn peeked at his face and saw his skin was a deep, dark green. *An orc! Why is he in White House?* The orc stood up and went over to the counter. He was enormous, and

Bryn noticed he dragged his left leg. *Is that why he's in White House?* Bryn was glad only one of these brutal-looking creatures was at the table. Orcs, he decided, were not his favorite.

Morlâ clasped Bryn's shoulder. "He could have been your roommate."

"That's Stinky?! You were going to put me in—"

"Enough staring, kid! He doesn't like it when people do that."

Filixx let Bryn calm down and then stood up. "Let's get some food. I'm starving."

So they each took a wooden board, a small bowl, and cutlery off the end of the counter and waited in line.

A ladleful of indefinable mash splattered into the bowl of the human boy standing in front of Filixx.

"Who's cooking this week?" he asked.

"Elves," said the boy, moving away.

Filixx watched the grey slop land in his bowl. It smelled like roasted nuts but looked inedible. Bryn thought it looked like glue.

"Those last five weeks flew past, eh?" Filixx pushed the bowl back over the counter. He turned to Bryn and Morlâ and, in a low voice, said, "Semesters always seem to start with weird elf food. Let's eat somewhere else."

Bryn was confused. "Filixx, what's the matter? It's finally our turn in line, and I'm ravenous."

"Trust me. You don't want to eat that. Elbendingen is on kitchen duty, which means grey mush and greens until they come out of your ears. And no meat! Not even a tiny bit." Filixx pushed Bryn and Morlâ toward the door.

"What do you mean, no meat?" Bryn asked. "You cooked some lamb."

Filixx and Morlâ laughed, and Filixx said, "All the fraternities, including White House, have kitchen duty alternately for seven days each. And to keep it fair, every fifth week, it's everybody's turn to cook, clean up, and set the tables. And all four fraternities—you'll excuse me, again, if I don't count us bastards—have their own tastes and traditional foods, and they cook accordingly. So this week, it's the elves' turn. They're so perfect and nice, they can't harm a living soul, which is fine in a way, but it also means they don't eat meat. Hence, the roasted nut mash abomination. They'll be serving raw greens, vegetable purées, vegetable casseroles—it's a meatless horror show all week."

Morlâ chuckled and patted Filixx on the back.

"So nothing if you're starving. Now, you might think it couldn't get any worse with the other three, but far from it. The humans' food is boring, but you can swallow it if you add some secret spices, but it gets truly horrible when the orcs cook. They only eat meat, which drives the elves crazy. But hardly any fresh meat. They bury it or leave it hanging in the sun until it stinks, and then they serve it. That's too much even for my hardened stomach. You can only get delicious food when it's the dwarves' turn to cook. Mushrooms, mutton and goat meat, well-ripened mountain cheese." Filixx had to swallow because his mouth watered. "Mmm, that's always a great week."

"What do we cook, when it's our turn?" asked Bryn.

"Since I do most of the cooking, I serve excellent dwarf food. However, the others in the house like to interfere, so we always have something on offer for all four fraternities," he remarked grimly. "The week we cook is probably the only thing the other fraternities appreciate about us. During this time, the dining room is fuller than ever."

They were now standing in front of the small ivy-covered door Bryn had entered the day before. Filixx took out a big golden key and opened the door. He came into the kitchen, and Morlâ and Bryn followed. Unlike their first visit, the kitchen was far from empty. Many elves were scurrying around gracefully, preparing the food being served at the servery counter.

"What are you doing here, Filixx?" asked a slim, blond girl Bryn recognized as Gwendolin.

"Hello, Gwenny! You know how much I adore that vegetable muck, so I'll make a proper breakfast for the three of us now." He then went to the big stove, where three elves were stirring huge pots, took a free stove plate for himself, and stoked the fire underneath.

"You shouldn't call me that," she protested, but Filixx had disappeared into the pantry.

"Hello, Gwendolin," said Bryn in a low voice.

"Hello … er?"

"It's Bryn."

"Oh, yes, I remember. You caused quite a stir yesterday," the elf said with a smile. She looked at his white sash. "The bastard house, eh? What a pity. After your performance yesterday, I would have expected more from you. But you seem to get on well with this riff-raff."

She nodded at Morlâ, whose face turned red. Just as he was about to respond, someone called Gwendolin from the dining room, and she flew out of the kitchen as if she had wings.

Filixx waved his two friends over to a small table in the corner. Soon, a big pan with scrambled eggs, mushrooms, and bacon landed in front of them. Bryn noticed almost as much bacon as eggs in the simmering pan, and it looked delicious and smelled tempting. Filixx came back with a fresh loaf of bread and, like their own, personal cook, had even organized a pot of herb butter. He served up large portions of scrambled eggs, broke off a large piece of the bread for himself, and handed the loaf to Morlâ.

"So, what did haughty old Gwenny say to you?"

"The usual," Morlâ replied, sighing. Bryn began to understand what it meant to be a White House member, to not belong to a real fraternity.

As the weather had improved, the three took the long way back to White House to enjoy the sunshine streaming through the gaps in the clouds.

"Today is the last day of the semester break; you have to make the most of it," said Morlâ and Filixx agreed.

Bryn, however, was looking forward to his first day of classes. He had never been to school, let alone university. His previous lessons with Gerald had been somewhat practical, except for the lessons in math and writing. Besides, the week was to start tomorrow morning with the main highlight—Magic. Once again, Bryn had goosebumps at the thought of what this subject might mean.

"How long does it take to graduate here?" he asked Morlâ once he'd come out of his musings.

"It depends on the strength of your talent. Normally, most students go to university for about ten semesters. A year always consists of two semesters, with the final exams and entrance test in the last semester."

"How do you know how strong your gift is?"

"I'm not the right person to ask," said Morlâ, looking grim.

Filixx intervened remarkably fast. Bryn had hit a sore spot with Morlâ. "I will not explain to you now how the gift works or what magic is; you will learn that from old Jehal in the morning. But to answer your question—there are different levels of magical ability. With elves, for example, the level is generally high. Humans are almost as good at magic. With the dwarves"— he threw a compassionate glance at Morlâ—"there is usually only a small percentage who are truly magically gifted. Many dwarves can only perform simple spells. The usual exceptions to this rule are us half-breeds as our magic level is hard to determine. And the orcs can't cast spells at all."

Bryn raised an eyebrow. "I thought being able to do magic was a prerequisite for admission to Âlaburg?"

"That is also true," Filixx admitted. "Orcs cannot use magic in the traditional sense, but some of them can summon, and all of them have one crucial advantage …" He paused theatrically.

"Which is?" Bryn asked impatiently.

"Orcs are immune to magic. They are not susceptible in any way to the magic of anyone with the gift."

Bryn's head spun. Magic seemed to be a complicated matter. But he would learn more about it in the morning.

Arriving at the tower, the three went down to the common room and spent the rest of the day together, chatting until they all went to bed.

Bryn extinguished the light and dropped his head on the pillow. He thought about what Morlâ and Filixx had told him about the university, including gossip about fellow students and Masters.

"I can't believe we've got Magic tomorrow!" he said, but Morlâ did not answer. Maybe he was asleep or perhaps was silent because of his bleak situation with magic. Bryn didn't know. However, he drifted off happily even though he couldn't wait until it was morning.

SEMESTER PLANS

Morlâ arched his back, stretched out his arms, and opened his eyes. He was about to sit up in the rumpled bed when he realized he was not alone. He rolled over and saw a person bent over the far desk, looking for something. He was instantly wide awake.

"Oh, rise and shine!" Bryn whispered.

"Man, you nearly scared me to death!" Waking from a deep sleep, Morlâ had forgotten he had a new roommate. "Why are you up already—and dressed?"

"Sorry, I just couldn't sleep anymore."

"Please tell me it's not going to be like this every morning," said Morlâ, half under his breath.

"I'll wait for you in the common room. Ok?"

Morlâ dismissively waved Bryn to the door with a limp hand, then rolled over, and shut his eyes.

Bryn grabbed his satchel and tiptoed out. The hallway was quite dark and quiet. The strange, round lamps on the wall now only had a faint glow. He ambled down to the common room, caught up in thoughts of what the day might bring, and ran smack into a girl rushing out of the bathroom—one he'd met the day before yesterday. It was Malin, and Bryn felt embarrassed seeing her wrapped in just a white towel, with another around her hair.

"Could you be any *less* careful?" she hissed, quashing any hope of further conversation, and pushed past him into room number eight, slamming the door.

Bryn continued down the hallway, mindful of every door he passed. The common room was quiet, except for the odd crackle from the fireplace, and it was untidy. Some of the armchairs scattered about the huge space were toppled over as well.

Bryn smiled to himself; the usual chaos of the morning was starting to feel familiar. But he noticed something different. On the walls, someone had hung huge semester timetables, similar to the one Tejal had given him but as big as a painting, for each of the students. Underneath each one was the name and a picture of the student. The first was Hela, the chubby girl in the group with Milan. *Her full name is Hela Demeter Papandrokolis. Sounds strange.*

The timetables listed the day and time of all the students' subjects and which assignments were compulsory to complete that semester. But they also included handwritten notes and reminders to the respective student. For Hela, it said, *More sports this semester! Finish a summoning for once! Less talking during the lectures!* Bryn had to smile when he read that. Curious, he looked at some others and discovered other reprimands, like *Learn more. No more dyeing anyone green! Work diligently! Stop setting fire to things! Do not get distracted so easily! When you summon a creature, clean up their droppings afterward!*

Now Bryn was curious about what had been written about him. He walked along the wall and looked for his name. There it was: Bryn McDermit. He was happy he could use Gerald's name, which he had long considered his own. The first thing he did was study his picture, amazed at how faithful the simple charcoal reproduction of his face was. He noticed his face looked much narrower than it did a few weeks ago. Fleeing here to the castle had taken its toll. But he also seemed more mature in the small picture. His hair was wilder, and his upper lip and chin had light charcoal strokes indicating some whiskers. Bryn was sure they hadn't been there a few weeks ago.

There were only three words of advice on his timetable, but they shocked him. *Control magic better!* Bryn could not make any sense of it. He had never tried to use magic before, so how could they know he couldn't control it?

Filixx popped his head in the door and disturbed Bryn's thoughts.

"Morning," he boomed. "Looking at our wall of shame, are we? What's old Tejal got to gripe about this semester?" He strolled over to study Bryn's timetable and made a long, peculiarly significant whistle. "Wow. *Control magic better.* You're one of the overly gifted, aren't you?" He laughed and squeezed Bryn's shoulder.

Bryn looked at him, astonished and disturbed.

"Oh, don't worry, it was just a remark. Every semester, the Masters need something to complain about—no matter how hard you try. Even if you're a new student who has yet to attend a class." Filixx moved away and read some of the other comments. He found Morlâ's. "… *keep working on your talent*—as if he didn't know that himself," he said, shaking his head.

Finally, Filixx found his timetable for the semester. Bryn followed behind him, peeking over his shoulder. *Filixx Streelman Renläer. So that's Filixx's full name.* The picture of him seemed old because Filixx looked a lot heavier now.

"There's nothing written on yours," said Bryn.

"Damn it, Bryn! Creeping up on me like that!"

Bryn could understand why Filixx was surprised, but not why he also looked embarrassed.

"Promise me you won't tell anyone about this."

"About what? That there are no comments? But that's a good thing, right?"

"Yes," Filixx stammered, "it is, yes, but not if you're the only student who never gets a comment. In my first semester, I was proud of it too, but then the others started teasing me, not only for being fat but also because they thought I was the teacher's pet. So now, I'm always the first one here at the start of a new semester so that I can add a few comments." He took a quill and a small inkwell from his pocket. "You won't say anything, will you?"

"No, of course not," Bryn assured him, shaking his head.

"Now, let's see … What could I improve on this year? Help me pick a good comment from one of the others, will you? I'll write that."

They searched through the semester timetables and called out suggestions to one other. *Arrive on time. Leave your toad at home. Work harder. Don't cast spells on the new students—more respect for the faculty. Stop dyeing the sashes of other fraternities in different colors.* But nothing was suitable for Filixx.

Then Bryn had an idea. "How about, *No more copying other people's work.*"

"Brilliant! If cheating to get those good grades doesn't earn me their respect, nothing will! Besides, at the start of every semester, I do copy their work," he added with a cheeky smile. Then he dipped the white swan feather quill into the pot and went to work.

"I do Tejal's handwriting quite well, don't I?"

"Looks fine to me. You're going to make the others very happy." Bryn chuckled.

And, as if on cue, they heard voices and footsteps in the hallway getting louder and louder. Filixx dropped the quill and ink into his satchel and slung it back over his shoulder.

Little by little, the common room filled with students, all airing their complaints about the Masters' remarks. Once that was over, most of them went to the dining room for breakfast.

Morlâ was one of the last to make an appearance. Already in a bad mood, he pushed back his disheveled hair, wiped the sleep from his eyes, and read Tejal's note on his timetable. Bryn and Filixx waited for a reaction.

"*Morlâ Bergstone … keep working on your talent; you will find it hidden deep inside you.* How original; three semesters in a row, the same old remark. She could at least think of some other way of saying it."

The three left White House and ran to the dining room for breakfast because Morlâ had made them all quite late, and Bryn had no intention of being late for class on his first day.

Because the elves were still cooking, Filixx ducked into the kitchen and prepared a massive breakfast, which they ate in the noisy dining room along with the other students. Bryn was so excited about his first Magic class that he hardly ate a thing.

When they stepped into Remter Hall, Filixx said goodbye and went up the staircase on the left. Although he and Morlâ had started at the same time, his progress was much more significant than that of his dwarf friend, and so the two of them did not have any lessons together this year. Filixx went to the higher classes on the second floor. Morlâ had to repeat the first semester, so most of his classes were with Bryn. Morlâ had only advanced in one subject, Math, but he was one of the best students in it.

Morlâ watched Filixx disappear up the stairs. "Well then … let's go through all this again," he reminded himself. "At least I can show you around, Bryn."

They took the staircase on the right; it was made of dark wood and recently waxed, with the steps almost completely worn out in the middle. It took them to a large hallway that had many doors and was teeming with students. Bryn saw that only a few still wore their house colors, unlike the day before, when it had been compulsory. Most of the students seemed to be content with subtle hints of their fraternity. One dwarf had a wolf tooth painted blue and red hanging from his left ear. A human student had her hair dyed red and yellow, and a tall elf, who didn't seem to like Bryn looking at him, had painted his fingernails alternately yellow and blue. Only the orcs wore their whole, black uniforms. They continued to march in menacing groups, and all the other students gave them a wide berth.

Morlâ pushed himself and Bryn through the noisy crowd toward their classroom.

Suddenly, he said, "Oh, shit! This can't be true. Oh, no …"

Bryn was bewildered. "What's wrong? Have you forgotten something? I can lend it to you. I stuffed my satchel this morning with more than I might need."

Morlâ shook his head and pointed down the hall to a group of blond students waiting outside a door. "We have Magic with them."

"With the elves. So what? It's better than with the orcs, isn't it?"

Morlâ sighed. "How I would love to have lessons now with students of Řischnǎrr. They are almost as bad at Magic as I am. But elves! Bryn, these are the most gifted beings in Razuclan. These giggling first-years can do more magic in an hour than I did all of last year."

Bryn didn't know what to say. He still hadn't entirely understood what magic was. Without a word, he kept abreast of his friend as he plodded toward the giggling, chattering elves.

Like the first time Bryn had met elves, they took no notice of students who were not of their nation. Surprised, Bryn noticed he and Morlâ were the only students who were not elves and asked Morlâ about it.

"Only two different fraternities have lessons together. Since you are the only new member of White House this semester, and I am the only one repeating, I guess we have to take on this bunch of first-semester elves alone."

After a moment, an older man came shuffling down the hallway toward them. He wore leather slippers and leaned heavily on a black cane, and his right leg dragged heavily. His long, grey hair hung tangled over his face, and in his expansive grey beard, Bryn spotted breadcrumbs. His head was bent forward, and it was near impossible to see his face. It seemed to take him an eternity to reach the room.

Is this the Master of Magic?

Silently, the man took a large, worn key, which he wore around his neck on a long, silver chain, and unlocked the classroom door. The elves pushed into the room after him to get seats in the front rows. This left Bryn and Morlâ with the last row of desks to themselves, which they were hardly sad about.

THE COLORS OF MAGIC

The classroom seating was arranged in five rows of five seats each. Each wooden folding seat was bolted to the floor with its desk. Morlâ pulled down one of the seats and slumped into it.

Bryn dropped his satchel on the desk and took the seat next to Morlâ. Several words were scratched on top of Bryn's desk, but he could read only the ones in the common language. *No more university! Magic is boring! Rezal loves Gystan*. The desk had an incline, and the top right corner had a recess to put the inkwell in. He placed his quills in the dip that ran along the end of the desk closest to him, pulled a papyrus stack from his satchel, and looked around the room impatiently.

The room had three large, stained-glass windows that filtered what little sunlight there was. A tall cabinet with many doors, each with a heavy lock, stood on the other side of the room. The floor was oak parquet and well-worn, and at the front, also having seen better days, was a big, wooden desk covered in burn marks and scratches. Behind that, a small, green chalkboard was propped up on a wooden stand that you could flip over when one side was full.

Bryn watched the old Master rummage through his desk and swivel about in his creaky leather chair.

While some students were deep in discussion and others were still fighting over the best seats, Morlâ chatted to Bryn. "I didn't expect Jehal would teach another semester. Rumors said the elves wanted to take back the position of Master of Magic from the humans because they felt he was too old, but he's stronger than I thought."

"Silence!" shot a powerful, thundering voice through the room.

Bryn wondered who spoke until he saw the old Master's lips moving.

"Don't students bow out of deference to their Masters anymore?" he growled.

Bryn looked at Morlâ, confused. Then the elves in the first four rows jumped to their feet and bowed deeply before the Master. Bryn and Morlâ followed suit, and then sat down again. The room fell quiet; all they could hear was the rattling sound of Jehal's breathing.

"That's better. Your manners get worse every decade. Well, we can fix that. You'll get to know me, and you'll see my classes respect the rules. As punishment for your disrespectful behavior, you will prepare a paper next week on *The Colors of Magic*. And one student will present theirs to the class. Now, if that person fails to bring it with them and has no excuse, they will remove themselves from my course for the rest of the semester. Do we understand each other, ladies and gentlemen? So do me a favor; be lazy this week. The class is much too full for me anyway."

Bryn and the elves scribbled down the assignment while Morlâ sat there and stared at Jehal, who was looking over a list of names.

"Let's see who we have here. Melvina Meadowstone?"

"Here," came a high, shy voice.

"Here, what?"

The girl looked at the Master in bewilderment. Then she seemed to understand. "Here, Master."

"That wasn't too difficult, was it?" growled Jehal. "With such astonishing elvish eyesight, you must have noticed I'm a little older than you and not so good on my feet, so bring your semester timetable to me!"

Red-faced and nervous, the girl approached the desk, the timetable scrunched in her hand.

The Master snatched it from her and smoothed it out. "Should anyone else wish to present me with such a tattered, dirty rag, you can take your leave immediately. Then wait a semester for the next beginners' class. I'm not signing another one like this!"

He pinched a tiny pair of glasses to the bridge of his nose, scribbled something with a small yellow quill, handed it back to the cowering elf, and shooed her away. She found her place and slipped into her chair, seeming desperate not to attract attention.

"Well, well, well, who do we have here?" said Jehal with cruel amusement. "Morlâ Bergstone!"

Bryn saw Morlâ stiffen.

"We had the pleasure of meeting last semester, did we not?"

"Yes, Master," said Morlâ, bowing his head.

"I hope during the semester break, you were able to discover even a tiny fraction of talent. Otherwise, this nightmare should end now. You could join Master Gerald in the garden instead and learn all about compost and hedge trimming and so on. I suspect you'll have more success there than here; let me remind you this course is for gifted students."

"Whatever you say, Master," said Morlâ, struggling to compose himself.

"Well, that's what I think," Jehal barked. "Now come forward so we can continue this farce."

Morlâ moved as fast as his tiny stature permitted, an immaculate looking semester timetable in his hand. Jehal took it without looking up, scribbled his signature on it half-heartedly, and passed it back.

He then read out the other names: *Herolin Mountainsprig, Ionius Birchlea, Klabier Pineberry, Oldo Brambush* … And one by one, the students went up. Finally, Jehal came to the last name on his list. "Bryn McDermit."

Bryn leaped to his feet. "Here, Master."

"Are you related to our new garden laborer by any chance?"

The belittlement of his foster father stung, but Bryn refused to let it show.

"Yes, Master. He brought me up."

"Ah … so family unknown … the bastard house. Have you used magic before?"

Bryn panicked. He couldn't remember how he had used magic in the forest, and Tejal had forbidden him from mentioning anything.

Jehal arched an eyebrow. "Well, boy?"

"No! No, Master," said Bryn.

"Perfect, the least talented have found each other and are seated in the back row. How appropriate. Well done. Can I ask one thing though?" His voice sounded less amused. "Over the next few weeks, don't attempt to disrupt my class or hinder the actual students' progress. Can you do that?" He waved his leathery hand for Bryn to step forward.

Bryn picked up his timetable and went to the desk. The Master grabbed it and scoffed. He flattened out the few creases, signed it, and flicked Bryn away with his hand.

"My name, as most of you know, is Ultar Jehal. You will address me as Master Jehal. Is that clear?"

The class nodded in silence.

"You are here because the Lekan Gate has chosen you. And because our esteemed Chancellor has tested you and given you her approval."

Bryn detected the merest trace of sarcasm in Jehal when he mentioned the Chancellor.

"But don't think that's why you can do magic. Being accepted here has nothing, absolutely nothing, to do with magical talent. As demonstrated by numerous examples." He stared long and hard at Morlâ and Bryn. "Even so, those who prove themselves gifted can perform great things if they learn to control magic and have it submit to their will." He paused dramatically. "Yes, you heard that right. You must control magic, compel it to work for you." His cold eyes drifted from face to face. "By the way, how are you going to do your homework if you don't write down a word of the immeasurable knowledge I'm imparting to you?"

Sheets of papyrus immediately unfolded, and everyone began scribbling notes. Much to Bryn's astonishment, however, Morlâ only pretended to.

Jehal pointed his scrawny arm toward the windows. "Millions of individuals out there believe magic can grant you every wish," he mocked. "They think all you need to do is mumble the appropriate phrase—preferably one that rhymes—and that's it." He snickered. "They have no idea about the nature of magic. It is pure science. Magic, like mathematical formulas, astronomical calculations, or medical findings, always works the same, regardless of where it is and who uses it.

"That's why it's predictable. And the better you understand it and its ways, the greater the magic you can do. So it's up to you how good you become. As with any subject, you need diligence, commitment, and superior intellect to do magic. If you have these three qualities, I guarantee you will do great things. If not, you will remain mediocre and end up a wizard in the court of some impoverished human nobleman, making fireworks and wart removal cream."

Bryn frowned and shook out his hand, which ached from writing so much. Then Jehal was off again.

"Non-gifted beings perceive the world using their five senses. But that is only one aspect of reality."

Bryn's ears pricked—finally, he would hear the truth about magic!

"When our esteemed Chancellor tested you ..."

Now Bryn was sure of Jehal's sarcasm.

"... you discovered that besides this present 'reality'"—he made air quotes around the term—"that we are experiencing now, there exists another. This is the magic realm, but only the gifted can see it. And just seeing it doesn't mean you can use it. To control and direct the flow of magic, one must first enter its realm."

Bryn filled his third sheet with notes, put it aside, took out a fresh piece, and continued, his inkwell all but empty.

"Magic is like the wind or a river—it flows continuously. And like these two natural forces, we can use them to our advantage if we know how. Ships sailing across the ocean take advantage of the wind, for example, and water from a diverted stream turns the mill wheel. But no one would claim this is magic. For thousands of years, the enlightened nations of Razuclan have used this natural phenomenon to make their lives better. Magic is but another part of nature, but only a few can perform it. This is the only difference. Are there any questions so far?"

No one dared speak.

The Master looked at them with suspicion. "Very well. Splendid, it seems you've understood everything. So I should assume the next lecture will also be easy for you?" Again, he looked around. Even the elves found him intimidating. The Master sighed. "And before I forget, I'm looking forward to next Monday's assignment. With genius first-semesters like yourselves, I'm sure to learn something from you myself."

This prompted an unusually large elf, whose name Bryn had forgotten, to raise his hand.

"Ah! One amongst you who understands they may not know everything. What a shame! Your question, Oldo?"

He already remembered the boy's name? Bryn noted with envy. Jehal's memory was impressive, and Bryn wondered if that was what happened when you spent your whole life teaching.

"How do you enter this magic realm, Master?"

The old magician's face lit up. "A brilliant question, Oldo, and a credit to the reputation of your people. If you want to do magic, you have to get to the magical energy first. Anything else would be complete nonsense. A dwarf would have asked me, first, how to turn stones into diamonds, and a human student, how to make someone fall in love with them." Jehal looked again at Bryn and Morlâ, triggering a relaxed giggle from the elves.

"Very well, you want to learn magic. Let's get started." He waved his hand in the air, and on the blackboard behind him appeared a bold, underlined headline in thick, white chalk, followed by a list of points.

Chapter 1: Seeing and entering the magic realm
A) Concentration
B) Blocking out the 'normal' world
C) Perceiving the cracks in the world (mostly visible as flickering)
D) Seeing the realm through the pure desire for it
E) Entering the realm (advanced and gifted students only)

Jehal looked at the students. "That's all it is. We'll try it together. But don't be too disappointed; no student has ever managed to see, let alone enter, the realm in their first session. If you should notice a slight flickering, then you have made fantastic progress today. Now, are we ready?"

All the elves nodded.

Bryn and Morlâ gave a tentative nod because Morlâ had tried this exercise a hundred times without success and was unwilling to try it again, and Bryn didn't understand what was going on.

But as neither of them wanted to draw the Master's wrath, they pretended to play along.

Jehal stood up from his desk. "Now, take a deep breath."

There was a deep draught from many throats.

"Concentrate on perceiving the realm. Nothing else matters now."

Jehal's voice seemed different. It was less bitter now, more reassuring. Even Bryn began to feel more confident.

"Free your mind!"

The classroom grew still; only the students' inhalations and exhalations could be heard.

"Keep your eyes on a fixed point and hold them there! Think only of the realm and your desire to see it!"

Bryn stared at the back of the girl seated in front of him and tried to concentrate. The Master's words seemed to wash over him, and his desire to enter the realm grew. Bryn took deep, relaxed breaths and kept his attention focused on the girl's satiny, green cloak and her thick, blond hair. Just as he began to feel self-conscious, he noticed a brief shimmering, like a heat haze you might see over a wide, empty plain on a summer day. In the next moment, his senses became significantly heightened like they had in the Chancellor's office. Now he could see that the girl's cloak was made of fine, silver-green threads and that her fine hair was not entirely smooth, each golden strand made up of tiny, overlapping plaits.

His nose filled with the smell of Morlâ's leather jacket but also, unfortunately, his armpits. Bryn's heartbeat got louder, and he could feel the blood coursing through his veins, but he was not afraid this time. The air that left his nose sounded like a hurricane. His right hand tingled again, but this time, it was pleasant. Suddenly, the room flooded with red, blue, and yellow bands, flowing around everything like water. Colorful ribbons swirled around his fingers and grew wider further up his arms. He looked down at himself and could see the thickest of the bands wrapped around his upper body. His insides glowed like a liquid rainbow. Yellow light flowed around the elves, while Jehal was bathed in glowing red. A sideways glance revealed Morlâ covered in a band of near-transparent blue.

So these were the colors of magic!

"Come back, boy!"

Bryn was watching himself again. Then, out of the corner of his eye, he saw a red hand on his shoulder. It was shaking him but in slow motion. It looked funny, but he could ignore it. He was only interested in the colors. This vision was the most beautiful thing he had ever seen. Bursts of magnificent red light shot from the hands clasping his shoulders. Energy whirled about the room; now, ribbons of brilliant red light also began to snake around his body. Bryn found that if he touched them, they vanished into thin air, making him laugh.

"Stop!" cried a strangely familiar voice. "What … What are you doing? Stop it now, Bryn! Come back! Concentrate on coming back to the here and now!"

If he had come back, he would have seen the abject fear in Jehal's eyes as Bryn casually obliterated the red bands of energy the Master was manifesting.

But Bryn was fine where he was; he didn't recognize Jehal's voice or what it was saying, and the surging energy around him consumed him.

"Please, Bryn, wake up!" roared another voice.

Morlâ! Though deeply lost in the magic, Bryn knew Morlâ meant something to him. His head turned painfully slowly over to his friend. He watched Morlâ's frightened face and the frantic movements of his lips. His friend wanted to tell him something. Morlâ reached out with both hands, and Bryn held them. The pale blue haze that surrounded Morlâ crept over Bryn's forearms. He felt the same fear Morlâ was feeling—the fear of losing a friend! Then, suddenly, inexplicably, everything fell silent. Bryn tried to open his eyes, but it was too painful. Utterly bewildered, he shook himself mentally and forced his eyes to open. Why was he staring up at the ceiling?

"What happened? Where am I?" he asked, his voice weak and hoarse. A greasy, grey shock of hair fell in front of his face, and whiskers with nests of crumbs tickled his nose.

"You're here in the classroom," said the Master. Bryn could smell his sour breath. Jehal then reached down and pulled Bryn to his feet. As he did, he noticed the fading black circle on the back of Bryn's right hand. The professor's eyebrow twitched, his surprise almost imperceptible. As quick as a flash, he regained his composure and ordered everyone back to their seats.

The elves hurried back to their chairs immediately. But Morlâ did not leave Bryn's side, even when Jehal tried to move Bryn toward the door.

"Sit down, Morlâ," he ordered.

"No," he shouted back.

Jehal turned to the dwarf, towering over him, but Morlâ stood firm. Something flickered in Jehal's eyes. If Bryn didn't know better, he would think he saw a mix of astonishment and respect.

"Morlâ, *please*," Jehal sighed. "I must take Bryn to the infirmary."

Morlâ was irritated at the request, and only when Bryn signaled with a weak nod that he was all right did he go back to his seat.

The student and the Master stepped into the hall, and Jehal closed the heavy door behind them. He stepped in front of Bryn and looked at him. Bryn saw the pupils of his tiny eyes contract. "What did you see?"

Bryn tried to look innocent. He did not give the Master an answer. After all, Tejal had warned him not to talk about the colors.

"Now, don't be so stubborn," growled Jehal. "At least tell me if you've experienced something like this before."

"Yes," Bryn whispered.

"When?"

"At the entrance exam in the Chancellor's office."

"And you suffered a similar episode there?"

"I think so. I don't remember everything. But when I came to, the Chancellor's office was destroyed."

"So she knew. Damn it, why didn't she warn me? For years I've been telling her it would happen again someday if she accepted every mongrel vagabond who passed by here."

"What would happen again?" Bryn asked, growing more alert.

"Oh, nothing … Did you also draw magical power from another gifted person in the Chancellor's office? Someone whose energy you could see?"

But before Bryn could answer, everything went dark, and he collapsed. As he fell, Jehal caught him and held him in his arms with unbelievable speed and strength.

SECRETS AND FRIENDS

Bryn opened his eyes.

"Good morning! Or should I say good afternoon?" quipped Morlâ, standing next to the bed. Bryn lifted his head off the pillow and smiled as best he could. "You've been asleep the whole day." Morlâ leaned in. "You know, at lunch, Filixx was so inconsolable, he ate your serving as well!"

"Where am I?"

"In the infirmary, where else? Jehal brought you here after your little performance. Wow, you sure flaked out, huh?"

The room felt so sterile. Everything was white. Bryn could see other beds, made up with white sheets and lined up along white walls, with a small, white table between each of them. The glare from the large lamps on the ceiling forced Bryn to turn away from Morlâ's big, smiling face.

"Yes ... the hallway ... I was in the hallway, and I passed out. One moment Jehal was speaking to me, then—"

"What, he was talking to you? The stupid jerk said he was taking you straight to the infirmary. If I'd known he'd stop to chat, I wouldn't have let him get rid of me so easily. What did he want?"

Bryn hesitated and turned away again.

"Never mind, keep your secrets. We hardly know each other, anyway—why trust a bastard like me, right?"

Bryn heaved himself off the bed to sit eye-level with Morlâ. "No, listen, I trust you, but you have to promise not to say anything."

"Not even to Filixx? He's too clever for that. He finds out everything anyway—something I still don't understand. No, we don't want to do anything that would put our close friendship with Filixx at risk—not to mention all that extra sumptuous food—without which, we wouldn't be able to survive here anyway."

Bryn laughed for what felt like the first time in ages. "All right, all right! We can trust Filixx! And I'm sure if he had any secrets," said Bryn, thinking of the notes on the timetable, "he would trust us with them as well."

Morlâ cocked his head to one side. He knew nothing about this, but something made him curious. But first, he wanted to hear about his new friend's secret.

Bryn lent over up and took a sip of water from a clay mug on the bedside table. He told Morlâ about the admission exam in Tejal's office, the colors, and what happened in Jehal's class after entering the magic realm.

Morlâ lowered himself onto the next bed. "Man, that's the craziest story I ever heard. Are you sure you saw all three colors?"

Bryn nodded.

"Of course, I have never seen them, that goes without saying, but every student of Âlaburg knows about the three colors of magic. Blue for the dwarves, red for the humans, and yellow for the elves. If a member of any one of these nations uses strong magic, everyone can see them even in the natural world—like in a Combat Spell. That's why the fraternities feature their own color and that of another nation in their official emblem. It's a symbol of peace between all the nations of Razuclan. Put simply, fraternity colors reflect the colors of their magic and the colors of all the nations on the continent. And those who cannot or are not allowed to use magic must, of course, distance themselves from magic. That's why the fighting machines of the Řischnǎrr fraternity wear black, and we bastards wear white."

Morlâ took a deep breath. "I have never heard of anyone who can see all three colors. Like all humans who have the gift, you should only see red when you're in the realm. Think about what you could do with this!" Morlâ's eyes danced with excitement. "But why wouldn't you return? And why couldn't Jehal's magic bring you back?"

The infirmary door opened and in stepped a beautiful, blond woman in a white coat. Bryn could see she was an elf. Morlâ jumped off the bed and gave her a slow, extended bow. *She must be special*, Bryn thought. *Morlâ doesn't show even Tejal this kind of respect.*

She nodded to Morlâ, smiled, and walked over to the bed. "Hello, Bryn. I am Mevira Winterblossom." He thought her voice sounded like a songbird chirping; it was high and soothing. "How are you?"

Bryn bowed as best he could. "I'm better now, Master Winterblossom," he declared, sitting up a little more.

"Well, let's see if that's true, young Bryn. I need to examine you. Should I tell Morlâ to leave?" she asked as if Morlâ wasn't there.

"No, please, he can stay."

At that, she flashed him a disarming smile and sat on the edge of the bed. Her scent struck Bryn as a mix of fresh, wet moss and a forest after a summer storm. He took a deep breath through his nose and unbuttoned the front of his gown. She tapped all over his upper body with a cold, silver disc that she'd warned him would be a little unpleasant. Then she placed her smooth, firm hands on his temples.

"I want you to clear your mind, Bryn. I want you to empty it of all thoughts. Can you do that for me?"

"That'll be easy. There's nothing in there!" Morlâ chimed in. But his wisecrack only produced a sharp, disapproving look from the Master. In the following silence, Morlâ shuffled back to the other bed and stared at his feet.

Bryn bit his tongue so as not to laugh and nodded at the Master; he would give it a go.

"Excellent," she said, stroking his temples again.

Bryn felt his eyelids grow heavy. Then, from somewhere, he could hear the faint tinkling of a bell. The clearer he heard it, the more he felt the weakness drain out of him. Whatever the healer was doing, Bryn found it intensely pleasurable. Next, Winterblossom's voice was asking him to wake up. "That's it, Bryn. Open your eyes, wake up now." The Master's face came into focus, and Bryn realized the little bell had stopped ringing. "Excellent, Bryn. You were under for quite a while, and you did well. How do you feel?"

"I … I feel …" Bryn stammered, and then gave up.

Winterblossom laughed. "It's all right, I've seen this before, after treating the new students for magic burns. Not to worry." She gestured a thumbs up, followed by a thumbs down. "Which is it?"

Bryn stuck his thumb up and smiled.

"Wonderful! Bryn, you may put your clothes on now." She stood and started for the door, then turned around. "By the way, your first Healing class this semester is in five minutes, and I want to see you both there. All right?"

Their Healing class was with the elves—or the 'magically gifted' as Morlâ liked to call them. Even though Winterblossom was strict, they both agreed she at least had a sense of humor. Bryn liked how she used it to explain the anatomy of humans, dwarves, elves, and orcs. From the heart to the brain, many things were similar, which surprised Bryn. He'd just assumed the differences would be significant because the people looked and behaved so differently.

Bryn hung on the Master's every word, and when the class ended, he felt like he'd learned something. The first day of the first semester was over, and it left Bryn in good spirits.

SUMMONING

When Bryn woke the following morning, he felt odd—like he'd been at the university for quite a while already. And somehow, rooming with Morlâ felt comfortable and familiar. He'd also slept much better than the previous nights. He jumped out of bed and went to the bathroom. Morlâ was sitting on his bed with his eyes closed, yawning, and a towel over his shoulder when Bryn returned.

"Man, you're an early riser," he grumbled and trudged past Bryn for the door.

While Morlâ was in the bathroom, Bryn put his notes from yesterday's Magic and Healing classes into a pile. He looked over at the stack of fresh papyrus Tejal had put on his desk that first day. *I wonder if there's enough for the rest of the week?* But when Bryn counted them, to his surprise and delight, it had the same number of sheets as the day before. *What a strange, funny place this is.*

At breakfast, Bryn and Morlâ had no choice but to eat with everyone else. Filixx had warned them the night before that he would be away preparing something for class. Even so, the sight of that light brown, nutty porridge was still a blow that left them both groaning.

"Who knows what those damned elves have put in here," said Morlâ, jabbing at the detestable mess with his spoon.

"Certainly not meat," teased Bryn, who liked it better with every spoonful. "Eat it; it doesn't taste that bad."

But Morlâ could only manage a few bites. He took a small wooden box out of his pocket and poured almost the entire contents over the cold porridge. He offered what remained to Bryn, but he politely declined after noticing the powder looked blue and smelled of rotten fish.

"Now it's edible!" Morlâ boasted.

After such a disappointment, the two didn't stay long and went to Remter Hall. But instead of taking Bryn to the first floor like yesterday, Morlâ took him out through the hall's massive front door.

"Summoning classes take place in the stable," Morlâ explained through gritted teeth.

Outside, Bryn struggled to keep his jacket collar closed to ward off the biting wind. Morlâ led him down the side of the hall and across several hundred feet of open space to a wooden building in a field surrounded by a picket fence.

Morlâ lifted the latch on the low gate and swung it open. "You ready?" he asked Bryn. But before Bryn could reply, Morlâ was sprinting over the grassy field to the stable, laughing. Bryn ran after him and reached the sprawling three-story building just as Morlâ did. Bryn looked up, panting.

"Is it new?" he asked. It wasn't, Morlâ assured him. The wood planking on the front wall looked smooth and stretched up to several great, open hatches huddled under the shingle roof. Bryn ran his hand over the stable's massive double door, which was like the ones he'd seen on the barns in Sefal. They heaved open one of the doors and stepped in.

The smell of fresh hay was typical, but Bryn couldn't believe how warm it was for such a big, open space. In the middle of the stable was a large, circular area covered in straw and enclosed by a woven fence of young saplings. *A ring? But where are the animals who train here—or live here? And no feed boxes or stalls for the cows. Another mystery, I suppose*, thought Bryn, more curious than concerned.

A group of dwarves had already gathered ringside, and many of them wore beards like Morlâ. Bryn was trying to avoid eye contact, but he could see a few girls. Morlâ saw this as well and was also observing them in secret.

As the two latecomers approached, they heard the words "Morning, bastard!" echo around them. Morlâ froze—his eyes narrowed. He had no doubt the insult was meant for him. Bryn glanced over at Morlâ and could see the veins bulging in his neck.

"Who said that?" Morlâ hissed. "Step forward! I'll show you if I'm a real dwarf or not!"

Before the conflict could escalate, a powerful-looking dwarf appeared on the far side of the stable, leaped over the fence from a standing position into the ring, and strode over to the students.

Bryn could see the confidence in his steps. And though he looked relatively young, Bryn could tell he was the Master of Summoning. After crossing the space, he leaped over the fence again and stood in front of his new students, beaming.

He was tall for a dwarf. His long, dark hair tied into a ponytail and full, dark beard gave him a rugged appearance, like an adventurer. But Bryn also noted how well-defined his beard line was.

The Master was wearing a sleeveless red and white checked shirt that exposed his muscular arms. Under that, he wore light brown leather pants. The shirt was wide open at the neck and revealed a chest covered in dark hair. Around his neck hung a big, white tooth on a leather string, and on his forearms were wide leather bracelets embossed with runes. Another thing that struck Bryn was how well-tanned he was, particularly for this time of the year.

On the whole, he was quite good-looking. Several female students noticed this too, exchanging meaningful glances as he approached.

All the students bowed deeply.

"Good morning, my friends. It's going to be my pleasure to introduce you to the great art of Summoning," he said, studying all the student's faces. "My name is Dorinda Underhil, but when we are in the stable, you are welcome to call me Dori. And the bowing—you don't have to take that too seriously either. All right?" He flashed them a dazzling smile. Several girls began giggling. Bryn glanced over at them. "All right, let's focus, please! First, I need to check the attendance."

While the Master checked who was present, Morlâ mentioned to Bryn that this was Underhil's first semester. The last tutor had been either mauled to death or eaten by some creature—he wasn't sure which.

"All right, everyone is here. So many eager faces—and all of you want to study the ancient art of Summoning!"

"He's not seen my face then," Morlâ quipped.

"First, who can explain what Summoning is?"

Nobody answered.

"Don't worry," he explained, "wrong answers won't affect your final grades. I'm of the belief that there's no such thing as a wrong answer."

A girl raised her arm, chewing on her bottom lip.

"Yes? Grüöletä, isn't it?" The girl looked delighted he knew her name.

"First, you contact the spirit world and then—"

"No. I'm sad to say that's wrong, my dear," Dorinda interrupted. "But not to worry." He shot her a smile. "Anyone else?"

Several more students raised their hands, but their answers were also wrong. Even so, they each received a smile and an encouraging nod from the Master.

Finally, tired of rolling his eyes, Morlâ raised his arm. "Summoning is the ability to materialize any creature in Razuclan, anywhere, and subject it to the summoner's will using the power of the gift. Skilled summoners can manifest herds of animals or swarms of insects and use them for their own ends. There is also the danger of losing control of the summoned entities, and they may attack the summoner. Hence, a beginner should summon only harmless creatures like worms or flies," Morlâ concluded.

Dorinda clapped his hands delightedly. "Excellent, Morlâ! Keep this up, and you can take over my job soon."

Bryn watched Morlâ struggle with the lavish praise. But when he looked closer, he thought he also saw the tiniest hint of pride in his friend's eyes.

"Let us begin then! Come into the ring," Dorinda urged. "The fence will prevent the animals you are about to summon from escaping."

The excited students scrambled over the fence or, in the case of a few dwarves, squeezed under it.

"Summoning is conditional on having the gift," the Master reminded them.

Bryn glanced at Morlâ. His shoulders looked even more hunched and rounded than usual.

"First, you will materialize your creatures here in the stable, and then you must learn to control them. You will use the gift to do this too. Now, consider how you should divide your power. For example, you don't want to summon something dangerous from the Fire Swamps only to find you've no power over it—and it has you for dinner."

Morlâ huffed under his breath. "He shouldn't joke. The Master before him was—"

"I want you to work in pairs," Dorinda went on, his voice more serious. "I want one person watching while the other is summoning, in case there's an emergency."

Moving with an undertone of apprehension, the class spread out through the ring in pairs. Dorinda waited until they settled and placed his left hand over his larynx. Immediately, his voice filled the space, booming from all directions. "Choose which creature you wish to summon. Imagine it in detail. Describe its appearance to yourself—its coat, color, smell, size, and so on. Once you've done that, I will talk to you about what to consider when summoning your creature."

Dorinda went from student to student as the murmuring in the class grew louder and louder.

Bryn and Morlâ paired up and talked about the task, but they became distracted and ended up shoving each other into the soft straw and throwing it at each other. When the Master joined them, they still hadn't chosen an animal. Dorinda looked at Morlâ and Bryn, whose hair and clothes were covered in straw, with a mix of curiosity and warmth.

"I see you two are having fun. Is the creature you've chosen the Straw Cootie or a Chafer Bug? I mean, were you searching for them in the straw to have me believe you had already summoned them or so you could study them?" he asked with his usual broad smile.

The two boys looked at each other and almost exploded into laughter. Straw Cooties and Chafer Bugs? Bryn was pretty sure those insects didn't exist. Plus, keeping a straight face was getting harder and harder, and he was turning red. Dorinda smiled at the two students but was annoyed.

Morlâ tried to salvage the situation. "We've opted for the Gnarf worm, Master," he said earnestly.

"Dori, please," he reminded him.

"Yes, yes, of course," Morlâ agreed, a little uneasy about it all the same. "Well, the worm lives in caves deep underground. It's quite small, but it can drill tunnels with its teeth, even into the hardest rock. I've seen them in the mines near my home. So I had the idea of summoning one. I tried to describe it to Bryn, like you were saying, in as much detail as possible."

Bryn gave a thoughtful nod, but tears were welling in his eyes.

"Very well then. Carry on. As homework, I want a three-page essay from you, with drawings, about this worm's life—you made it sound so interesting."

And then Dorinda moved on to the next pair. When he was finally out of earshot, Bryn and Morlâ erupted into laughter. Shortly after that, their first Summoning class was over.

Bryn didn't feel like he'd learned much, but it had been a delightful morning, even if the extra homework spoilt it. Nonetheless, the two friends had a spring in their step as they took off to meet Filixx for lunch.

STARBALL

Remter Hall was now a sea of hungry students, but the boys quickly found Filixx, deep in conversation with an enormous orc. This seemed odd to Bryn. He thought nobody mixed with students from Řischnărr. As they approached, the orc thudded his left hand on his chest, Filixx bowed, and the muscle-bound giant disappeared into the crowd.

"Hey, Filixx," Morlâ cried out, a worried look on his face, "what did he want with you? Do you have a problem with Řischnărr? Just remember, there's nothing we can't handle—especially with Bryn here …" He grinned wryly, dying to tell Filixx about his roommate's extraordinary abilities.

Filixx looked at the two in confusion. "No, no, everything's fine. I had to clarify something with Řälärm—about the lessons. Now, what's this about Bryn? Did he conjure up a Galbanofant this morning?" He laughed loudly. "But tell me, was the new Master any good?"

Morlâ put his arm on Filixx's shoulder and leaned into his ear. "You will never believe it. But yesterday, Bryn here performed magic!"

Bryn interrupted him. "Not here, Morlâ!"

"You're right! I'm sorry." He turned back to Filixx. "Isn't there a warm, secluded spot in the kitchen we can go to? And some meat? Breakfast this morning was, well, a little too elvish."

Filixx nodded in solidarity. "Come with me. You like roast duck, right?"

Bryn's and Morlâ's faces lit up. Once again, the three friends went to the small, ivy-covered door and stepped in. Filixx led them to a small, cozy, disused storeroom, ushered them inside, and headed to the kitchen.

Lunch consisted of roast duck served on a bed of red cabbage, apple, and cinnamon, with potato dumplings tossed with bacon and parsley. After they'd finished eating, Bryn told them all about defeating the Vonnyen and his experience in the magic realm.

The room fell silent. The combination of lunch and the stories from Bryn left them all feeling heavy and deep in thought.

"I've never heard anything like it—wow!" Filixx exclaimed. "This is extraordinary, Bryn. You're something special! The Chancellor did well, telling you to keep this a secret. And it's safe with me. The fact the Vonnyens are back is more than worrying though. Their last appearance heralded the beginning of two great wars. It's depressing news. I only hope Tejal has advised the Order to watch for any new developments in the Arell region. Then again, I may be worrying too much; she is extremely capable."

"What do you think is wrong with me?" Bryn asked, his eyes widening.

"I can't tell you anything—not yet, anyway," Filixx replied, squeezing Bryn's arm. "I will do some research in the library. And I'll ask the Five Wise Ones—without, of course, revealing your secret. They may know something—"

"I have an idea!" Morlâ cried out. "For the moment, while we're trying to help Bryn find answers, why can't he help us? You see, Bryn, our Starball team needs to play a lot better this semester, and …"

"Starball? I don't know how to play—"

"Now, now. No false modesty," Morlâ said brightly. "And … I would like you—both of you—to try out for the team. What do you say? Training starts this afternoon."

"Oh. Well, the try-outs shouldn't be difficult as I'm sure we'll be the only ones there," said Filixx with more than a hint of sarcasm.

Morlâ looked at him, heaved a deep sigh, and the conversation tapered off. On a flimsy pretext, Filixx excused himself but promised to come to training later.

In the afternoon, Morlâ and Bryn set off for the tower. Once inside, they flopped on their soft, warm beds to talk over the morning's events but soon nodded off.

Bryn yawned and eased his head an inch off the pillow. The afternoon nap had left him even more tired, and he didn't want to get up.

Startled by movement right next to his bed, Bryn opened his eyes. Morlâ was leaning over the bed with a big grin, staring at him. In one hand, he held the Harel Star, which looked almost twice as big as him, and he was motioning wildly for Bryn to get out of bed. Bryn fell back into the pillow, one eye on his roommate. Then Morlâ launched into a ridiculous tirade about him staying in bed and letting down White House, the university, and … his family. Bryn shook his head and gave in with a wry smile.

He and Morlâ set off for the training ground behind the stable. To stay awake, Bryn focused on the sound of the snow crunching under his boots as he trudged along behind Morlâ.

Morlâ stopped abruptly and turned to Bryn. "Each fraternity has one training day per week. That's it," Morlâ warned. "This means you must keep Tuesday afternoon free for the rest of the semester. Is that clear?"

Bryn nodded silently and wiped more snow off his nose. *It's a good thing I put on my thick fur clothes*, he thought. *Otherwise, I'd have hypothermia by now.* The bitter cold didn't seem to bother Morlâ though. He reminded Bryn more and more of Gerald, which made him smile, and they set off again.

"Almost there," said Morlâ, stopping to catch his breath. "I wonder how many will turn up? I hope the try-outs won't take too long. That way, we can practice a bit afterward."

The two boys set off again. Suddenly, the Harel Star slung over Morlâ's shoulder caught the wind, and he had to grab the long staff with both hands to stop it from flying off.

Finally, they stopped.

"This is it!" Morlâ said, looking excited.

Bryn looked around curiously. He was staring at a large, muddy field, which was slowly being covered in snow.

Morlâ looked around. "Hmm … We're a little early," he said. "Well, the others will be here soon. In the meantime, I'll explain the rules of the game."

Bryn was now wide awake. Sports at Âlaburg were a long way from the games he'd played in Sefal—marbles and catch.

"I'm all ears, Morlâ," he said brightly.

"Very good! That's the level of enthusiasm our team needs. If you're also a halfway decent player, I'll put you on the team," Morlâ added with a grin. "But first, the rules. A team consists of a maximum of five players. Only one can be used per round. Each game consists of a maximum of three rounds. There is always one player fighting for his fraternity against a player from another fraternity. Attack and defense alternate between the two players in the first two rounds. This means they both have to play an attack and a defense round, which are always three minutes long. A successful defense for three minutes earns you one point, and so does the conquest of the opposing star during your attack round. My job, that is, that of the team captain"—Morlâ seemed proud as he explained that part—"is to decide when which skill and, therefore, which player should be used. The overall aim is to prevent the other team from touching our Harel Star—and theirs is to stop us from touching their star."

Bryn raised his eyebrows incredulously. "That's it? No race or magic contest? No dragons to defeat? No magical flying skills?"

"Slow down, Bryn. Some things you just described can happen—except dragons, of course. How old are you anyway to believe in such nonsense?" Morlâ snorted, amused. "Next, you'll be talking of flying broomsticks …"

Bryn blushed—he'd been thinking about flying broomsticks.

"So, as a team," Morlâ continued, "we can choose any spell, incantation, or martial art—basically any non-lethal defensive or offensive trick—as long as it prevents the opponent from touching our star or helps us touch theirs within three minutes. The game is over when one team wins at least two rounds. But if the score is 1–1 after the first two rounds, a decisive third round is played. This time, it's an 'open' round, meaning both Harel Stars are on the field, and you have to choose between offensive or defensive tactics. After the third round, there is always a winner because there is no time limit. Understand?"

"No, not really," Bryn admitted.

"No problem. Just think of me as the designated player for White House. Everyone is only allowed to play one round against one opponent in a tournament. As each player in a team plays only one round at a time, it's crucial who's selected. For example, imagine I'm playing against Elbendingen. In the first round, I have to defend our star. Of course, the little pointy-eared one conjures like mad all the time. With our star in my hand, I have to be fast enough to escape his spells and him until the three-minute first round is over. Then we would already have the first point. Round two is where White House attacks and they defend. I'm playing the same cursed elf again. Now, for example, I could run toward him roaring, so he gets scared and forgets his little tricks. Then I could hit him over the head and touch their star"—he giggled—"and that's the second point for us. We've won the game. Understand now?"

Now Bryn thought it sounded exciting. Success depended on the quality of the players and the captain's tactics. Yet, he was still a little uncertain. "But I can't cast any spells or summon anything …"

"You'll learn all of that. There are still a few months until the tournament. It always takes place on the first weekend after the spring full moon. I have no idea who will show up for the try-out session today, but I think you'll make a great fifth man. That's important because there are five fraternities in total—including White House. Of course, you're not playing against yourself," he added with a wink. "This is why there are only four players in the Spring Tournament. The captain decides which player to use when and against which fraternity, depending on the tournament's course. And as the fifth man, you might not play at all.

"You would be good because the other houses haven't gauged your skills. But I'm sure the word is out about your performance in the Magic lesson, so the other captains will keep one of their best people in reserve to play against you. The first players of White House should have won their games by then. Your presence alone helps us." At these words, Morlâ's eyes shone. Then he looked around and put one hand in front of his eyes against the snow. "The other applicants should be arriving soon," he said excitedly.

Another twenty minutes passed. Bryn was getting colder. "Morlâ, I think …"

"Yes, yes …" he defiantly interrupted, "I know what you want to say. Let's wait for another five minutes. I thought at least Filixx would have turned up …" he muttered into himself.

The two friends huddled together. The snow was falling heavily, and the wind had picked up. The training ground offered no protection from the harshness of the weather, so the two stood there, covered in snow, waiting while looking at the approaching blizzard.

After ten minutes, just as Bryn was about to give up, he saw two figures walking toward them. "I think someone's coming."

Morlâ squinted at the blurry figures. "Ha, I knew I could count on Filixx," he exclaimed. "Who else is he dragging with him though?" He had to shout to be heard over the gust. "I don't believe it, that's—"

But Bryn had already seen him. "That's Stinky!"

Morlâ did not know whether he should be happy or worried. "How did Filixx get him here? Last semester, he didn't even answer when I asked if he wanted to join the team."

"Filixx, my friend," Morlâ called out when the new arrivals were a few yards away, "I was afraid you wouldn't come."

"Of course I did. What else did you think I was going to do?" Filixx asked, gasping. Having to keep up with the orc had strained him greatly.

"And you even brought someone with you … Hello, Ûlyėr!" Morlâ greeted the orc.

The giant orc didn't answer. Morlâ, looking a bit helpless, glanced over at Filixx.

Filixx turned to Ûlyėr. "We talked about this … You want Ŕälärm to lobby the Řischnărr fraternity on your behalf, right? Because they'll accept you if you're a great warrior, right? Well, now you've got your chance to prove it! That's why you're here—to play the game."

Ûlyėr hesitated, then pointed a large, claw-like hand at Bryn, and exploded into a rant. Ûlyėr was speaking a language incomprehensible to humans and dwarves. To them, it sounded like a deep, rumbling hiss instead of than speech. Then, without warning, Ûlyėr's face twisted horribly, and he hit the ground with tremendous force, as if an enormous, invisible hand had pushed him down. Bryn was utterly perplexed. Filixx stepped forward and offered to help him up, but Ûlyėr shrugged it off and began to heave his hulking frame out of the icy mud on his own.

"What happened?" Bryn whispered.

"Stinky broke one of Âlaburg's most important laws and spoke in his native tongue," Morlâ whispered so as not to upset Ûlyėr further. "You have to use the common language, or you'll be immediately punished. Trust me. The spell is agonizing. On my third day here, I swore once in my own language, you know, for fun. And I've never spoken it here since! Be thankful you've only got the one language to use."

Ûlyėr steadied himself on his feet and turned on Filixx. "You never mentioned humans on the team. You know what they did to my people in the Second War of the Nations …"

"Yes, you've told me many times, but Bryn had nothing to do with that," Filixx replied, which Bryn found brave of him to say. "Besides, I never told you who was on the team and who wasn't. And, by the way, you didn't ask."

Bryn could see the cogs turning inside Ûlyėr's massive, ugly skull. *I'm fine if this thing doesn't want to play*, he thought, irritated by Ûlyėr's accusation.

"Very well. This team is my only chance to join Řischnărr. But don't think we're going to be friends, human," he snarled at Bryn. "I want nothing to do with any of you outside of training. Understood?"

Morlâ seized the moment to rally the group. "All right, Ûlyėr, that's good, and thank you for sharing … But remember, if we're going to give it everything we've got, we must play as a team. And as captain, you must follow my instructions. Are you fine with that, Ûlyėr?" Morlâ asked him softly.

The giant orc bent down and looked Morlâ in the eyes.

Bryn watched, impressed, as Morlâ stood his ground.

They stared at each other in silence until Ûlyėr broke off, looking satisfied with something. "I will give everything I have to win the championship—you just get us there. Because if you can't …" he paused, and two huge tusks slid out of his mouth, "I will find a new captain who can."

Morlâ swallowed loudly and took a deep breath. "Well … I don't think anyone else is coming, so let's start training. At least we can field a team! But as we are only four—and I'm sure I don't need to say this—we can't afford anyone getting hurt."

Morlâ stomped out to the middle of the field with the Harel Star still hanging over his shoulder. The other three followed their captain through the icy wind and heavy snow in silence.

Morlâ halted and stuck the pole carrying the star into the near-frozen ground with a force that few would have expected from him. Bryn noticed a light flash from the star itself.

"Is it still calibrated to you?" asked Filixx, who had seen it as well.

"Sure. We didn't play last semester, and your spells work," Morlâ replied, finally smiling again. "Well, folks, this star belongs only to White House. Nobody will get at it this season! Not even with the tiniest finger. Is that clear?" he shouted.

"It's clear," the three players murmured, unmotivated, although Morlâ did not let that upset him.

"Very good. But to do that, I need to know what your skills are and develop the right strategies. It's best to start with mock contests. Filixx against Stinky—I mean Ûlyėr." The orc shot Morlâ a dark look. "And me against Bryn. All right?"

The only human in the group got a bit frightened. How could he stand up to Morlâ when he had no spells at all and was undoubtedly inferior to him in battle? But Bryn didn't have time to think about it any longer. Morlâ was already giving more instructions.

"Filixx, you are defending, and Ûlyėr is attacking." Then he stomped through the snow to what seemed to be an arbitrary spot on the field. "That should be fifty yards—the right attack distance," he shouted over the wind but could hardly be heard. "Come here, Ûlyėr." He waved his arm for emphasis.

Without a word, Ûlyėr went to Morlâ. Bryn noticed he was limping.

The two talked briefly, then Morlâ went back to the Harel Star, in front of which Filixx had already positioned himself, and spoke to him. Morlâ touched the star with both hands, and it began to shine brightly. Then he came over to Bryn, took out a small hourglass, and turned it upside down.

"Begin!"

Immediately, Ûlyėr ran toward Filixx, his limp no longer noticeable. But Filixx didn't seem bothered. He was firmly planted in front of the glowing star and moved his lips silently.

"Morlâ," screamed Bryn, "he will tear Filixx to pieces. Do something!"

But Morlâ only smiled to himself. "The fat man is not as harmless as you think. Wait and see."

Bryn turned back to the field. Ûlyėr had nearly covered the fifty yards and was almost on Filixx. Still in full flight, he lifted his huge arms to grab the dwarf-elf. Before he could catch him, a fog wafted over the ground, savagely swift, and completely enveloped Ûlyėr. For a few seconds, neither of the contestants were visible. Then came a bloodcurdling roar. Ûlyėr broke out of the fog, running so fast that small, grey wisps of fog trailed behind him.

Bryn looked baffled. How could the situation change so fast? Now Ûlyėr was the one getting attacked. But why?

Once more, the roar sounded, and then out of the mist came the being that made that sound. A huge, scaly body appeared; the protective plates of the animal shimmered green-yellow. The garish color clearly stood out from the grey of the day. A split tongue shot out of the creature's elongated head, aiming for the orc. Three relatively short, muscle-bound pairs of legs could soon be seen through the mist, taking the creature quickly toward the fleeing orc. Again, the beast roared, exposing three rows of razor-sharp, filthy, yellow teeth. It pushed through the snow like a plow, leaving a deep furrow behind it. Its only purpose was to put an end to Ûlyėr, who was trying to evade the monster by running and jumping in all directions. It was an unequal fight.

"Morlâ, do something! That brute is going to kill Ûlyėr."

"Take it easy. That's Starball. It gets a little rough sometimes," said Morlâ, not taking his eyes off the action.

In the meantime, the demon had almost reached the orc; its caustic tongue had already left painful-looking welts on Ûlyėr's back and lower legs. It tried to catch its victim with its tongue again, but with a long leap to the side, Ûlyėr escaped, and the monster's long, slimy, red tongue snapped back into its mouth.

But this evasive maneuver had its price; Ûlyėr slipped and fell in the muddy slush.

Bryn noticed the snow on Ûlyėr's legs turning blue, and he thought about what the Master had said in yesterday's Healing class—something about orc blood not being red like human blood. Whatever Filixx had summoned, from whatever godforsaken corner of Razuclan, roared triumphantly—at least that's what it sounded like to Bryn, and stopped him thinking about the color of orc blood. The creature spun around and sprinted toward Ûlyėr's fallen form. Bryn could see the beast's gaping mouth and fearsome teeth, all headed for Ûlyėr.

Bryn tried to plead with Morlâ, whose expression changed all at once into concern.

"Filixx," he roared. "Filixx, call your monster back immediately. Ûlyėr has had enough."

But Filixx didn't hear Morlâ due to the howling blizzard. He was still standing next to the Harel Star with his eyes closed and lips moving, maintaining his Summoning Spell.

"Filixx!!!" Bryn and Morlâ yelled.

No reaction.

Hopeless, the boys realized they would not reach Filixx in time—nor Ûlyėr before the beast ripped him apart. But regardless, the two ran toward the lizard beast. Morlâ pulled a wooden stick covered with metal out of a sling hidden under his clothes. They sprinted as fast as they could, but the thick snow made progress slow. They watched, frozen, as the giant creature launched itself at Ûlyėr, its mouth open and dripping with saliva.

What occurred next happened so fast that Bryn had to piece it together later that evening from the others' recollections. From what Morlâ could recall and the few words that Ûlyėr uttered to him, despite his attitude toward Bryn, the following picture emerged:

Bryn was still about twenty yards away from Ûlyėr when he stopped. His lungs were on fire, and he was gasping for breath. He saw the lizard lunge at Ûlyėr. But to both their surprise, Ûlyėr had vanished, and the ferocious creature bit into snow and mud instead. The animal went into a frenzy. Roaring, it twisted and turned, looking for its victim, as fast as its short legs allowed. Enormous masses of churning snow splattered around. Ûlyėr had fled. Suddenly, something exploded out of a snow pile and landed with a crunch on the green lizard's back. Ûlyėr!

At first, Morlâ and Bryn, like the summoned creature, had no idea what had happened. The lizard seemed not to react and just stood there in the driving snow—a big mistake. Ûlyėr suddenly grabbed the creature by its short neck and began to strangle it with his large hands. The lizard reared up like a headstrong stallion, but Ûlyėr had it in a vice-like grip. The demon started to sink into the snow, its attempts to defend itself growing weaker. It struggled to get up and stopped trying to bite Ûlyėr, still riding on its back. Its aggressive roar had turned into a feeble croak.

Ûlyėr listened but remained unmoved. He wasn't interested in his opponent surrendering; he was going to kill it.

Bryn felt sorry for the creature. It was here by magic, torn from its life and forced to fight under another's will.

The fog billowed up again, this time directly around the lizard. The creature started to fade until it vanished right in front of Bryn. Filixx had stopped the Summoning Spell and given the animal its life and freedom back.

"What's this?" yelled Ûlyėr in a state of frenzy. Then he saw his chance. The Harel Star was still shining, and Filixx, standing beside it, was helplessly exhausted. Ûlyėr ran toward it, but just before he could touch the golden, shining trophy, it faded. The three minutes were over. The last grains of sand had trickled through Morlâ's hourglass, and the star's magic was no more.

Ûlyėr roared in anger. He raised his giant fists, and it seemed as if he wanted to hit Morlâ, who, oddly, looked calm and relaxed. But Ûlyėr soon resigned himself to the outcome and stood there in silence. Within a few seconds, he'd had two victories snatched from him.

Even though it was Ûlyėr, Bryn could understand the anger he was feeling. He knew well enough how it felt to return home after a long hunt without a catch.

Morlâ pulled the Harel Star out of the ground. "Congratulations, chef," he said, his face drenched in sweat. "It's been a long time since I've seen such a thrilling Starball contest.

A huge compliment to you as well, Ûlyėr—you did a fantastic job."

"I have lost!" The great orc left the field without another word. His limp was visible again.

"Well… ah … I guess orcs aren't good losers," said Morlâ. Then he looked at Filixx, beaming. "That was so great, big boy."

"Thanks," said Filixx, plopping down in the snow. The wet and cold didn't seem to bother him, but something else did. He leaned forward and, his voice low, said, "I went too far. It was a Farel lizard. I never conjured a dangerous creature like that before, and I almost lost control over it. Could have killed all of us …"

For a while, nobody spoke.

"Yes, but he didn't, did he?" Morlâ finally said. "Come on, let's play another round. Bryn, you against me."

Bryn's mouth went dry, and his head grew hot, but Filixx saved the day.

"Look, I think it's enough for today. Let's go back. When the weather's better, we'll train again."

Bryn wasn't sure if the weather was the only reason why his friend didn't want to continue. Still, whatever it was, it meant he wasn't going to embarrass himself in front of friends he'd only met this week.

Morlâ threw the Harel Star over his shoulder and stomped back to the tower through the snow, his head bowed.

Bryn held out his hand, and Filixx grabbed it warmly. As he pulled Filixx to his feet, he saw a flower fading on the back of Filixx's left hand. They looked at each other without saying a word. Morlâ was hard to see now, so they set off through the flurries of snow, following their captain's footsteps.

UNIVERSITY LIFE

Bryn's classes on Wednesday and Thursday were more academic than his class in Magic.

The Master of Bryn's lesson in Religion was a human called MacKamell, and he spent the entire time trying to convince the class of the righteousness of the Kajal faith. He warned of an apocalyptic doomsday unless all beings worshiped the Great and one God. Since religious education was divided into denominations, Morlâ chose a different class only attended by dwarves. Bryn knew a little about Morlâ's religion, which worshipped the Eternal Stone and the Earth's Mother. He'd even tried to convince Bryn to come with him to his class.

But Bryn had refused, laughing. Although he had never been a devoted churchgoer, his faith belonged to what little he'd taken with him from his old life. So Bryn found himself with a few other human students, feeling ignored. He soon began to regret not having gone with Morlâ. Bryn listened to more threats of eternal damnation from MacKamell if the students were not firm in their faith. But his thoughts finally drifted off after the Master repeated the supreme Commandment of Damnation for the fifth time.

The afternoon was devoted to History. Morlâ had already warned him this subject would be incredibly dull. The classroom was full of students, some of whom had been in Bryn's Religion class. As before, his fellow human students made every effort to pay him and Morlâ as little attention as possible. Even though he didn't like it, Bryn was getting used to it. He felt like a person with a chronic illness, adapting to a new permanent ailment but unable to forget what things had been like before.

Master Tieffenor, the History lecturer, was tiny—even by dwarf standards. His head was shiny and bald except for a few warts and dark spots, and Bryn figured he was quite old. He wore his grey beard long, plaited into three thick braids, which made him look sort of comical. Bryn chuckled as the Master tried to hoist himself onto the raised platform behind his desk to begin the lesson.

But when Bryn pointed out how funny Tieffenor looked, Morlâ shook his head and admonished him, telling Bryn not to be disrespectful. Bryn had rarely seen him react like this to a Master. Usually, Morlâ was always the first to mock or sneer at them for a peculiarity or weakness.

Bryn found the lesson and the way the Master taught it interesting. He learned about the real history of Razuclan—and not just from the humans' perspective—as well as about the breaches of treaties, the skirmishes, and why all the nations had gone to war. Bryn also noticed how the Master's enthusiasm for his subject made him appear ageless. The afternoon soon flew by, and after the class, Bryn began to feel like History might be as enjoyable a subject as Magic.

It was late afternoon, and Bryn wanted to work on the pile of homework from the first three days of classes. He persuaded Morlâ to come with him to the library in the university's basement, and he was glad he did. Their joint assignment—an essay on the life of the Gnarf worm—would have been impossible to do alone. Nowhere in the library, in any book, could they find a creature even close to Morlâ's Gnarf worm. So Bryn wrote down everything Morlâ claimed to know about the worm. Then Morlâ made two clumsy sketches of the Gnarf worm eating and mating, and Bryn attached them to the essay.

That evening, Filixx organized another excellent dinner for the three of them, only this time in his room. As they ate, Bryn asked Filixx if he'd found anything in the library about his condition or learned anything from the five sages.

Filixx kept chewing and took his time before answering. "I'm sorry, my friend. I haven't made any progress yet. I couldn't get an appointment with the Five Wise Ones, but that's normal. In the first few weeks of the semester, all the first-semester students have questions. Unfortunately, they do not make exceptions when it comes to allocating appointments. So we will have to wait a little longer for their assessment. I didn't make any progress in the library either. But I am sure I am on the right track because the administration has blocked the books I wanted.

"This is a sign that Tejal is doing her own research. Even standard textbooks like *The Way of the Magician* or *The Colors of Magic* have a temporary block on them. These are indispensable for first-semester students. So if you want to do your usual first-semester homework for old Jehal, you'll have to find other ways," Filixx added with a grin. "Or you can copy my essay—the old grump had shown a lot of enthusiasm for it."

Bryn and Morlâ looked at each other, delighted; it was one less assignment to do.

"But, of course, that won't help you, Bryn," said Filixx gravely. "I'll try to get permission to release these books. We have to start somewhere. I could talk to Tieffenor too. He's the best when it comes to the history of magic. He may seem a bit quirky at times, but he's smart. He's also technically retired, so over the last twelve semesters, it's been almost impossible to get an appointment to see him. The administration can't find anyone qualified enough to replace him, especially for the few guilders they're offering per month. But I promise you I will keep at it."

"Thank you for all you're doing," said Bryn. "But maybe it's just as well. The sooner you find out what a freak I am, the less soundly you'll sleep at night."

"Cheer up, kiddo," Morlâ told him. "Whatever we find out, we'll handle it together."

Filixx nodded.

Bryn's grim mood lifted. At least he was sure of one thing: he'd found two true friends.

They all began to clear the table.

"Oh, Filixx?" said Morlâ, putting away the leftovers. "How come you still don't have a roommate? You've been living alone here in your little kingdom for ages now. I thought, as student head of the house, I would have some say in the matter. Yet, every time there's a new arrival, I tell the administration we've got a bed available in room number three, and they always tell me, yes, we know, and not to worry."

Filixx shot Morlâ a glance. "Pure luck, Morlâ, pure luck. Gosh, is that the time? It's late. We've got a long day tomorrow. Can you both leave me now? Thanks. I have homework to do." He gestured toward the door as if to remind them where it was.

Morlâ left with Bryn behind him.

"I'll find out your little secret one day, Filixx," Morlâ whispered to himself.

Math was on Bryn's timetable on Thursday, so he wouldn't have Morlâ with him in class that day.

When Bryn woke that morning, he found Morlâ was already up, whistling, and drying his hair, much to Bryn's surprise.

"Good morning, sleepyhead," said Morlâ, grinning.

Bryn tried to stifle a huge yawn. "Morlâ, why on earth are you up so early?"

"Oh … I couldn't sleep anymore," said Morlâ, finishing his hair. "All right, I'll be off now—sometimes, Master Sterlingheart needs help setting up the classroom."

Morlâ walked out the door and went whistling down the hallway.

Bryn had never seen this side of Morlâ before. It seemed he had no problem getting up early for classes as long as they were ones in which he excelled. *Funny person*, thought Bryn, smiling. He hoped Morlâ would have even more reasons for getting up early this semester.

Bryn yawned again and went to the bathroom. Once dressed, he made his way to the front door. But before climbing the stairs, he popped into the common room to look at his semester plan on the wall. It had some new comments scribbled on it in several colors. What had Tejal said? But to his disappointment, it was the same remark from the start of the week but this time in triplicate—in red, yellow, and blue. *Control magic better!* He turned away and, in his frustration, failed to see Karina standing behind him.

"Well, new boy," she said, "no progress this week, then? But don't despair; you're not alone. You and Morlâ do a great double act. *The Talentless Ones!* One can't do magic, and the other doesn't know how to do it without fainting." She roared with laughter. To Bryn, she sounded like a horse, if horses laughed, and he tried to step around her to leave. But her three friends, Malin, Elina, and Hela, appeared at her side and began to join in. Bryn stared around helplessly. But he did notice that Hela was the only one who looked even remotely uncomfortable.

Confused by this unfriendly attack on him, Bryn's face turned red.

"Look," Karina shrieked, "the kid's turning red too!"

The other three started laughing again. Bryn had to do something. Without saying a word or looking at the four girls, he left the room and went up the stairs.

"Where are you going?" Karina demanded, calling after him.

He didn't react. Karina called again, "Bryn, Bryn, I'm talking to you. Come back here! Bryn!"

All they heard was the door at the top of the stairs closing. For a moment, she and her friends stood in stunned silence.

They're not used to being ignored, thought Bryn, breaking into a smile at his small victory. He patted the old gargoyle's head, which was now part of his routine, and set off to Math.

Bryn entered the classroom and searched for a seat. The Master who taught the first-semester Math class was an elf by the name of Snowflower, and she had yet to arrive. Bryn could see a handful of orcs were already in there, waiting for class to begin. Unlike the students from Elbendingen, Ølsgendur, and Bond-of-Faith, who only ignored him for not being one of them, the orcs were hostile, with their dark cloaks and hateful expressions. Bryn wished the Řischnărr students would completely ignore him as well. A few even began to flex their muscles at him.

But before the situation deteriorated further, an attractive blond elf entered the room, and Bryn's first Math class began. After a few minutes, though, Bryn realized he didn't understand anything. Though Snowflower was pleasant and helpful, he could not make sense of the complex numbers and calculations. By the end of the lesson, Bryn was relieved that last night, Morlâ had offered to help him if he needed it.

At lunchtime, he and Morlâ met in the dining room, and from there, they went to the library. Morlâ tried to help Bryn decode the secrets of Math—but with little success.

MASTERING THE MAGIC

It was the final day of their first week, and Bryn and Morlâ were sitting in the dining room, tired, and peering at their breakfast. They'd both forgot Elbendingen was still on kitchen duty. Bryn could see Morlâ was searching for something to say. Bryn picked up a spoon and drew his bowl nearer. It held slices of odd-looking red, yellow, and sky-blue fruits tossed into a salad with some ground nuts.

Bryn thought the food tasted quite good, even if it was a bit tart. But out of solidarity with Morlâ, he pushed it around his bowl with his spoon, taking a bite only now and then. Even so, Morlâ appeared to be in a particularly bad mood today, and Bryn thought he knew why. They had hand-to-hand fighting this morning in Combat class. Bryn knew Morlâ had excellent close-combat skills, but he couldn't defend himself against attacks of magic, let alone counter them, so the university had made him repeat this subject.

The combat arenas were located a few hundred yards behind the Starball field. They looked just like small amphitheaters. Bryn could see three of them, all oval-shaped with rows of seats for spectators that curved down to a wooden stage and was protected by a roof. Morlâ led him down the steps into the arena where their class was being held this morning. There, they realized who they would have lessons with for the rest of the semester—the orcs. They were about to train in close combat with the best warriors on the continent!

A door on the far side of the arena slid up.

"Well, Bryn, here we go! Prepare yourself for a regular bruising. And if you think it can't get worse than that," said Morlâ, pointing to the door, "you're wrong."

Bryn looked over and saw a large orc dressed in black making his way to the arena stage.

Master Ñokelä, like the orc students, had his dark hood pulled so far over his head that his face—if you could call it that with orcs—was not visible. With only a few steps, the Master had crossed the wooden fighting area and now stood in front of the first-semester students waiting in the audience seating.

As if on command, the darkly dressed orcs bowed, which made a loud rustling sound.

Bryn and Morlâ bowed too but without the reverence.

The new Master pulled the hood off his face.

Bryn stopped breathing. He did not make a sound and was thankful he didn't attract any attention. The big man was horrible to look at even by orc standards. Apart from his small horns and prominent fangs, he had a large, deep scar that ran like an enormous dark-brown growth down across his right eye and over his right cheek. The eye itself was missing, and Bryn could see the empty socket behind a fold of mutilated, sagging skin. It looked like a red-hot blade had burnt out the eye. Bryn got goosebumps. One thing was clear about Ñokelä; his combat knowledge wasn't theoretical.

Ñokelä scanned the class with his one good eye.

"The rumor is," whispered Morlâ, "the scar is a souvenir from the Second War of the Nations. One of your leaders allegedly gave it to him during the Battle of Oak Mountain. They say he paid for it with his life."

Bryn saw the Master's yellowish, wolf-like eye darting about in its socket. It seemed to be absorbing every detail and was quite disconcerting. Then the Master raked his eye over the sole human student in the class. Bryn could have sworn his gaze lingered on him longer than on any other and with more menace. But when the Master turned away, Bryn wasn't sure whether he had imagined it.

Though Ñokelä spoke Razuclan's common language, he had a halting way of speaking and a heavy accent, making everything he said sound harsh. Bryn found his voice frightening.

"Well, well … the first-semester students. Let us see whether the Lekan Gate was correct. Will you make fighters worthy of defending Razuclan or not? My course is about the high art of Combat. Remember that! You won't learn any hocus-pocus nonsense here! No bright colors, cute little animals, or bubbling potions." He pointed to the circular stage. "Here, in the arena, no number of tricks or illusions will help you. Only your strength and ability count. And one thing is certain—there is only ever one winner and one loser."

Again, he gave the students a dark look. "Remember—even if I regret it, we forbid any form of lethal attack. You will learn how to defeat your opponent without injuring them permanently. Fighting is an art; remember that. It has existed for thousands of years for a reason. When you know what you are doing, one touch can send your opponent to the ground. If your technique is better, you can defeat even the strongest opponent. Likewise, strength can also be a decisive factor for victory. It all depends. Here, you will learn to fight in a way that best suits *you*."

The orcs thumped their chests with their left fists. It made Bryn even more nervous.

After attendance was taken, the students formed a semicircle around the Master. He showed them a complicated sequence of incredible strikes and kicks, which they had to copy.

To his dismay, Bryn found that the other students, including Morlâ, were all able to do the intricate movements—and in perfect unison. He felt like a red apple in a basket full of green ones. His awkward contortions stood out in stark contrast to the others' smooth, flowing movements.

"Stop!" yelled Ñokelä, storming over to Bryn. "What are you doing?"

Bryn's face burned. "I … I, um—"

"What did you say?" Ñokelä's huge head dropped until it was level with Bryn's. He could see the yellow eye, wild like an animal's and filled with hate, scouring his face. "Speak up, you pathetic human slug."

"Master, I—"

"A clear case of laziness. But we'll soon knock it out of you. I'm sure, little human, that after you get beaten black and blue in your first practice fight, you'll try harder. Oh, yes, I almost forgot," he said with a vicious look. "Your first fight, boy? It's now!"

Bryn's heart leaped into his throat.

Morlâ eyes widened. "But Master—"

"Silence! If I want to hear from one of you midget bastards, I'll rattle the bucket!"

The orcs, who had gathered around, erupted into cruel laughter.

Morlâ ignored them, but his face was grave. "How can Bryn do a practice match without any lessons?"

Ñokelä became incandescent with rage.

"I thought I told you not to speak. It seems you could do with a lesson in humility yourself. Kuelnk, Pyzu," he yelled, and two of the largest orcs stepped forward. "Give our two honorable students from White House a demonstration of the art of orc combat."

The two orcs gave their fellow students a sinister grin and bowed low. "With pleasure, Master."

The class immediately began to shuffle into a tight ring around the four students.

Bryn was up first. Morlâ tried to put himself at the front of the line, but a pack of orcs forced him back. The whole class began to chant back and forth to one another. To Bryn, it sounded like a loud, aggressive drumbeat. It echoed around the ring, filling the arena.

The orc standing before him was huge, at least two feet taller than him, rippling with muscle, and angry. Bryn was a reasonably good hunter, but without a bow or knife, all he had was his physical strength, and—if he was honest—it wasn't exactly great. He was helpless. The orc's eyes were wide open, watching him, and then they narrowed to crinkled slits.

"Begin!" Ñokelä's deep voice roared across the stage.

Kuelnk bent his knees, crouched forward with his arms bent, and made his way toward Bryn with slow, steady steps. From nowhere, a gust of wind caught the orc's cloak, the swirling black cloth distracting Bryn for a moment. But he also saw the fearlessness on the orc's face; in a few steps, he would be on top of Bryn.

The orc was dragging out the moment, catering to the cheering crowd and relishing every second. Bryn could see no escape. He felt cold and was sweating profusely—a trickle ran down his neck, over his shoulder, and down his back. The hair on his body stood up as the orc took a step closer. His heart beat so hard, it hurt. But Kuelnk was still playing, circling his victim predatorily, slowly getting nearer and nearer. Bryn thought he could taste copper in his mouth, like blood.

The orcs were whipping themselves into a frenzy, yelling "Řischnărr-Řischnărr!" over and over.

"Come on, show the human scum what we are capable of," one called out.

Bryn understood that attack was imminent. Still, he closed his eyes and took a deep breath, trying to think of a way to avoid getting too injured—but in vain. He opened his eyes and not a second too soon; Kuelnk was coming straight at him with a murderous look on his face. His tusks were dripping saliva.

The time for games was over. Escape was not an option.

Bryn prepared himself to receive a brutal beating. But—*No! I don't deserve this!* The realization hit him like a blow to the stomach. Without warning, a mighty rush of anger shot through him, overwhelming him. He stopped shaking. He wouldn't surrender to his fate without a fight. Before Kuelnk could smash into him and tear him open with his claw-like hands, Bryn swerved to the side and spun around, and as he did, he saw Kuelnk trip over his own momentum and crash to the floor.

Kuelnk howled in rage, further incited by the sneers from his fraternity. The moment Kuelnk regained his footing, he ran at Bryn once more, but again, Bryn evaded him.

"You're here to fight, not play games of tag!" boomed Ñokelä's voice.

Heartened by this, Kuelnk changed tactics. This time, he lurched toward Bryn with his long arms spread wide open. Bryn backed away, and the ring of students behind him parted. He was moving back up toward the edge of the stage. The gap between the two fighters became more and more narrow. Then Bryn hit something hard behind him. He had forgotten about the high wooden fence between the stage and the seating. He looked at Morlâ. It was over. He couldn't run anymore. Bryn waited for the first blow.

I should have let him beat me up right away because now, he's fuming. Suddenly, his right hand began to tingle. In his panic, Bryn thought he imagined it, but it grew stronger and stronger until the feeling became more familiar to him. *I remember* ... Suddenly, everything in front of him melted with a splash into a spectrum of color. Bryn's senses sharpened. *I remember now* ...

He watched himself raise his right hand—the mark on its back was glowing.

"Your magic tricks can't work on me," he heard Kuelnk grunt before he struck out with his mighty claws.

A multicolored, dazzling beam of light shot from Bryn's hand, illuminating the whole arena.

Kuelnk flew high into the air and slammed into the perimeter fence on the other side of the arena. His massive body lay motionless. A thick splinter of wood from the fence had pierced Kuelnk's upper arm, and the wound was spurting blood. A puddle of it was also spreading out from under his head. Again and again, Bryn's bursts of energy screamed over the arena and into Kuelnk's unconscious body, causing it to spasm and jerk about violently.

Bryn! Bryn! called a voice in his head. *Control the magic! Do not let it control you! Leave the realm! Now! You'll kill Kuelnk.*

Bryn recognized the voice. It was Tejal. But he didn't know how to do what she wanted, and nor did he want to. He saw the world through a thousand swirling colors, and with every sensation flowing through him, all he understood was that he belonged here; he was home and didn't want to leave. He wasn't interested in Tejal, and the Combat class was just a distant memory. But with each attack on Kuelnk, his magical power grew stronger and stronger. Bryn was the center of everything, and he'd never felt more alive.

Then, unexpectedly, the floor of the arena rose to meet him, and everything went black.

Opening his eyes was slow and painful. Where was he? All the colors had disappeared, and his senses had returned to normal. His memory was slow to return though.

The arena. Kuelnk. How was he?

Bryn was overcome by the fear of having done something he couldn't undo. He struggled to his feet. Every bone in his unsteady body seemed to be aching.

"Bryn, you're back!" said Morlâ. His worried face came in and out of focus in front of Bryn. "I thought Tejal had knocked you out."

What's Tejal doing in Combat class? wondered Bryn. But before Bryn could voice his question, the Chancellor rushed over to him. Behind her, Bryn could make out a group of orcs standing around Kuelnk's unconscious body, which was now enveloped in a large, translucent, shimmering shell that looked like a bubble made of out of water.

"Now it gets serious," whispered Morlâ as he noticed the look on Tejal's face. "You are the first person, in the history of Razuclan, who has been able to use magic to harm an orc."

She's going to expel me from the university, Bryn kept thinking until everything went black again.

PRIVATE LESSONS

"Bryn. Bryn!"

He could hear a voice calling him. He should answer, but it sounded so beautiful that it made him think of the mountains instead. He was in a meadow, wet with dew, covered in wildflowers. He could smell their fragrance and taste the frosty morning air on his tongue.

But the voice came again. "Wake up, boy!"

This time, the tone was impatient and bossy, but he ignored it, preferring to stay in this idyllic world.

Ice-cold water splashed across his face.

"Thank you, Gwendolin. Take the bucket back with you. I'll mop up."

Bryn came to and tried to get to his feet but stopped. He had no idea why his face and hair were soaking wet. He looked up to see two faces hovering over him. One was Tejal's. Her hair was pulled back, tight as usual, and she was wearing a purple cloak. The other was Gwendolin's. She was wearing a tiny yellow and blue hat tilted back stylishly on the side of her head. Bryn blinked hard at her several times. She leered at him. Then, with the tin bucket in her hand, she left the room, her blond hair billowing behind her.

"Nice to have you back, Bryn," Tejal whispered. "I'm sorry I had to resort to such an unorthodox method."

She handed him a soft, white towel, and Bryn dried his hair as best he could.

"In case you're wondering where you are …" Tejal made a sweeping gesture at the room. Bryn looked about and recognized the strange paintings and the massive desk. He was in Tejal's office.

"Why am I here?" he asked carefully. All of a sudden, he remembered the events of the last hour. "How is Kuelnk?"

The Chancellor stared at him sternly. "I'm glad you asked that because I can see you're becoming aware of what your powers can do. He lives. That's all I can say for now. He has been taken to the infirmary, and Master Winterblossom is treating his relatively severe wounds." Less gravely, she added, "But orcs are tough. I think he'll recover completely. Tell me how you did that, Bryn. How were you able to attack an orc with magic? Even I cannot do that, and neither can any other wizard in Razuclan."

Bryn gave her the only answer he could. "I don't know."

Tejal looked at him thoughtfully. "I thought you might say this—or I should say, I hoped you would."

Bryn looked at her questioningly, but she wasn't ready to tell him more.

"Tell me exactly what happened. Everything you can remember."

Bryn spoke of his fear of fighting against the seemingly invincible orc and the uncontrollable reaction his body had. Tejal listened quietly and nodded now and then.

Once he finished, she said, "I wrote it down on your timetable the first day itself. You must learn to control the magic that flows through you. At the moment, it is still the other way around—your magical potential controls you. Most students at Âlaburg have the opposite problem. They are not able to call up their magical talent, whereas you are a special case because you cannot stop yours. But just as we can help almost all students awaken the magical power within themselves, I am sure that I can teach you to control yours."

Bryn wondered if he'd misheard her. The head of the university wanted to teach him herself? The Grand Master seemed to guess his thoughts or, even more frighteningly, read them. Though he hadn't yet heard that this was possible, maybe it was—magic was still new and puzzling to him, and its potential seemed endless.

"Yes, you heard, right. This semester, you will have special classes with me so you can't hurt another student. Every Friday afternoon, you will come to my office, and I will try to teach you techniques commensurate with your great strength and help you practice your talents in a controlled way. It has just been added to your semester timetable," Tejal said with a smile.

Bryn swallowed. *Individual lessons with the Chancellor! What will the others think of me?* He thought briefly about the problems Filixx had faced because his achievements were too good.

"Of course, Grand Master," Bryn stammered, giving her a deep, formal bow as he should have earlier.

Tejal took notice and smiled to herself.

An exception to the protocol is permissible when you are unconscious, Bryn thought. He then decided to leave the office.

"Where are you going?" Tejal's sharp voice sounded somehow amused.

Bryn turned around, confused. "I thought we were to start next week."

Tejal looked him square in the eye.

"Well, maybe it's better to start today," he said, a little disappointed that he would lose his Friday afternoon.

"Well understood. You don't want to hurt anyone else, do you?" A chair magically slid up behind him and nudged the back of his knees. "Now, sit down."

"So, young McDermit, these training exercises, which you will do every week until you have complete mastery of your powers, are designed to show you the limits of your abilities. While magic is available to us without restriction thanks to the earth's energy field, using it exhausts anyone. Your great powers show that you can channel and use this energy in a unique way. Why this is so and how far these abilities go are not entirely clear to me yet, but at the moment, that is not so important."

Bryn looked blankly at her.

"Oh, I always forget you're so young, and that useless Gerald raised you like a normal human. Let's try a simple example. Imagine you are the best cross-country runner in Razuclan. All right?"

Bryn nodded dutifully although he still didn't understand what Tejal wanted from him at all.

"Good. So you're the best runner in the land. No one can beat you. But now you'll have to face the five next best runners from all the other lands. All five in a row without a break. What do you think will happen?"

Bryn answered without thinking about it. "I'll lose to the second or third runner since I'm exhausted."

"Very good. I want you to experience this. I want you to realize how much energy you can let flow through your body until you are physically exhausted. Hopefully, over time, this will allow you to judge for yourself how much magic you are using and regulate it in your interactions with others. Do you understand so far?"

Bryn nodded. "I have one more question—if I may," he said, hesitating.

"What is it?

"How do you exhaust a magician?"

Tejal laughed. Bryn never expected such a beautiful laugh from such a stern woman. "You ask the right questions, my young fellow. Keep it up, and you'll go far. I'll be your opponent in the race. My powers are superior to yours because of my experience dealing with magic, even if I don't have your extraordinary abilities. Besides, the special energies and beings of Âlaburg are available to me as Chancellor," she added quietly and mysteriously. "Because of that, it is probably fair to say that I am the most powerful magician in all of Razuclan, at least as long as I stay within the walls of the university."

Bryn eyebrows lifted in amazement.

"By the way, this is not something the entire university needs to know. Do we understand each other?" she asked firmly. After Bryn assured her of his discretion, Tejal explained how they would practice controlling his powers. "I'm going to put an energy bubble around you that will contract further and further. You'll feel it, and if you don't build up counter-energy in the form of a spell, it will crush you. Think of it as a big press."

Bryn swallowed hard. He didn't like the idea of being crushed. Not only did he fight an orc earlier today, but now he had to fight the most powerful magician in all of Razuclan!

She saw what was going on inside his head. "Do not be afraid. I can control my magic. The appropriate counter-spell is relatively simple. Enter the realm and take the ribbon," said the Grand Master, observing him closely, "or all the ribbons. Wrap them around your body. You can do it mentally or use your arms. Imagine wrapping yourself in large strips of cloth, like a mummy from the Cameo Desert. Except, of course, the cloth is made of energy. All right?"

"I ... I ..." Bryn's stuttering earned him an austere glance.

"Stop stammering!" she said harshly. "You are a student of Âlaburg—something granted to but a few. It's time you acknowledged how privileged you are. What if, in a few years, in service of the Driany Order, you must settle a dispute between two nobles? You can't be afraid or timid then. The people expect courageous protectors. So start acting like one."

He blushed but took a deep breath. "I still have no idea how to enter the magic realm," he said, his voice firm.

A sparkle appeared in Tejal's eyes. "All the better then. You can practice this as well. You seem to have no trouble entering it under pressure." Then she gestured with both arms as if she wanted to wave something away.

The next moment, the air was being forced out of Bryn's lungs. He couldn't breathe—such was the pressure on his body. It was as if Filixx had sat down on his chest, with Ûlyėr about to join him. His eyes felt like they were being pushed out of their sockets, and his head was pounding terribly. He thought he would suffocate. Excruciating pain filled his whole body. He was losing consciousness. He couldn't concentrate, and everything started going dark.

Suddenly, thousands of different colors appeared, and Bryn's vision became clear again. His senses instantly heightened. He had entered the realm, and, instinctively, his inherent powers went to protect his body. The pressure eased. Bryn tried to work out if Tejal's spell was crushing him physically or only acting on his mind. But he had no answer, especially now with Tejal's voice in his head.

Welcome! Well, that's a good start. Now we can try some real magic.

Immediately, the pressure grew even stronger, and hundreds of yellow bands of light flew toward Bryn. They formed a yellow sphere around his body, which began to squeeze him tighter and tighter. Suddenly, Bryn could see all the other shimmering colors swirling around him too. Instinctively, he tried to grab them to create a protective cover for himself. But Tejal's magic was strong, and his arms were stuck to his sides. He looked down at his hands to see the magical currents of energy run through his fingers like water and began to panic.

As Tejal's sphere closed tighter around him, it seemed to suppress his bands of multicolored energy. Bryn feverishly tried to grab hold of the bands close to his hands, but his fingers went right through them again. Then he noticed that in the spectrum of colors, the red bands stood out. And the more Tejal's attack intensified, the more they stood out. He concentrated on grasping them, but these too melted between his fingers. The pressure from Tejal increased, and he was struggling to breathe.

Then Bryn saw a fine, almost transparent band of red energy near his hand. Desperate, he tried to grasp it with his fingers. He could hold it! The thin red band immediately wrapped around his forearm and whirled itself around his whole body. Again, he used his fingers to grab more of these wisps of energy, and suddenly, his right arm was free. He made a circular motion with it, whipping the red bands around him, making them more concentrated and forming a sphere of protection around himself. Bryn felt the pressure on him grow weaker, but it didn't let up entirely.

Once he had initiated the protective sphere, he began to use his arms to gather more energy to strengthen it. It was difficult because of the resistance from Tejal's crushing yellow sphere. Meanwhile, he could see the other colors were growing stronger and beginning to flow around him more freely. Bryn grabbed them and drew them to him. The strength of Tejal's sphere began to diminish, and Bryn was able to push it away from himself and replace it with his protective layer of red energy. Now, not only red, but all the colors were whipping around him, incredibly fast and intense. He tried to lift his arms once more to direct an attack on Tejal, but his strength failed, and his knees began to tremble. His arms felt heavy, and he could feel the sweat, if such a thing existed in this realm, running down his back.

The bright colors ebbed away from him, but he noticed this gave him more physical strength even though his magic seemed to be weakening. *Is this what Tejal meant by controlling magic?* He relaxed his attention on the red bands of energy and found he could lift both arms again. But this wasn't of much use to him without any magical energy in reserve. Unsure what to do, Bryn grabbed all the bands of energy he could, and, in an unbelievable feat of strength, thrust them all at Tejal's yellow sphere. It shrank and moved further away, but Bryn struggled to stand up; the last thing he saw was the floor coming closer and closer.

"Very good, Bryn," he heard Tejal say and opened his eyes. She was beaming at him. "In a few weeks, you might be able to break the energy bubble before you pass out."

Bryn felt a lump on his elbow and realized he had also collapsed in the real world. He got to his feet slowly, certain he'd have other bumps and bruises from the fall. His shirt was dripping wet, and his legs wobbled like he'd sprinted several hundred yards. He was just glad he could still hold himself upright.

"Don't look so sad," said Tejal, putting a hand on his shoulder. "That was a good start. It'll get better. I promise." Then she pointed her hand toward the door. "See you next Friday. And Bryn …"

He turned back to her. Tejal saw the depth of weariness in his eyes.

"Remember ..." Her face softened.

"Yes, Grand Master?"

"Remember ... your punishment tomorrow morning with Gerald in the garden." And with that, she returned to her desk and began looking through one of the drawers. "And please try not to annoy any orcs next week."

Bryn staggered out of the Chancellor's office. Orcs were the last thing on his mind—he just wanted his bed.

IN THE GARDENS

Bryn tiptoed out of the room. The night before, after a long discussion about Bryn's unprecedented feat of magic against the orcs, Morlâ had told him not to wake him under any circumstances; otherwise, he'd not get enough sleep. As Bryn passed Morlâ curled up in bed, it struck him that the dwarf was like a cat—he certainly took every opportunity to sleep, especially on weekends, when he loved to sleep in until late!

Bryn patted the gargoyle without thinking as he passed by. During the night, it had snowed again. The university grounds looked like it was covered in a fresh layer of powdery sugar. The temperature had dropped too, but since the wind had died down, Bryn didn't find it quite so piercing anymore. Besides, the sky was bright blue, the sun was rising, and it would be a beautiful winter's day. He stopped and looked about; nobody else seemed to be outside. He could see some light in the windows in the Elbendingen house, but even those early risers were staying inside this morning.

He continued on and came across a meticulously cleared path in the snow. *Someone's up, after all.* He followed the path as it headed in the direction of the gardens. After a few hundred yards, he passed the Bond-of-Faith house. The sight of the timber buildings, so familiar to him, still left him with a slight twinge. He surveyed the dark beams, white-painted clay walls, and leadlight windows. A few of the windows had light in them.

Finally, Bryn reached the sprawling, densely wooded gardens of the university. To his surprise, he found several trees had been pruned, and sections of the perimeter fence had been repaired and given a new coat of paint. Bryn opened the small gate and made his way down the narrow path deeper into the forest garden. *I wonder where Gerald is?* At first, he didn't notice the soft ringing; when he did, it sounded as if his ears were playing a trick on him. But then he recognized it—the melodious laughter of the Samuusen.

"Oh," the little fairy creatures giggled. "Who is this, coming to visit us so early in the morning?"

The friendly little creatures darted about Bryn's head. He could hardly focus on any one of them. Their transparent wings beat so fast the air above them shimmered. Their melodious laughter made Bryn smile. This pleased the little creatures, and, one by one, they began to settle on his head and shoulders. Some held on to his ears or swung from his earlobes while others tugged at his hair. It tickled unbearably. He noticed that groups of three or four of them were also twisting his hair into small braids. They kept saying the same things to him over and over in unison and giggling; it was amusing now, but he figured they could be extremely annoying sometimes.

"Please, tell us, young Bryn …" spoke those little mouths. "What are you doing here in the garden? Are you here to make sure we're looking after your grumpy old Gerald properly?" All of them broke into laughter. "No, we didn't think so. It looks like you're being punished!" Again, they erupted into giggles. "Never mind, our Chancellor is wise; at least she knows why you're here even if you don't. But then, perhaps we asked her to send you?" Once more, they burst into laughter.

Every time the Samuusen moved or tugged at his hair, it tickled Bryn almost to the point of distraction. Several adventurous Samuusen even tried to crawl into his ears, and Bryn had to fight the urge to scratch himself for fear he'd crush one of them.

"Why won't you talk to us, Bryn? You're becoming so tiresome—or maybe you don't know how to?" they teased.

"Of course I can talk," Bryn replied gruffly.

The little fairies laughed as if they'd never heard anything funnier. A few of them were pounding on Bryn's head with their tiny fists and rolling about, which made him even itchier.

"So, you can speak! Well, I guess that's a start. Can you also do some magic for us?" It must have been a serious question because they all fell silent, stopped scampering around, and waited for him to answer.

The abrupt calm unsettled him. *Why the hell is it important to the Samuusen if I can do magic or not?* he wondered. But before Bryn could speak, they launched themselves at his hair and earlobes again, and the thought evaporated.

"I cannot yet control the gift," he finally admitted. "But I am working on it with the Chancellor," he added, more to reassure himself than them.

"That is good, Bryn, and important," they answered in one voice. "Much, if not everything, depends on how well you master your power, Bryn. Razuclan needs your special gift—you are the last one to have been given it. The last one left alive—"

"What? What do you mean by that?" Bryn demanded.

Their response was only laughter, and they went back to tittering amongst themselves. The brief moment of seriousness was over, and so was the Samuusen's visit. In an instant, they were fluttering around his face once again. One after another, the little creatures flew off into the bushes and shrubs. Only one tiny fairy remained, and she was floating, entirely still, right in front of Bryn's eyes. Now he could see how pale and delicate her facial features were—and she had flaming red hair. Was this what made him think of strawberries the first time he had met them?

Her face turned serious. "Control the gift, Bryn. Don't let it control you." Then she pinched him on the nose with her tiny hand and flew off into the gardens' depths.

Bryn stood there for a while, bewildered. Without their laughter, the world seemed less beautiful and cheerful.

"What happened to your hair?" a deep voice boomed behind him.

Bryn flinched in shock. Gerald was standing behind him with a hammer and a saw in his hands. Bryn ran his hand through his hair and felt the little braids. He must look like a hedgehog.

"The Samuusen," he said, shrugging.

Gerald nodded and placed his hand firmly on Bryn's shoulder. "They've got nothing but mischief on their minds, Bryn. Please don't listen to them when they start flapping around you—they're just little pests. Everything they say is nonsense; they're only interested in playing games."

Bryn wasn't sure if Gerald was right, but he nodded anyway. But later, while he and Gerald were repairing a section of the fence, Bryn couldn't stop thinking about what the fairies had said to him.

Much, if not everything, depends on how well you master your power, Bryn.

NEW ARRIVALS

Bryn felt as if the last several weeks had flown by. Winter felt shorter this year too, especially now, after seeing the first buds on the pussy willow while working in the garden.

Bryn was still at White House, but he had become so close to Filixx and Morlâ that he couldn't imagine life without them. He often wondered how life would be without their jokes, encouraging words, and advice.

At the university, Bryn was an outsider in two ways. As he belonged to White House, the students of the real fraternities acted as if he was invisible or made a point of treating him with contempt.

At the same time, news of his fight against the giant orc had spread all over the university. The strange bastard boy, with the magical right hand, was now the object of public attention. Bryn felt this on countless occasions. The mysterious private tuition from Tejal contributed to this as well. She tried her best to teach Bryn how to control the gift better but with varying success. Entering the realm became more natural to him. But Tejal still had to withdraw her magical attacks if Bryn could not summon his powers. And often, Bryn would faint, expending too much energy on his counterattack.

He also had varying success with his subjects. When it came to Magic class, old Jehal would not even allow him to attend. Instead, he would get Bryn to fetch cups of tea or deliver empty envelopes to the secretary's office. On his return, the other students had usually finished the practical part of the lesson. One day, before class finished, Bryn summoned the courage to talk to the Master about it.

Jehal turned white in response. "I … I told the Chancellor years ago something like this would happen. Years ago!" Then he abruptly ended the lesson and sped off.

The following week, Magic was canceled.

But Master Underhil seemed delighted with him. Bryn and Morlâ had succeeded in summoning a Gnarf worm—even if Bryn wasn't sure how they'd managed it. Although he could enter the realm, he could still not materialize the creature. But after one attempt where he passed out, he came to with Morlâ holding a thick, gray worm in his hand. It was writhing on his palm and tried to bite the dwarf's little finger. Everybody was euphoric over the class's first successful summoning. Only Bryn noticed the finger-sized holes in Morlâ's leather satchel. He did not say anything, preferring to bask in the Master's praise with his friend.

Master MacKamell turned out to be a sentimental, pious man—the students called him MacCaramel. Bryn learned it was best to repeat his lessons back to him verbatim. MacKamell seemed happy with that, and Bryn thought he should get a C for the subject.

History was one of Bryn's favorite subjects. He especially liked Master Tieffenor's classes on how Razuclan came into being. Tieffenor noticed this and brought Bryn books and yellowed scrolls to study.

Unfortunately, Bryn failed to discover anything about his circumstances. Filixx also found nothing.

Bryn only survived Math because Morlâ tutored him, and he knew it would never be one of his strengths. Morlâ's remark that it was a question of logic never made sense to him.

Like most of the male students, Bryn had a small crush on Master Winterblossom. But his thoughts would always drift back to his true love, Drena. Still, Bryn always looked forward to Healing, which had also become one of Bryn's favorite subjects. Winterblossom was friendly and her knowledge about the body impressed him.

However, since his fight with Kuelnk, Master Ñokelä had tried to make his and Morlâ's lives as miserable as possible. Ñokelä had taken the young orc's defeat as a personal affront. So, in every class, out of shame, he would make the boys run extra laps around the castle, send them on obstacle courses, or make them lift weights until they were both exhausted.

Bryn was never again allowed to fight an orc. Since fighting Morlâ was out of the question, they could only study the

Řischnărr students' fighting, exercise, or have play fights with each other. Still, Bryn noticed there were advantages. His arms had become bulkier, his shoulders were broader, and his stomach was a lot firmer. He'd also had a growth spurt of almost four inches over winter, which bewildered Morlâ and upset him a little.

Starball training was not going well either, and the Spring Tournament was only around the corner. It had been hard to persuade Ûlyėr to continue playing on the same team as Bryn, but they promised him he'd never have to play against him in a practice match. Once, during training, the orc pointed at Bryn and uttered a long word in his own language. The response from governing powers of Âlaburg was immediate, and Ûlyėr dropped to the ground, writhing in agony. Since Bryn's fight with Kuelnk, students often whispered it behind Bryn's back. Those who were not orcs especially liked to use it as they were never punished for it. Bryn had asked Filixx what it meant and was told it translated into 'Realm Shadow.'

Other than the fear Bryn's name could arouse, he was not much help to the team. He fainted a lot on the training ground and couldn't concentrate enough to enter the realm. So it was easy enough for Filixx to enchant him or for Morlâ to throw him into the dirt. Apart from that, Bryn fit in like any other student at Âlaburg.

One sunny, school-free Sunday, an incident caused quite a stir throughout the castle.

Bryn didn't want to spend the first day of spring in a dark cellar, so he convinced Filixx and Morlâ to help haul up three armchairs from the common room to the front courtyard. Bryn insisted the effort would be worth it, but Morlâ and Filixx were cave dwellers and struggled to understand Bryn's enthusiasm. They swore the whole time. Still, they were soon lounging in the sun and sipping the ice-cold elderberry juice Filixx had snatched from the kitchen. Filixx even put a straw hat on the head of White House's stone sentinel.

He stepped back to admire his handiwork and turned to the others. "Well, we shouldn't forget him either with weather like this."

They imagined what Gerald, their House Master, would say if he saw them like this and laughed. Then, out of the blue, they heard the thundering of horses' hooves.

Curious, they stood and looked at the castle entrance. The Lekan Gate appeared locked, so the riders would not be able to pass. Yet, everyone who heard the sound knew something big was happening and fixed their eyes on the gate.

Suddenly, Bryn realized what bothered him about this. *Why did we hear the horses? There's never a sound from outside when the gate is closed.* At that moment, the two mighty iron gates opened. Bryn had to blink. It seemed as if the stylized ornaments decorating the entrance were moving. The big stone in the bearded old man's magic wand was shimmering in all the colors of the spectrum. But when Bryn took a closer look, the vision had disappeared. He narrowed his eyes and waited for the newcomers.

For a while, nothing happened, but then the clatter of hooves sounded again. Bryn spotted four shapes. Three of them galloped into the castle courtyard on massive, black warhorses. Then a much smaller person on a stout, gray pony trotted through the gate. The three faster riders were very different in shape and bore varying equipment. One was a giant and outdid even Ûlyėr by at least two or three heads. Despite his size, he dismounted swiftly, albeit with a lot of clattering that drew attention to his pitch-black armor. He carried an enormous broadsword. Bryn knew there was no way he could lift it, let alone swing it. Most impressive of all was the metallic black helmet covering the warrior's face. The thick, greenish-brown horns protruding on either side gave him away. He was an orc.

A petite woman jumped out of the saddle next. She had golden hair and the beautiful, even features of an elf. In stark contrast to her orc companion, she was not wearing any armor, only a green cloak woven through with red threads over simple, white linen clothes. As she turned to grab her horse's halter, the wind blew her cloak back, and Bryn saw two long, dangerous-looking daggers tucked into a wide, yellow belt.

The third newcomer was dressed like a human. He wore leather trousers, black boots, a white shirt, and a sweeping black hat with a large red feather tucked into the brim. It gave him a bold appearance. His only protection seemed to be a gnarled walking stick.

The strangers immediately began to talk excitedly, apparently unaware half the university was watching them.

The gray pony halted in the middle of the courtyard. The rider was remarkably stout even for a dwarf, with a gray beard that hung down to his chest and a veiny red nose. Bryn had often seen this in people in the Laughing Boar, especially the ones who spent too much time drinking the 'heavy red one,' as Gerald liked to call the wine. Altogether, he looked a bit shabby. His leather pants, torn in many places, barely reached his knees, and, on his bare torso, he wore a rusty chain mail vest.

Filixx—who had an eye for such things—noticed the newcomer was chewing on a roast chicken leg. He reached for his saddle with his other hand, took out a greasy-looking flask, and took a big gulp.

Bryn was pretty sure it didn't contain water.

The dwarf burped and tossed the gnawed chicken bone behind him. His pony trotted over, without any prompting, to the other three newcomers. Groaning, he dropped to the ground and looked around. Unlike his comrades, he noticed all the spectators who had gathered around them. Swaying a little, he bowed to the crowd, like an actor after a successful performance. The blond woman said something to him in a sharp tone. The dwarf seemed to accept the criticism at first, only to shake his head and throw kisses into the air. The students answered him with cheers and applause.

Moments later, Tejal hurried toward the party, her hair tousled as if she'd only woken up. Her usually stern look had given way to an even more tense and agitated expression. She pushed through the crowd, issuing harsh words to some of the students blocking her way.

Bryn, Morlâ, and Filixx joined the crowd to get a better look, just in time to hear Tejal greeting her guests.

"Welcome to Âlaburg, Grand Knights of the Driany Order. It's an honor to finally welcome a delegation of the Order to this university."

Tejal made an elaborate hand gesture, and a small, silvery swirl flew out of her palm and split into four. Bryn had seen this strange shape before, when he'd opened her welcome letter. Each guest, in turn, caught one with the back of their left hands. As they did, each swirl turned from almost colorless to red, yellow, and blue and then dissolved into thin air. The swirl released no colors when it touched the back of the orc's mighty paw. The magic was absorbed by it.

The four knights bowed as one. "Hail, Tejal, Madam Chancellor, Grand Master of Magic, Keeper of Seals, Supreme

Keeper of Peace, and Healer. We are all delighted to be back in Âlaburg."

Tejal put her hand on her larynx, and her voice magically amplified. "Silence. Everybody return to your fraternity houses immediately. There is a curfew until dinner. I will hold the student heads personally responsible if students do not adhere to this. Now, get a move on!"

Bryn heard the occasional angry murmur as the gathered students dispersed. Bryn grabbed his armchair and was about to go down to White House when he saw Tejal embracing the elf. He watched, stunned, as the women wiped tears from their eyes with white handkerchiefs. Then Bryn heard Gerald's voice: "Do it now, not tomorrow!" So he turned away and went down to the common room with his chair.

MAGIC FIRE

Contrary to the Chancellor's announcement, the curfew lasted all night. Accompanied by the student heads, a few students were allowed to go to the cafeteria and fetch dinner for the others. Returning to their excited housemates, they reported not seeing anybody else out there. The university was deserted. As the evening progressed, rumors about the sudden appearance of the knights became increasingly fanciful.

Bryn was having trouble falling asleep. His mind was busy with the events of the day. *Why are the knights here? Why didn't Tejal know they were coming? And for someone usually so calm and collected, why was she crying?* But while he tossed and turned, Morlâ was snoring softly.

The next morning, Bryn woke up tired and in a bad mood. It was Monday, and the week started with Magic. Again, he would have to play errand boy for Jehal.

Morlâ was already up, and he'd left his bed unmade as usual.

Bryn put on some trousers and trudged down the hallway to the bathroom. *It's so quiet. Where is everybody? Damn, I must have overslept!* He splashed ice-cold water on his face and rushed back to the bedroom. It smelled of stale, dead air, and he dressed as quickly as he could and left. With his leather school satchel over his shoulder, he ran down the hall and through the common room. As he passed the timetable on the wall, the words *DON'T BE LATE FOR CLASS* suddenly appeared on it. Bryn winced like he'd been kicked in the backside and belted for the stairs.

He was winded and panting by the time he made it to the university's main building. The sweat down his back began to cool him slightly. Remter Hall was deserted, and all the corridors were empty. Classes had already started. Bryn cursed himself. *Why didn't Morlâ wake me?* Rushing up the stairs to the first floor, he found the door to his classroom shut. From inside, he heard subdued mutterings. Bryn took two deep breaths and knocked. No reaction. His heart beat faster. Just as he was about to knock again, he heard a voice.

"Enter ..." said Jehal, with his usual threatening undertone.

The golden door handle was smooth from years of wear but felt icy cold. Bryn opened the door a little and found all the Elbendingen students smirking at him. They were waiting for the punishment Jehal would inflict on him. As he opened the door further, Bryn spotted the Master's grim face, staring venomously at him. To his great surprise, someone else was also standing there. *The human Driany Knight from yesterday.* He was wearing his bold hat again, and, unlike Jehal, his face lit up at the sight of Bryn.

"Sorry I'm late, Master," Bryn said, bowing hastily. Then he tried to reach his seat in the back as discreetly as possible. But, of course, Jehal, the old fox, wasn't satisfied with that. Bryn should have known.

"Good morning, Bryn," he said. "I hope you had a good night's sleep and a hearty breakfast? On behalf of the class, I would like to apologize for starting without you."

Bryn spun around. "Oh … that's fine, that's all right." But no sooner had he said the words than he regretted every syllable.

"If you think you're something special, Bryn McDermit, you have come to the wrong place!" Jehal shrieked. "I guess I haven't made my position clear enough over the last few weeks. I won't tolerate this kind of behavior from anyone, especially you." Jehal lifted a wrinkled hand and shooed Bryn away. "Sit yourself down!"

He lowered himself into the chair next to Morlâ, who glanced at him sideways but didn't dare say anything.

Jehal regained his composure and waited for Bryn to unpack his satchel. "So, you still don't understand the rules. But you'll learn them, my boy," he said, his voice so low that it was almost impossible to hear. Jehal thumped his desk and stood up. "The entire class will each hand in essays on the following topics: *Blacking Out from Magic, Problems Controlling Magical Power, The Realm of Fire,* and *The Unresponsiveness of the Orc Body to the Effects of Realm Energy.* These essays are due next week and will account for fifty percent of your final grade."

Nasty murmurs spread around the classroom.

"Why are we being punished along with the bastard? It's too much; it can't be done! Only those from White House should be made do it!"

Jehal listened to their protests and smiled to himself. He had just made Bryn's life at Âlaburg even more difficult. That was obvious from the hateful glances he was receiving from the other students. Even Morlâ was struggling to look him in the eye.

Bryn tried to salvage the situation. "Master, I think they're right. I should be the only one being disciplined."

But Jehal would have none of it. "You still don't understand!" Jehal narrowed his eyes. "You need more to do—to train your memory. Therefore, each student will also write a paper on *Freaks and Magic*. Does anyone else care to comment on the assignments?" he bellowed.

Nobody made a sound.

Jehal looked pleased with himself. "All right ... now, where was I?"

The knight cleared his throat loudly.

"Oh yes ... our guest," said Jehal, frowning. "As I was saying ... Grand Master MacRallen here is considered one of the most brilliant exponents of magic—for a human being—"

"The most brilliant, in fact," he said and winked at the class.

Dumbstruck, Jehal tried to unpurse his lips. "Our *short-term* guest will help me perform some simple spells," he said eventually. "Normally, I would have shown you these myself. But our esteemed Chancellor believes that somebody new might help grab your attention, but—"

"Thank you, Master Jehal! Thank you for such a kind introduction. But I think I can explain the rest myself. After all, I am a Grand Master."

Jehal's eyes bulged with rage. Not even Bryn's inappropriate remark had done that. MacRallen's eyes, instead, wandered over the sea of faces and gently paused on Bryn.

"My brothers and sisters, I am part of a delegation to Âlaburg, here to teach you some simple, yet highly effective, protective spells. These were recently developed by some of the Order's most talented Grand Masters—including myself." He again smiled playfully at the astonished students. "They will be distributed as quickly as possible among all our magically gifted students, in case you ever need to defend yourself." At that, MacRallen's cheerful demeanor shifted, becoming slightly more serious.

Bryn wasn't sure if anybody else had noticed this subtle change. He was the only other human in the room who could see MacRallen's face as Jehal was standing behind the knight. Bryn sometimes found it difficult to interpret the elves' and dwarves' facial expressions, so they probably had the same issue with humans. Bryn was also curious about MacRallen. *The knights are here to teach us spells to defend ourselves. But what do we have to defend ourselves against?*

After a moment, MacRallen once again looked cheery and optimistic. "But, to be clear, we believe your greatest danger, studying away in your rooms and so forth, will be the possibility of a late lunch."

The knight now had everybody's attention—some of the elves were even giggling.

"All right, let's begin." The new Master looked deep into the eyes of the students. "Who among you can enter the realm on their own?"

About two-thirds lifted their hands.

MacRallen gave an appreciative nod. "So many? Good. That's an outstanding achievement for a first-semester class. Well done, Master Jehal," he said, looking over his shoulder at Jehal, who was slumped in his chair. "Today, I want to show you how to ward off most magical and physical attacks in a simple but effective way. Those who cannot yet enter the realm should try again. I will assist you. Those with more problematic magical abilities are my specialty!"

Morlâ looked up, his eyebrows steeply arched.

"The spell I'm about to show you is called the Coat of Protection. I realize the name is not too imaginative. But my suggestion, the Warrior's Overcoat, failed to win a majority in Council," he said with a wink. Then he took a long, deep breath and started to focus his thoughts. In an instant, his body became wrapped in a shimmering, milky cocoon. Only an outline of

MacRallen was visible. "This," came a metallic voice from within, "is the Coat of Protection. Master Jehal has agreed to use his magic to attack it to demonstrate its protective power. Jehal, would you be so kind?" The white cocoon bowed slightly in Jehal's direction and began to swell in size.

Now it looked like Jehal had regained his former vigor. In no time, he positioned himself before MacRallen, and red beams of energy shot out of his hands. But the magical shield simply absorbed them, neutralizing the spell.

"You see," came MacRallen's voice again, "your Master's strikes were powerful. But the Coat of Protection absorbs the attacker's energy and even strengthens the one under assault."

Jehal flinched, and then he started hurling small, red-hot knives at the Grand Master. Hundreds of them smashed into the shield. This assault was fiercer than the last, for the milky-white cocoon suddenly became transparent. Bryn could briefly make out MacRallen as if through clear, flowing water. Then Jehal stopped his attack and wiped the sweat from his forehead.

MacRallen seemed to have less strength too. His voice sounded slightly shaky and was puffing loudly as he spoke. "Master, I did not know that you, too, could cast the Fireblade Spell." He paused to take another breath. "Anyway, you can see that the shield is impenetrable, so now, I think we should—"

But Jehal did not let his guest finish. His face was distorted with hatred, and he raised his arms and pointed his palms toward

MacRallen. Instantly, a burst of thick, yellowish-red fire, like flying lava, shot out with a loud crack. The protective cover was immediately surrounded by flames and seemed unable to absorb the spell.

From inside came a stifled noise; MacRallen didn't seem to have the strength for anything else.

Jehal was now covered in sweat, and his face was bright red. But neither of them had any intention of giving up.

The room had become suffocating and searing. All the students got up and huddled together in the back of the room to escape the heat. Bryn could smell burning. The wooden floor was smoking, and some of the furniture was about to catch fire.

MacRallen was barely visible under the disintegrating protective cloak. Bryn saw him drop to his knees. Jehal held onto his desk with one hand, the Flame Spell shooting out of the other. It was a dangerous situation for both of them, especially with the Grand Master engulfed in flames. Jehal's eyes were closed, concentrating on maintaining his spell. He wouldn't even have noticed if his opponent had lowered his protective shield.

"Morlâ! We have to do something; they're going to kill each other!" Bryn said.

But Morlâ was standing away from him and could not hear him over the chaos. Not only were the Masters in danger now but so was the entire class as the flames had cut off an escape through the door. The windows were too high for anyone to jump out of safely. Panicking, Bryn turned to a tall elf student next to him, Ionius Birchlea.

"Ionius?" The much larger elf looked at him, startled, and nodded. "We have to do something, or this is not going to end well."

Ionius gave him a doubtful look, but Bryn stared, unflinching, into the boy's eyes. Ionius relented, asking, "You're right, but what can we do?"

Bryn thought for a moment. "We have to attack Jehal!"

Ionius's red, flushed face turned pale. "We can't do that. If we attack a Master, they will kick us out of the university."

"Maybe, but it's the only way. An attack on Jehal will drain him; he won't be able to continue."

Ionius's eyes darted back and forth, and then he stepped back, trying to get nearer to the back wall of the room.

Bryn was struggling to breathe—the flames had consumed much of the oxygen. He could not wait any longer. He had to try it alone, even if he was expelled from the university and lost his best friends—and maybe even Gerald. If they did kick him out, he would lose the thing that had given his life a new purpose, and something he knew he could be good at one day.

A cry sounded behind him. Through the smoke, Bryn could see an elf girl in great distress, patting out her smoldering hair. The decision was made. He had to shut out everything and concentrate on entering the realm. Although it had been getting easier for him to do this, he was far from mastering it. But to his astonishment, the realm opened up to him immediately.

As he entered the magical in-between world, a completely different picture presented itself. Again, the room filled with a variety of colors. All the colored bands headed toward where the two Masters were fighting. That area glowed an impossibly bright red, with thick bands of energy shooting all over it. MacRallen appeared as a light red, rounded shape, surrounded by glaring red hues that shot around the paler red dot with insane speed, trying to penetrate the knight's protective cover. Bryn saw some of the bands hit their mark. Jehal was also immersed in red. His color no longer pulsed in different hues but remained one solid color.

MacRallen staggered forward. Bryn now understood what blacking out from magic meant. *It'll be hard to get Jehal to stop. This battle only ends when MacRallen has no physical life force left—upon his death.* Bryn was determined not to let that happen. Though Bryn had never managed something like this before, he gathered a few of the thinner red bands of energy and tried aiming them at Jehal. Though it produced an intense focus in him, and he could feel his strength becoming more concentrated, nothing happened. He tried again. Then three more times. Nothing! MacRallen remained trapped, on the verge of losing consciousness. Large pieces of the protective cover were coming loose. In a matter of seconds, it would be destroyed, and MacRallen would be defenseless against Jehal's blasts of fire.

Bryn wracked his brain, unaware he was also motioning with his hands. Somehow, the red, yellow, and blue energy lines responded to this and began flowing toward him—especially the red ones. First, it seemed as if he was pulling them away from MacRallen and Jehal. The red merged with the other two colors. Bryn wasn't paying attention to that anymore. He was becoming overwhelmed with how great and energized he suddenly felt.

The colors wound around his wrists and arms by themselves, merging into an even thicker strand of energy. This gave Bryn an idea. *What if I could break the connection between the two of them?* With a smooth gesture, he shot a yellowish-blue band of energy at the red implosions. It slid between the two Masters like a wall. Immediately, the red band intertwined with the other two to form a multicolored band. Bryn held on to it and felt, for the first time, that he was able to control it—he was deliberately controlling magic!

Had Bryn left the realm at that moment, he would have seen a torrent of water surge out of his hands and extinguish the fire.

With the two men no longer surrounded by their magical power source, Bryn let the currents of energy slip away. Again, the three colors scattered throughout the realm, as if these dramatic events had not even happened.

When Bryn returned from the realm, he noticed the classroom was cooler. He stared at the puddles of steaming water covering the floor. *Where did this …?* But before he could finish that thought, the other students pushed past him in a panic, rushing out the door. Only Morlâ stayed. He was trying to pull the Grand Master to a sitting position.

Bryn approached Jehal and shook his shoulder. His eyes opened and he tried to focus. "I warned her years ago this would happen. Years ago," he said in a feeble voice, blacking out just as Tejal and Master Winterblossom hurried in. They stared aghast at the charred, sopping wet room. Then their professional training as healers kicked in, and they ran over to attend to MacRallen and Jehal.

At this point, Bryn and Morlâ tried to leave. But they were not discreet enough to escape Tejal.

"My office this afternoon—both of you," she said without taking her eyes off the unconscious body of Grand Master MacRallen.

AN UNCERTAIN FUTURE

Bryn and Morlâ sat on the uncomfortable bench in the anteroom to Tejal's office. He noticed that Morlâ's feet could not touch the floor, so this bench had to be even more irritating for him. The two friends had not spoken to each other after the morning's events. Bryn wasn't quite sure why. If Morlâ had asked him something, he would have been glad to answer. But the dwarf seemed withdrawn and hardly acknowledged him.

The two of them resigned themselves to a long wait and dwelt on their thoughts. There was a restlessness in Bryn that made his stomach ache. *Will they throw me out of the university today for using magic against a Master?* He was sure Morlâ was also thinking the same thing. *But why was Morlâ ordered to come here as well? Does Tejal suspect he was involved? Does she want to punish him too? I will not let that happen. It was all my fault, and I will tell Tejal that,* he decided. *Morlâ should not be punished for being my friend.*

Suddenly, Gwendolin walked through the front door and into the reception. Morlâ and Bryn turned around. She gave them a haughty look and strutted to the reception desk, sorting through some documents. But she couldn't fool Bryn. He was sure she was doing everything but ignore him and Morlâ.

At some point, Morlâ's patience ran out. The tense and uncertain situation had made him frustrated. "Come on,

Gwenny. I can see something is wrong. Spit it out so we can get this over with."

"Don't get too cocky, dwarf. This isn't about you and your lack of talent."

"What is it then?" Bryn asked. Was he wrong, or did the elf wince a little when she heard his voice?

Gwendolin glared at Bryn. "You'll find out when you step in there. Don't think the whole university revolves around you— Realm Shadow," she scoffed in a baby voice. Again, Bryn thought he saw an uneasy flicker in the eyes of the otherwise self-assured elf. "I knew from the first day that you two bastards with your impure blood would not succeed. And I was right. I heard they're kicking you out as soon as the Chancellor patches up the Masters you attacked."

Bryn couldn't believe it. Before he could say anything, Morlâ spoke in a deep, threatening voice that Bryn had never heard before. "Shut your blasphemous mouth, Gwenny, or—"

"Or what?" The young elf leaped out of her chair to confront him. She was so agitated that the Elbendingen fraternity's flower had appeared on her pale, flawless skin.

Does she expect us to attack her? What were the students thinking about him and his friends now?

"Cool it! Both of you," Bryn shouted, making both of them flinch.

Gwendolin sat down again, and Morlâ went back to studying his dangling feet.

"What's gotten into you? You want to brawl in Tejal's office?" Bryn asked him.

To his surprise, Morlâ replied to him, just loud enough to be overheard. "I know this much. Gwendolin fears the day of the spring full moon. That's when the Starball tournament is held. And she's terrified Elbendingen will lose to us bastards."

Gwendolin leered at him. "You and your ragtag bunch will never beat us. It's a miracle you found three other idiots willing to spend the whole day getting clobbered with you."

"We shall see, we shall see …" said Morlâ, putting on an air of mystery.

At that moment, Tejal's harried voice echoed in the room. "Gwendolin, please send Bryn in!"

Gwendolin regained control of herself in an instant. "Of course, Chancellor."

She led Bryn to the office door, opened it, and gave Bryn a gentle push.

Bryn bowed hastily and prepared himself for a savage lecture from Tejal. To his great surprise, nothing happened. The Chancellor sat behind her desk in silence, looking somewhat lost. She looked pale, with dark circles under her eyes, and her usually tightly pinned hair was disheveled. It was the first time Bryn recognized traces of exhaustion in an elf. After Bryn straightened up, Tejal looked at him for a long time.

Then the stillness of the office finally broke. "Thank you."

At first, Bryn couldn't believe his ears. *Thank you!* Gradually, its significance sank in. They wouldn't be kicking him out of the university. Bryn wanted to hug the entire world. Since he couldn't hug Tejal, he just smiled shyly and made a slight bow.

"I don't know how to thank you, Bryn. Because of your bravery, Master Jehal and Grand Master MacRallen are still alive. Well, barely. A few minutes later, and we couldn't have helped them. You also pulled your fellow students out of danger. I should never have allowed this demonstration." The last sentence was directed more at herself than Bryn. "How did you even manage to interrupt a magical duel between two of the continent's best wizards? Experienced duelists seal themselves off in the realm so nobody can influence them. This is also the reason why deaths occur after blacking out from magic. Many talented ones have never come back from the realm, dying there."

Bryn explained to Tejal how he had used the colors to separate the two wizards. Tejal listened to him with closed eyes, hands clasped in front of her face. She took her time before she spoke again.

"It's the colors. The colors of magic, which you can control. They seem to give you unimagined powers. I'm not sure I would have been able to separate the two. If I had been able to, it would've only been because of the special powers Âlaburg gives me. Whether this is good or bad for you and the magical community remains unknown."

She was looking at him with profound sadness. Bryn shifted from one foot to the other. He wanted to ask a question that had been plaguing him since the day he first entered the realm in Jehal's class and fainted. He cleared his throat.

"What is it, Bryn?" Tejal asked.

"I have a question for you."

"I will answer as best I can—if I am allowed, of course."

Bryn wondered what she meant. But now was not the time for that.

"Master Jehal said he warned you about me," Bryn said tentatively. "He said he knew that something like this would happen. What did he mean?"

"Is that what he said?"

"Yes! Well, something like that," Bryn admitted, a little embarrassed. "I gave you the short version. But he always mentioned it in extraordinary situations."

Tejal looked at him again for a long time before answering. "Without knowing what Master Jehal said, I cannot be one hundred percent sure what he meant … but I have an idea."

Bryn would never have thought that elves could age. But now, under the lamplight, Tejal appeared old and sad. Her flawless skin seemed wrinkled, her eyes dull and feeble. Elves were also subject to nature's laws—even if it affected them less than the others of Razuclan.

"Bryn, the roots of the First and Second Wars of the Nations were not only the quarrels and jealousies between the four nations. They were also an excellent opportunity to mobilize their battle-ready hordes. But in the background, the magically gifted were always involved in these ever-changing alliances. Sometimes, human and elf wizards teamed up against the orcs. On other occasions, the humans fought the elves along with the dwarves. The three magically gifted nations guarded their special abilities and new spells. However, the great scholars soon realized how powerful spells could become when they connected two different energies while within the realm. But, unlike yourself, they needed at least two wizards from different nations to do this.

"This kind of magical intervention was rarely used. When it was, the result was often devastating. Usually, when nations combined to cast a spell, it would hold the key to victory in the great, epic battles." She paused, and Bryn could see a memory flicker over her face. "But the cost was horrific. Thousands died. There are still completely inaccessible territories in Razuclan. And murderous creatures, beyond the control of their creators, roam the land. These monsters are one of the reasons for the founding of the Order."

Tejal straightened up in her chair before continuing. "Some great sorcerers and magical talents used the energy of the realm like this. But their goals were all wrong. Even before the Great Peace Treaty, the most powerful magicians had a meeting and established rules for using the energy of the realm. They forbid some spells and instituted a general ban that meant no nations would be able to combine their magic again. It is the Order that controls and enforces these rules. Severe punishments, even death in the realm, were also pronounced and are in effect still. The peaceful, magical world abides by these rules. But there is a group that breaks them, though unintentionally."

"The children with parents of two different nations!" Bryn exclaimed.

Tejal nodded. "Yes. Nobody knows which magical powers the offspring of these couples will develop. This is why the founding of White House and acceptance of students of undetermined background have taken so many years. Many of us here fought for this. Razuclan needs every talented person it can get. It doesn't matter whether they know who their ancestors are or not. Yet, others,"—she hesitated for a moment—"like Jehal, are utterly opposed to admitting so-called 'impure' students. They maintain that the mixed-blood would disrupt the magical balance and undermine the peace."

"So that's what Master Jehal thinks I am," cried Bryn, interrupting the Chancellor, who didn't react to his rudeness.

"He believes I am a threat to magical harmony and peace. That's why he refuses to teach me. Because he doesn't want to be guilty of a crime against the Order. Or worse, against the realm itself."

Tejal nodded, but her face was set into sorrowful lines. "It seems those are his reasons. And I can't blame him. Jehal knows from experience what magic can do when misused. Back then—" Tejal hesitated again. "But this is not our concern now." She stood up slowly and came around the desk to Bryn. "You have my full support and are a valued student of Âlaburg. I will see to it that you can complete your education. Nobody should be held responsible for their origins or the skills nature gave them. If you work hard, Bryn, you will make an extraordinary magician. What you did today proves to me that you can use the powers you've been given responsibly. That is all I need to know."

Tejal was starting to resemble her old self again. The strictness was back in her voice.

"As soon as Jehal has regained his strength, I will remind him of his duty as a Master to treat all students equally. You will get the same education as everyone else here at Âlaburg, I promise you. Do not worry about the special things you can do. The realm has always been in flux, and changes have been part of the magical world since Razuclan came into existence. Study diligently, listen to your Masters, and respect all people. Then, you will succeed and become a great wizard."

Bryn's shocked expression drew a smile from Tejal.

"Yes, Chancellor!" It was all he could say.

"Right. You can go now and send Morlâ in. I'll see you Friday afternoon."

Bryn walked into reception with a big smile and told Morlâ he could go in. Bryn made his way to the front door without even a glance at Gwendolin. Since Morlâ seemed to prefer being alone today, he decided not to wait for him but walk to White House on his own. Heading back, he repeated to himself what Tejal had said to him. A tingling sensation shot through him.

I am going to be a wizard.

AN ENCOUNTER WITH GRAND MASTERS

On his way to White House, Bryn stopped to breathe in the air. It smelled of spring for the first time this year—like early blossoms, green buds, and the first, warming rays of the sun. There was no other way to describe it, but it felt like life was awakening after a long winter. Lost in thought, he enjoyed the scent and the tranquility. As it was dinner time, the university lay deserted. The students were probably enjoying the food of the Řischnǎrr fraternity in the dining room. Bryn was not sorry to miss out on that. He'd had enough of giblets and blood pudding for the week.

"Oh, young McDermit," a deep voice boomed to his left. "What are the odds of us meeting here?"

Bryn jumped in fright. He had been sure until now that he was walking all alone. Cautious, he turned to his left and saw—nothing.

"Down here," the baritone teased. Bryn glanced below and saw a dwarf—not just any dwarf but one of the Driany Knights who had arrived Sunday afternoon.

Bryn apologized right away. "I'm sorry, Knight. I didn't notice you."

"It happens, but most people never forget me after one encounter," he said with a wink.

Bryn continued on his way together with his odd companion. The stout dwarf was eating something bloody and greasy, and shreds of it were hanging from his beard—definitely orc cuisine.

Bryn's first impression of the knight proved right. Up close, his clothes looked shabby and unkempt, full of stains and holes. He had swapped the chainmail vest he wore on his arrival for a colorful floral shirt that fell to his knees. It had also seen better days. His hair, like his beard, was gray, and his face was furrowed with wrinkles. He must be several decades old.

His bulbous, red nose indicated he was quite fond of drinking, but he didn't reek of alcohol. Either he hadn't been drinking tonight or was stuck with a big, red honker.

"Do you mind me walking with you?" he asked guilelessly, looking up at Bryn and right into his eyes for the first time.

Bryn's breath caught. In those brown eyes glowed infinite wisdom. The dwarf seemed to be looking straight into his soul. Next to him, Bryn felt stupid and insignificant. Now he understood why the fat, unkempt dwarf was a Driany Knight. He had to possess a wealth of knowledge and understanding of the world that few living beings on Razuclan did. Bryn now remembered dwarves lived much longer than humans. Morlâ even claimed that some of the oldest of his nation were over five hundred years old.

All this crossed his mind in such a bewildering flash that he almost forgot to answer. "Certainly not, Knight! It is an honor to have you walk with me."

"An honor, Elmar, did you hear that? Clearly, he doesn't know you yet," said a female voice, this time to Bryn's right.

Bryn turned around once more. There stood the elf who had arrived on the weekend. She beamed at him, then the wind blew some golden strands of her long hair into her beautiful face, and Bryn started blushing. It bothered him a lot, but he hoped nobody would see it in the twilight.

The elf, dressed in plain, tight, white linen clothes, didn't seem to notice. She was merrily chatting as if they had known each other for ages.

"I hope our esteemed Grand Master Boulderstone is not boring you, Bryn? Sometimes, he can be quite soporific, particularly when he meets strangers who dare not interrupt him."

Boulderstone snorted loudly but did not attempt to defend himself.

"No, no, Ms …" Bryn didn't know how to address the elf and blushed again.

She gracefully managed the situation with a sweeping movement of her hand and a short bow. "My name, young Bryn, is Isilmar Morningsky. Like our mutual friend, I am also a Grand Master—only taller!"

Only now did Bryn realize his mistake. *A Grand Master. And two of them!* He stopped and bowed, but he'd halted so abruptly, the others kept walking. Both Grand Masters turned around to look for him. Bryn's face was red, and he bowed once more.

"There you go!" said the dwarf. "And I thought Tejal said these new students hadn't been taught anything."

"Leave him be, Boulderstone. The three of us met by chance on an evening stroll—don't spoil it now. And little did Bryn know what illustrious acquaintances he would make today." The three then resumed walking, and Morningsky continued talking. "It's good to be out. The Řischnǎrr evening meal is lying heavy in my stomach. Tonight's menu seemed even more gory and putrid than when I was at Âlaburg."

"I found it tasty," a deep voice boomed from the shadows a few yards ahead.

Bryn was too startled to hide it from his two companions. The abrupt appearance of a stranger shrouded in darkness brought back memories of his encounter with the Vonnyen in the wintry Arell Forest.

Morningsky looked at Bryn and smiled. "Orr, you're scaring our young companion. Not everybody knows that an orc three-yards tall with arm-length horns and finger-sized fangs can be as tame as a cute little wood mouse. Step out of your dark corner."

Bryn struggled to avoid flinching again when the giant dark orc appeared from behind a tree. He towered above them all by several feet. His twisted horns were painted red, making him appear even more dangerous. When he tried to smile—Bryn hoped it was a smile, at least—bright white fangs shimmered in the growing darkness, meant for more than just feeding. In a few long strides, the orc stood in front of them. His every move exuded tremendous strength. Bryn could see the numerous muscles under his dark skin. It had not occurred to Bryn that someone this big could move so gracefully and silently.

"Sorry, young McDermit, I didn't mean to scare you," he said, offering Bryn his right-hand claw.

Bryn took hold of the massive hand with both hands but still could not fully grasp it.

"I don't want to nitpick," Boulderstone said, "but Orr is also a Grand Master, Bryn. So …"

Bryn immediately bowed, and Orr flashed his brilliant white fangs at him again.

Morningsky glanced at Boulderstone. "I told you it was best not to have Orr speak to him first," she said, giving Orr a good-natured nudge.

Bryn realized then that his encounter with the three Grand Masters was no coincidence.

What do they want from me? he wondered. But since he dared not ask them, he just walked alongside them. They wandered across the vast, darkening grounds of the university in silence. The Grand Masters had distracted him somewhat, and he soon found himself at the rear of the mighty tower with his small group, still quite a way from the entrance to White House.

Finally, Grand Master Morningsky broke the silence. "Well, I never expected the four of us to go for a stroll together."

"Let's stop playing games," Boulderstone gruffly cut in. "The boy must have realized by now this is no chance meeting."

"Are you sure, Elmar?" She gave Bryn an inquiring look, but he couldn't utter a word. The whole situation was just too strange.

"Are you all right, little human?" Orr inquired, which intimidated Bryn even more.

"Yes," Bryn whispered.

"See," Boulderstone teased Morningsky, "Orr does have a gift for handling humans. We should have made him talk to Bryn first!"

"Nonsense. I should have been first. All humans love elves." The Grand Master spun around, her golden hair flying seductively around her head.

"We should have intercepted him at Tejal's office straight away," the orc said in his deep voice.

"I've had too many bad experiences in that office," Boulderstone countered. "Nobody will ever make me go in there again. Taking him out of his room at night when he's fast asleep, as I suggested, would have been the best solution. But we also—"

But Bryn had had enough of listening to their secret plans, and he erupted angrily, "What do you want from me?"

"Well, well, well. There might be more to you than meets the eye," Grand Master Boulderstone said with some delight.

The group had come to a halt, their focus on Bryn. Three different pairs of eyes studied him carefully.

"Apologies for our little charade, Bryn," Morningsky said. "We didn't want the other students to know we had to talk to you. This whole situation seems, well, complicated enough as it is."

"Utterly!" Orr snorted. "The two human fools—no offense to you, young McDermit," he added, "would have killed each other, if—"

"—if," interrupted Boulderstone, "you had not saved their lives with your remarkable abilities."

Bryn fumbled for something to say. Uncomfortable being the center of attention, he didn't feel like a hero at all. And he still didn't know how he had done it.

"Anybody would have done the same thing," he mumbled.

Orr put his heavy hand on his shoulder, causing Bryn to crouch a little. His big head dropped down close to Bryn's face. "No, young human, not everybody would have done that. No one acted, except you. No one! Like it or not, this is a heroic deed, and I want …" He looked briefly at the other two Grand Masters. "We want to thank you. What you did for MacRallen was huge and deserves credit. He is not only our brother in the Order but also our friend, and you have saved him."

The other two now approached Bryn and put their hands on his shoulder. Filixx had once explained to Bryn that this was considered a great honor in the magical world. When gifted people came directly into contact, their energies briefly merged and surrendered to the others' power.

The Grand Masters spoke as one. "We thank you, Bryn McDermit. The Peace Keepers of the Driany Order owe you a debt of gratitude."

Bryn was speechless.

"Is there anything we can do to thank you? Being Grand Masters, we have considerable influence," Boulderstone said.

A million ideas raced through Bryn's mind. Maybe now he could transfer to the Bond-of-Faith fraternity and be among humans again? Or no more kitchen duty? But Bryn had only one true desire, which he hoped the learned Driany Knights could grant him.

"I want to know who I am and what I am."

His three extraordinary companions glanced knowingly at each other.

"A wise decision, young human," said Boulderstone, "and one that shows great character. Only by knowing about ourselves can we fully live our life and define and share it with others." He was silent for a moment, but neither Morningsky nor Orr seemed willing to add anything more. When he spoke again, his voice was so soft that Bryn could hardly hear him. "Knowledge, young Bryn, can also be a burden. Are you sure this is what you want?"

Bryn's short, firm nod was answer enough for the Grand Master, who sighed. "Very well then. What you are is not so easy to define, but I will share what I know of what it means to be a Seer of Colors."

Excitement coursed through Bryn. So that was what the magical community called beings like him. He was a Seer of Colors!

"As you know," the dwarf continued, "the three magical nations on Razuclan can only access their respective magical energies in the realm. For humans, the color of their magical energy is red; for elves, it is yellow, and for us dwarves, it is blue. This is mainly due to the origin of the energies scattered across the continent."

Bryn nodded for the Grand Master to continue.

"So much for the rule. The exceptions that confirm it are those known as Seers of Colors. But only a few have appeared over the centuries. I do not know of a single student of Âlaburg who possessed this ability. Except you, of course," he added, smiling. "This is why the Chancellor didn't find anything on similar cases in the university archives. She deliberately withheld her limited knowledge about what it means to be a Seer of Colors, as it is one of the best-kept secrets in the magical world.

Only a few Grand Masters know and may share this information. Luckily, one of the leading experts in this little-explored field of magic stands right before you." Boulderstone grinned. "A Seer of Colors is capable of extraordinary feats of magic. Though I've never heard of one being able to attack an orc with their powers."

Orr made an indefinable noise, which gave Bryn the shivers.

"If any of them ever abused their power, the consequences for the magical balance throughout Razuclan would be disastrous. The same danger exists in your life. You have to learn to follow the true path of magic and avoid being tempted by the realm's exciting possibilities. Moreover, every enemy of free and peaceful magic on Razuclan will also become your enemy, as you already know from painful experience."

Images of that icy cold night, the deserted clearing, and the murderous Vonnyen flickered through Bryn's mind.

"More than any other gifted being, you must be careful about controlling your abilities to avoid irreversible damage to Razuclan," Boulderstone advised him.

Bryn realized what he'd meant by burden. Taking care not to be the reason for the world's end was more than one person could bear. Now he understood Jehal's reaction. But he couldn't accept what he was hearing.

I didn't choose this, Bryn thought grimly.

"The Order, therefore, imposes a vow of silence on anyone who possesses this information," Boulderstone finished.

"And, of course, my diligent sister adhered to that," Morningsky remarked, winking at Bryn.

That explained why Tejal hadn't told him straight away he was a Seer of Colors and why she was crying after the Grand Masters arrived at the castle. Hopefully, the sisters were only shedding tears of joy then, but Bryn doubted it. He remembered an old human saying that he had never understood as a child: *When elves cry, hard times follow.*

"You, too," the old dwarf continued, "should share this knowledge only with the ones you trust. I will not commit you to silence because being a Seer of Colors is part of your nature, and you cannot hide it from everything and everyone for the rest of your life without losing your true self."

Bryn was grateful because he had to talk to somebody about it. He could hardly wait to tell Gerald, Filixx, and Morlâ, even though he didn't know whether his roommate still trusted him unconditionally.

"The science behind a gifted person becoming a Seer of Colors is a matter of debate in the magical community. Some believe that the so-called 'impure or bastards,'" said Boulderstone, "absorb both of their respective nations' energies. An explanation that is almost certainly impossible in your case. Another explanation is that gifted ones who have spent a long time away from their own people's realm absorb the energy of their respective locations to become a Seer of Colors. But this, too, is out of the question. You are too young for such a transformation to be possible. Furthermore, since you began to live with Gerald, you have always been in human territory." The dwarf sighed. "You see, I can tell you what you are but not who. The source of your extraordinary talent lies in your provenance. Unfortunately, we have no information about that either."

Bryn's high spirits evaporated. He had wanted to learn about his origins, but the Grand Master's words crushed his hopes.

Orr sensed Bryn's disappointment. "Let us clarify one thing. We may not know yet, but one day, we'll find out." The giant orc crouched down to look Bryn in the eye. "I promise that on our travels and missions, we will always keep our eyes and ears open to find out the secret of your origins."

For a long time, Bryn said nothing and just stared into the orc's black eyes, watching his small yellow pupils constantly dilate and constrict. Still devastated, all Bryn could manage was to thank him.

Nothing more needed to be said or done, and the Grand Masters and Bryn continued their evening walk in silence. As they got closer to the door to White House, they bid him goodbye, one after the other. The last to depart was Grand Master Boulderstone.

"Bryn, even if you don't know where you're from, you know who you are."

The boy looked confused.

The dwarf laughed. "Think about it. In your short time as a student here at Âlaburg, you managed to be the first gifted being to defeat an orc with magic. Your powers terrified Master Jehal; he no longer wants to teach you. You became part of a Starball team and saved the life of a Grand Master, a Master, and several fellow students. And you still wonder who you are? For me, it is simple. You're an excellent young wizard."

The old dwarf chuckled again and disappeared into the dark, leaving Bryn alone but with a smile working its way across his face.

SOMETIMES IT HELPS TO TALK

That evening, Bryn did not share his exciting news with anyone. Filixx was not in his room or anywhere else in White House, and Morlâ was already asleep when Bryn returned to their room. Even though he was pretty sure Morlâ was only pretending to sleep, Bryn left him alone. He hoped his roommate would become less suspicious of him, less distant, and eventually talk to him when ready.

When Bryn woke, Morlâ was already gone. He had left quite early, his unmade bed the only sign someone had slept there. He usually stayed in bed as long as possible. Bryn was now quite sure Morlâ had a problem and was deliberately avoiding him. The recent events must have made Morlâ turn away from his friend. Sadly, Bryn stood up.

I have to talk to him, he decided. *Best before lessons!* He hurried to the dining room.

At this early hour, the hall was still reasonably quiet. There were no long queues at the food counter, and the tables were not overcrowded. Bryn searched the spacious room and spotted Morlâ sitting in a corner behind a large, dead potted plant.

Morlâ sat by himself at one of the few tables for two, playing with his food. The reddish lump on his spoon meant only one thing. One of the orcs' favorite dishes, blood soup, was on the menu again.

Determined, Bryn walked over and took the chair opposite Morlâ.

"Good morning!"

Morlâ looked dumbfounded. "Uh … uh, good morning. How did you …? I mean, I couldn't sleep, so I decided to have an early breakfast. I thought you might sleep in after your exciting day yesterday."

Morlâ smiled, but Bryn could see it wasn't real. Bryn wasn't in the mood for lame excuses. His friendship with Morlâ meant too much for him to pretend everything was fine. Something had come between them.

Bryn's heart was pounding. "What's wrong? Why are you avoiding me?"

Morlâ's eyes widened, and he dropped his wooden spoon into the bloody soup. It splattered on both boys as well as the table. Morlâ pulled a dirty cloth from his pocket and cleaned up the mess. Bryn thought that Morlâ, who'd never before exhibited much concern for neatness, was trying to avoid him again. Finally, Morlâ put the cloth away and looked up.

"I have no idea what you're on about," he insisted, clumsily patting Bryn's arm. "Everything's fine." But he couldn't look Bryn in the eyes.

Bryn said nothing and just looked at Morlâ. But his friend kept avoiding his gaze.

Morlâ eventually caved, running a hand through his hair and asking, "What do you want from me?"

"I want to know why you're being so weird!"

"I am?"

Bryn just looked him in the eye.

"Oh, hell!" Morlâ exclaimed. "Damn, little human. Dwarves are not into talking about our feelings and all that human stuff. Nobody does it. We avoid each other, or we fight. That's how we solve our problems. Not by talking through everything like you scrawny beanpoles do."

Finally, Bryn could recognize his friend again. But though Morlâ was wrong to suggest all humans found it easy to talk about their feelings, he was wise enough not to interrupt him now.

"Look, it's not your fault. It's just … it's …" The look on Morlâ's face revealed his inner conflict. He sighed deeply and slumped against the back of his chair. "The thing is, your problem is that your magic is too strong and that you have too much of it, whereas for me—and you're in and out of the Chancellor's office, and at night, you're having secret meetings with some of the continent's most powerful wizards." Morlâ took a deep breath.

Surprised, Bryn raised an eyebrow. *How did Morlâ know?*

"And ..." Morlâ laughed cheerlessly. "I'm always on the side. The dwarf without talent. The bastard who somehow managed to sneak past the gate into the university. The friend of the Realm Shadow. The one who hasn't worked a single spark of magic his entire time here. The one who brings in a Gnarf worm and pretends to have summoned it."

It hurt Bryn to hear this, but he understood only too well. Being so busy with himself, he had forgotten entirely about Morlâ's particular situation. During the last weeks, the two of them were more often discussing *his* problems. Morlâ had always been sympathetic and never complained. Even though he might have to leave the university if he didn't develop his magical powers before the final exams, they had considered ways to solve Bryn's problems and never talked about how Bryn could help Morlâ. Nor did they discuss what would happen if Morlâ never found the gift within him. After his short outburst, Morlâ had fallen silent again, examining his fingernails. Bryn felt sad for his friend.

He drew in a breath. "Without you, I would still be getting lost here. You're the one who makes sure I won't starve. You're the one who runs White House so all the residents, from all nations, don't tear each other apart. You're the one who's going to lead White House to the Starball finals this year. You are ..." Bryn hesitated briefly. "You're my best friend."

Morlâ looked at him with wide eyes. Something seemed to be the matter, though, because he kept rubbing them.

Bryn had the good grace not to mention it.

The dwarf cleared his throat. "Oh, you sentimental humans. So dramatic, the lot of you." He rose from his chair, reached out over the table with his short arms, and gave Bryn a cumbersome hug—an expression of friendship the two had previously never shared.

Bryn returned the honest, firm embrace with a broad grin, hugging his little friend heartily.

UNSPORTSMANLIKE BEHAVIOR

Now that Bryn and Morlâ had talked things over, Starball training was better than ever. The team was now allowed to train almost every day as it was only one week until the first spring full moon. The following Saturday, the first part of the university competition would be held.

After one of their many practice sessions, Bryn told Filixx and Morlâ all about his meeting with the Grand Masters. As usual, Ûlyėr left immediately after training, so the three could discuss Bryn's news. They did not come up with extra insights. Still, Bryn was glad he finally had someone to talk to about being a Seer of Colors.

In the evenings after training, the boys usually collapsed into bed. That night, Bryn lay there thinking that at least they wouldn't come last in the tournament this year, which would be much better than the achievements of the previous residents of White House. Gerald's training tips had proved to be incredibly useful. Bryn was amazed that his foster father was such a great Starball coach. With his help, they could perhaps surprise one or two of the other fraternities.

More than once, Bryn dreamed of lifting the trophy while the rest of the university cheered for White House team. When he woke up, it always seemed highly unlikely. But the idea was deeply ingrained in his subconscious.

Thursday rolled around—the last day on which the players had to attend lessons. The Friday before the tournament weekend, they were supposed to get ready for the competition.

Bryn was more than happy about it. For the last few weeks, classes had been even more strenuous, something he would never have believed possible. But the great rivalry among the House Masters had resulted in them favoring the students and players in their respective fraternities and harassing everyone else whenever possible. Since Gerald did not take classes, the White House team was at a particular disadvantage. There was no one in the university to protect them from the other Masters or pester the other fraternity teams on behalf of White House.

Jehal, the head of Bond-of-Faith, presented some magical artifacts in his class. He ordered Bryn and Morlâ to look into their capabilities. Alas, he had conveniently forgotten to mention that some of them could cause severe damage. One artifact was a particularly harmless-looking dried troll ear, still adorned with a sparkly earring. Bryn was pretty sure that its effect was to petrify his opponent. That the two friends survived this class unscathed was pure coincidence.

Even the prudent Master Tieffenor couldn't resist the challenge of the competition. Ølsgendur hadn't won a title for generations. Being their House Master, he wanted to support his players as much as he could. According to Filixx, the Master had asked him after a lesson to search the archives in the university's basement. He had to look for scrolls about the Rebellion of the Wolf Men in the interim between the First and Second War of the Nations. As it happened, the doors were closed earlier than usual on that day. After a futile search, Filixx found himself locked up in the huge basement vault. Only his resourcefulness, which included getting hold of some fake university keys, had saved him from spending the tournament weekend underground, surrounded by dusty scrolls of papyrus and mice.

Even Ûlyėr was not safe from being messed with. After his seminar on Healing with Master Winterblossom, the House Master of Elbendingen fraternity, his appearance in the university dining room seemed far too cheerful and happy. Filixx recognized it as the symptoms of an elvish love potion, given 'accidentally' to the giant in class. But the orc soon recovered, and by evening, his familiar bad attitude was back. When Bryn greeted him in White House hallway with a friendly 'hello,' the orc pushed him aside and stepped into the bathroom without a word.

Master Ñokelä, the House Master of Řischnärr, was his usual self. He treated the students of White House with the same unfairness and severity they had grown accustomed to in the past months. An increase in his bullying was just impossible.

Bryn's great advantage in the current situation was that Morlâ, Filixx, and even Ûlyėr were all affected. At least the team members could bond over the bad behavior of the Masters.

The four players were in the dimly-lit common room, sitting around the fireplace. None of them noticed that the fire was about to go out. They wore anxious expressions, and Morlâ even had beads of sweat on his forehead. The only one not showing any sign of anxiety was Ûlyėr—at least Bryn couldn't detect any in his dark face.

They had the room all to themselves for the night. It was one of the things Gerald had managed to arrange for them. But it was the end of a long, hard day and the last evening before the tournament, and their team captain was once again lecturing on rules and tactics.

"Morlâ, we know the rules," Bryn protested.

"Listen up, everybody," Morlâ replied with renewed tension in his voice. "The other teams are just waiting for it—one single rule violation, and they'll exclude us from the tournament. So, one more time."

Bryn glanced at Filixx, who rolled his eyes, and they went on pretending to listen. Both boys knew Morlâ needed to reassure himself, and he droned on and on about all the tournament proceedings.

"We're playing a total of four games, and we're going to win them all if we can. All of us will have to play because we don't have a fifth man." His eyes lingered on Bryn. "Each of us is only allowed to play once. For every victory, two points will be awarded. The top two teams will play against each other in the final on Sunday to decide who wins the University Cup. Always remember to defend our Harel Star or touch the opponent's. You have to defend or conquer the star at least twice in three rounds tops. Attack and defense alternate in each round. The third round is open. Any more questions?"

The others shook their heads.

"Fine," Morlâ said, still somewhat nervous. "Now, off to bed. We start early tomorrow."

Morlâ remained in the common room. He unfolded a stack of papyrus, all covered with arrows, player's names, and fraternities, and started fretting over potential strategies and game plans like he had done hundreds of times over the past months.

THE SPRING TOURNAMENT

It was the morning of the tournament, and the four White House players sat in the university's dining room in silence. Although Filixx had prepared several exquisite dishes from each of their home regions for breakfast, nobody seemed hungry. Even Filixx was so nervous that he struggled to eat something.

Bryn stared into his bowl and poked his breakfast with a fork. But a block of ice formed in his stomach when, out of the corner of his eye, he saw Gerald, wearing his white coach's cape, pushing through the mass of students. The tournament was about to begin!

Gerald broke into a huge grin.

"Good morning, White Team!" he roared over the other students. "I realize that you need to eat a lot at your age, but you should be finished by now. The tournament starts in an hour, and teams must be in their arenas on time to get ready for their games. If you're late and miss the deadline, you automatically forfeit. And as you may have noticed, our Chancellor, virtuous as always, is meticulous in her application of the rules," he concluded with a wry smile.

On hearing this, Morlâ woke as if from a trance. "Oh, damn! Come on! We have to go!"

Without waiting for anyone, he snatched up his white cape, which the players had to wear on the Starball court, and was about to run out of the room when Gerald grabbed him by the shoulder.

"Slow down, Morlâ. There's plenty of time to finish your breakfast."

Bryn took a sip of water; his mouth was so dry. "I think we're ready, Gerald. We're all done with breakfast, aren't we?"

"As ready as one can be," muttered Filixx, leaning on the table to ease his heavy frame out of the chair.

They left the dining room and Remter Hall and headed to the stadium; as they did, Bryn noticed Ûlyėr's limp seemed more pronounced than usual.

On the way, Gerald explained how things would proceed. "Two games are played across the stadium's four arenas at the same time. Team members are not allowed to watch other games. Of course, this does not apply to other fraternity members and fans of the four fraternities or White House. We might want to assign someone to watch the other games and report back with the results and any insights," he recommended.

Morlâ nodded calmly. "That's what the twins will do. Rulu and Ulur have a kind of telepathic ability, enabling both of them to see and hear what the other does. While we are playing, one of them will always be with us and pass on any important information. I discussed this with them months ago."

"Well done," said Gerald. "Excellent planning. Then you can tell them now to go to arenas one and three, where the first two games will take place. I received the schedule for the games this morning. Tejal …" He cleared his throat and blushed slightly. "I mean, the Chancellor, of course, always makes a big secret about the order of the games, and since this season is the first time in years that five teams will play, I guess the planning wasn't easy either. Ten games is utter madness," Gerald, muttered, more to himself than the team.

"And … the schedule?" said Bryn, gently interrupting him.

"Oh, yes. Sorry." He fumbled about under his cape and eventually pulled out a small, wrinkled piece of papyrus with the list on it. "You're not supposed to know the schedule before the tournament opens—not until it's been published for everyone. But I know for sure the other four House Masters have already …"

Gerald did not complete that thought, but it was clear what he was going to say, and the team was grateful that their House Master had committed this small infraction on their behalf.

Gerald rechecked the list. "Yes. We're not playing the first round."

A moan went through the team. Now they would have even more time to go crazy listening to the noise of the other games.

Gerald didn't seem to notice the team's reaction at all because he continued, unmoved. "First round, Řischnărr will play Ølsgendur and Bond-of-Faith will play Elbendingen. Now, I've no idea if the dwarves will be able to win this time. Tieffenor told me that last year—"

"Gerald!" Bryn interrupted him again.

"Oh, yes." Squinting, he held the note close to his face. "Our first game is against Elbendingen! And the opening ceremony takes place in arena two. Come on then. Let's head there first!"

From her podium in the spectator seating, Tejal finished her formal opening speech with a reminder to all the teams. "The purpose of the Starball tournament is to show how all the nations can compete peacefully rather than slaughter one another in war. Respect this basic idea. And one final point—anyone who deliberately injures another student should expect the harshest consequences, including expulsion from the university."

Morlâ and Bryn listened to the speech surrounded by a sea of students in colorful capes.

"Expulsion? Well, that would be something new. If she does that, there would be hardly any players left on Monday," Morlâ said as they waited for Tejal to finish.

"I wish everyone an exciting Spring Tournament. May the most talented team win!" she said, finally stepping down from the podium.

The students immediately rushed to the stadium entrance, where the game schedule now appeared on a colossal poster. Bryn noticed not one of the opposing players were involved in the jostling.

Arena number two was soon empty. Most of the students had made their way to the other venues to watch their teams play. Some were already singing their battle songs like *Bond-of-Faith Hold Your Head Up High!* or *Ø … Ø … Ølsgendur, we might be small, but we always win big.* The orcs resorted to military marching, which was no less impressive than the other fraternities' songs or the thousands of colorful flowers conjured up by the elves, which fell over the students' heads like confetti.

Gerald and the team were the only ones left in the arena.

"Now we wait," said Filixx. The small group huddled together and looked out over the circular wooden court. A roar went up from one or other of the arenas, but nobody could tell from the crowd's response which way the game was going. They had to wait for the twins to report.

"2-0 to Řischnărr," reported Rulu as soon as he returned. "The orcs didn't give the dwarves a chance."

The whole team gathered around their fellow student. He swallowed hard, exhaled quickly, and then closed his eyes. His chest dropped, and his narrow nostrils widened.

"Who was playing?" Morlâ asked, holding a pile of messy notes in his hand.

Rulu opened his eyes on hearing the question and replied joltingly, as if his mind was somewhere else. "Zsac for Řischnărr and Diorit for Ølsgendur." The last word was hard to understand as Rulu spoke so softly. And then he fell completely silent.

"Why did he stop speaking?" Bryn whispered impatiently to Filixx.

"Oh, he's speaking all the time." He chuckled. "You just can't hear him. He has established a connection to Ulur. Rulu is probably receiving the report of the Elbendingen and Bond-of-Faith game."

Rulu opened his eyes again. "1-2 to Elbendingen. Maal Lionkress scored two points for Elbendingen, but the decisive match was the open round. And Martin MacEntalen, the captain of Bond-of-Faith, injured himself so badly in his attack that he could not continue. He wanted to, but Winterblossom forbade him; he could barely hold himself upright at the start of the third round, so Elbendingen won the open round almost without a fight." Rulu looked paler than ever and leaned against the fence around the court.

"Thanks, Rulu. Tell Ulur to stay at his post. I need to know how the orcs are faring against the humans," Morlâ said, looking up only briefly from his notes, which he was completing with the information he had just gained.

At that moment, masses of elves dressed in yellow and blue flooded the arena—but there were also a few in the crowd dressed in white.

To Bryn's surprise, he saw Karina, Malin, Elina, and Hela in the crowd, looking excited and proudly wearing white capes like the ones the players wore. The Five Wise Ones were also mingling with the enthusiastic crowd. Toulin, Houlin, Kaneg, Worin, and Lebos not only wore their white sashes but had also made themselves hats that looked like White House's Harel Star. They were trying to unroll a massive banner of Morlâ looking like an ancient hero with flowing hair and muscular arms, looking into the distance and confident of victory.

When Morlâ saw it, he turned slightly red but said nothing. He was too busy concentrating on the game.

Master MacKamell walked into the arena. He would referee the game and make sure the students did not kill each other. He called the team captains to join him center court and greeted them.

"Morlâ, Gwendolin, you know how it's done. Gwendolin, heads or tails?"

Without thinking twice, the elf chose heads. The Master tossed the ancient coin in the air. It turned over and over, morphed into a tiny silver ball for a moment, and landed on the court's wooden boards as a coin again, with a light, sharp *clink*.

"Heads! You've won the toss, Gwendolin. Morlâ, who's on the court first?"

Gwendolin shot Morlâ a cheeky grin.

"Morlâ?" MacKamell repeated.

"Oh … up first? Ah … I am," he replied a little too firmly, not wanting to look weak in front of Gwendolin. Nevertheless, he was aware of the disadvantage of not knowing which player Elbendingen would put up. Now Gwendolin could choose someone she believed could defeat him.

"Gwendolin, who are you putting up?"

"Myself, my esteemed Master."

Master MacKamell smiled at being addressed with such reverence.

Damn, she's good, Morlâ thought. *Now she has the referee on her side.*

"Well, let us begin. Elbendingen has chosen to attack! Bring the White House Harel Star into position." MacKamell left the court and went to the giant hourglass standing nearby.

Ûlyėr came onto the court, passed Morlâ the pole with the sparkling Harel Star on top of it, and went back through the gap in the fence. Morlâ walked over to the right side of the court and smashed the pole into the wooden floor.

"Elbendingen team, are you ready?" MacKamell cried to Gwendolin, who was standing at the court's far-left edge.

Gwendolin nodded slightly. Then hundreds of voices started to shout, and a yellow wave went around the stadium.

"White House team, are you ready?"

The elves immediately shouted down the few isolated cheers. Morlâ nodded. The Master turned the hourglass over, and grains of sand began to trickle down the narrow neck from the upper glass chamber to the lower one. The White House Harel Star began to glow brightly.

"Your three minutes starts now!"

Bryn, Filixx, and Ûlyėr could do nothing but stand behind the small perimeter fence around the court. All eyes were on their captain. Morlâ stood rigidly in front of the star.

From where Bryn was standing, he could see that neither Gwendolin nor Morlâ were moving, though the sand continued to run down the hourglass. Just as Bryn was feeling a little hopeful about an easy first point, Gwendolin charged Morlâ at breakneck speed. Her body was barely perceptible—a yellow flash of light bolting across the court.

Morlâ was expecting her attack and pulled out his iron-sheathed wooden club from under his cloak. He swung at her as she came close, confident he would land a blow, but he hit only air and fell over due to his momentum. It was not the *real* Gwendolin.

"What happened?" shouted Ûlyėr.

Bryn ignored his teammate. He was too engrossed in what was happening on the court. Sadly, he was now watching the *real* Gwendolin leap over Morlâ, lying sprawled on the ground, and touch their unguarded Harel Star, which immediately went out.

The arena went wild.

"1-0 to Elbendingen," shouted MacKamell.

"A magical illusion," Filixx said under his breath. "The oldest Starball trick in the book. I can't believe Morlâ fell for it." But there was no time to criticize him further; Gwendolin had just thrust her Harel Star into the court, and the Master had turned the hourglass over again. Round two had begun.

Now it was White House's turn to attack. Morlâ yelled, angry with himself, and charged toward Gwendolin.

Gwendolin heard Morlâ's anguish. Unconcerned, she wrenched the pole out of the court and, holding it in one hand, coldly stared down her attacker. Just as Morlâ was upon her, Gwendolin somersaulted at least four yards into the air and landed behind Morlâ with a soft thud, the star still in her hand.

Bryn had to admit it was not an easy jump. No description could ever do it justice.

Morlâ, once again unable to escape his momentum, ran full speed into the court's wooden fence. He lay there dazed for a few seconds but then stood and ran toward Gwendolin, albeit slower. A few steps before he reached her, he pulled out several heavy wooden discs and hurled them at her.

Gwendolin froze. She managed to avoid the first two, but the third hit her head with a loud *clonk*, and she fell to her knees.

Morlâ increased his pace and reached out to touch his opponent's star. He was only five steps away—then four, three …

Gwendolin felt the blood run down her face and gasped. Opening her arms, she took a deep breath. She and the Harel Star disappeared. Morlâ pulled up as quickly as he could and looked for her. All he saw was a faint flickering sphere where she'd been standing. She had cast a Protection and Invisibility Spell.

Morlâ approached the shimmering bubble, tried to grab it with both hands, and then struck it with his club. But nothing happened. The spell held. As unexpectedly as Gwendolin had disappeared, she became visible again. Morlâ froze; the Harel Star was no longer shining. Their three minutes were up, and Morlâ conceded the game immediately.

"2-0 to Elbendingen. Elbendingen has won the game," announced Master MacKamell.

The arena erupted. Gwendolin lifted the star over her head with both hands.

"El-ben-din-gen! El-ben-din-gen!" thundered hundreds of voices. The Starball court was suddenly covered with flowers.

Morlâ trotted back to his team. He was greeted with a few comforting words, but none of his teammates could hide their disappointment; they'd worked hard all semester for this.

Only Gerald said something encouraging. "It's all right, Morlâ. We can still get to the final." He patted the despondent captain on the shoulder.

"You're right, Master," said the dwarf after taking three deep breaths. "How did the other teams play? Where's Rulu?" When he spotted the twin, he rushed over to him to get the other teams' scores and scribbled down some more notes.

White House's next game was against Ølsgendur. Ûlyėr was up, and the giant orc was working himself into a fervor in front of his opponent—a third-semester dwarf named Akn Olivin. Everyone could see Akn's eyes held the glaze of terror.

Despite his impediment, Ûlyėr made short work of Akn, and Ølsgendur was defeated 2-0. Bryn could not imagine the trembling dwarf playing Starball next season.

What a pity Gerald didn't see this, thought Bryn. But Gerald had just been assigned to referee the match between Řischnǎrr and Bond-of-Faith and was not in the arena. *Hopefully, he will have the chance to see us win.*

Bryn feared Morlâ might nominate him to play next. However, the captain wanted Filixx to play against Bond-of-Faith. The humans had their backs to the wall; they had lost their captain in the first game against Elbendingen and still had no wins. Just like White House, they had to win this game to have a chance of making it to the final.

Morlâ spoke at length to Filixx before the game, and so did Gerald. But all the tactical advice and encouragement seemed to have an unexpected effect. Morlâ won the toss and told referee Master Winterblossom his 'well-upholstered friend Filixx' would be playing. When Morlâ came off the court, he found Filixx ready to start but extremely pale. As Filixx walked to his side of the court, Bryn and the others could see his legs trembling. And his cape was wet with sweat, although the day was quite cool.

"White House, are you ready?" Winterblossom asked in her beautiful voice.

Filixx failed to react at first but nodded his head wildly after Morlâ yelled at him.

"Bond-of-Faith, are you ready?"

"Yes," answered a stocky human with cropped red hair who was in the fifth semester. His name was McFlaherty, and Filixx could not find a trace of fear in his opponent's face.

The Master turned over the hourglass, and the game commenced; Filixx was defending.

As Filixx wiped the sweat from his eyes, a burst of red energy shot from the human student's hand and wrapped itself around Filixx's chest. More blasts followed, and Filixx was soon tied him up like a roll of roast pork. The applause from the audience was deafening but increased when his opponent slowly walked toward the Harel Star. Stepping over Filixx, he bent down and whispered something in his ear. The way Filixx's face changed color told Bryn the words were decidedly unfriendly. McFlaherty touched the star, and immediately, it stopped glowing.

"1-0 to Bond-of-Faith," declared Master Winterblossom. "And should I see or hear such unsporting behavior from you again, McFlaherty, I shall disqualify you. Do we understand each other?"

McFlaherty gave her a cheeky grin and promised he would do better.

Now free from the spell, Filixx got to his feet. Bryn couldn't believe his eyes because a tremendous transformation had taken place in Filixx and a different person seemed to be standing on the court. He fixed his counterpart with an evil stare, all traces of his trembling and trepidation having disappeared.

"Ready for round two?"

It was Filixx's turn to attack, and he immediately began casting spells. First, he placed a Protection Spell around him; second, using a Deception Spell, he created three identical versions of himself; and third, he summoned several rat-like creatures with sharp teeth and sharp-looking claws to attack McFlaherty. Bryn had never seen so many magical spells in so few seconds. His friend was truly gifted!

McFlaherty cast his Bondage Spell once more, but it was ineffective against Filixx's magic. He found himself in a hopeless situation, forced to defend himself from the rat creatures while simultaneously defending the Harel Star from four Filixxes coming from four different directions! Just as McFlaherty leaped to tackle one of the Filixxes coming directly at him, the real Filixx swerved in from behind him and touched Bond-of-Faith's star.

"Point for White House. 1-1. Well summoned, Filixx," Master Winterblossom praised him.

"You can always rely on the big fellow! Now we just have to win the open round," Morlâ said to Bryn and Ûlyèr. "And watch this. You're about to see an old acquaintance," he added mysteriously, as Winterblossom let the third and decisive round begin.

Both glowing Harel Stars had been set up in the arena. The audience was quiet. The fans on both sides knew this round was crucial for their team. Whoever lost now had no chance to be among the first two teams.

But Filixx did something odd and flopped down on his backside in front of the Harel Star, putting his head in his hands. A murmur rippled through the crowd.

McFlaherty took this as a sign of weakness and sprinted toward Filixx. He no longer trusted his magical powers and would rely on his physical prowess instead. With his head down, Filixx could not see how fast McFlaherty was approaching him and the star.

"Filixx," Bryn roared in horror.

Morlâ smiled and patted Bryn's shoulder.

Then a fog began to appear, rising off the court; with tremendous speed, it spread a thick, silvery veil over the entire court.

McFlaherty stopped just before the fog completely rolled in. He could somewhat make out Filixx's outline sitting in front of the Harel Star and started running toward him again. But from the thick, rolling fog that now enveloped both of them came a deep roar that made the arena tremble—a sound only too familiar to Bryn. Seconds later, blood-curdling human screams echoed in the arena.

As the fog cleared, Bryn's suspicions were confirmed. The Farel Lizard was back! And like their first training session, the huge monster was attacking Filixx's opponent without mercy. McFlaherty screamed again, and the beast kept chasing him.

Morlâ grinned. "I told you you'd see a familiar face! An ugly one, admittedly, but effective all the same."

Bryn could see how Ûlyėr clenched his big, clawed hands upon seeing the beast's, a murderous look on his face. But he couldn't worry about that now. Filixx had just got up and started staggering toward the Bond-of-Faith Harel Star. His face was covered in sweat, his eyes were narrowed to slits, and his hands were clenched into fists. Each step seemed difficult for him.

Mastery of the summoned beast demanded his full concentration.

In his peripheral vision, Bryn saw Master Winterblossom jump from her stool. She, too, was agitated and seemed to wrestle with herself about intervening.

But Filixx spared her from having to decide and touched the unprotected star. Immediately, it stopped shining, and the creature vanished into thin air.

If McFlaherty's face was relieved, it was impossible to determine because he had a nasty gash on his leg and was screaming in agony.

"2-1 to White House. The game goes to White House," Winterblossom announced in a fragile voice, wiping the sweat from her brow with her yellow robe sleeve.

"Very good, Filixx. Exactly as we discussed," said Morlâ, greeting the returning hero. "I knew that after the first round, that arrogant human would think he could walk all over you."

"You planned it this way?" asked Bryn, astonished.

"Of course," Morlâ replied, slightly offended. "That's my job."

Rulu then returned to the arena. Morlâ went over to his informant and came back beaming.

"Ølsgendur lost 2-0 to the pointy ears. So Elbendingen won all their games and are now leading with eight points. Ølsgendur and Bond-of-Faith are still playing against each other, but they have no chance of finishing second. Řischnărr and we are now both tied for second place with four points each. Our last game against the orcs will decide which one of us makes the final tomorrow."

At that moment, all eyes turned to Bryn.

The remarkable success of White House and especially the tie between the two teams, which made the game between the bastards and the orcs look like a semi-final, filled the arena almost to bursting. Bryn couldn't believe the number of students streaming in. The team was happy to play here again, as everyone secretly felt arena two brought them luck. Bryn was the only one not happy. There was too much pressure on him.

Even so, he could not see any orcs, or anyone dressed all in black, in the large crowd. Bryn couldn't understand it. *But their team's in this match!* Bryn noticed plenty of elves coming in and looking for somewhere to sit. He watched them laughing and twirling their golden hair. Each of them wore something yellow or blue in support of their fraternity. He noted they all smelled of spring flowers and wondered if it was a clever diversionary tactic. It certainly had a beguiling effect on him.

The Bond-of-Faith members were also present in large numbers, filling the space with red and yellow clothes decorated with images of the ankh. The humans cursed a lot and made fun of one another as they made their way to their seats. Even the dwarves, who came in last and without a single victory, brought their banners. They also ensured that the small snack bar run by some of the students was set up within minutes. All White House students, who had been cheering for their team all day, had also come. Bryn even thought they sang the White House songs a little louder now than in the previous games.

Morlâ also noticed the absence of the Řischnărr fans.

"No orcs among the spectators?" he asked the group. "What is going on? Ûlyėr, do you have any idea?"

Ûlyėr gave an unfriendly grunt, which probably meant he also had no idea.

"Strange," said Filixx, agreeing with his captain. "Who knows what tricks they've cooked up." Then he shook his head slightly and turned to Bryn, smiling. "It doesn't matter, though, does it? It's nothing our Realm Shadow can't handle."

Ûlyėr started to say something when Filixx mentioned the orcs' name for Bryn, but the arrival of the Řischnărr Starball team interrupted him. Bryn was deeply unhappy, and his stomach was churning.

The entire team, consisting of five players, and Ñokelä ran in military formation toward the referee, Master Underhil, with their black capes fluttering behind them. Underhil flinched when he saw the tall, muscle-bound delegation of orcs running toward him. Only after the team bowed to him did he seem to relax.

Bryn could see, however, that this changed immediately when Ñokelä, with his fearsome appearance, bent down to talk to him.

After a brief conversation, Underhil shook his head, at which point the orc's House Master bared his fangs and gestured wildly with his arms.

"Then let Tejal decide," they heard the orc Master say, his voice rising.

Underhil grabbed his larynx and talked as if to himself.

Shortly afterward, Tejal appeared with a tense look on her face and rushed toward the small group at center court.

A murmur went through the audience. Then it became unusually quiet. Everyone could clearly understand there was a dispute between the Masters.

"Every student of Âlaburg is allowed to take part in the games," the Chancellor told Ñokelä, loud enough to be overheard.

"But not this abomination of magic." Ñokelä pointed at Bryn, whose face turned red. "I cannot expose my students to such danger," the orc Master continued.

"But he is the only one who hasn't played yet," Underhil intervened. "According to the rules, he must play. White House only has four players. They have no other choice."

"You're right, Master," said Tejal. "Ñokelä, you know the rules as well as I do. This is the way Starball has been played for centuries. When a team brings a player onto the field who has already played, the Justice Spell prevents them from touching either their star or their opponent's, so they can't win."

"Then you must change the spell!" Ñokelä cried. "None of my people can be expected to fight such a magical freak."

Tejal's gaze hardened. "Bryn is a student of Âlaburg; the Lekan Gate found him worthy. It's not for you to be their judge, Master."

"But—" the orc started, but Tejal cut him off.

"As the university Chancellor and, therefore, the referee with the highest authority, I determine Bryn McDermit to be a legitimate player. And since he is the only one from White House to not have played today, he will play now! Who on your team will play against him, Master Ñokelä?"

Ñokelä snarled at Bryn, expression twisted with hatred. "Nobody!"

Tejal brought her hand up to her larynx, looking at Ñokelä and then Bryn.

"2-0 for White House." Her voice shattered the silence in the arena. "Tomorrow's final between Elbendingen and White House starts at four o'clock. In such exceptional circumstances, tomorrow, the fifth person from each team must play—or the fourth."

Tejal looked over at Bryn and his team. The stunned crowd of students then watched her leave the arena, her cloak billowing behind her.

THE FINAL

Bryn threw up in the sink again.

"Take it easy, son," said Gerald, patting his back.

The enormous pressure on Bryn and all the excitement were taking their toll. Bryn nodded and tried to focus on something other than the awful taste in his mouth.

"Feeling any better?"

His stomach did feel calmer, but that was probably because there was nothing left to come out of it.

"Get yourself cleaned up, and I'll see you in the common room."

Bryn lifted his head and caught sight of himself in the mirror. His eyes were bloodshot, his skin yellowish and pale, and a bead of sweat was running down his forehead. Anyone might have assumed—and reasonably—that he was seriously ill. But Bryn knew otherwise. Tejal's decision yesterday had taken the pressure off the rest of the team but not him. Bryn was sick from worrying about this afternoon's game.

After their win yesterday, the supporters from White House and, much to Bryn's surprise, many humans and dwarves had formed a crowd and cheered the team to the tower. Everyone knew making the final was White House's most outstanding achievement to date.

Even so, Bryn knew that not winning the title would be an unmitigated disappointment.

Bryn also thought about Morlâ, Filixx, and Gerald. They had all spoken to him at length on the way back and assured him no one would be angry if he did not win. But they never forgot to add what it would mean for the despised bastard house to win the Starball title. Bryn wanted this victory too. Everyone who had looked down on him and his friends, the pure and the perfect, the ones with a family, a home, and a nation and fraternity that wanted them—Bryn wanted to show them all.

Bryn also wanted the victory for himself. He wanted to make history. He wanted to be among the first from White House to win the title.

Bryn shuffled into the common room and found the whole team waiting for him.

"Bryn!" Morlâ cried. "You're looking so much better!"

Bryn acknowledged his captain and lowered himself into an armchair. "Thanks."

"Bryn …?" Bryn frowned and looked over to see Filixx standing near the door, the Harel Star in his hand. "We have to leave immediately … you spent quite a while in the bathroom—otherwise, we'll lose because we're late."

With his other hand, Filixx brought out a snow-white cape from behind his back and gave it to Bryn.

"I ironed it myself."

Bryn realized it was late when he saw that the castle courtyard was empty. A few students still roamed around, but most of them had gone to the stadium.

My friends were waiting for me! It warmed Bryn's heart. His teammates had given him time to collect himself, and moreover, nobody had put him under pressure—not even Ûlyėr. He couldn't disappoint them now. Bryn started walking faster to get the air into his lungs. Although he still had a sour taste in his mouth, his courage was returning. Whatever happened, he knew his friends would remain his friends. And that was the most important thing.

The small delegation rounded the last bend before the stadium.

"Well, look who we have here," came a deep, halting voice. "It looks like a pack of cheats."

Kuelnk was standing in their path, along with Pyzu and two other enormous orcs Bryn had not seen before.

"What do you want?" Morlâ growled, reaching under his cape to ensure his club was still there.

"What do we want?" Kuelnk sneered while the others laughed. "We want our team in the final. Not a team of cheats and bastards. Řischnărr would have swept you away if we had entered."

"But you didn't," snapped Filixx.

Pyzu glared at him, and the other two flexed their muscles; then, like a pack of wolves, they began to circle the boys.

"It wasn't our decision, Kuelnk," said Morlâ, trying to placate them. But it fell on deaf ears. "It is what it is."

"No, dwarf. None of you are going to the game—especially not this freak. That will be how it is," said Kuelnk, pointing his claw at Bryn.

At that moment, a huge claw landed on Bryn's chest, startling him. It gently pushed him back. It was Ûlyėr, maneuvering himself between Bryn and Kuelnk.

Ûlyėr straightened up and took another step forward. For the first time, his teammates could see he was much taller than the other orcs facing them. And, somehow, he seemed even more threatening than usual.

"Nobody touches Bryn!" roared Ûlyėr at a volume Bryn thought impossible for even an orc. Ûlyėr crouched into an attack position, claws clenched, and bared his huge yellow fangs.

Bryn's eyes widened. After their lousy start that first day of training, he'd assumed Ûlyėr would remain hostile toward him forever. Yet, since then, all Ûlyėr had shown Bryn was a complete lack of interest. He would never have expected Ûlyėr to defend him!

"Stay out of this, Stinky," Kuelnk spat. Ûlyėr did not react, staring steadily at Kuelnk like a hunter readying for the kill. "You can't interfere here because you don't exist. You're dead to us, Ûlyėr. And Řälärm will never accept you into our fraternity. Even as I speak, it's like I'm talking to myself!"

The other Řischnärr students roared with laughter.

Before the situation could escalate, they heard Master Tieffenor's raucous laughter. He had turned the corner with Gerald. Immediately, the four orcs ran off and disappeared into the commotion in front of the stadium.

Without delay, the team also made for the stadium. And when they appeared in the arena, a thunderous applause rose from the crowd. Most of the students seemed to be there for the otherwise unpopular bastard house. However, the elf supporters, all dressed in yellow and blue, did not join in. Instead, they showered the spectators with beautiful, scented flowers.

"I think that's their way of booing us," Bryn quipped.

The only one Bryn could see in black was Master Ñokelä; the other orcs were boycotting the game. In solidarity, Ñokelä refused to sit with the Chancellor in the official stand, but that didn't seem to dampen the atmosphere.

Jehal was refereeing the game and called the captains to the court to nominate the players. This was a farce as everyone knew who was going to be playing.

"Representing Elbendingen," announced Gwendolin, "is Mahir Cedarseed."

She was a young elf from the second semester and the fifth member of their team. For White House, Morlâ nominated Bryn.

With his teammates' words of encouragement in his ears and the Harel Star in his hand, Bryn walked into the court. Only now, as he positioned himself on the left side of the court, did he notice how heavy the star was.

An unusual calm came over Bryn now that the game was about to start. He had blocked out the cheers and noise from the crowd to such a degree that he hardly noticed his opponent.

"Are you both ready?" Jehal's harsh tone tore Bryn from his daydream. Without waiting for the players' answers, Jehal turned the hourglass over. The finale had begun.

The slim elf stood there, not moving. Mahir closed her eyes and mumbled something. *She's summoning some beast*, Bryn thought. His panic rushed back. His heart was pounding, and his blood pulsed in his throat.

What can I do? The elf still had her eyes closed and was reciting some verse. *It's probably some huge, elvish beast that'll tear me to pieces.* Bryn tried desperately to enter the realm, but it was no good.

For the spectators, two players standing around not doing much was boring. They had been looking forward to a gripping and eventful finale. Bryn could hear the first boos.

I can't listen to this. I must concentrate!

His left foot suddenly sank into the wooden surface of the court. *How is that possible?* It destroyed his concentration, and the realm closed to him. Then his right foot also sank. *What is going on here?*

Bryn turned to the Harel Star, relieved to see it still standing there, radiating light. Then Bryn sank down to his waist.

The ground beneath him gave way further, leaving only his head above the surface of the court. *So this is her spell!* Being swallowed by the Starball court must have made a grotesque sight. Dread overwhelmed Bryn. Moving his limbs or breathing was becoming more and more difficult. Enormous pressure was building up around his body; he began to panic. Until now, he hadn't realized he was claustrophobic! Freeing himself from this spell was all that mattered now. He thrashed about as best he could and twisted and turned his head, but nothing helped.

Bryn let out a spine-chilling scream.

"1-0 to Elbendingen," cried Jehal. "Well done, Cedarseed. I had no idea you were so good at using the Hypnosis Spell." He didn't bother to look at Bryn but yelled in his direction, "You can stop squirming, McDermit. No one hurt you—or should I say, no one ever hurt you," he snickered, much to the audience's delight.

Bryn realized he'd only been lying next to the extinguished Harel Star, thrashing and screaming, *believing* the ground was swallowing him. Now he wanted the ground to open up and swallow him. If he could have quit the university then and there, he would have. Bryn stood up and tried to ignore the mockery and laughter from the crowd.

"Concentrate," Morlâ whispered to him. He grabbed the Harel Star and ran back through the gap in the perimeter fence.

Easier said than done, thought Bryn, feeling even more depressed. But Jehal didn't give him a second to think. Without waiting for Bryn to signal he was ready, Jehal turned the great hourglass over again. Bryn had three minutes to touch Elbendingen's star. He attempted to enter the realm one more time and failed. He quickly realized that to have a chance of winning, he had to rely on himself and not magic. The timer continued to run down mercilessly; a third of the sand had gone through already.

Mahir seemed utterly calm and composed, and Bryn's thoughts became more fraught. While he straightened his cape and regained his footing, she shot a spell at him so quickly that Bryn only avoided it by diving desperately into the air. Then she retreated to her position in front of her shining Harel Star, her tactic effectively keeping Bryn at a distance.

Bryn thrust his hands into his trouser pockets, as he always did when thinking. A glance at the hourglass told him more than half the time had already passed. He had to do something, or he would lose the final. He found something hard and round in his pocket—a hazelnut. Last night, Gerald had talked him into eating some for the game because they were energizing. He had one left over and took it out.

It reminds me of Drena. The thought of her reawakened Bryn's fighting spirit. *I must touch the Harel Star any way I can.*

Once again, he looked at the little nut. Bending down, he picked up a splinter from the hole the star had made in the court. Pricking his finger with it, he covered the hazelnut in a thin layer of blood. With fifteen seconds left, the stadium had turned into a frenzy of yellow and blue.

Bryn ran toward the elf; again, she unleashed a spell on him, which he managed to avoid. He feigned left, and the second flash of angry yellow energy hit the floor next to him, leaving a black, smoking hole. Now he was ten steps from the star, and the last grains of sand were in the timer's neck.

Knowing he had only one shot, Bryn aimed. Just as he did, a charge of energy came straight at him. Time seemed to still. The shimmering golden spell crawled toward him. Bryn knew it would hit him. Closing his hand around his little projectile, he squeezed his eyes shut and threw it with all his might.

The elf's spell hit Bryn and hurled him several yards through the air. He landed hard on his back, winded and with a painful burning sensation in his chest.

I didn't make it was all that flashed through his mind.

But Morlâ, Filixx, and Ûlyėr were in each other's arms, screaming with joy.

Bryn sat up and saw that Elbendingen's Harel Star had gone out.

Jehal examined the hourglass and kicked it. But the spell that stopped it precisely when the star was touched had left some grains of sand in the neck of the clock.

"1-1," said Jehal, "though more than likely the result of foul play."

Gwendolin yelled at Bryn, "How much more cheating are we going to see from you in this tournament?"

But the rules were clear. A player had to touch the opposition's star. Which part of the player touched it did not matter—even if it was only a drop of blood.

Bryn would have liked to go over to his teammates, but he still had to survive the decisive open round.

Gwendolin brought out Elbendingen's star and sent Bryn a look far fouler than he would have expected from such a pretty face. Now both Harel Stars were on the court.

"Are you ready?" Jehal asked.

Both players nodded, not taking their eyes off each other. It was now down to the two of them. No timer, no excuses, and no mistakes that could be corrected. The decisive game for the Spring Championship was about to begin.

Bryn watched Mahir start to put a Coat of Protection Spell around herself—like MacRallen had in that memorable lesson.

But she needed several attempts to do it. Bryn tried, without much hope of success, to enter the realm. But almost immediately, he began to feel the familiar tingling in his right hand, and on its back, the black circle appeared. His senses sharpened abruptly, and the world filled with flickering bright colors.

Bryn could see that Mahir had also entered the realm. Yellow streams of energy were flowing toward her, swirling playfully around her slim frame. Her Coat of Protection Spell was almost finished. Bryn had to hurry so she didn't attack him first. He could well do without another encounter with one of her spells.

Bryn also began to spin a Coat of Protection Spell around himself—and not a second too late.

The first golden flashes of energy hit his protective sphere. For a moment, he felt he was looking through water. As Bryn struggled to see, the elf ran across the court to touch the White House star. Only at the last moment did Bryn notice this and remedy his mistake by including the star in his Coat of Protection Spell.

Mahir tried to break through the translucent sphere, but it was impossible. But Bryn was also growing weaker from her magical and physical attacks. Simple perseverance would not be enough to win, not with unlimited time. He had to attack her.

It was slow and challenging, but Bryn dragged himself and the star toward the elf's unprotected star. Like Bryn, Mahir now quickly put her star within her Coat of Protection Spell. But it weighed her down, restricting her movements.

Bryn also found walking extremely difficult. Again and again, he had to stop and take a deep breath, but this exposed him to Mahir's attacks as she circled him.

To Mahir, it seemed Bryn was tiring, so she summoned a flock of small birds to hack at his protective sphere with their sharp, tiny beaks.

Bryn began to sweat; he would not be able to keep his spell working much longer. A bird penetrated the sphere but vanished instantly once inside, deprived of Mahir's magic. Bryn knew time was running out, and his opponent's Harel Star was still several yards away. Mahir was showing no such sign of fatigue. Bryn realized he had to change tactics again.

A sudden and powerful bolt of energy struck Bryn and lifted him off his feet. His Coat of Protection Spell evaporated, and he was back in the real world, leaving him and the star unprotected. Again, he heard the roar of the crowd. The elves leaped from their seats and screamed and cheered their player, while the faces of White House's supporters filled with horror and disbelief.

The elf, engulfed in her Coat of Protection Spell, slowly but steadily made her way toward Bryn and the White House star. *How do I stop her now?* Bryn did the only thing he could think of. He picked himself up as fast as his aching muscles would allow, grabbed the Harel Star, and ran. The Elbendingen supporters mocked him, calling him a coward. But at that moment, he didn't know what else to do.

Mahir was not impressed. She changed direction and moved faster toward Bryn, firing bolts of yellow energy at him that he just barely dodged.

I have to go back to the realm. I don't stand a chance out here! He had never been able to dive into the magical world under duress, but this was his only chance. And, to his immense surprise, he succeeded. But there was a price—he was too weak to hold on to the Harel Star. It lay at his feet. But being in the realm, he could see the yellow bands of energy surrounding Mahir as she ran toward him. One band broke away from her and shot straight at Bryn. Bryn threw his arms in front of his face—a blind reflex. Helplessly, he braced for the impact and closed his eyes.

But nothing happened. When Bryn opened his eyes, he realized his arms' sudden movement had created a multi-colored band of energy that wrapped around his hands and forearms and then separated again and split into red, blue, and yellow. Somehow, he had succeeded in stopping Mahir's magic.

But how?

Mahir fired another charge at him.

Bryn raised his arms once more, but this time he concentrated on what was happening. Bryn could sense his movements more than see them as he pulled more and more of the colored bands toward him—first, the blue and then the red, but he was having difficulty attracting the yellow. It felt like pulling sticky resin from trees. However, Mahir's next bolt of yellow energy immediately wove itself into the other two colors, creating an even thicker, multi-colored strand without harming Bryn at all. By connecting the blue and red bands of energy, Bryn had neutralized the elf's dangerous yellow energy.

But Bryn had no time to think before Mahir changed tactics. As Bryn had no protection at the moment, she tried to attack him physically. He made the split-second decision to grab the yellow energy streaming from Mahir, as if he were reeling in a thick, heavy rope. The energy seemed to attach itself to his hands. Immediately, he realized he was drawing energy not from the realm but from Mahir herself!

Mahir's eyes rolled up, and her face filled with fear. She couldn't understand what was happening. She felt ill, and her body started convulsing. Her beautiful features twisted into an expression of pure horror.

But Bryn kept drawing more and more of her energy. All the colors of the realm obeyed him and him alone.

Mahir fell to her knees. Around her, Bryn could see only a faint, flickering yellowish light.

He kept going.

She let out an agonizing scream. Only then did Bryn recognize the fear in her eyes.

As she collapsed, her head hit the court's wooden surface, and the sound sent a shiver through the crowd.

Bryn heard it too, but he had an overwhelming desire to continue. The game, the victory, and even the girl did not matter to him. Power flooded through him, and it was intoxicating. He had never felt more alive.

But her scream began to haunt him. He knew that if he drew any more energy from her, he would drain her life and kill her. He struggled with himself to look at her unconscious body.

Suddenly, he remembered what Gerald had always taught him. Life was precious and worth protecting. He finally looked at the girl lying near him and flung his arms open, and all the energy he'd been holding spun away from him. The colorful braid dissolved, and yellow streams of energy began to flow back toward the motionless elf.

Bryn withdrew from the realm, and the mark on his right hand vanished. With his mind clearer, he ran over and kneeled next to Mahir. Even though he couldn't see it now, the energy continued to flow back into her body.

"Mahir? Mahir! Wake up," Bryn pleaded. "Did I hurt you?"

I almost—but Bryn didn't dare finish that thought.

Mahir didn't answer.

Bryn lifted her gently and held her.

As he did, the young elf's bright blue eyes flew open, and she gasped for air as if she were drowning. She looked at him, trying to focus, but Bryn had to turn away. She lifted her hand and brought his face around to hers.

In a frail voice, she said, "I don't know what you've done, Bryn, but you've beaten me. I know that much. Go and get your prize. You've earned it." And with that, Mahir's eyes closed, and she lapsed back into unconsciousness.

Bryn didn't know what to do. The spectators were shouting all sorts of things. Morlâ was beside himself. Most of the Masters were up on their feet, yelling at him. But none of them realized what Bryn had done. He lay Mahir down on her side, smoothed her hair, and got to his feet. Slowly, his head bowed, he walked over to Elbendingen's unprotected Harel Star and touched it.

The arena erupted into sheer chaos.

Jehal appeared unable to speak and call the win—or refused to—until he saw Tejal's stern look.

"2-1 to White House. The winner of this year's Spring Tournament is White House."

EVERYONE HAS THEIR DEMONS

Wild cheers broke out in the stadium as Morlâ, the White House captain, received the winner's trophy from Chancellor Tejal. He lifted the particularly ugly, chunky silver-handled pot into the air with his short arms and held it over his head. The students of White House, Bond-of-Faith, and Ølsgendur burst into thunderous applause. All the elves had left the stadium, insulting Bryn and White House. So out of five houses, only three were present when the winners of the Spring Tournament were honored.

Frowning, Bryn mused on how the student body of Âlaburg was deeply divided; it was not simply a matter of his victory. There must be some complex reason why the fraternities had drifted apart so much. If these hostilities escalated one day, they would endanger the founding idea of the university—securing peace in Razuclan.

"Don't make such a face," Filixx shouted at him, drunk with joy, shaking Bryn out of his heavy thoughts.

Then Filixx pushed him forward and onto the stand, which had served as a VIP box for the Masters until a moment ago. The celebrating crowd chanted Bryn's name loudly. Happily, he lifted the cup into the air. His dream had come true, and he had to admit that the cheering and attention felt good. His insecurity vanished, and arm in arm with Morlâ, Ûlyèr, and Filixx, he celebrated their victory.

At the end of the ceremony, they even performed some improvised dwarf dance, swinging their legs high in the air. The audience was thrilled.

The party continued in the cellar of the defense tower well into the evening with no end in sight. Bryn had never seen Gerald so happy and relaxed. The former hunting master was going around slapping shoulders and congratulating all the students; he even joined in the cheers when Morlâ and his teammates were carried around on the other students' shoulders.

At one point, the students joined forces and even lifted Ûlyèr up. And it spoke to his good mood that he did not tear anyone's head off when they dropped him. Later, Morlâ and Filixx recounted the best moves from the game, accompanied by expert commentary from the others. Afterward, they hugged everyone they could get their hands on.

The only one no longer in the mood to celebrate was Bryn. The hero of the final sat alone in the far corner of the common room. He stared into a glass of raspberry juice Filixx had brought him. Occasionally, he took a bite from the piece of roast beef in his hand, dripping thick, brown gravy on his cape. The potato casserole, freshly-baked bread, roast loin of pork, and pan-fried liver all piled up on silver platters on the table in front of him held little interest. Filixx also set out an assortment of elvish chocolate treats, which Bryn had yet to try. Hela came over and inspected Filixx's chocolate-coated pickled pears, candied red apples, and honey-coated blueberries on sweetened cream. She gave Bryn a smile. He just nodded, and she grabbed another piece of cream cake and retreated back to her friends.

"You're spoiling the party for everyone," said Gerald, dropping into the chair next to Bryn. "What's wrong? You've done great things today and should be proud of yourself!"

Bryn took a gulp of the juice.

Gerald knew the boy all too well. "Is it because of how you defeated the elf girl?"

Bryn almost dropped his glass. "How do you know that?"

Now it was Gerald's turn to take his time. He stared at the food in front of them for a suspiciously long time and decided on one of the chocolate pears. Once he had eaten it and licked each one of his fingers, he turned to Bryn and lowered his voice. "Well, where should I start? As you may have noticed, I don't do magic."

Bryn nodded. He sensed Gerald was about to reveal something he'd been keeping secret from him—something that had somehow always stood between them.

"I do not use magic but not because I cannot. I almost wish it were so," Gerald continued in a low voice. "The opposite is true. In my time as a student and member of Bond-of-Faith, I was considered a gifted magician. By the way, I was the fifth man in my second semester here, and I was in the finals as well." He put his hand on Bryn's shoulder, smiling. "But we lost 2-1 to Řischnărr. I got my first university mission early on and proved myself. The years went by. I became Gerald McDermit, a member of the Driany Order and even a Master here at Âlaburg. I was a Peace Keeper." Gerald snorted in amusement. "Anyway, wherever there was trouble between the nations of Razuclan or reports of raids by the Vonnyens …"

The mere mention of those creatures gave Bryn goosebumps.

"… me and my little band of men would be sent out. We had quickly earned a reputation for solving any kind of problem. And so we were on the road for most of the year. The Order sent us from one source of trouble to another. During this time, I spent so many miles on horseback and soon began to think I'd been to every corner of the continent. We crossed between the four territories regularly and were well received and respected by orcs, elves, dwarves, and humans alike. At that time, the Order was highly revered; the devastation of the last great war was still fresh in the minds of the people of Razuclan. We promised a degree of stability and hope for a peaceful, normal life."

Bryn watched Gerald's gaze drift away as he stared into the fire.

"On one of these missions, I found a little girl in the cellar of a burnt-out inn in the extreme north of the territory held by the humans. A bunch of marauding Vonnyens had raided it. She was the only survivor, sitting in the dark crying and terrified, her face covered with ash from the fire. All she had with her was a rag doll. I still remember thinking her eyes lit up when she saw me. But it was just the whites of her eyes—the only thing not covered in ash. Since all the other people in the inn were dead, we assumed that the girl's parents must have been among them. The child was so frightened, she could not speak.

"After we secured the area, we went to the next village to find someone to take her in. Easier said than done. The war had hit the people there hard, and they could hardly make ends meet. Their harvests had been utterly destroyed, and the winter had been long and severe that year. All the villagers regretted the girl's fate, but they also made it clear to us that they could not afford an extra mouth to feed over the winter. We discussed what to do with her.

"A solution to our problem arose sort of by chance. Jack O'Kelly, one of my companions, tried to light a fire in one of the ruins in the village during a blizzard one evening. That was when he realized the girl had the gift. When she brushed her fingers over the dry kindling, a crackling little yellow flame flared up. She must have done it to help us. She would reach out to the wood in the fireplace, and it would ignite. It seemed as if the girl used magic as a matter of course—and not for the first time. She hadn't spoken to us until that day. So I tested her. It was proven beyond doubt that she was gifted. We decided to take her to the castle. I believed she could be a strong magician, and I was not mistaken ..."

Gerald sighed and poured himself a large glass of raspberry juice. Bryn was sure his foster father would have preferred something stronger.

The bustle in the common room had subsided, and the dinner table was now almost empty. Bryn and Gerald were alone except for a couple snuggling in the corner, looking like they'd just found each other. Gerald put a log on the fire, drank his juice, and wiped his thick, black beard with the back of his hand.

"After a few weeks, we finally reached the university. Caoimhe—that was the girl's name—had begun to speak and was let in by the Lekan Gate. The then Chancellor, Grand Master Jaspis, tested her. Only after great discussion was she finally admitted. Caoimhe was only fourteen at the time. She was also assigned to White House since her test results were not clear, just like yours. The villagers told us the innkeeper, in whose cellar we found her, had no children. Her parents may have been travelers abducted by the Vonnyens. I never found out—which, in retrospect, was perhaps a good thing."

Gerald studied his glass of juice and swished the liquid around. He sighed again and looked at Bryn for a long time.

"Caoimhe made great progress in her first few years here at Âlaburg. She was one of the best students to attend this university and achieved excellence in all Seven Wisdoms. But one thing made it difficult—she had no friends or could not have any. She was extremely quick-tempered and also arrogant. I never found out if it was because she was afraid of rejection. She showed everyone, at every opportunity, how much more talented she was. It was one reason why the other students refused to associate with her. There were some unpleasant incidents between her and students of the other fraternities. She had especially fallen out with the orcs and dwarves, but her enormous talent protected her from greater harm. But …"

Gerald took a deep breath. "That did not protect others from her! One evening, outside the dining room, she got into a dispute with a group of dwarves—two boys and a girl. The argument became heated, and Caoimhe began to attack them with magic. Initially, the three of them fended off her attacks quite successfully. It was only one versus three. But then, as the eyewitnesses testified, one by one, they became unconscious and fell."

Bryn felt as if someone had thrown a bucket of ice-cold water in his face.

Gerald saw Bryn's face and nodded.

"Finally, when all three had stopped moving, the others ran for the Masters. They were afraid of Caoimhe. But for one of the dwarves, it was too late. Melkin Carnelian, a second-semester student, was already dead. The other two would not have survived Caoimhe's wrath either if Jehal and Tejal had not overwhelmed the girl with a massive counter spell. I was also there. Later, Tejal admitted they could never have defeated the girl without my help."

"What did Caoimhe do?" Bryn asked.

"She drained the poor boy of his magical energy, and, as a result, he died."

When Bryn heard those words, the room began to spin, and he slumped sideways in his chair.

"Bryn? Bryn?"

Gerald's deep voice slowly brought him back to his senses. Bryn opened his eyes. Gerald held Bryn's head in his two huge hands and helped him sit up.

"I should have told you this story after your test in Tejal's office, but I didn't dare. I'm sorry. But I know I wasn't wrong about you. You're in control of your talent. The rush of power does not leave you numb to those around you. Cedarseed is alive because you can control yourself."

Gerald grabbed the boy and hugged him. Bryn let himself fall into the embrace. But one thought rang in his head: *Can I control myself next time?*

"What happened to Caoimhe?"

"She was banished forever from Âlaburg and was to be put under a spell to prevent her from using magic again. This is the worst punishment the Order can impose. But before the spell could be cast, she disappeared in the night. To this day, no one can explain how she breached the gate or the walls. I have never seen Caoimhe again, nor have I cast another spell."

"Why?"

"Why did I stop using magic?"

Bryn nodded.

"Well ..." Gerald let out a shuddering exhale. "I was expelled from the Order because I had brought discredit upon the magical world. Caoimhe's presence in Âlaburg, which came about because of my initial test, eventually led to a gifted man's death. And this is one of the worst transgressions a member of the Order can commit. Of course, I was only indirectly involved. The Council judged this in my favor, together with everything I had done for the Order and for peace on Razuclan. That is why my magical abilities were not taken from me. But I had to swear not to use them until I had rectified my mistake."

"How can you do that?"

Gerald looked deep into Bryn's eyes. "My task was to find an exceptionally gifted person who will commit to serve the peace of Razuclan like no one before them."

FILIXX'S MISSION

In the weeks after the final, the dwarves and humans treated Bryn like a student from a real fraternity. The elves and orcs, however, openly despised him, which made classes with them torture. Bryn also sensed students were smiling at him a lot more, but he didn't know how to respond to them. He also thought a lot about Drena.

Master Jehal continued to be hostile toward him. But after what Gerald had told him about Caoimhe, Bryn understood that Jehal was afraid of him.

Jehal wasn't the only one. Bryn was afraid of himself! Rarely now did he enter the realm, although it got easier and easier. Bryn still feared unintentionally hurting someone because he lacked perfect control over his powers. Only in Tejal's Friday afternoon lessons did he feel safe enough to use magic, and these classes were improving his abilities enormously.

Bryn's relationship with Tejal also improved considerably. She was glad Gerald had finally told him the truth, although she never said so openly. There must have been an agreement among the Masters, which was why Tejal had not told Bryn of Caoimhe herself. Even Jehal had kept quiet, which made Bryn all the more aware of the importance of those past events.

The next day, Bryn recounted Gerald's story to Morlâ and Filixx; in fact, Gerald had encouraged him to do it. And when Bryn finally got an appointment to see the Five Wise Ones, which seemed to have been expedited due to his victory in the final of the Starball tournament, they were able to add something to Gerald's story.

They knew that Caoimhe was never known as a Seer of Colors. To those who saw them, her spells always appeared red. Bryn had assumed Toulin, Houlin, Kaneg, Worin, and Lebos wouldn't know much about seeing colors since the Grand Masters had emphasized it was a great secret. But the Five Wise Ones seemed to find nothing unusual about Bryn's unique magical ability and made no secret of their findings. They assured Bryn what they knew would never leave their circle without his permission.

They also knew Caoimhe had quite a few friends at the university, something which had escaped the Masters' notice. Credible statements from former students would prove, according to Toulin, that a secretive community had gathered around the talented girl, one that most likely shared her hatred of dwarves and orcs. The clandestine group was unusual because it included both humans and elves—a rare case of cooperation between the fraternities but one with malicious intentions. Kaneg was convinced, however, that this loosely knit group had stopped meeting soon after Caoimhe's disappearance.

On a Wednesday evening, Bryn was sitting with Morlâ, who was tutoring him in Math. He was hoping Morlâ would do his homework for him, which he had to hand in the next morning. Rondo, the Gnarf worm that now lived with them in a small wooden box, watched the two friends and chewed happily on a piece of granite, which he particularly liked to eat.

Suddenly, Filixx raced in, sweaty and out of breath, without knocking.

"It's time!" he roared excitedly, waving around a wrinkled envelope. "At last! And in the third semester! I still can't believe it."

"Steady there, big boy," said Morlâ. "Calm down, calm down. You nearly scared us both to death. What happened? You're now officially allowed to eat twice as much dessert as everyone else?" He grinned at Bryn, who winked back.

"What are you talking about?" Filixx asked.

Bryn and Morlâ burst out laughing.

Filixx wasn't sure whether to be offended or join in. Fortunately, he decided on the latter. "No, little man. It's much better!"

Now he had their attention.

"Now, stop teasing us," Morlâ demanded, "and tell us what you've got there."

Bryn recognized the seal of Âlaburg—the dove with the snake in its claws—on Filixx's crumpled envelope, but the red wax was glowing. Unlike his letter from Tejal, he could also make out a circular inscription under the seal: *PEACE AND FRIENDSHIP*.

"All right," said Filixx excitedly. "I didn't want to open the letter by myself, so I came here as soon as I could."

Physical activity was something Filixx liked to avoid, but he must have hurried to them because his clothes were drenched in sweat.

"What's so special about this letter?" Bryn asked. "I recognize the seal, but—"

"Yes, the seal—because the Chancellor just gave it to me." But Filixx could not get any more words out and had to swallow hard and take a deep breath. "The university … the university has given me …"

"Filixx!" yelled Morlâ.

"The university has given me my first mission!"

Bryn's jaw dropped, and Morlâ's eyes popped open. A mission! It was the most incredible honor a student could receive. Only a few of the best students were chosen every semester to help the Driany Order maintain the peace. Those selected would then pick a small group of fellow students to accompany them. Their mission could take them into any of the four nations of Razuclan—the evergreen forests of the elves, the ice deserts of the orcs, the high mountains and deep mines of the dwarves, or the human territory, which, of course, Bryn knew only too well.

Filixx stared at his friends' expressions. "I thought you'd be more pleased," he said, hesitating for a moment before saying anything more. "I was thinking … of taking both of you, you know, with me."

Bryn and Morlâ realized what Filixx's news meant. They would leave the university and go on an adventure together. The boys broke out in cheers, throwing themselves at Filixx to hug and congratulate him.

Once they calmed down, Morlâ tried to put his arm on Filixx's shoulder. "There, you see, my big one. All your studying, the sucking up to the Masters, and those extra chores have finally paid off."

Filixx and Bryn laughed. But Bryn had an important question. "Where are you—I mean, where are we being sent?"

Filixx slipped his thumb under the flap of the envelope to break the wax. As he did, the small, silver swirl of protective magic in the seal was released. He read the letter to the others.

To:
Mr. Filixx Streelman Renläer
Âlaburg University of Peace and Friendship
White House

Room three

Dear Mr. Renläer,

We are pleased to inform you that, based on your outstanding achievements over the last two semesters, you have been chosen to support the honorable Knights of the Driany Order in a peace-keeping mission.

To ensure that you bring this assignment to a successful conclusion, you are now obliged to choose three fellow students to support and accompany you. The selected students will be released from their regular classes for the duration of the mission, but, just like yourself, they will be graded at its conclusion. These grades will make up fifty percent of your final marks in all subjects for the current semester.

At this point, Filixx stopped reading and grinned at his friends. "So two of the three positions I could fill right now, if you're both …?"

"Yes!" Morlâ and Bryn shouted together.

"Well, that's settled then!" Filixx said happily. "But who else should we take? Should we take a girl?"

For a moment, there was silence. All three began to talk at once, but one name kept coming up again and again—Ûlyėr.

"Alright," Filixx said as they slowly calmed down. "So the dream team is reunited. Let me just head over to number four and ask Ûlyėr!"

Filixx grabbed the letter and rushed out.

"Do you think this is a good idea?" Morlâ asked. "Ûlyėr hasn't been too unfriendly since the tournament, so …"

"So you feel he would be a good fit, that it's a wise choice to take him on such a mission," said Bryn, finishing Morlâ's sentence.

"Yes!

"Well, he's the best candidate, I think," said Bryn. "Filixx does too. So I think it's a good idea."

In the next moment, the door opened. Filixx came back to the room, and Ûlyėr followed after him, bending down to avoid the door frame.

"Ûlyėr wants to hear about the mission first and then decide," said Filixx. He sat down on Morlâ's bed, smoothed out the letter, and read on.

Ûlyėr didn't say a word but stood near the door, his colossal frame casting a long shadow over the others.

So choose your group wisely, Filixx. Your companions, like yourself, should all be exceptionally talented if your mission is to succeed.

Destination:

Your mission will take you into human territory. Be aware that many humans reject the idea of magic even though it is integral to Razuclan.

Therefore, be cautious using it around them, and keep the marks on your hands hidden.

Your destination is a small village in the shadow of the Arell Mountains called Sefal.

Bryn felt as if someone had punched him in the stomach. His friends noticed his reaction and tried to comfort him.

"Don't worry, Bryn," said Morlâ. "We don't know what's going on there yet. If they're sending students, it can't be too bad, can it?"

Bryn nodded silently, but the worry and fear for all the people who lived there and whom he had known all his life still weighed heavily on his mind.

"Read on," he told Filixx in a scratchy voice.

Filixx cleared his throat.

Reports have been coming in for some time that wild animal attacks have been increasing in the woods near there. Groups of traveling merchants have also been attacked and disappeared without a trace.

An image of Drena popped into Bryn's mind, and his heart lurched in his chest. He began to tremble, thinking Drena might have been in one of these groups.

Go to Sefal and investigate what happened. If there is any evidence that magical intervention is the cause of these phenomena, stop your investigations immediately and contact the Order.

P.S: The university will provide all the equipment you require.

You may not ask any questions about the mission to any of the Masters of Álaburg; otherwise, your performance will be judged as fraudulent and insufficient, with corresponding consequences for your grades this semester. The aim is to prove yourself in a real situation, thereby demonstrating your suitability for further involvement with the Order.

We wish you good luck!
Yours in peace and friendship,
The Council of the Seven

Bryn tore the letter from Filixx and read through the part about Sefal again.

"We have to leave immediately. My home is in danger and maybe the girl I love too."

"I will accompany you!" came a deep voice.

Bryn had almost forgotten Ûlyėr was there. But the big, powerful orc's words could not have made him happier. Ûlyėr was coming with them!

DEPARTURE INTO UNCERTAIN ADVENTURE

Two days later, the four friends were ready to set out on their mission. Bryn could hardly wait. Since they weren't allowed to talk to the Masters about the mission, Bryn couldn't inform Gerald, although he would have been just as interested and shocked as Bryn about the developments in their former home town.

The morning was cloudy, and a light rain was beginning to fall as Tejal bid them farewell. They had spent Thursday planning their trip; they had all been released from regular classes since Filixx received his letter. Their absence had earned them several envious looks and pointed remarks from Karina, Malin, and Elina in the common room, who assumed the four were skipping classes.

The fact that Bryn had traveled the route to Sefal—though in the opposite direction—only a few months before made things a lot easier. Bryn's insights enabled them to get a good idea of the distance and terrain that awaited them. Accordingly, the four arranged for the university to provide them with provisions, blankets, clothing, horses, and other useful equipment.

Morlâ had to make do with a fat, somewhat headstrong grey pony that, even before their departure, tried to stick its head into the sack of provisions on the back of Bryn's black horse. But a deep growl from Ûlyėr stopped the animal in its tracks. However, for the rest of the journey, the pony had a name—Thief.

Filixx had decided on a sturdy brewery horse, with thick tufts of hair around the hooves. He thought it would be able to carry his weight over a long distance. Ûlyėr insisted he would be much faster without a horse, and the others had no choice but to believe him.

Morlâ, Filixx, and Bryn wore their new, brown cloaks, which would give them some protection from the rain, and also a pair of fine leather gloves. These would hide their magic mark if they had to resort to magic in an emergency. Morlâ called this measure laughable in his case, but Filixx insisted on it. However, nobody had told them how to hide an orc. They would cross that bridge when they got to it.

The three boys mounted the loaded-up horses, while Ûlyėr stood next to them, carrying a huge knapsack. Together, they listened to Tejal's farewell speech in the otherwise empty courtyard, as the other students were in class.

"Filixx, be aware of the honor this mission involves as well as the responsibility that comes with it," she began.

Filixx bowed his head, and when he lifted it, Bryn saw a brooding, serious expression on his face.

"You chose your companions well, Filixx. And your group is the embodiment of the fundamental principles of this university."

Then she turned to Bryn. She looked at him for a long time. "I want you to trust yourself."

Although Tejal's words touched him deeply, he could not think of anything to say to her, so he only nodded.

"Morlâ," Tejal continued, "the Lekan Gate has never been wrong. You will find your talent."

Morlâ mumbled a few words of thanks, dismounted, and bowed to her.

Finally, she came to Ûlyėr. "Live the life that was given to you, Ûlyėr! It was always meant to be this way!"

Bryn didn't understand what Tejal meant by that and saw his confusion reflected on Morlâ's and Filixx's faces. But Ûlyėr dropped to his knees, opened his muscular arms, and tilted his huge head back, exposing his throat. This gesture of submission, extraordinary for such a warlike creature, was something Bryn had never expected.

Tejal acknowledged Ûlyėr's gesture with a magnanimous smile. Then she handed Filixx a document with several seals on it. The edict identified the group as official Peace Keepers of the Driany Order. Every inn or guesthouse would be obliged to provide free food and lodging for an official delegation of the Order. Everyone in the enlightened nations had to give them protection or assistance, as set out in the Peace Treaty of Âla.

Filixx carefully put it under his cloak.

"And remember, you cannot cross the Panra Pass until noon tomorrow. That is when the Order has stipulated your mission officially begins, and when the protective spells will be suspended for you. Since your group already possesses friendship, all that remains is for me to wish you good luck, and may peace be with you all."

They spurred their horses forward, and Ûlyėr fell into a light trot that allowed him to keep up with the others without effort. Bryn turned around several times, hoping to see Gerald somewhere to secretly wave goodbye to him. But the Chancellor had obviously not informed him of their departure. Finally, they passed through the gigantic Lekan Gate, which the Âlaburg had silently opened for them.

FAREWELL, MY STUDENTS! BRING GLORY AND HONOR TO ÂLABURG, resounded the Lekan Gate's voice inside their heads as they crossed under its mighty archway.

If Bryn had turned around once more, he would have seen Gerald walk over to Tejal.

"Was it necessary to send the boy on this mission?" he asked her as the gate finally closed.

"Yes, it was, and you know it," she said, walking off.

As Tejal cleared the courtyard, she turned around to see Gerald standing still, staring at the locked gate.

"Don't you have some pruning to do, Gerald?" she called out.

He didn't look at her, just nodded his head and went off in the other direction toward the garden.

ÛLYĖR'S STORY

Morlâ came out of the forest undergrowth with the only dry wood he could find and dropped it near the small fire they had lit.

"I was thinking—am I the only one who finds it scary that Tejal always seems to know everything about us?"

But the others were busy setting up camp, and Morlâ's question went unanswered.

Since they couldn't cross the Panra Pass that day, the four would spend the night in the valley in the middle of the mountains. The temperature was pleasantly mild compared to the last time Bryn was here. Their fire was not for warmth but for illumination. By early evening, it had already become quite dark under the forest's dense, green canopy. There were no dangerous animals in this part of the woods either. And at least until tomorrow, they were still under the protection of Âlaburg.

With the camp set, the four made their way to the fire and sat down on the soft, scented forest floor. Bryn lay back to see if he could spot any stars through the dark leaves and branches. While he marveled at how relaxed their adventure had been so far, Morlâ and Filixx began to speculate on what might lie ahead.

Bryn listened to them for a while, then reached into his pack, and took out a piece of bread. He skewered it with a stick he'd picked up and toasted it over the dancing flames, but his mind drifted back to something Morlâ had said.

"No, you're not the only one, Morlâ! I have felt that about Tejal too. Somehow, she always seems to know you better than you know yourself. Do you know what I mean? I can't describe it properly."

"You're right, Bryn," said Filixx, sticking some bacon on a stick. "I know what you mean."

Bryn watched Filixx prepare his dinner and remembered something he'd once said: *It does not matter how bad things get as long as you've got bacon!*

"Tejal knows our fears better than we do," Filixx continued, checking his bacon. "Either that, or she's got a damn good mind-reading spell."

"Whatever it is, her farewell speech put shivers up my spine," said Morlâ, shuffling up to the fire with a stick full of bread. "When she spoke to me, it was obvious she was talking about my little problem with magic." Morlâ sat up and looked at the other three. "Somehow … she gave me hope. I don't know why I felt that way, but I did." Morlâ placed his bread back in the flames and chuckled wryly. "I hope she remembers that after the final exams, when Jehal tries to have me expelled."

None of the others laughed. They knew what Morlâ meant. If he could not show any aptitude for magic by the end of the mission, his time at Âlaburg was over. He would not be allowed to repeat classes a second time.

Filixx muttered something, threw some wood on the fire, and stared into the flames. No one said anything, but Filixx glanced at Bryn. They knew they would both miss Morlâ if he had to leave.

Bryn wasn't sure if Ûlyėr felt the same. The orc was a mystery to him. The whole day, Ûlyėr had walked a few yards in front of or behind the other three and had hardly spoken a word to them. But he surprised Bryn when he sat down by the fire with them and appeared interested in the conversation.

I wonder if I'll ever figure Ûlyėr out? And why did he want to come with us? Bryn knew Ûlyėr had joined the Starball team because he'd thought that if White House won the tournament, he would be asked to join the Řischnǎrr fraternity. But they had both heard Kuelnk say that that would never happen. None of it made any sense to Bryn, and his curiosity was getting the better of him.

Finally, after weighing everything, Bryn turned to Ûlyėr, who seemed even more eerie than usual in the flickering glow of the fire.

"Ûlyėr, what did Tejal mean when she said you should live your life? Don't you do that already? Somehow, I don't understand—" Bryn faltered when Ûlyėr raised his head and locked his piercing eyes on him. His mouth became dry, and his heart began to beat faster, but he kept going. "Tejal's words seemed to have a great effect on you."

Filixx and Morlâ supported Bryn with a nod and looked at Ûlyėr. He did not react to them but fixed his eyes on Bryn, who was getting a bit annoyed about his companion's unwillingness to share.

"I don't mean this in a bad way, and I'm not curious just for the sake of it either. Let us get to know each other because we might have to rely on one another in a dangerous situation. Right now,"—Bryn made a sweeping movement with his arm—"this is reality, not a game of Starball. Out here, we have to stick together to survive. And there will be dangers; I'm quite sure of that. For example, the Vonnyens who attacked me in winter— why wouldn't they be still out there? I'm sure they are."

When Bryn mentioned the Vonnyens, Ûlyėr growled and bared his tusks—the first emotion he had shown all day, but Bryn could not work out whether it was directed at him or the Vonnyens. Yet, Ûlyėr refused to speak.

Bryn dismissed Ûlyėr with a wave of his hand, lay back on the ground, and stared up at the night sky. *Stinky's a dead loss*, he thought. *If it comes to a fight, I'll rely on Filixx and Morlâ, not him. That's for sure.*

His angry thoughts were interrupted by Ûlyėr's deep voice and halting way of speaking, and he sat up.

"The other three nations on Razuclan believe orcs and Vonnyens resemble each other and that maybe one is even descended from the other. This is wrong! We orcs are enlightened beings with gods, stories, songs, art and culture, and our own language.

"The Vonnyens, however, are uncivilized beasts who possess none of this. Like animals, they can only follow their instincts, which command them to kill and destroy. These creatures cannot create; they can only destroy. Vonnyens have no compassion, no sense of the beauty and uniqueness of any life. Although some of you might believe the same about orcs."

Bryn had never heard Ûlyėr say so much before and so eloquently, but he had to push him further. "What do you mean by saying all this?"

Ûlyėr seemed to be wrestling with himself. "I am to live my life because I am dead," he said cryptically and fell silent once more.

The crackling of the fire and the sounds of the forest were all that filled the silence. Bryn caught the distant noise of a branch snapping under the weight of a deer or wild boar. A curious, sniffing hedgehog approached their fire, and from the darkness above them came the hoot of an owl flying off to catch something for supper.

Ûlyėr looked at Bryn. "To the orc nation, I am dead!"

Now Bryn remembered the exact words Kuelnk had said to Ûlyėr before the final.

"Ûlyėr, before the game, Kuelnk said you can't interfere here because you don't exist, because you're dead to them," said Bryn pressing him one more time. "What did he mean?"

Ûlyėr took a deep breath. He found it difficult to talk about this. "I was born the son of a great warrior, even though I never knew his name. I was born in the blood-blue birth tent of the Çawakï clan, one of the strongest and largest orc clans in the nation. Thus, I was destined to be a defender of my clan's glory and honor. But …" Ûlyėr trailed off, staring into the fire. "But I was a freak!"

The word made Bryn flinch.

"My birth dragged on for several days. My mother must have been in unbearable pain, but she did not make a sound. She was an orc! After they pulled me out of her womb, everyone marveled at my height and weight until …"

Ûlyėr threw some wood into the embers. The sparks that shot into the air were reflected in his eyes.

"… until they saw my left leg. It protruded from my body at some unnatural angle, just skin and bone. The muscles hadn't developed in the womb. It looked like a stick compared to the rest of my body. The old birth helpers spat in the fire and made superstitious protective signs against the evil eye when they saw my deformed leg. My mother wanted to know what was wrong. But the women blocked her from seeing it.

"One of them fetched Karï, the chief of my clan, from the village. Typically, males are not allowed to be present at a birth. Pregnant females must leave the community to give birth. Often, that means they are several thousand yards away from the village. Only the old helpers are allowed to accompany and help a pregnant orc during labor.

"After a few hours, Karï finally arrived at the tent. The old attendants had sent my mother into a dreamless sleep with poppy milk. Karï immediately decided I could not become part of the magnificent orc nation. The Rocks of Gohul would be my destiny. My nation has lived like this for thousands of years. We are a community of warriors. We spend our first seven years with our family; then, we are sent to a separate community with other young orcs. There, under the care of the Farang—the Masters— we learn to break away from our family, to break every personal bond, and to concentrate only on fighting. We enter adulthood as superbly trained warriors who know no mercy and are yearning for battle.

"Since this kind of education can also be carried out at Âlaburg, at least to a large extent, the wise men of my people agreed to the establishment of the university in the Peace Treaty of Âla. Our ancestors believed the additional training in Âlaburg would make the orcs even better warriors and enable them to study their enemies better. The University of Peace."

Ûlyėr made an odd snorting sound. Bryn thought that was how orcs expressed sarcasm.

"Ñokelä is currently the Farang responsible for our training. Each clan is allowed to select the strongest from the separate community of youths, and they then fight against each other in a big ceremony. Only the winners can become students at the university. Strength and the absolute will to win are what we call the gift, not magic like the other nations of Razuclan. But this is not the only thing that distinguishes us from humans, elves, and dwarves.

"We orcs never live on our own but always in a community. The young orcs live together. Warriors live in close connection with other warriors. The Circle of Brothers is another. And, of course, the whole clan is also our family. A single orc is nothing without others. We always bind ourselves to the group, not to other individuals. If a warrior chooses a female to mate with, this bond is rarely strong and never for a lifetime. The time a warrior stays in the world is too short to attach themselves to a single thing or individual.

"But fate had foretold another path for me. The path of shame! Karï himself took me to the Rocks of Gohul. This is how my clan describes the canyon in the middle of the Ëægÿ ice desert; it is hundreds of yards deep. He laid me down on the edge of the abyss, wrapped only in a simple fur blanket, and left me to the will of the gods, as generations of his ancestors had done with the children who would never be able to fight for the clan.

"But he had not counted on the strength of my mother's will. When she came to her senses, the old ones in the blue tent told her what happened. She killed two of them and fled into the cold, stormy night. She never told me how she reached the rocks without help, but she found me—buried under a blanket of snow. She told me my hand broke through the snow when she called my name. She took it—and me surviving the brutal cold—as a sign from the gods and decided to raise me.

"My mother then fled with me far out into the lonely, endless Ĕægÿ ice desert. After several weeks, she found a suitable place for us, far away from civilization. Because if others of my nation had seen us, our fate would have been sealed. They would have killed both of us.

"As I grew older, I began to test my strength in the vastness of the ice desert. Alone, I ventured deeper and deeper into the white infinity of Ĕægÿ and fought with snow leopards and polar bears. But eventually, I began to ask my mother questions about our fate because I instinctively felt it was not right there. I longed for the company of other orcs. Eventually, she told me the story of my birth. At first, I hated her for it. I became convinced I should have died as a newborn."

Ûlyėr paused again. When he continued talking, he was much quieter. "Only after my mother died did I realize the sacrifice she had made so I might live. I was not the only one who was alone. My mother also abandoned her orc community to save me. I realize that now."

Now Bryn understood Ûlyėr better. After all, Bryn had many people who accepted him—at least outside the university. But Ûlyėr was an outsider, not just in Âlaburg but in Razuclan as well. He was destined to be separated from his fellow orcs for the rest of his life.

"Well, the rest is quickly told," Ûlyėr continued. "After I buried my mother, I set off for more populated areas. She had given me a map before her death and warned me that the orcs would not accept me. And that's precisely what happened. I was met with hatred wherever I went since everyone knew a single orc had to be an outcast.

"I was beaten up more than once, though an opponent never defeated me if they fought alone. So I moved from village to village until I finally met an elven delegation of the Order trying to settle a dispute between two hostile groups. One of the chiefs told them my story. It must have softened the knights' hearts. I was allowed to join them as a servant. So I lit the fire for them, went out to hunt for their food, and groomed their horses. As chance would have it, they wanted to stop at Âlaburg on their way back to prepare for another mission.

"They had organized somewhere for me to sleep outside the castle walls. But I quickly carried some goods from their trip up to the castle, intending to leave them in front of the Lekan Gate because they told me it would be locked. But as I approached the gate, I suddenly heard a voice in my head. When the four knights arrived, they were shocked. I was taking their things through the opening gate."

When Ûlyėr stopped speaking, there was silence for a long time. Each of the friends let their thoughts wander. Then Filixx spoke up.

"Ûlyėr?" he began hesitantly.

But the orc, now his usual self again, just hissed at him. "Save your pity, Filixx."

"No, wait," said Filixx, trying to soothe him. "I want to ask something. Must a Circle of Brothers be made up only of orcs?"

Ûlyėr frowned at him but eventually answered. "No, there is no such stipulation, but who else would join an orc circle but other orcs?"

"Is there a ceremony? How do you cement the bond between the brothers?" Morlâ asked.

Ûlyėr eyed Filixx and Morlâ thoughtfully, tilted his head back and pointed to his throat. "We make a blood bond."

Now Bryn understood what Filixx and Morlâ were getting at and stood up. Filixx and Morlâ did the same. The three went around to Ûlyėr.

"Ûlyėr," Bryn began. "I hereby ask to join your Circle of Brothers."

Filixx and Morlâ echoed the words. All three friends tilted their heads back and bared their throats to Ûlyėr, just as they had seen him do.

The orc slowly rose and dragged one of his sharp claws across his neck; blue blood trickled out of the cut. He scraped the same claw lightly over the throats of Bryn, Morlâ, and Filixx.

Bryn felt a brief stinging across his throat.

"Our blood has been mixed," said Ûlyėr. "You offered me your life. I offer you mine. We will fight and live together as a Circle of Brothers."

THE PANRA PASS DOES NOT FORGET

After the night's intense conversation, the group's dynamics had changed, and in the morning, everyone was in a good mood. It was sunny too, and they teased each other and made jokes while they cleaned up the campsite and got ready to leave.

A fine mist gathered about them, and the sun glinted through the dewy drops clinging to the leaves, dribbling golden light over the students as they packed. Even without the birds chirping, it was a perfect morning.

Once they'd finished, the three riders mounted their horses and took off. But unlike yesterday, this morning, Ûlyėr ran alongside them. He hadn't said much so far, but after his emotional outpouring last night, it didn't bother the other three.

Filixx, however, talked non-stop. Everything they saw or passed by led to a lecture on geography, culture, or history.

"The Panra Mountains are one of the highest mountain ranges in all of Razuclan," said Filixx. "The pass Bryn has chosen for our crossing is at an altitude of roughly twelve thousand feet. Trees and other plants have a hard time surviving at this altitude, and when they do, they are vestigial and only a shadow of what they would be lower down. Only a few conifers manage to put down roots in the barren, rocky ground. There are only a few animals up here too. At most, there are groundhogs and small mountain goats." He glanced at Morlâ. "Possibly a few Gnarf worms as well, if Morlâ hasn't caught them all for his Summoning class."

The boys burst out laughing, and even Morlâ joined in.

"But it's not quite true what you say, Filixx," said Bryn, wiping away a mix of tears of laughter and sweat with his shirt sleeve.

"What do you mean?" said Filixx, not used to someone doubting his words. "You told me about the worm yourself!"

Morlâ eyed Bryn reproachfully.

Bryn looked at him, embarrassed. "I thought you had already told Filixx," he said half-heartedly. "Anyway, that's not what I meant. It was what you said about animals. When I crossed the pass last winter, we came across a snow fox. It was still small, but they can grow into quite large adults."

"And what became of your furry little friend? Gloves? A warm hat?" Morlâ asked, to everyone's amusement.

Bryn remembered how the little creature had kept him warm on one of the coldest nights of his escape. It seemed a lifetime ago now. *I hope you are doing well, little one, and have grown into a fine-looking young fox.*

The group fell silent again, and everyone concentrated on the strenuous ascent and conserving their strength. The three riders knew that they would have to send their horses back once the ascent became too difficult. The narrow path continued to rise steeply and was littered with countless stones over which the horses stumbled again and again.

After hours of climbing, Bryn's black horse slipped again, acquiring a bloody wound on its ankle. He pulled on the reins.

"Whoa, big fella." Glad to get some rest, the horse stopped abruptly. "Alright, folks," said Bryn to the two riding in front. "That's it. From now on, we walk. Speaking of which, where's Ûlyèr?"

Filixx, red-faced and sweaty despite his horse having had done most of the hard work, pointed to the narrowing path in front of them. "He disappeared behind the turn there. Wait."

Filixx was panting so hard that he needed to take a deep breath. Then he put two fingers in his mouth and let out a shrill whistle, which was amplified a hundredfold by the mountains.

Morlâ and Bryn clapped in agreement at Filixx's impressive performance.

Filixx threw their approval back at them with mock scorn. "It means nothing to you that I can calculate the fourteen-sequence algorithm of the Tamir. Your highest compliment, and only compliment, is asking to copy my homework. But whistling with two fingers—that you find amazing!?"

"Yes!" shouted Morlâ and Bryn.

Once the laughter died down, Filixx showed the two how to do it. But try as they did, neither of them could make a sound. Filixx was sure they would be busy with it every spare minute of the journey from now on.

"What's wrong?" came Ûlyėr's deep booming voice. No one had noticed him approaching from behind.

That could have been a Vonnyen, thought Bryn, giving up trying to whistle. *We must be more careful.*

"Ûlyėr, the horses cannot make it from here on. We have to leave them behind."

Bryn dismounted and shoved the supplies from his saddlebag into his knapsack. Filixx and Morlâ, unhappy at having to walk, got off their horses and repacked their bags too. Then they slapped the horses on their flanks and sent them back into the valley.

"They will find their way to the university. I'm sure they've brought many students safely into the mountains," said Bryn. But a great sadness came over him as he watched them go, thinking about where Reven and Olander were right now.

Morlâ muttered a string of curses as he lifted his heavy pack. "Maybe the horses should have learned to take students across the Panra Pass while they were at it," he said.

And with that, they began the steepest, most challenging part of the crossing.

Bryn estimated they'd need two hours to get to the pass and then another two to cross it and make it back to an altitude where they could set up camp. So he urged them to hurry, wanting to avoid doing any of this in complete darkness.

Walking now was only possible in a single file. Ûlyėr led, followed by Morlâ, who struggled with a knapsack nearly as big as him. Sticking out from under it, though, was a heavy, two-handed steel bludgeon. Filixx was next and sweating profusely. He was having trouble even keeping up with Morlâ. His head looked like a dangerously overripe tomato. Bryn was last. He'd slung his bow over his back and was keenly watching the surroundings as best he could. He thought about the terrible cold and snow from his last time here to help him stay cool.

For a while, the only audible sound as they trekked up the mountain was Filixx wheezing. Though their progress had been slow, they were now close to the pass. In the meantime, it had become cold and windy, and they wore their cloaks with the hoods pulled over their heads.

Visibility got worse the higher they went, and low-hanging clouds were now obscuring the top of the ridge in a milky fog.

Bryn's legs were burning, but he knew he had stay focused on just putting one foot in front of the other. In what felt like a trance, Bryn watched his feet labor their way over the sharp rocks and deep furrows in the path; he counted every step. Under his cloak, his shirt was soaked in sweat. Suddenly, Filixx's heavy knapsack hit him in the face. Filixx had stopped in front of him. He grabbed Bryn by the forearm and put a finger to his lips.

"Ûlyėr has seen or heard something. We're supposed to wait here!"

Bryn grabbed his bow and nocked an arrow. He saw Morlâ pull out his heavy bludgeon and remove the white cloth tied around it. Filixx sat panting on a small rock, wiping the sweat from his forehead. Then he closed his eyes. Bryn knew he was about to enter the trance-like state from where he could cast a powerful Multiple Spell.

The three companions stood ready to defend themselves on the narrow mountain path. But they were sandwiched between a ravine some two hundred yards deep on their left and an unassailable wall of jagged rock on their right.

"We have to keep going. We have no chance here," he whispered to Filixx and Morlâ, both of whom nodded. They moved forward quickly and quietly, always in danger of slipping on the loose rocks and falling down the mountain.

Ûlyėr was nowhere to be found.

The clouds became thicker the higher they climbed, wetting their skin and clothes.

Bryn flinched at the sound of a small rock sliding. In fear, he looked around frantically, not sure if it came from behind or ahead of him.

Eventually, the path led to open terrain, which let the three move as one and allowed them a 360-degree view of the plateau. There was a stillness here, born out of the wind. Bryn knew they were getting close to the Panra Pass, but he could also see a mass of low-hanging clouds heading swiftly in their direction.

Again, they heard the sound of rocks falling nearby. Above them, a bird cried, spooked by the noise, but no one could spot it due to the clouds.

Morlâ pulled the other two into a back-to-back circle with him because of the twilight and worsening visibility.

"To protect us against an attack from any direction," he said in a low voice. "And where the hell is Ûlyėr?"

"No idea," Filixx whispered. "But—"

"If everything were fine, he'd be here already," said Bryn.

Suddenly, a yellowish light lit up the gray mist surrounding them. Filixx had conjured a werelight.

"If we're not alone up here, any attacker should know they're dealing with magicians."

Morlâ agreed. "I don't want to feel like I'm being hunted. I'm not going to hide!" He stepped away from the circle and spun around slowly with his hands in the air. "Who's there? We are just peaceful wanderers. Tell us who you are."

At that moment, they heard a roar. Morlâ stopped twirling and fell silent. It was Ûlyėr. They heard it again, closer this time.

"Where is he?" Filixx asked.

"I don't know," said Morlâ, lifting his bludgeon with both hands.

"I can't see anything in this thick soup," Bryn complained, straining his head left and right. But in the hazy twilight, all he could see was the glow of Filixx's werelight in the heavy mist. Even it could not light up the darkness in this weather.

They heard another rockslide but nothing from Ûlyėr.

Bryn's nerves were strained to the breaking point. "What's going on here? Can you—"

Something hit him in the chest, and he fell to the ground, hitting his head.

Morlâ and Filixx yelled.

Then Ûlyėr appeared, running through the mist roaring.

Dazed and confused at the sudden turn of events, Bryn tried to stand, but something hairy pushed him back and pounced on his chest. Bryn struggled to free himself from the beast, but his knapsack was snagged, and he couldn't move.

Ûlyėr roared again. The furry head of the attacker went for Bryn's face. Reflexively, Bryn raised his arm, shut his eyes, and prepared for a bite.

Then he heard Morlâ and Filixx laughing and felt soft fur on his neck. His attacker's smell reminded him of something strangely familiar. Bryn opened his eyes.

It was a small, thin snow fox, and it was trying desperately to crawl under his cloak. Bryn could now see Ûlyėr standing in front of him with his arms raised above his head. He saw the little fox's tail disappear under Bryn's cloak, but then his head popped up under Bryn's arm, and Ûlyėr screamed.

Morlâ and Filixx pissed themselves laughing.

Ûlyėr lowered his arms and stared around, confused.

"You made short work of the monster, oh great warrior. It could have jeopardized our whole mission," said Filixx before bursting into laughter again.

Ûlyėr thought for a moment and then bent forward to pat the little predator, but it disappeared again behind Bryn's shoulder.

"Ûlyėr, wait a moment," said Bryn, sitting up as best he could. He flung open his cloak, and up popped a small, furry head. The fox's clever, dark eyes looked at Bryn, and it immediately began to lick his face with its rough, pink tongue.

"Yes, yes, my little one," he said, stroking the soft, white fur of his unexpected guest. "I haven't forgotten you either."

RETURN TO THE FOREST INN

Once Bryn, Morlâ, and Filixx had managed to talk Ûlyėr out of his bad mood, they continued on their way. They had finally reached the pass. Now they were slowly but steadily descending, which Bryn soon felt in his knees.

The snow fox never strayed far from Bryn and would often walk in between his legs. As if the terrain was not challenging enough, now he had to be careful not to tread on his new friend. Morlâ and Filixx stroked it after Filixx gave it a piece of bacon, but when Ûlyėr tried to get near, it growled. Nevertheless, Bryn had taken to the animal. Recognizing the light gray streaks in its white fur, Bryn was sure it was the same fox that had frightened him in the mountains before.

After several hours, they arrived at a small grove of trees. As it was almost dark, they decided to camp for the night as the low bushes and stunted pines offered some protection from the biting wind, and with the dead branches scattered about, they could make a fire. That was all they were capable of tonight. Exhausted and curled up in their cloaks around the fire, they made themselves as comfortable as possible on the rocky ground.

Ûlyėr wasn't tired and offered to keep the first watch, which the other three gratefully accepted.

The snow fox lay next to Bryn and seemed to enjoy the warmth of the fire, which dispelled the darkness and the clammy, wet cold at least a little. Bryn stroked the animal behind its ears and fell asleep.

Ûlyėr had stood guard the whole night, and at dawn, he woke the others.

Bryn opened his eyes slowly and saw the fire was out. All that remained were the cold gray ashes. He was shivering. He pulled back his cloak and touched his sweat-soaked shirt—and noticed the snow fox had disappeared. Bryn got to his feet.

"Have you seen it?" he said, turning to Ûlyėr, who was busy giving Morlâ a little kick as a reminder to get up.

"Do you mean your cuddly new toy?" said Ûlyėr.

"If that's the way you want to put it," Bryn said, walking toward Ûlyėr. "I can see that you know something. Have you done something with it?"

Ûlyėr raised himself to his full size and sniggered at Bryn.

"Answer me!"

"Calm down, Realm Shadow."

What happened to it?"

"Listen, you two—" said Filixx, but Ûlyėr silenced him with a wave of his hand.

"Calm down, brother Bryn," Ûlyėr insisted.

Bryn took a few steps back and took a deep breath.

"Thank you," Ûlyėr said, with a nod.

"There's not much to tell. The little guy disappeared just before sunrise. I saw him trotting back toward the pass. He even said goodbye to me." Ûlyėr lifted his knapsack and showed everyone the wet pee on it.

Morlâ and Filixx laughed.

"But …" Bryn began.

"That's what happened, Bryn. Blood of my blood, eh? Thought you trusted me," Ûlyėr scoffed, turning away.

Bryn felt ashamed. "I'm sorry, Ûlyėr. Of course I trust you. I don't know what I was thinking."

Ûlyėr stopped for a moment and turned back. He seemed satisfied enough with the apology, but when he passed Bryn's knapsack, he kicked it so hard it flew through the air and landed in some bushes several yards away.

Bryn shrugged; if this was how orcs reconciled their differences, then so be it.

After this inglorious start to the day, the four made a concentrated effort to raise their spirits. Bryn understood how ridiculous his suspicions had been.

"Too bad the little fellow is gone. But I'm pretty sure I won't have any more problems in Summoning in the future," he said in an attempt to lighten the mood. "I only have to close my eyes, and I can see and feel the little critter right in front of me. Underhil will be thrilled come final exams."

The others laughed, and with that, the issue was finally settled.

After a while, the conversations ebbed away. The descent from the Panra Pass was strenuous, and everyone was struggling. They missed their horses, and Bryn's knapsack was poking him hard in the back. It had a small bulge underneath that refused to go away, no matter how often he repacked. Morlâ and Filixx did not seem much happier with their situation either. Only Ûlyér—as always—seemed to manage everything effortlessly.

Slowly, as they descended, the weather turned summery, and vegetation became more abundant. Bryn looked at the vast forest of giant trees in the distance. The tree line looked like a huge green curtain, but he struggled to see where it opened.

"What do we do now?" Filixx asked, taking a gulp of water and pouring the rest of the bottle over his head.

"We must find the Royal Trail," said Bryn. "Gerald used to say it is nowhere near as grand as it used to be, but when we traveled along it, it was still wide enough for two grown horses to go comfortably side by side."

Bryn shaded his eyes with his hand and scoured the edge of the forest from east to west, but he still couldn't see an opening.

"I guess there's no signpost?" Morlâ muttered to himself and dropped his heavy knapsack with a loud crash.

"We'll know where to go once we're closer to the forest," said Bryn.

"Great! I thought you knew where you were going?" Morlâ demanded, raising his voice. "Here's an idea. Let's all go and get lost in the forest! Come on!"

Before a fight broke out, Ûlyėr came to Bryn's rescue. "No, we won't. I can see the path."

Bryn looked where Ûlyėr was pointing but could see no path, only an endless line of dark green trees. He thought Ûlyėr might have been pointing to some random part of the forest, but then he remembered what Ûlyėr had said to him about trust.

"I'm impressed! You orcs have great eyesight. Come on, let's go! From now on, Ûlyėr's in charge!"

"I thought we were going to have lunch," Filixx said sadly. He'd just unwrapped some smelly cheese and had been sniffing it dreamily.

But Ûlyėr was already running toward the forest, and Bryn had taken off after him. Morlâ slung his heavy knapsack over his shoulder with a clang, and Filixx had no choice but to postpone his meal and stow the cheese away—after a small bite. The two then climbed down the last stretch of the mountain to join the others.

Ûlyẻr was right! Bryn could see they were heading directly toward a wide, well-trodden path that opened like a dark mouth into the forest.

Soon, they reached the edge of the forest and decided to rest and eat. Filixx found his cheese again and took a large bite.

"How far is it to Sefal?" he asked Bryn.

Bryn blew the air out of his cheeks. "I guess two or three more days. If we hurry, we can get to the Forest Inn today, so we don't have to spend another night outdoors. From there, it's about a day's journey home."

Home. Did I say that? Bryn thought. *It used to be. Not anymore, but the village means a lot to me—and Drena. I have to know how she is. We're taking too long. We have to go faster!*

Bryn leaped to his feet and urged the others to set off again.

A few minutes later, they found themselves in the subdued light and cool, fragrant air of the forest. The thousand-year-old Royal Trail would lead Bryn back to his old life—and Drena.

"We can't be far from the inn now," Bryn insisted. The sun had already set half an hour ago, and under the thick canopy of the forest, it was getting darker and darker.

"Let's rest here," said Morlâ.

"No, I want to sleep in a bed again," Filixx objected.

Ûlyẻr stayed out of the discussion, but he seemed unusually tense and looked carefully around into the darkening night.

"But it's just a little further," Bryn said and began walking faster.

"You've been saying that for ages," Morlâ complained, trudging behind Bryn, who had meanwhile disappeared behind a slight bend in the road.

Bryn could make out the shadowy outline of a building up ahead, but as he got closer, instead of warmly lit windows and chimney smoke he saw last time, he found a dark building with no fire. Maybe he'd made a mistake. But the forest had been Bryn's second home not long ago, and he didn't understand how he could have misjudged it.

What is going on?

Before he could ponder further, Filixx and the others were standing next to him.

"Are you sure this is an inn?" Filixx asked. "It looks pretty deserted to me."

"Well, when I was here in winter, it was an inn. Let's go closer."

"We should be careful. Something's not right. It's too quiet, and there is no life in this house," said Ûlyėr, who had not spoken in a while.

Now the others could feel it too. The forest seemed to be filled with an oppressive, eerie silence. Shivers ran up Bryn's spine, but he wasn't sure why.

Cautious and vigilant, they approached the inn. All the windows had been smashed, and the inn sign, which used to hang by the door, was missing. Only half of the beautifully carved oak door was left hanging in the frame. Behind it was the main bar—or used to be. Poking his head in the doorway, all Bryn could see was darkness.

"It smells too. Should we go in?" Bryn asked quietly. "We can't spend the night here."

"Our mission is to investigate what is going on here," said Filixx. "And we'll start right now." He conjured a werelight, and the front of the building and the doorway lit up.

Bryn tentatively conjured a werelight too, though it was a small one. Immediately, the multicolored light began hovering above his head, obediently following every movement of his right hand.

One after the other, they stepped inside; the glass from the shattered windows crunched under their feet. Their incandescent lights barely lit the room and were certainly not strong enough to drive the shadows out of the corners.

Nevertheless, the werelights were sufficient enough to give them a glimpse of the scale of the destruction. All the tables and chairs were smashed, the pieces scattered around the place. The once beautifully polished bar was severely burnt. But what Bryn found more worrying were the deep notches in the heavy wood.

He knew only big swords or massive axes could have inflicted such damage.

Bryn went toward the stairs that had led to the guest rooms, while the other three remained close together near the entrance. The sign that was missing lay near the stairs. Bryn moved the werelight directly above it and read what had been scribbled on it.

~~This house is under the protection of the Peace Keepers.~~

DEATH TO THE ORDER

Breakers of Oaths are ~~not~~ welcome.

The rest of the sign was missing and probably somewhere in the chaos, but the message was clear. Bryn looked closer at the small brown trickles that ran from each letter and was sure the new words had been written in blood. Bryn wondered about the poor suffering soul whose blood had been spilled here.

"We have to get out of here now!" Bryn snapped, moving toward the entrance.

Though unsure what he meant, the other three nonetheless followed as quickly as they could. Outside, Bryn told them what he had seen and why they had to leave. He feared those who had torn the Forest Inn apart might still be in the area.

The Royal Trail was now pitch black, and the four were running as fast as their tired legs could carry them. They headed north, away from this cursed place, but Bryn wasn't sure if their destination would look any different. Presumably, the inn's destruction was part of the unimaginable horror that had spread like a black veil over the Arell Valley. Bryn hoped this veil was not a shroud. But he had a feeling the center of this nightmare was probably not here but the only settlement in the entire valley—Sefal.

SUDDEN DWARF DEATH

Bryn had no idea how long he'd been running, and his legs and lungs were burning, but, haunted by images of Drena and the Vonnyens who'd attacked him, he knew he had to keep going.

He was drenched in sweat, and his shoulders were raw from rubbing against his knapsack. His throat was parched, a throbbing ache, but he shook his head in an attempt to ignore it and ran even faster. After the Forest Inn, he was sure something horrific was going on in the valley. Only a miracle would save his home and village from it—if they were still there at all.

Gerald and I should not have fled from these creatures, he thought, despairing. *He knew how dangerous the Vonnyens could be, and the misery they could cause. We have betrayed the village and our friends! We should have stayed here and fought, or at least warned them!*

But in his heart, Bryn knew Gerald had acted out of panic. Or maybe he had believed the attacks were isolated incidents and would end after the two beasts' deaths. What Bryn had witnessed at the inn, though, proved that this had been a fatal mistake.

The humidity was making Bryn nauseous, but he would not stop. On and on, he ran furiously through the night. Suddenly, a dark claw touched his forearm.

Bryn cried out and then realized it was only Ûlyėr trying to get his attention.

"Bryn!" he shouted. "Bryn, we must rest!"

"No! We must go on! My village! My friends! Drena!" Distracted by Ûlyėr, Bryn stumbled over a branch, but with astonishing speed, Ûlyėr caught him before he hit the ground.

"Brother, you must stop, just for now."

All Bryn heard was the word brother, and it forced him to stop.

Bryn tried to speak, but he felt he was about to pass out and bent over with a hand on his knee to catch his breath. Ûlyėr took the water bottle from his belt and handed it to him. Bryn took several large gulps and gave it back, his hand shaking.

"Ûlyėr, we cannot stop."

"I would follow you anywhere tonight, and Filixx and Morlâ would do the same … but they cannot take it. They won't say it because they know what's at stake for you, but they can't stay on their feet any longer. The last few days have been exhausting for all of us. If we both keep running ahead at this pace, these two will be left alone in the forest, and the group will be split. This leaves us more vulnerable to danger than if we stay together."

It took Bryn a moment, but he realized Ûlyėr was right. Bryn touched his forearm in acknowledgement. And much to Bryn's surprise, Ûlyėr neither flinched nor pulled away.

"What do you suggest, brother?" Bryn asked, straightening.

They decided to get off the trail and make their way into the thick undergrowth to make camp. No one spoke, and no one lit a fire, so the four huddled together in the dark, eerie silence, believing the slightest sound might attract the assailants—the creatures, perhaps—who had wrecked the inn. Ûlyėr gestured that he would take the night watch again.

Bryn looked for a halfway comfortable sleeping position and put his head on his pack. Ûlyėr's large, shadowy outline loomed over their makeshift camp, and for a while, Bryn watched him rake his bright yellow eyes over the darkness. Bryn marveled at his stamina and was grateful for the lesson in leadership Ûlyėr had given him earlier.

Filixx and Morlâ curled up on the ground and fell asleep straight away. Bryn's eyes were heavy. He thought of Drena. As he drifted off, he hoped he'd see her in his dreams. But instead, his sleep was plagued by nightmares about her and his home.

Ûlyėr observed him as he tossed and turned, and he hoped for everyone's sake that whatever Bryn was going through, he wouldn't cry out or make a sound.

The sun was now rising, so Ûlyėr went to the other three as quietly as he could and shook them gently. Bryn opened his eyes to find Ûlyėr standing over him with a concerned expression. Though he'd had a rough night and felt as if he'd pulled all his muscles, Bryn was pleased to see the orc's big, green face. Filixx and Morlâ stretched and yawned without making a sound and hobbled about on their aching legs. But Ûlyėr, as usual, showed no signs of exhaustion.

Eating as they packed up camp, they decided to head back to the trail. It was clear they were an easy target there, but the risk of getting lost in these ancient forests seemed greater than that of being discovered.

Despite the hour, it was already warm, and as the day went on, the heat became more and more oppressive. Ûlyėr, Bryn, and Morlâ had taken their shirts off, but Filixx insisted on wearing his even though it was drenched in sweat and sticking to him.

For the hundredth time that morning, Bryn swiped at an insect that had landed on his face.

"Damn storm flies," he muttered to himself.

"Agreed," Filixx said from behind him and took a sip of water. Looking through the forest's dense, green canopy, Filixx tried to gauge the weather. "I think we've got a lot of rain on the way. We should find somewhere dry and soon. I hope your cabin—" But he caught himself and stopped.

Bryn glanced back at him. He preferred not to imagine what was left of his old home.

"We'll see," he said. "I think we should reach it in two or three hours. Maybe the rain will wait till then."

As the day wore on, more clouds gathered, and the wind picked up. The temperature was dropping too, so the group had to drag their cloaks out of their packs. The trees began to sway as if they were dancing to some sad song, accompanied by the first flashes of lightning and the sounds of thunder.

"I think I felt a drop," said Morlâ, holding his hand out. As if on cue, heavy drops of rain began to hit the ground, leaving small dark craters on the dry, sandy trail. Seconds later, the rain started pouring and ran in small streams over the parched forest floor.

"We have to find shelter," Morlâ roared over a tremendous clap of thunder. Without waiting for an answer, he ran toward a mighty oak tree that must have stood there for centuries.

"No!" Filixx yelled after him.

But Morlâ couldn't hear him. Like all dwarves, he had an aversion to water and wanted shelter from the rain. But before Morlâ's short legs could carry him to the tree, there came a loud boom and a sharp shock of white light.

All the hairs on the back of Bryn's neck stood up; he knew, too well, the sensation of energy being discharged. And he could smell something burning.

"We're under attack!"

Filixx and Ûlyėr were next to him, looking around frantically, but no one could see Morlâ through the torrent.

The giant oak Morlâ had tried to reach was on fire, and the flames were growing bigger even in such heavy rain. To his left, Bryn saw something on the ground a few yards in front of the tree.

"Morlâ!"

He was unconscious and lay face down on the path, his arms and legs flung out to the sides.

"Stay here!" yelled Bryn, hurrying across the muddy ground to his friend while Filixx and Ûlyėr scoured the area, even though this left him exposed. *Hopefully, they can hold off any attackers until I get Morlâ out of here.*

"Quick, Bryn! Hurry up!" Ûlyėr shouted, but the warning threw Bryn, and he stumbled face-first into the mud.

Bryn spat the dirt from his mouth, wiped his eyes, and crawled toward his fallen friend, rolling him onto his back.

"Morlâ, say something!"

The rain pooled under Morlâ's eyes and washed the mud from his face. Bryn could see he'd turned a ghastly white, and he shook him, but there was no reaction. He put his ear to Morlâ's chest and became sick with fear—there was no heartbeat!

Another tremendous explosion burst above him, leaving his ears ringing. But he could not pay attention to any of that right now. The others had to stop the attackers. All he could think about was Morlâ.

No heartbeat, and he's not breathing.

Bryn's frantic thoughts paralyzed him. He knew if Winterblossom were here, she'd know what to do, but they'd never covered this type of thing in class. Bryn clenched his fists and pounded on Morlâ's chest.

"Morlâ!" he shouted, but the only response was the rain roaring around him. "Morlâ, wake up!"

Bryn's eyes began to sting, and he leaned over his best friend. Without thinking, Bryn placed his palms in the center of Morlâ's chest and pushed down hard and relentlessly in quick intervals, but Morlâ didn't stir. Bryn looked at Morlâ's lifeless body, hopeless and horrified. Still, he pushed down one last time—a small hand grabbed him by the wrist!

"Ow! Ouch! Stop! Can't a dwarf even get sudden dwarf death from being struck by lightning without getting beaten up as well?"

Morlâ was alive!

Bryn sat back, wide-eyed and unable to speak. Morlâ stared at him for a moment, then wiggled an eyebrow, and the pair burst into hysterical laughter. Filixx and Ûlyėr came over, looking confused, and explained that they'd not been under attack; it was only lightning that had hit the old oak tree and Morlâ.

KRELL

Long after the thunderstorm ended, Filixx continued lecturing the other three on the numerous and fantastic self-defense mechanisms particular to dwarves. One of them was a protective response that momentarily reduced all of the body's functions to a minimum. Dwarves called this sudden dwarf death, and it allowed them to survive all sorts of emergencies unharmed.

Launching into yet another history lesson, Filixx said this natural and spontaneous ability to respond to something life-threatening meant dwarves were also protected against many spells, which had saved many lives in the First and Second Wars of the Nations. Now Bryn understood why Morlâ was always so fearless in the Starball games, regardless of whether his opponent was gifted or not.

Bryn knew exactly where they were and signaled for the group to halt.

"We're close to my old place, but I think we should leave the trail here, circle around, and approach it from the rear."

"Are you sure?" Ûlyėr asked. "The cabin would be an ideal place for an ambush, but they might also be expecting us to predict that and go around."

Nevertheless, he and Bryn got off the trail and crept into the undergrowth. Morlâ and Filixx followed them, but they were also uncertain if this was the right thing to do. Bryn retook the lead; this part of the forest was as familiar as his room in Âlaburg.

"Better be quiet," he warned his companions when they were near the cabin.

If it were autumn, the cabin roof and its dark brown wooden shingles, covered in moss, would have been visible through the trees, but right now, all they could see was a green wall of leaves.

"We have to get closer," Bryn whispered. But the other three seemed to hesitate. "What's the matter with you?"

This time, Filixx tried to explain. "Bryn, please don't be mad, but we're not sure if seeing your old home is worth the risk of being discovered or attacked. We did want to do this because of everything you've been through, but now we're not sure." Filixx fiddled with the hem of his shirt, struggling to know what to say in the awkward silence. "Maybe it's better and safer to go straight to Sefal? Yes, it's your home, but you know, there's no one living there now for us to protect."

Bryn chewed on his bottom lip and stared at each of his companions. Naturally, he wanted to return to his old home and spend a memorable evening in the safety of the cabin. He had been looking forward to standing once more in his old room and staring out of the window into the garden, as he had done many times before. He wanted to lounge around with his new friends in the old living room. But he was also aware of the price his homesickness might demand. Again, he remembered the bloody sign at the inn.

What have I been thinking? Finding Drena is far more important than an evening spent reminiscing in my old home.

"You're right! It wasn't reasonable for me not to think of it. The cabin isn't my home anymore. My home is with you at Âlaburg. Let's go then. It's too big a risk, especially if the Vonnyens are looking for me. Let's find out what's going on in Sefal."

If anyone's left there who can give us an answer. Bryn's chest tightened, and nausea swirled in his stomach. He led the group the other way round the cabin, further and further north, and straight to Sefal.

It took them around three hours to reach the edge of the village.

"And now?" Morlâ asked as they hid behind the trunk of a mighty fir tree. "We can't just wander down the main road, asking if everything is fine."

Filixx agreed. "If the Vonnyens are around, we will run straight into them. We have to sneak in somehow and find villagers we can talk to without anyone else noticing we're here. Who would you go to, Bryn? Any idea?"

"Let's try and find Krell the hermit. He lives in a hut just outside the village on the other side of the Heling River. He collects precious stones there and sells them at the market. It's not far from here, but I think we should wait until dark to cross the river."

They crept through the forest around the village until they got to the river. As it was flowing somewhat sluggishly, Bryn suggested they wade upstream so they wouldn't leave any footprints on the riverbank. Once they saw Krell's hut, they would look for a place to hide in the undergrowth and wait until dark.

The hours stretched on endlessly as the four huddled behind a few bushes near the river. Bryn kept thinking about Drena. He prayed to all the gods that she had taken her mother's advice and stayed away from the valley and Sefal.

To be condemned to inactivity so close to their goal tore at their nerves. There was also a tiresome discussion with Ûlyėr about him staying away from Krell's place for the time being so as not to frighten him. In the end, they agreed he should cross the river with them but wait in the shadows near the hut while they talked to Krell. He would only reveal himself if the situation became dangerous.

Finally, behind the snowy mountain tops, the orange afterglow of sunset faded to black, and the four were able to make their move. Luckily, the narrow crescent of the waxing moon reflected little light, and crossing the river went without a hitch—except for Morlâ cursing about being in it.

Bryn turned to Ûlyėr when they reached the other side. "I think it's better if you hide now. We're nearly there."

Huge and heavy as he was, Ûlyėr disappeared without a sound into the darkness.

Bryn knocked softly on the door of the hermit's thatched hut, but nobody came or spoke.

"There must be someone there," Filixx insisted. "I'm sure I just heard something. He's probably too scared to light a lamp."

Bryn clenched his fist and hammered on the weather-beaten wooden door.

"Let's just go in," Morlâ suggested, and before Bryn could stop him, he pushed the door open with a loud creak and stomped inside. His two friends followed him.

"Hello?" Morlâ cautiously called into the darkness.

"Go away, you beasts," a voice cried out. Then something came out of the dark toward them—a feeble old man, brandishing a heavy wooden truncheon he could barely carry. Bryn thought he looked more sad than frightening.

If he hadn't been standing in Krell's hut, Bryn wouldn't have recognized him. The hermit, who had always looked healthy and happy and had given Bryn a colorful stone on many a market day, looked terrified and his body showed signs of grievous neglect. His clothes hung in rags on his emaciated frame. Under his wide, terrified eyes were dark rings, and his long gray hair and beard were matted and filthy.

"Go away. You won't get me, too."

Krell struck out at Morlâ, whom he considered the weakest opponent, probably because of his size. But the dwarf lunged forward, and Krell lost his balance, his massive wooden club falling from his hands.

The old man broke down crying. "Go away, you monsters. You've done enough harm already. What do you want from us?"

Bryn knelt and put his hand gently on his shoulder. "Krell. It's me, Bryn."

The old man lifted his head off the floor, and Bryn could see his eyes were filled with tears.

"Bryn?" he asked, struggling to speak. "Is it really you?"

Bryn caught him under the arms and lifted him to his feet. Krell stared at the boy for a moment. Then he took a candle stump out of his pocket, dropped it into a soot-blackened glass to shield the flame, and lit it. As the little flame grew, Krell went over to check all the shutters were tightly closed. After he felt he'd secured the place, he turned his attention to his visitors.

"Bryn?" He touched the boy's face with his dirty hands and held the candle right in front of his eyes. "I can't believe it's you! We thought you and Gerald were the first ones killed out there." He hugged Bryn long and hard. "Thank Kajal; you're alive. Where is Gerald? How is he? Where have you been all this time and—" Suddenly, he swung the candle around to Filixx and Morlâ and squinted. "Who are they?"

"Gerald is well," Bryn began, telling him of their escape and his new home in Âlaburg. While Bryn did not mention much about the university and its many secrets, the hermit still looked at him in pure amazement.

"You boys are representatives of the Order?" He laughed briefly and cheerlessly. "Even if I believe in the old stories more than many others, I can't imagine young fellows like you belong to an organization that is more myth than reality nowadays. No living person has ever seen a Knight of the Driany Order, and if you talked to people in the village, most would laugh at you, thinking you still believe in fairy tales."

Filixx stepped forward without a word, took out the document Tejal had given him, and handed it to Krell, conjuring a werelight to help him read it.

Tears shimmered in Krell's eyes as he read.

"By Kajal, it's true! The Order does exist!" Then he noticed the small, spinning golden ball following Filixx's left hand. "I thought you had lit a candle. By Kajal, magic still exists in Razuclan!" Krell then took a closer look at Morlâ. "And you must be a—"

"Yeah, yeah, yeah," Morlâ interrupted him. "I'm a dwarf. It's hard to overlook. And my prodigious friend here, Filixx, is a dwarf-elf who can also do magic—and is also an incredible

429

cook—but that's not the point now, old man. Tell us what's going on! We need answers! Why are you hiding here in the dark all by yourself like a—well, like a hermit?"

Bryn looked at Filixx, who rolled his eyes.

But Krell nodded silently. "You're right, little friend. If you're here to help, you must hurry. Tonight, they'll come for some of us again and drag us into the old mine. No one has ever come back from there. That's why I'm hiding here. It's the first time I've been here in weeks. I was lucky enough to get away and hide in the forest when they first appeared on New Year's Eve. Since then, I've been living out there best I can," said Krell, pointing out the door. "It's pure coincidence you met me tonight, but I was in desperate need of some things. Some clothes, for one thing, as you may have noticed."

Bryn put a hand on his old friend's shoulder. "Krell, who are *they*?"

"All I know is they're beasts. And they can speak!" Krell whispered and blew out the candle.

CROSSES OF BLOOD

"Vonnyens," said Bryn.

One by one, the others turned to him.

"But Vonnyens cannot speak," said Filixx. "It's one of the first things we learn in Magic and History. In the great wars, the Vonnyen combat units were all under the control of a spell and never once showed anything resembling independent thought or intelligence. They are only created by magicians to fight and destroy—that is their sole purpose. And no one has ever heard them speak. If they could, it would mean they possessed reason, and with that, they could elude the magician's influence and pursue their own agendas. So far, this has never happened."

"But I heard them speak," Bryn said calmly. "One of them even asked me a question."

"If it's true, Razuclan is about to face its greatest threat," said Morlâ. "Vonnyens who can communicate would threaten the entire continent. If they can speak, it means they can think, and if they can think, they might stop doing others' dirty work and seize power for themselves."

"Exactly," said Filixx. "They will come to realize how all nations have exploited and sacrificed them to create havoc and fight their battles for them. Hundreds of thousands of them have died. And—"

"—and if they are intelligent beings," said Krell, hobbling over to Filixx, "they will no longer want to live crammed into dungeons underground, subject to someone else's will, but—"

"—but try to conquer a territory for themselves," Bryn added.

"And why not begin here," came a deep voice, "in a small, remote village with only a few people?"

Bryn could only see Ûlyėr's yellow eyes in the doorway.

Oh no, Krell will faint for sure.

But Krell's face lit up as he watched Ûlyėr squeeze through the door. "A night of miracles and prophecies fulfilled!" he said, shaking his head in wonder at seeing a huge, muscle-bound orc in his home. "I never thought I would ever meet a son of the warrior nation."

To everyone's surprise, and Bryn's relief, Krell tilted his head and bared his neck to Ûlyėr.

Ûlyėr looked at the human for a moment, unmoved, and then returned the gesture and stepped into the room proper.

Bryn went to introduce Ûlyėr but bumped his shin again on some furniture. Muffling a cry, he instantly conjured a werelight, which filled the dark hut with bright colors.

How does Krell know so much about Razuclan? thought Bryn, rubbing his leg.

"We're here to stop them," said Ûlyėr, rising to his full height.

Krell put his hand over his eyes and glanced around at his young guests. "One human, a dwarf, an orc, and a dwarf-elf, united against the greatest enemy of all free people of Razuclan! Nothing like this has happened since the ancient days of Tamir. But you must hurry. Tonight, these monsters—these Vonnyens—plan to take the remaining villagers to the mine and wipe out Sefal once and for all.

"Over the past months, with every new moon, they would enter the village and mark a cross in blood on certain houses. The following night, those in the marked houses were taken to the abandoned silver mine. The villagers followed the Vonnyens like sheep, but the next morning, those left acted like the others never existed. No one seemed to remember they once had neighbors, friends, or even siblings after they disappeared.

"Before, more than forty families lived in Sefal, and now, only six are left. Last night, red crosses were painted on all their houses. Around midnight, these people will also be imprisoned or worse in the mine, and then all of Sefal will belong to the Vonnyens."

"Why do these humans stay in the village?" Ûlyèr asked with a hint of contempt in his voice. The warrior found it hard to understand why they didn't leave or fight back.

"I cannot tell you for sure. But it seems the people of Sefal no longer have free will. They have behaved like this ever since the Vonnyens first appeared. The villagers go about normally as if nothing has happened. Nobody pays attention to the crosses or asks about the fate of the ones who have disappeared. Once a week, they even hold a market, only there are fewer and fewer stalls and customers."

"A spell!" said Bryn and Filixx together.

"Either the Vonnyens somehow possess the gift, or somebody who does is helping them," said Morlâ.

"Someone who can cast such a powerful spell on so many and maintain it over a long period would be a powerful magician," Filixx said, looking worried.

"Why are *you* not under this spell?" asked Morlâ, narrowing his eyes.

The old man sighed and nodded. "I guess I was just lucky. I can spend days in the forest or up the river collecting herbs and stones, and I was not here when the Vonnyens appeared. And my hut is quite far from the village, so they probably didn't discover it right away, although I'm sure they've been here since." Krell shuddered at that thought.

"Since then, I've been in hiding, but I sneak into the village from the forest to watch what is happening. In the beginning, I tried to warn others, but nobody listened to me. They did not even notice me! Once, I found the McKensey boy fishing in the river. I know him, and he's fond of me. I wanted to save him, take him here to the other side of the river, but he started to scream and kick me—like he'd never seen me before."

Krell became unsteady and sat in a chair.

"I did get him across and into the hut, but when I woke the next morning, the boy was gone. I saw him again that night, along with his parents and two sisters, walking toward the mine with several Vonnyens. I've not seen him again." A tear trickled from the old man's eye. "After that, I lost all hope. Tonight, I just wanted to get some things, and then make my escape and never come back. What is the point of staying? I can't help anyone, and by tomorrow, there won't be anyone left in Sefal anyway."

Krell wiped his eyes.

"But now all that's changed." One by one, he looked at the four companions, as if to remember this moment, and smiled. "It will be midnight in an hour. That's when they come. The beasts always come back the night after the crosses of blood appear."

"Then we will save the villagers," said Bryn, with a steel in his voice the others had not heard before. Bryn knelt in front of Krell, who seemed even more frail and tired. "How is Zeffi?" he asked.

"Zeffi?" Krell asked, rubbing his forehead. "No, Zeffi is still around, but there's a cross on his door."

Morlâ could see Bryn getting anxious. "Krell, look at me. What about Drena, his niece? What happened to her?"

Krell frowned, then shook his head slowly and closed his eyes. Bryn's heart sank. It was clear to the others his whole world was collapsing.

Suddenly, Krell's eyes popped open.

"Is she the pretty niece who comes to visit?"

"Yes, yes, she is," said Filixx, glancing at Bryn.

"She should be with him then! The girl came here for the New Year's Eve party."

Bryn stared at Krell in blank amazement.

"The next day, the Vonnyens raided the village and must have put a spell on her too. Since then, she's been living with Zeffi, and like everyone else, she doesn't see what's going on."

Bryn's hands began to tremble from the adrenaline, making his werelight flutter. *Drena is not safe, but she's still here. I can save her. I must save her!*

"We have to go!" he cried. "We have to save the rest of the villagers—and Drena."

"I agree," said Filixx. "Although, according to our mission, we're supposed to wait for support from the Knights of the Driany Order if we believe people who possess the gift are involved. But I think, in this case, the First Law of Magic negotiated in the Peace Treaty of Âla applies: *Every gifted person must always commit their abilities in the service of peace for all living beings of Razuclan.* Wait a moment."

Bryn noticed a brief flicker in the room when Filixx entered the realm. A second later, a tiny, yellow, glowing ball rushed out the door.

"I sent a message to Tejal and told her everything we know. Any help will arrive too late, though, but at least we'll be sticking to the rules. Plus, this is about much, much more than semester grades."

The four helped Krell find his things and bid him farewell. They watched him follow the river into the forest until he disappeared, and then they set off for Sefal.

AN IMPROVISED PLAN

"Do you think Krell will manage on his own?" Morlâ asked as they crept toward the center of the village.

"I'm sure of it," said Ûlyėr. "He has managed to take care of himself in the past months. Although I still cannot understand how you fragile humans manage to survive in Razuclan at all. Your bodies have no means to defend yourselves with." He directly addressed that to Bryn. "No scales, claws, or fangs. Besides, you are small and have so few muscles."

A quick sideways glance from Bryn silenced the orc, but the others chuckled despite, or perhaps because of, the seriousness of the situation. How could they know when and if they would have something to laugh about again?

"Stop," exclaimed Filixx.

"Why?" Morlâ moaned. "We have to save Bryn's darling as soon as possible." But it was his kissing noises that earned him a nasty look from Bryn.

"We will," said Filixx, not reacting to Morlâ's joke, "but we have to protect ourselves. I think they're using some kind of Hypnosis Spell."

At the mere mention of the word hypnosis, memories of the Spring Tournament flooded Bryn's mind, and his face turned bright red from the humiliation.

"I think I can conjure a Protection Spell that will cover all of us, but this only works as long as you stay close to me."

Filixx closed his eyes, and immediately, Bryn noticed the sounds around him were quieter and more muffled. And the dark landscape momentarily blurred as if he was looking through water, but that faded after a few blinks.

"What did you do?" Bryn asked.

"I put a protective dome over our heads. If your hearing is a little affected, then it should be working."

"What?" Morlâ asked.

"I asked you, how is your hearing—"

"What?" said Morlâ. "Crows wore your earring?"

He and Bryn burst into laughter, which they immediately tried to suppress. Even Ûlyėr was amused at Morlâ's nonsense and flashed some teeth no one had seen before.

"Very funny, shorty!" Filixx tried not to laugh, but the corners of his mouth were twitching. Fear was making them all a little silly.

Soon after, the students reached the edge of the village. The small, wooden Church of Kajal and its circular courtyard were surrounded by several small- to medium-sized buildings. Only a few lights were lit, but the small windows glowed valiantly against the overwhelming darkness.

Bryn quietly pointed out the buildings. "That crooked cottage belongs to the Graham family. They're weavers. Next to that is

Hay's house. He's a butcher. That's Kerr's mill, and behind that, you can see the light next to Ramsay's herb garden. Marel still seems to be here. I can smell smoke from his distillery. That's it over there." Bryn strained to see better over the small bush they were using as a cover. "There. That's Zeffi's roastery, with the painted golden hazelnut on it."

At that moment, a young woman appeared in the only window with light in Zeffi's house, which was directly behind the roastery. Bryn anchored his attention on that distant window. The young woman held back her long dark hair and blew the candle out, but she turned her face toward the window in that split second before the light died. *Drena!*

A shock, like a bolt of lightning, went through Bryn's body. The feeling of seeing Drena again after such a long time was indescribable. On the one hand, he was incredibly happy to finally be so close to her again. On the other, his heart almost wanted to burst because he couldn't be with her, given the present danger.

"Pretty difficult to see at that distance. Are you sure that was Drena?" asked Morlâ. Bryn nodded without looking at him. "She looks lovely. I prefer blondes, as you know, but still—"

"We'll do everything we can to save her," said Filixx, elbowing Morlâ in the ribs.

"Yes, everything we can—and, yes, absolutely lovely," said Morlâ, glancing at Filixx.

Ûlyėr grunted in agreement and flexed his powerful muscles. "But we need a plan. Remember Krell and the McKensey boy? Just entering Zeffi's house and taking Drena out won't work."

"You're right," Bryn said desperately, "but what else can we do?"

"It's like a Starball game," said Morlâ, putting on his captain's voice. "It depends on the right tactics. Just warning the residents won't work; the old man tried that and failed. Besides, our goal should be to save all villagers or at least find out what's happened to them."

The other three nodded.

"Good. So, we wait here until the Vonnyens fetch the last of the villagers. Remember, their magic can't harm us. Then we'll join them," Morlâ said with a wicked grin.

Filixx gasped at the audacity of that plan. "Voluntarily?"

"Let me finish, big boy, and then you can poo-poo my idea. All right?"

"I'm sorry. Go on. Your plans did win us the Starball Cup after all."

Morlâ gave him the tiniest of bows. "Thank you. We'll stay put until the Vonnyens have visited all the houses. We'll find a good spot to lie in wait for the villagers to pass by, and then we'll fall in with them. I don't think Vonnyens can distinguish between dwarves or dwarf-elves and humans, so we should be fine." Morlâ glanced at Ûlyėr. "Though orcs, I'm not so sure."

"Don't worry, Captain. I'll stay hidden and follow you. No one will see me."

Ûlyėr had surprised them several times by how effortlessly he could disappear silently into the night, so they knew he could easily do the same tonight.

"Very good," said Morlâ. "The rest of us behave like everybody else, pretending to be under a spell and so forth. The Vonnyens will then lead us straight to their hideout." Morlâ paused and looked blankly at his friends. "And after that, we'll have to improvise!"

He pulled out his iron-reinforced bludgeon and attached a shiny ax blade to the end of it.

Bryn noticed the stench first—how could he ever forget that horrible smell of death and decay? His hands shook as he held his bow. He tried breathing through his mouth, but it was too late; the reek of death had already filled his nostrils. He knew there was no turning back now.

"At least they're punctual," Morlâ whispered and pulled his shirt up over his nose. Filixx and Bryn did the same, but Ûlyėr didn't need to.

Suddenly, a small group of large figures dressed in black appeared ahead, barely visible in the darkness but moving quickly toward the Ramsay family's house. One of the five Vonnyens opened the door and disappeared inside the house. The four remaining pairs of glowing red eyes began looking around until the Ramsay family came out, with the other Vonnyen behind them.

The Vonnyens visited four more houses, and then entered Zeffi's home. The people inside stepped out to join about fifteen others walking down the street. Bryn tried to see if Drena was among them, but it was impossible.

The sad procession headed toward the edge of the village.

"Come on!" whispered Morlâ, turning to see Bryn and Filixx right behind him.

They all knew this was their only chance to merge into the group of villagers. Until now, the three had been following slightly behind the procession, creeping through front yards, climbing over fences, and using any cover they could find, in the hope that there would be an opportunity to join the group unnoticed. The accompanying smell was becoming unbearable, and the last house was just ahead of them. It was now or never!

In the meantime, the Vonnyens had split up. Two now walked at the front, one at the back, and one on each side of the group. They passed the last house before Bryn and the others could reach it, and they lost their final chance to join the procession. Two hundred yards of flat, open field now lay between them and the edge of the forest. Morlâ's plan had sounded so promising, but now it was in tatters, and he and Filixx went back behind the house, their shoulders slumped.

Bryn stepped behind the corner of the house and looked at the other two for inspiration. His mind raced desperately for a solution. He peered around the corner to see if he could spot Drena, but the captives had already passed by the house.

Seconds later, an enormous crash sounded from Bryn's right. Looking up the street, he could see that the large wooden barn on the corner had collapsed entirely.

Ûlyėr!

The Vonnyens reacted with unbelievable speed. Four of them left their posts and, within seconds, were at the scene with weapons drawn. However, the one who had stayed seemed oblivious to the chaos, and the captives continued to walk on.

As Bryn marveled at the brilliance of Ûlyėr's diversion—even though it was too late—old man Ramsay and his wife appeared, passing slowly right in front of him. He grabbed Filixx and Morlâ and dragged them back to the corner of the house.

"This is our moment," he urged them.

They ran as fast and quietly as they could over the front yard and into the street to fall in behind the two stragglers. All they could do now was hope the four Vonnyens, who were sure to rejoin the procession, would fall for it. Like the rest of the unfortunate troop, they trudged toward the mine, heads bowed, staring at the ground.

A few minutes later, the stench grew strong again, and out of the corner of his eye, Bryn saw the four Vonnyens resume their posts. It didn't seem like they'd caught anybody either—at least there was no sign of Ûlyėr.

Then came the decisive moment. A Vonnyen at the rear ran past them to flank the group. The vile-smelling creature didn't notice a thing.

But the worst was yet to come. They were heading to an old silver mine full of Vonnyens, where people disappeared and never returned.

THE MINE

After an hour of walking, the group reached the entrance of the old silver mine. Despite the situation, Bryn was relieved. Walking with a group of people in silence had felt strange. It was so quiet that all Bryn could hear was Morlâ breathing next to him and the familiar squeak of Filixx's leather pants. The Vonnyens seemed to have silenced even the sounds of the forest. It was clear the Vonnyens' presence here meant only death.

The mine had been shut down many years ago, and since then, the folk in Sefal considered it a place to be avoided. The old people told stories about children and adventurous souls who went into the mine to explore its deep underground caves and numerous branching tunnels, only to never surface again. Bryn had never believed those stories, but Gerald had forbidden him from going to the mine. Nonetheless, Bryn ventured in once, but he never went so deep into the dark main shaft that he could not see daylight. He hadn't reached the bend in the shaft further up that led steadily downward.

At the mine entrance was a small fire, and a lonely sentry was standing next to it, handing out torches to the Vonnyens at the front of the group. The slender Vonnyen paid no attention to the villagers and kept his face hidden under a black cloak hood. He did not communicate with his comrades, or if he did, Bryn was unable to notice. So far, he hadn't heard any of these Vonnyens speak.

Maybe only a few of them can speak.

With their torches lit, the lead Vonnyens led the group into the damp tunnel. Inside, it was much cooler than the summer night. Bryn touched the walls of the mine, careful to avoid being seen by the Vonnyens behind him. The rock felt slimy. Some algae were growing on it, covering the walls with a damp, slippery film.

The tunnel became more and more narrow. Soon, the group could only walk in a single file. Bryn didn't know who was in front of or behind him now because the torch light in front of the group barely reached him. However, he could tell the tunnel was leading steadily downward.

Meanwhile, they had passed many side tunnels and gone around several bends. *I will never find my way out of here alone*, thought Bryn. He wondered if he could contact his friends surreptitiously in the darkness now that the tunnel had widened a little, but he had no idea where they were. Starting to panic, he broke character and looked about frantically.

And, of course, as luck would have it, a Vonnyen somewhere behind him reacted immediately and pushed through the tunnel of villagers until he was behind Bryn, sniffing the back of his head. Bryn held his breath; the stench of decaying flesh was unbearable, but he had no escape route, and the villagers in front of him were moving slower than ever.

Bryn grew desperate. If they discovered him now, their mission would fail, and they would have sacrificed their lives for nothing. In the dark tunnel, he had no chance against the ruthless monsters, and using a spell on them might hurt the innocent people around him. His eyes stung from the sweat running down his forehead, and then he felt a waft of air on the back of his neck. The Vonnyen had raised his deadly, clawed hand, and Bryn expected the worse.

Oh, no! He's got me!

But neither of them expected the intense flash of light that surged through the tunnel.

It forced Bryn's eyes shut, but the Vonnyens had it worse—it caused them severe physical pain. The one behind Bryn went into convulsions and collapsed on the ground, screeching and trying to shield his ugly red eyes with his claws. The spellbound villagers did not react; they just stopped and stared with expressionless eyes.

"Come on, we're not here to see the sights," Morlâ said in Bryn's ear. Then he kicked the Vonnyen in the face with his heavy boot and pulled Bryn into one of the side tunnels, where Filixx was waiting for them. "Well done, Filixx. A nice, impromptu performance!"

Dwarves, perfectly adapted to life underground, could see much better in the dark than humans. So Bryn ran after Morlâ and Filixx, letting them lead him down the dark tunnel.

Soon, the screams of the Vonnyens faded away. Bryn thought of Drena and hoped she was all right. But, at the moment, there was not much he could do for her.

"Stop," said Filixx, panting at a junction. "I've lost my way."

"What? I thought—" Bryn began.

"No time for that," Morlâ cut in. "We must get to where they're headed before they do. Our only option is through one of these side tunnels. Quickly, Filixx, you need to read the rocks!"

Filixx put his palms on the tunnel wall and closed his eyes. Morlâ patted Bryn encouragingly on the shoulder. Filixx took a deep breath and pointed into the darkness.

"This way!"

Morlâ saw Bryn had no idea what was going on, so as they moved swiftly down the tunnel, he explained their plan to Bryn. "Gifted dwarves can read the currents of energy in stone and rock; it's called a Rock Reading Spell. I can't—which goes without saying—but our genius here, Filixx, has just enough dwarf blood to do it. He can see the energy flowing through the stone by merely touching it. This energy is the same energy that allows anyone with the gift to do magic. These currents are much stronger in the rocks than in the air because they originate from deep underground. Filixx forms a kind of map of the tunnel network in his mind. And when you add this to our excellent dwarf sense of direction as well as a life spent mostly underground—ta-daaa! We know where to go."

Bryn almost stumbled, processing all that, but he quickly caught up with Morlâ again.

"How do you know where the Vonnyens are taking the villagers?"

"Well," Morlâ said brightly, "we're improvising!" Bryn couldn't see Morlâ grinning in the darkness, but he knew that he was. "We're sure we are on the right path. Filixx has spotted a huge cave at the bottom of the mine. There seems to be a strong source of magical energy there too. We think this is where the Vonnyens are going."

Running through the dark tunnel, Bryn lost all sense of time. After what felt like an eternity, he noticed the way led slightly upward. They rounded a ninety-degree bend, and the tunnel filled with a pulsating reddish glow.

"We're almost there," said Filixx, puffing. He went ahead but had to crawl because the roof of the tunnel had become so low. The source of the red light was directly ahead of them and growing more intense. Filixx had to cover his eyes.

Bryn and Morlâ negotiated the low tunnel with varying difficulty; Bryn had to crawl, but Morlâ could walk comfortably.

When they reached Filixx, he pointed to a gap in the tunnel wall. A vast cave opened up about thirty yards below them.

"Are all of those …?" Bryn whispered.

"Yes," Morlâ said grimly.

"I'm afraid so," Filixx added. "I wonder if anyone has ever seen so many Vonnyens in one place."

The colossal cave resembled an anthill. Everywhere, the disfigured monsters moved about. Some of them fanned massive fires, in which weapons were being forged, while others hardened the blades in huge barrels of water and then placed the heavy, lethal weapons in a large pile, before which other Vonnyens waited in long queues, greedy to pick them up. Others were armed with pickaxes, tirelessly chipping away at the rock face to make the cave bigger. None of them wore cloaks, roaming around naked.

Bryn could now see their skull-like heads. Most of their facial features were partially decayed, their faces devoid of any expression or emotion. Their red eyes glowed, but there was no life in them. The rest of their bodies consisted of rotting flesh, some of which hung in thick, dark strips from their arms and legs. They still looked powerful and dangerous. And the stench was indescribable.

One Vonnyen, who seemed to be the overseer, screamed at the others, urging them to work faster and keep order. Although Bryn didn't understand precisely what they were up to, one thing was clear—this chaos was well organized, and Vonnyens could speak. Bryn turned and looked at the other two, who grimaced for doubting him.

"By Tamir!" Filixx cried suddenly, stepping back from the gap and pulling the other two with him. Thankfully, the tremendous noise in the cave drowned out his unexpected exclamation.

"What's the matter?" whispered Morlâ.

"Have you seen the light?" Filixx asked.

"Of course. The whole cursed cave is blood-red," Morlâ replied.

"No," Filixx sighed and wiped the sweat from his face with his filthy shirtsleeve. "I mean where it's coming from—the origin of the light."

Then he crawled cautiously back to the gap to look over the edge, and the other two followed him. Filixx pointed to a crack in the ground that looked like a deep wound in the rock; the pulsating red light came from it. Dozens of Vonnyens with picks and shovels were busy removing large chunks of rock, trying to widen the opening.

Bryn couldn't say why, but everything inside him wanted to stop these monsters from enlarging that opening. It felt like they were inflicting a wound on the underground that would never heal. But he couldn't talk to the others about it because the next moment disrupted everything. The villagers arrived in the cave, pushed along by several Vonnyens. Each villager now had at least one heavily armed Vonnyen guarding them. And the unknown magician likely considered it a waste of their powers to keep the new arrivals under a spell after they arrived in the hideous cave because fear and bewilderment crossed the villagers' faces, followed by horror Bryn could not begin to describe.

"They're forcing them toward the red light," Morlâ said.

Bryn ached when he saw Drena. She looked confused, and her cheeks were wet with tears. Her beautiful dark hair was messy, and her face had a long, bloody scratch on it. She had been beaten.

"We must do something," Bryn whispered.

"Yes, but what?" Morlâ asked. "They're a hundred times more powerful than we are, and even you, Bryn, could not stop them alone, especially if your fear …"

But Morlâ did not need to say anymore. Bryn knew what he meant. His fear of using magic had grown steadily since the Starball final, and since then, he had only used it under Tejal's supervision. The fear of unintentionally hurting someone or making a situation devastatingly worse had been growing in him since he had drained the young elf of her energy, nearly killing her and *enjoying* it.

Bryn grabbed Morlâ's arm.

"I don't have a choice. Not anymore." He glanced again into the cave. "It's time to use it. The Vonnyens will feel my anger, and I will spare none of them. I promise you that." His voice had an edge that Filixx and Morlâ had not heard before, and it made them nervous. Then Bryn remembered what Tejal had said, and he took a long, slow breath. "But right now, there are far too many of them, and without Ûlyėr, we also lack an invaluable warrior. But—"

A man's screams drowned out all other noise in the cave.

Horrible things were beginning to happen below, and the villagers started to scream at what the Vonnyens were doing to one of their own. Helplessly, they watched two broad-shouldered Vonnyens drag an old man from their group and throw him into the fiery opening.

Nothing seemed to happen to him at first, and the old man crawled back to his feet. But then he started to scream in agony. The red light surrounded his body, shooting up through him. First, his skin blistered and turned red, then brown, and finally black. Seconds later, all that was left of the man was ashes, which floated around in the opening.

"Did you see that? Why are these monsters doing this? So this is what happened to the rest of the villagers," Filixx whispered anxiously, turning away from the cruel spectacle.

Moments later, Filixx looked down at the scene again. Roars of joy and rhythmic stomping were coming from the cave. Shocked, the three friends saw that a Vonnyen had crawled out of the glowing gap, frenetically greeted by his new brothers. There was nothing left of the man. Now he was one of them.

"So this is how you create a Vonnyen. By Kajal, we must do something," Bryn begged his friends. He knew all the villagers down there. He'd never felt so helpless.

"There are too many," Morlâ insisted. "It would be suicide. They will do the same to us in the end if their swords don't kill us first."

But Bryn wasn't listening. The two Vonnyens had gone back to the villagers to choose their next victim. The sound that Bryn heard next would haunt him forever.

Drena was screaming for her life.

COURAGE BORN OF DESPERATION

"We can't wait any longer," cried Bryn.

He entered the realm in a flash and wrapped himself in a Coat of Protection Spell. He grabbed his bow, took a running start, and jumped into the cave. Midair, he shot several arrows at the two Vonnyens holding Drena. The arrows were slow to pierce through the flickering protective cover, but once they did, they shot like lightning into the skulls of the vile creatures, killing them instantly.

Filixx and Morlâ watched as their friend plunged into the hellish nightmare. They knew the Coat of Protection Spell would protect Bryn from magic and swords but not the fatal impact of falling from such a height.

Morlâ shouted for Filixx to do something.

Instantly, the mark on Filixx's left hand began to glow, and he fired a bolt of yellow energy at Bryn's falling form.

Bryn didn't notice the force slowing him down until he landed gently and safely on a small ledge a few yards above the cave floor. Above him, Filixx and Morlâ looked a little less anxious, but about a dozen howling Vonnyens were coming straight at him with their swords drawn and their faces distorted with hate. But as they got closer to Bryn, one by one, they fell to the ground, motionless. Filixx and Morlâ looked at each other, stunned.

Bryn was robbing the approaching Vonnyens of their magic and life force.

As the Vonnyens near him collapsed and died, Bryn also shot powerful, multi-colored streams of energy at the Vonnyens further behind. Those that were hit sank to the ground but rose again almost immediately. The stream of cursed creatures was relentless, with hundreds coming at Bryn and trying to strike him with their deadly weapons. Completely outnumbered, Bryn now found himself encircled by them.

Bryn's protective spell blocked the first of their merciless strikes, but it steadily drained his strength. To compensate, he kept drawing on the Vonnyens' energy force, but this was not comparable to a gifted being's magical power. Their grayish-colored energy felt somehow wrong, like eating a roast of rotten meat. Initially, Bryn did feel strengthened by it, but seconds later, it started to weaken him. The more energy he drew from these creatures, the less powerful he became. Still, he couldn't stop if he wanted to keep up his protective spell and continue his attacks.

No matter how many Bryn killed, more and more kept coming. Only the ledge he was standing on prevented more creatures from attacking him, as only two could climb the small slope toward him at once. But with these numbers, this tiny advantage was becoming less useful to him. Bryn also needed to stop his magical attacks because he was close to blacking out. Drena's safety was all that had kept him going, but now he was starting to doubt if that would be enough to save him—or her.

He struggled to keep his Coat of Protection around him. One or two more heavy blows, and Bryn was sure his only barrier between life and death would fail. He dropped to his knees and stared at two Vonnyens jostling to be the first to plunge their sword into him. In a few seconds, the winner would climb up on the ledge and kill him.

Vonnyens streamed in from all the side tunnels. Hundreds pushed each other out of the way to reach him, climbing over their fallen brothers without any consideration.

A giant Vonnyen had made it up the ledge and thrust his rusty, jagged sword toward Bryn's chest. Bryn's protective spell was still able to deflect one more blow, but that was it. He was too exhausted to maintain the spell. He raised his head to look at Drena one final time, but he could not find her. Out of the corner of his eye, Bryn saw the Vonnyen raise his giant sword above his head, ready to bring it down with all his might.

I wish I could have told you I love you, Drena.

"Not a good place to rest, my friend!" shouted Morlâ, blocking the Vonnyen's deadly strike with his ax. Then, gliding backward while raising his arms, Morlâ struck the Vonnyen's wrists, severing them from his clawed hands. Bryn saw the sword fall over the ledge with the twitching claws still grasping the handle, oozing greenish-yellow blood.

"Hey, Filixx," shouted Morlâ, "it's quite hard to see through your Coat of Protection!"

Then, with his massive ax, he threw himself at another wave of attackers and left Bryn sitting on his little ledge.

Bryn's vision began to blur, and tingling magical energy began to flow through his body. *Filixx!* Bryn saw him sitting, eyes closed in the middle of the chaos, surrounded by dozens and dozens of dead Vonnyens. He had woven a Guardian Spell around Bryn. His friends had saved his life!

Risking their own lives, they had followed Bryn into the cave, and what had started as a rescue plan was now falling apart reasonably quickly. Filixx and Morlâ stood below Bryn with their backs to him. From his ledge, Bryn could see the Vonnyens had surrounded them in an arc. The monsters stepped cautiously toward the three, closing ranks, wary of being struck by Morlâ's ax or a deadly Attack Spell from Filixx. But it was clear to Bryn these beasts would sacrifice themselves for victory.

Suddenly, a wave of movement went through the Vonnyens' ranks. Something was attacking them from the rear. In their confusion, the first rows of Vonnyens became distracted and immediately fell to dwarf steel and elven magic. But as soon as they fell, they were replaced by others.

What is going on? Bryn thought, standing up to see better.

A roar boomed through the giant cave, amplified by the echo, and hundreds of Vonnyens began to scream. Bryn gave a tiny smile. *An orc battle cry*. Ûlyėr had found his Circle of Brothers!

Encouraged by this, Bryn jumped down and threw himself back into the fight.

None of them could tell how long they had been fighting, but suddenly, they were standing next to the glowing opening, still fending off the masses of Vonnyens incessantly attacking them. The unequal battle had brought them all together again in a final, hopeless fight.

"Glad you could pop in," Morlâ shouted to Ûlyėr between swings of his ax.

"I thought you and your delicate little physiques could use some help. Unfortunately, most of the tunnels were too small for me, so it took me a bit longer."

The monsters swarmed toward them, pushing them closer and closer to the edge of the opening. But Bryn sensed something new was happening around them. He could feel a strong magical presence.

In the next moment, his Guardian Spell was gone, which meant the others weren't protected either. Frantically, Bryn tried to enter the realm but found himself unable to. A sideways glance told him Filixx was facing the same problem. And another change was happening. The Vonnyens had stopped advancing about five yards away from them, forming a semicircle behind the bodies of their dead comrades and staring at the four.

"The gifted one," whispered Filixx, exhausted, "is preventing us from using our magic. Only a mighty magician can intervene directly in the realm and block us from accessing it."

"Come out, coward!" screamed Morlâ, angry at the interruption. "Face me like an adult and stop your dumb magic tricks."

But nothing happened.

Bryn wondered why his ears were ringing and realized the cave had suddenly become silent.

The solid wall of Vonnyens before them didn't make a sound, and the only movement was the pulsating red glow reflecting off their rotting skulls.

"Come on, my little magician," Morlâ shouted into the silence. "Look, he doesn't dare attack us directly, so we'll continue to fight his lackeys."

Morlâ leaped over several of the dead and swung his ax at one of the Vonnyens standing in silence. It sunk into the creature's hideous skull. Morlâ yanked the blade out of the beast, and a gush of greenish-yellow blood spurted from the wound. The Vonnyen stood for a second, and then fell forward onto one of his dead comrades. However, none of the other Vonnyens intervened.

Morlâ went to strike the next victim, but his ax stopped above his head mid-swing. Morlâ looked dumbfounded. It left his hands and flew in a high arc through the cave, landing behind their attackers. Suddenly, Morlâ was lifted off the ground by an unseen force. Unable to move, he hovered about two yards in the air.

"Is this all you can do?" he sneered despite his predicament.

Ûlyėr wanted to help him, but he, Filixx, and Bryn were also under some spell and could not move.

Morlâ then flew slowly toward the red opening in the ground. "Is that all? Come on. You must have better tricks up your sleeve—a rabbit, maybe a colorful handkerchief?"

But whoever the magician was, they were not provoked by Morlâ, who was steadily floating toward the deadly opening. Ûlyėr tried to grab him as he went by, but Morlâ was too high even for him. Now, hovering directly above the pulsating light, Morlâ was released from the spell and fell straight into the narrow opening.

Bryn gasped. He had to help his friend; otherwise, he would meet the same fate as the old man from the village. But he still could not move. Again and again, he tried to enter the realm to protect his friend, but he could not break the magician's powerful spell.

Because it had become routine in Tejal's magic lessons for Bryn to try and try again when he failed at something, he made one last concerted attempt to enter the realm. To his great surprise, it opened to him! Now, with his heightened awareness, he turned his attention to the tremendous bright red energy coming from the glowing opening. The light was almost blinding, but, squinting hard, Bryn saw a glimmer of faint blue light flickering within it. Morlâ!

Bryn was sure the intense red energy was about to consume the weaker blue. He was also sure that in the real world, his friend was already suffering. Not knowing exactly what to do, Bryn tried several spells in a row. He tried to put a Coat of Protection around his friend; then he tried to pull him out of the opening. Finally, in desperation, he tried to summon Morlâ like you would an insect or an animal. But all his attempts failed.

Now Bryn could hear Morlâ's shrill cries of pain in the realm, and they brought tears to his eyes.

I can at least shorten his suffering.

He began to carefully draw the faint blue lines of energy away from Morlâ and to himself. Bryn felt Morlâ grow weaker and weaker.

In that moment, Gerald's face appeared behind his eyes, and a shocking thought came into Bryn's mind: *I have become just her, like Caoimhe.*

No! No! He could not kill Morlâ!

Bryn furiously cast back the bands of energy he had just drawn from his friend—and the unexpected happened. The blue light around Morlâ was no longer transparent but intense and powerful. Bryn didn't think twice, just grabbed as many blue energy bands as he could and shot them toward his friend. Morlâ's magical aura grew and turned dark blue. Suddenly, the aura exploded before Bryn's eyes, and he was thrown out of the realm by the powerful discharge of magic.

Now back in the real world, Bryn could not believe what he was seeing. Morlâ lay on the ground next to the opening, surrounded by smoke but alive. And on the back of his left hand glowed a black hammer. The protective magic powers that had saved Bryn back in the forest had also protected his friend. Instinctively, Morlâ must have drawn on this new energy—he had finally discovered his gift! That, along with his sudden dwarf death defense, had saved his life.

From out of nowhere, a metallic yet commanding voice echoed through the cave.

"Kill all of them!"

Immediately, the Vonnyens began attacking the four friends.

Since Morlâ's dramatic rescue, everyone was free from the Binding Spell and able to move again, and could feel their strength slowly returning.

Filixx covered them all with another Coat of Protection, but Bryn could see it was almost transparent. Until Filixx had fully recovered, it wouldn't fend off more than one or two blows.

Having lost his bow and now drained of his magical powers after saving Morlâ, Bryn was struggling to defend himself. He closed his eyes tight and imagined Drena was standing before him. Then came the loud sound of heavy footsteps. It was four against hundreds, and he knew this was the end.

Bryn opened his eyes to face the inevitable but couldn't believe what he saw. The Vonnyens weren't running toward him and his friends—they seemed to be fleeing. And then he saw intense flashes of various colors at the far end of the cave, and row after row of Vonnyens fell in piles, struck by powerful spells.

The four tentatively made their way through the piles of dead Vonnyens in front of them and began to give chase to the beasts fleeing in several directions.

As Bryn began to run, from out of nowhere, he saw a huge, bluish ax dripping with Vonnyen blood stop a Vonnyen's sword that was coming straight at Bryn's head. Bryn stopped, utterly stunned.

"I would have thought you could handle a few little Vonnyens," said a familiar voice in his ear.

Gerald! Bryn turned and stared at him, wide-eyed and unable to speak.

"I can't see the other two, but you and Morlâ stay here while we drive the rest of these monsters away." Gerald promptly disappeared into the chaos.

Only now did Bryn realize he and Morlâ were now out of harm's way. He couldn't see Filixx, but poking out of a corner of the cave was a huge, colorful lizard tail, accompanied by the fearful cries of Vonnyens, so he had a fair idea where he was.

He also found Ûlyér off in the distance, towering over the Vonnyens and hurling one of them headfirst into a bunch of others, knocking them all down. They were then beaten down and destroyed by an even bigger orc wielding an enormous metal staff.

Who is that? Bryn wondered.

Suddenly, an oversized hat with a blood-red feather in it dropped out of the air and landed at Bryn's feet. He looked up to see its owner save a beautiful elf from an approaching black arrow and then shoot a barrage of lightning bolts at a horde of Vonnyens, reducing them and their bows and arrows to a smoldering mess. The elf wasted no time thanking him but continued, unmoved, and slit the neck of a Vonnyen with her throwing knife. That Vonnyen had just tried to cut off the head of an unkempt dwarf, who, in turn, had been fending off five opponents with a small ax while holding a leg of roast chicken in his other hand.

Bryn suddenly understood who had saved them.

The Grand Masters of the Driany Order! The human Tal MacRallen, the beautiful elven healer Isilmar Morningsky, the battle-hardened giant orc Orr, and the wise dwarf Elmar Boulderstone, together with Gerald, had been sent by Tejal.

HAPPY AND SAD

The overwhelming strength and experience of the Grand Masters and Gerald were decisive in quickly ending the battle. The Vonnyens could not defend themselves against their intense attacks, especially since their own magician appeared to have made a hasty retreat after Morlâ's rescue. They had correctly seen defeat coming early and fled while they still could. The Vonnyens tried to follow but most could not escape the wrath of the Knights of the Driany Order.

Gerald had his arm around Bryn's shoulders as they exited the cave through a smaller side tunnel. Behind them, Orr was carrying Morlâ in his arms like a child. Ûlyėr and Filixx were also on their way to the surface.

"Did you find Drena?" Bryn asked Gerald. "And what about the other villagers?"

"I'm afraid I don't know anything about Drena, son. You saw the chaos down there. And we're bringing the villagers out of the mine now. They were lucky! Old Ramsay had once worked in the tunnels and took most of them to a long-forgotten maintenance shaft, so they missed most of the battle. MacRallen and Morningsky are searching all the tunnels, and Boulderstone is taking care of the villagers as they come to the surface. Someone will know where Drena is."

Bryn managed a half-smile, but Gerald could see he would be fearful for Drena until he saw her again. He patted the boy gently on the back.

Ûlyėr and Filixx waved to Bryn. "There you are!" said Filixx. "How are you? The stench in the tunnels was overpowering. It's good to smell the fresh forest air again."

Then Orr laid Morlâ gently on some soft moss next to an old, gnarled tree, and Filixx rushed over to him. "Morlâ, are you all right?"

Morlâ's eyes flickered open and scanned the overhanging branches. "A nightingale …" Filixx nodded and knelt next to him. "I guess the Vonnyens have been driven away then," he said, mustering a smile for Filixx.

They listened to the bird's beautiful song in the darkness. Then came the reassuring hoot of an owl. It felt as if life was coming back to the Arell Valley now the Vonnyens had been defeated.

Bryn sat next to Morlâ. Orr decided to leave the three and went back into the tunnel to look for any more survivors—or Vonnyens.

"Have either of you seen Drena?" asked Bryn.

"No," Filixx replied. "I immediately went over to the group of villagers MacRallen and Morningsky brought up first, but there was no sign of her." Gerald pointed over Bryn's shoulder. "Look! There's another group coming out of the tunnel. I'll go over and ask them if they've seen her."

"No, I'll go," said Bryn, getting to his feet. His friends watched him hobble over to the villagers. When they saw Bryn coming toward them, their dirty, bewildered faces lit up. Everyone wanted to shake Bryn's hand, and they hugged him over and over for freeing them from their underground prison. But Bryn's shoulders indicated to his friends all they needed to know; no one had seen Drena.

Finally, Bryn spoke to Zeffi. The nut roaster was the only one who hadn't thanked him. Bryn didn't expect anything else, but he was stunned when Zeffi yelled, "Where is my niece?"

An icy lump formed in Bryn's stomach. "Isn't she supposed to be with you?"

"No," Zeffi shouted. "This is your fault! She only came here for New Year's to see you. Her mother didn't want her to come. And now—" Zeffi began sobbing and turned away.

"Zeffi! Could she still be down in the mine?"

But Zeffi walked back to the open arms of his wife, who tried desperately to comfort him.

Bryn became distraught at seeing the usually stern man crying. He wanted to cry himself and had no idea what to do. Then Boulderstone came out of the smaller tunnel, and Bryn ran to him and hastily bowed.

"We are not in Âlaburg, Bryn. There's no need for this out here, especially after what you and your friends have experienced."

"Excuse me, Grand Master," said Bryn, "but I am looking for a girl, Drena. Have you found her? She has dark hair, beautiful eyes, and her smile—"

"I'm sorry, Bryn," said the Grand Master, looking at him sadly. "MacRallen, Orr, Morningsky, and I have searched the entire mine. We also used several Locating Spells. I can tell you, there's nobody down there."

"This can't be. You must search again," said Bryn and took off toward the main entrance to the mine.

"No!" Boulderstone yelled after him.

Bryn had no intention of stopping, but at his next step, he was forced face down on the ground, which shook violently beneath him. He lifted his head and watched helplessly as the dark mine entrance collapsed. In some places, the ground around it also sank by several yards, and he knew the vast cave, its horrors forever burnt into his memory, had also collapsed.

"Are you all right?" Boulderstone asked, reaching for Bryn's hand and pulling him up.

"No!" he roared. "No! Drena is gone forever!"

Bryn burst into tears and thumped his fists on the dwarf's broad chest.

"Calm down," the Grand Master said gently. "We had to make the mine collapse. This was the only way to prevent the source of the magic from being misused again to bring forth more Vonnyens. But I assure you, Bryn, no human was left in that mine. You have my word."

Gerald, Morlâ, and Filixx tried to comfort Bryn, but he was inconsolable. Tears streaming down his face, he called to her over and over in his mind; *Drena … Drena … where are you?*

INTERLUDE OF EVIL

The giant Vonnyen bowed deeply before the small, slim figure that stepped into the clearing from the shadows of the forest.

"We have lost the boy, Massster!"

The figure raised their right arm, and a red-hot beam shot across the clearing. It struck the Vonnyen in the chest and followed the beast as he collapsed, screaming in agony.

"Mercy, Massster! Mercy!"

"I don't reward failure," said the figure in an icy yet beautiful feminine voice. "Years of planning have been lost. And all because you and your kind are unable to defeat an underage student and his pubescent friends. Twice now, the boy has escaped your warriors. You promised Kaull's mistake would not be repeated."

The mighty Vonnyen groaned and was struggling to breathe against the powerful spell.

"Please, Massster! Pleassse! I have someone elssse for you."

The figure lowered her hand, and the beam vanished. "Speak if you want to save your wretched life."

The monstrous creature got to his feet and limped to the edge of the clearing and into the shadows.

The woman folded her arms under her cloak.

After a moment, the Vonnyen returned with an unconscious young woman over his shoulder and dropped her in the center of the clearing.

The woman knelt next to the delicate creature and turned the girl's head so she could see her face. "A beauty indeed. But how can she help us?"

"She means sssomething to the boy. I heard him call her name. Hisss thoughtsss are also only for her." The woman's eyes flickered. Noticing her interest, the Vonnyen ventured a step forward and pointed to the young woman on the ground. "She is called Drena."

"I sense you are telling me the truth. And that is good. It's what I expect from you," said the mysterious woman, smiling. "The boy will look for her. Yes, you have done well."

The Vonnyen relaxed somewhat and bowed. "He will not essscape me again, Masssster. I give you my sssolemn oath."

The woman smiled and breathed deeply; Drena's body lifted off the ground and floated in mid-air.

"I believe you. I know the boy will never escape you again— of that I am certain."

With the casual cruelty of swatting a fly, the woman shot a spell at the Vonnyen, which sliced him in two. The top half of the creature fell backward and thudded to the ground. The bottom half stood for a moment, then fell to one side.

The woman glanced at the fallen creature. Then, with Drena floating a few feet off the ground in front of her, she walked back into the shadows of the forest.

EXAM RESULTS

The journey back to Âlaburg went by quickly, and traveling in the company of four Grand Masters also had some unexpected benefits that the friends enjoyed.

Bryn had followed behind the others with a heavy heart. Gerald, who had again slipped back into his foster father's role, told him a search party went to their old cabin, only to find it a smoldering ruin. The Vonnyens had destroyed it. Bryn knew now his old life was finally over.

"I know you're sad, son," said Gerald, "so I have a surprise for you."

Putting his fingers in his mouth, he gave a loud whistle, and out of the thicket trotted Olander and Reven.

Bryn stumbled forward and pressed his head into the neck of his faithful horse. "I thought I'd never see you again, boy," he whispered. "Where have you been?"

"I told them to head to the Laughing Boar," said Gerald. "I knew Marielle and her stable boy would look after them."

Bryn's tears trickled down Reven's mane. He smiled to himself—but still felt the impossibility of ever being truly happy again.

Nevertheless, with the help of Gerald, the Grand Masters, and his three friends, Bryn found his way back to something like a normal life. But he vowed to keep looking for Drena because, in his heart, he knew she was still alive.

Morlâ pointed at the small pile of brushwood he'd gathered and let it spark into flames.

"I still can't believe it," he told Bryn with a huge smile.

For days now, he'd been experimenting with his newly discovered abilities and making remarkable progress. After all, he was in the company of four of Razuclan's finest Masters, who were happy to share their knowledge.

"I just wanted to thank you again, Bryn," Morlâ said, placing a piece of wood on the campfire.

"You don't have to. You do realize I wanted to kill you, right?" Bryn joked, trying to finally put a stop to Morlâ's constant thanks.

"Yeah, yeah, I know. But what you did, …" Morlâ was whispering because they had agreed not to tell anyone except Filixx and Ûlyėr about Bryn's extraordinary ability. "No gifted person has ever done that before. You have unleashed magic into another being."

"Well, you already had a bit of it in you," Bryn said, trying to play it down.

"No, think about it. Not only are you a Seer of Colors, but you can also give magic to people who have the gift—or take it away from them. That means infinite power, but it's also a great burden. Until now, chance has decided who is gifted and who is not. Now you can change that."

Bryn had thought about this. But it was when Morlâ said it that he understood what his ability meant. And he certainly no longer considered it a curse, something that only harmed others. Knowing he could give or take away magic in case of an emergency reassured him immensely.

"I am grateful to you. You have changed my life. I no longer have to feel like I'm a fish out of water. The university will finally be my home."

Morlâ clumsily patted Bryn on the shoulder and went into the undergrowth to collect more firewood.

Now he can finally live with the dwarf fraternity, Ølsgendur, thought Bryn, sad about losing his roommate. *The hammer on the back of his left hand gives him every right to do so.*

The next afternoon, the small group reached Âlaburg. The Lekan Gate opened majestically, but nobody was waiting for them inside, except for a single, blond figure standing in the distance.

Gwendolin? We're not off to a great start then, Bryn thought, giving Reven a light spur.

Gwendolin bowed deeply to the Grand Masters. "Tejal has asked you to come to her office as soon as you can. She wishes to discuss the mission and the grades of the four students with you," she said, shooting a snide glance at Bryn, Morlâ, Filixx, and Ûlyèr.

"The four students with you?" Morlâ asked, mimicking her. "Gwenny, have you forgotten our names already?"

"Morlâ!" Gerald shouted, reminding them all that in Âlaburg, he was still their House Master.

"Of course, we will gladly comply with Tejal's request," MacRallen said with such politeness that Gwendolin blushed a little.

"Are you coming with us, Gerald?" asked Boulderstone.

"No, no, no. I have to tend to the horses."

"Oh, not that old excuse again, Gerald," Morningsky said, winking at him. "I suppose she will call for you when she needs you."

And with a small laugh, the beautiful elf turned and followed the others, leaving Gerald staring about in embarrassment, much to Bryn's amusement.

Gerald cleared his throat and gave a short whistle. "Um, well, I'll take care of the horses then." Then he raced off, the animals trotting behind him.

As Bryn watched them head toward the stable, he marveled at how the Grand Masters' levitation spells helped get the horses over the steep Panra Pass. The knights, trying to cheer Bryn up, had thought that if Reven and Olander were with him in

Âlaburg, they might comfort him in a way even his friends couldn't.

"It feels strange to be back home again," said Filixx. "I can't imagine sitting in class again tomorrow, can you?"

"I hope they don't think we failed our mission," Bryn answered. "To me, it doesn't look like we conducted ourselves with glory. Without the Grand Masters, we would have been a pretty sorry sight. And we failed to find out what was going on, except that someone was using magic to turn the people of Sefal into Vonnyens. And nobody knows who they are or why they're doing this."

Morlâ looked over at the Ølsgendur fraternity house for a moment, clapped his hands and rubbed them together. "Well, hopefully, we'll get a C," he said. "After all, we did come back in one piece. And I can use magic now!"

A few hours later, Rulu and Ulur burst into Bryn and Morlâ's room. They found the two fast asleep on their beds, still in their dirty clothes. They'd brought a message—Tejal wanted to see Bryn and Morlâ immediately to give them their grades.

Bryn got up after the twins left, but he was in a bad mood, with a headache and a foul taste in his mouth. Morlâ had fallen asleep again after the boys had delivered their message.

"Morlâ." Bryn shook his shoulder. "Morlâ, we have to go to Tejal's office. Get up!"

Ten minutes later, they finally emerged from their room, glassy-eyed and with tousled hair. Filixx and Ûlyėr were waiting for them in the hallway, beautifully attired in their best clothes and looking like they'd scrubbed themselves to within an inch of their lives.

"Look at the state of you two!" Filixx cried.

Bryn and Morlâ just blinked at him.

"We're going to the announcement of our mission grades. This moment will determine our final grades for this semester, and, who knows, maybe none of us will even be selected for a mission on behalf of the Order again! Tejal expects us to receive our grades respectfully to honor the university."

It took just five minutes for Bryn and Morlâ to drape their grayish, wrinkled sashes over their dirty clothes and somehow plaster their hair flat with some water.

"There you are! Finally!" Gwendolin hissed from behind her reception desk. "You will be given your grades individually. Ûlyėr, you are to go in first."

Ûlyėr gave Gwendolin a particularly unpleasant look, which prompted the otherwise haughty elf to add a "Please!" before she went ahead to escort him into the Chancellor's office.

Bryn, Morlâ, and Filixx sat on the infamous bench, which always made waiting for appointments with Tejal painful.

Bryn was not used to sitting so straight, and his back started to ache after only five minutes. Filixx and Morlâ looked pained as well. Yet, nobody spoke. They were all deep in thought, occasionally looking over to Gwendolin, who was dealing with a mountain of papyri.

The current semester would end for them with the announcement of their mission grades, and in a few days, their report cards would be issued. Half of their final grade would come from their performance in the Seven Wisdoms, and they would get the other half from the Chancellor in just a few minutes.

Today's results were crucial to Filixx's future. They would mean the difference between being a magician exceptionally skilled in magical theory and one who could wield his tremendous talents in the real world. Morlâ needed a good grade to get him into the next semester. Jehal would certainly give him the worst grade in Magic, and he was desperate to make up for that. If he were to be given an overall F, he would have to leave the university.

Bryn had all these things on his mind. But mainly, he thought about how much his life had changed this last half-year. A hunting apprentice who thought magic only existed in fairy tales had become a student of Âlaburg and could now use magic himself. Although the loss of Drena still haunted him, the incredible and fantastic things he had experienced in the last semester gave him some comfort. Bryn had also made friends—exceptional ones who would walk through fire for him; their adventure had proven that to him several times.

And I would do the same for them, Bryn thought, smiling.

Gwendolin called Filixx to the Chancellor's office next. Then it was Morlâ's turn.

It was early evening before Bryn entered. Tejal had spoken at length with the others and let them out one by one through the side door of her office.

Bryn bowed deeply and reverently.

"Sit down," said Tejal.

Bryn slouched in the comfortable brown leather armchair in which he had sat so often during his private lessons with Tejal. It was still warm from Morlâ.

Before speaking, Tejal looked closely at Bryn for a long time. Just as he was starting to feel discomfited, she asked, "Well, how did your adventure go? Is there anything significant you would like to reveal to me before I grade your achievements based on the Grand Masters' observations?"

Bryn grew hot and uncomfortable. Tejal had a disturbing habit of always asking the exact question he didn't want to answer.

"No," he said softly.

"Are you sure? You know what can happen if you reveal your skills too late."

Bryn conceded with a nod and told her about the intervention he had performed on Morlâ, which allowed him to call upon his magical potential.

"Thank you for trusting me. Your abilities are indeed unique, and generally speaking, it is wise to keep them to yourself or share them only with a select Circle of Brothers," Tejal said with a wry smile. "Just so you know, none of the others told me anything about it—of course, they wouldn't." Tejal sat back in her heavy leather chair. "The four of you have become close, haven't you? I am proud of that. You are the first mission team since Orr, Boulderstone, Morningsky, and MacRallen to consist of members from all four enlightened nations. The four of you also embody the principle idea behind Âlaburg.

"As far as your unique talents are concerned, this development is also extremely positive. Now it is entirely up to you how you use them. You can decide for yourself whether you use magic for good to help others or cause great harm with it. The responsibility lies with you." Tejal looked at him sternly across her large desk. "I expect you to make the right decision when the time comes. Razuclan may have been waiting for someone like you—a gifted person who can activate the gift in others. For decades now, fewer and fewer gifted students have been coming to us. Nobody knows exactly why, but there seems to be fewer and fewer manifestations of the gift across the continent over time. Maybe you can bring it back. However, you can also strip another gifted person of their abilities, so you could also be the end of magic in Razuclan. You must think hard about that!"

Bryn didn't know what to say. The Chancellor's words weighed heavily on him.

"Now." She smiled. "I almost forgot your mission grade."

Bryn's heart jumped again. Tejal was good at creating suspense.

"You can probably guess what I have done, Bryn."

Bryn's shoulders slumped, and he sat back in the chair, staring at his feet.

Tejal smiled at him. "I have given your companions a good grade and will give you the same. Not only did your heroic efforts save the lives of several people, but you also solved the mystery of who attacked the merchants traveling to Sefal. You discovered the whereabouts of the unknown magician's source of power and how they created so many terrible Vonnyens. Even if the price for this was high." Tejal's face darkened. "May those poor souls of Sefal, who were transformed into monsters by corrupted magic, rest in peace."

Bryn remembered how they had transformed the old villager into a Vonnyen, and a shiver went through him. A great sadness came over him at the loss of so many whom he had known.

"And because you were personally affected by what happened, your commitment is all the greater. You will receive the highest possible grade for all your subjects, the same as the others. I have given you an A. Congratulations, Bryn, you have passed your first semester at Âlaburg with great success." Tejal stood and shook her stunned student's hand.

Completely overwhelmed, Bryn wandered to the door, but Tejal brought him back.

"Bryn," she said somberly, looking at him with a serious expression, "I know you have suffered a particularly great loss, and I do not wish to give you too much hope, but"—she paused briefly—"not far from the entrance to the mine is a clearing. A scouting party from the Order found a Vonnyen there who had been torn in half by magic. We know no one from the Order did this. But there was something else. They discovered the imprint of a human body in the flattened grass. And somebody then magically lifted the body off the ground. This evidence means the foreign magician, whoever it was, escaped us and took someone with them. And Drena is the only one among the kidnapped villagers who is missing."

Suddenly, Tejal looked tired, and she fell back heavily into her chair.

Bryn could see she was thinking about something but took this as a sign to leave the office. *Drena could still be alive!* Hope flooded over the sadness in his heart. *If she is still alive, I will find her!*

He walked past Gwendolin, oblivious to her contemptuous gaze, and headed out into the warm evening. At that moment, he saw Morlâ, Filixx, and Ûlyėr walking toward him. A smile crossed Bryn's face as he looked at his companions, and something shifted inside him.

No, we will find her!

"I got an A. I don't think I've ever got an A here for anything," said Morlâ as the four walked to the tower. "And I—" Morlâ halted for a moment, and then kept on walking.

"And you what?" asked Filixx. "What's up? Don't tell us that all of a sudden you've got secrets from us?"

"Well, I can finally join Ølsgendur fraternity," Morlâ said, stopping again. "Tieffenor was with me in Tejal's office, and when he saw the mark and heard about my heroic deeds"—he winked at the other three—"he immediately made me the offer to join them. Today, if I want to."

Morlâ's news was met with silence; it would mean they would no longer have classes together next semester, and the Starball team would break up. Someone from Ølsgendur could hardly take or accompany White House members on any possible future missions either, if he wanted to avoid jeopardizing his newly won status as a full member there.

Bryn was the first to speak. "Have you made a decision?"

Morlâ looked his friends in the eye one at a time.

"I have, yes." From under his shirt, he pulled out the chain with the small golden disk that allowed him access to White House—until now. He tore it from his neck and threw it away as far as he could.

Bryn was so disappointed that he could not look at Morlâ. "I see. It's Ølsgendur next semester then."

"Well, you know, Bryn, after much consideration," said Morlâ, putting his left hand in the gargoyle's mouth, "I've decided the colors blue and red don't suit me after all."

Then, suddenly, the White House door opened, and Morlâ ran in and disappeared downstairs. For a moment, Bryn, Filixx, and Ûlyėr looked like they were under a spell—frozen, wide-eyed, and speechless. Then, they rushed to the door, trying to squeeze through together, hollering and laughing, and clambered down the stairs to find their friend.

The end.

The adventure continues :

The Legend of Âlaburg (coming soon)

www.greg-walters.com

Printed in Germany
by Amazon Distribution
GmbH, Leipzig

23626093R00288